A STRAWBERRY SPRINGS NOVEL

AS I GROW

ELLE RIVERS

Cover Design by Summer Grove

Developmental editing by Mae Peredo, Wildwood Author Services

Copyediting by Kasey Kubica, Basic Behemoth Edits

Proofreading by Mae Peredo, Wildwood Author Services

 Formatted with Vellum

A NOTE FROM ELLE

As I Grow contains mature and potentially triggering content that some people might find upsetting. Please be advised that the following content can be found on-page unless otherwise noted.

- explicit sexual content
- unprotected sex
- accidental pregnancy (main character)
- childbirth (short, not detailed, no complications)
- discussion of parental loss/abandonment
- non-consensual kiss (not committed by main characters)
- physical assault (not committed by main characters)

Please take care of yourself and your mental health while reading any novel.

To anyone who feels like they have to be what everyone else needs
—you deserve someone who takes care of you.
Welcome back to Strawberry Springs.

PLAYLIST

A Night To Remember—beabadoobee, Laufey
Nothing Breaks Like a Heart (feat. Miley Cyrus)—Mark
Ronson, Miley Cyrus
mirrorball—Taylor Swift
Into You—Ariana Grande
Never Getting Laid—Sabrina Carpenter
Espresso—Sabrina Carpenter
Ruin My Life—Zara Larrson
Rumour Has It—Adele
Wi$h Li$t—Taylor Swift
Everything Has Changed—Taylor Swift, Ed Sheeran
The Man Who Left Too Soon—beabadoobee
I Lived—OneRepublic
Carry You Home—Alex Warren
Father Figure—Taylor Swift
Still into You—Paramore

STRAWBERRY SPRINGS
COMMUNITY GUIDE

Jackie Anne Tyler—Owner of Hair Haven salon
Kerry Winsor—Stay-at-home mom, resident gossip
Nicole Rudder—Teacher at Strawberry Springs Elementary School
Mollie Wilson—Owner of Bennie Grove Farm
Cain Smith—Farm Manager at Bennie Grove Farm
Tammy Jane and Ron*—Married owners of Center Point Diner
Hugh Jeffries—Retiree, resident grump
Marjorie and Henrietta Brown—Married librarians
Dr. Atticus Thompson, DVM—Veterinarian
Jade Clark—Owner of Jade's Goodies gift shop
Grace Day—Owner of Treasure Trove clothing store
Brooke Day—Aspiring singer
Dale Garrett—Owner of Food 'n' Things grocery store
Mike Finch—Sheriff of Strawberry Springs
Dr. Henry Connor, MD—Clinic doctor
Mark Bell—Owner of Bell's Brews bar
Theo Murf—Owner of The Reserved Bean

Wren Hackett—Local general contractor
Kelsey Marie*—Barista at The Reserved Bean

*Tammy, Ron, and their daughter, Kelsey have not consented to the inclusion of their last name in this guide at this time.

DEAN
EIGHT YEARS AGO

The house was quiet when I woke up.

That was something I'd never get used to. Just a few years ago, I would always hear Mom laughing with Dad in the kitchen as they made breakfast. I never remembered what it was about, but I did remember the joy the house was filled with.

I had never realized how much life Dad had brought to things. Over the last few years that he'd been gone, our default had been reset, and it never stopped feeling out of place.

Most mornings, I could ignore the feeling and walk to the dining room with a smile on my face. This time, I had to sit with it. Thoughts of Dad didn't always pop up, but the grief counselor Mom took me into town to see had warned both of us that this was normal, that grief wasn't a constant stream of sadness, rather, a trickle.

Taking a shaky breath, I got out of bed and pushed away the thoughts. This was going to be a good day, and I didn't need to be mulling on the past when my future was in front of me.

I found Mom eating waffles in the dining room. They were the frozen kind from the store. Neither she nor I could cook, so we'd relied on eating out and processed foods ever since Dad passed away. My memories of getting served big home-cooked meals on special days were fuzzy, but they were bright ones nonetheless.

"Morning," she said. "Hungry?"

"A little," I replied. "Thank you."

I took the frozen waffles and refused to complain. She gave me a smile before looking back down to her schedule. She used one of those leather-bound planners to make sure she never forgot anything. It was full of notes and things to do.

Mom didn't know, but I'd snuck a look at it the other day. I needed to make my plans perfect, and I needed her to have a rare day off.

"Can I drive the truck today?" I asked as I sat up straighter. "I wanna take Julie out to dinner."

I rarely got to use the vehicle Mom and I shared. Being a one-income household meant that we didn't have the funds for another one. I wanted to get a job to help out with money, but she refused to let me, saying I needed to focus on school and being a kid.

"Sorry, but I can't let you have it today. I need it for work."

My eyebrows immediately furrowed. "Isn't it your day off from cleaning?"

"And how would you know that?"

My eyes flicked to her planner and back up. "No reason."

"You looked, didn't you?"

My cheeks heated. "I just needed to know your day off."

"Things change. And honey, I never have a true day off. Not as a mom."

I hated it when she said that. She deserved rest.

"Today would have been good day to try. I'll be at school and busy with Julie. Just stay home."

She shook her head. "I have a job."

I scoffed. "What job? Cancel it."

"The Mullins are moving out so they wanted me to clean their place," she said. "They paid extra."

I frowned. She seemed to carry exhaustion around her wherever she went. It didn't feel right that she did it all while I was only going to school and hanging out at home.

Then what she said hit me. "Wait, the Mullins have been here for years. They're moving out?"

"They don't like the new houses across the road from them and I can't blame them for it. It's a whole subdivision."

I rolled my eyes at the mention of the new subdivision. We weren't the smallest of towns by any means, but ever since people figured out that we were close to Nashville, they seemed determined to move here in droves. They all said it was cheaper, that there were less taxes than the city.

But as I saw fields that I used to run in as a kid get flattened for houses, it felt like an invasion.

"Dean, I know you hate all of the change, but more houses mean more for me to do."

I groaned. She still didn't get it.

I didn't want her killing herself for me. I didn't need a fancy life like some of these other people did. Did I get looked down on in school sometimes? Yes. Did I hate that the rumor mill here only seemed to grow as more people arrived? Also yes.

I would deal with it, though. She didn't have to do so much for me.

"You still need days off, Mom."

"Dean," she cut me off with a flat look. "We're not having this talk again. I've got this."

She didn't, but she wouldn't let me do anything about it. I gritted my teeth and went back to my food. I hated feeling powerless.

I couldn't wait to start working. Then she'd never have to do this much again.

"I'm sorry about your plans with Julie, though. What if I drove you to whatever you had planned?"

Yeah, that wasn't happening. Mom driving me in would be a total mood killer.

Besides, kids at school already looked down on me for being as poor as I was. In this town, there was a divide between the people who'd lived here for years because it was cheap and the newer ones who'd moved in with money.

All of the new people wanted it to be like the cities they came from. They wanted strip malls and amenities. It looked like they were getting what they wanted.

I didn't care what they thought, but I also didn't want to give them more ammunition either.

I shook my head and forced my voice to be level. "I can make my plans happen at school. Should I walk home?"

"I'll come and get you on a break. It's fine."

"You should use your break to relax," I said. "I'll walk. It's a nice day."

Mom tilted her head to the side, smiling softly at me. Sometimes she would say that my giving nature reminded her of Dad.

I didn't know if I could hear that today.

In my head, I reworked my plans with Julie.

Today was going to be good. If all went well, Julie would be my girlfriend by the end of the day. She would be the *one*.

Just like when Mom and Dad met in high school.

I'd always looked up to them. Their love was like the sun. Bright and warm. It still was, even though Dad had never come home from the last call he'd responded to.

"And what'll you be up to then?" Mom knew I was messing around. Weeks ago, I'd come home to a pack of condoms on the table and had to endure the worst conversation of my *life*, but she was mostly supportive as long as I was safe. And I would be.

I knew she wanted me to have a great love story like she and Dad did, and hopefully, that was about to start.

"We'll be at school, so nothing *too* wild can happen." I shoved the last bite into my mouth. "But it'll start with me giving her something this morning. I just need to go see if the wildflowers are still blooming."

Mom's eyes lit up. "Flowers, huh? Are you making it official?"

I nodded, ignoring the fluttering in my chest. I'd been feeling this ever since I wanted to go steady with Julie, but I knew us dating was the natural next step.

Hell, it sure seemed to make Mom happy.

"Picking wildflowers for a sweetheart," she said with a smile. "Just like your dad."

I tried to hide the way I stiffened when she mentioned him. People were well meaning when they would compare me to him, and I *did* look a lot like him with my lighter hair and eyes. But some days, the reminder that he was gone made all that grief come back. These days, I liked to focus on what I shared with Mom, since she was the one who I saw all the time.

"Yeah, I guess."

Normally, Mom would pick up on my tighter tone, but she was lost in memories. "You know, that's how he asked me out. It worked. I bet it'll work again. Julie is a sweet girl."

She always had been. We'd grown up together, and she was one of the few people in town that had been here since birth. I thought she was pretty, but she'd always been a part of the popular crowd, and I couldn't believe she was going for me. But she'd pulled me into a closet and had her way with me, and we'd been messing around ever since.

Technically, the field I was in wasn't ours; it belonged to the owners of the massive house next door. But they had more than enough to go around, so I grabbed flowers and arranged them the best I could, and then went inside to get dressed.

"I'm ready," I said as I walked in.

"That looks nice. Julie's gonna love them." Mom grabbed her keys and tightened her ponytail before we walked out the door.

It wasn't a long drive to the high school, but I grew more and more nervous as time went on. I liked Julie. A lot. I hoped she said yes; I really wanted this to work.

"Go and get 'em, kid." Mom patted me on the shoulder.

"Thanks," I said. I took a breath before hurrying out of the car.

Julie was by her locker surrounded by her friends. She'd gotten in with all of the new kids in town, the ones who had nice clothes and fancy cars. I knew none of them cared that much for me, judging by the way they stared and whispered when I walked by, but I wasn't one to be scared of someone's opinion of me. Love conquered all of that, after all.

Her eyes were wide when she turned to me. Up until now, our rendezvous had been a secret. She would catch me either before anyone was around when Mom had to drop me off early or after most of the kids had left for the day. Sometimes, she would drive me to the movies and we'd have fun there. We were never around her friends, though.

But if we were doing this, it was time to come out of the shadows.

"Oh, hi . . ." Her voice was unsure, but I smiled at her anyway.

"I got these for you," I said.

"Oh . . . Thanks. Where are these from?"

"I picked them for you from my backyard."

One of her friends coughed. It sounded suspiciously like a laugh.

Julie's eyes darted to her friends and a blush settled on her cheeks. I wasn't sure why she cared about what they thought. I knew they all talked about each other.

Julie had a gap in her teeth, and the one staring me down had been talking to another girl about how she needed braces. Hell, I'd caught Julie's last boyfriend, a guy who'd just moved to town, talking about how she didn't put out enough.

I'd punched him in the face. The in-school suspension was so worth it because I had a feeling that was when Julie finally noticed me.

We all only had one summer together before we went to college. I was going to a trade school in Nashville, and I knew she was planning to go to a college in the city too. Once she said yes to being my girlfriend, I wanted to show her how a man should be. I wouldn't talk about her behind her back. I would stick around and be with her for exactly who she was.

"Can I walk you to class?" I asked.

"Why would you wanna walk me to class?" She laughed, looking in between her friends. "Thanks, though." I frowned as she walked away.

The girls walked close together, talking about whatever they had going on. The flowers were still in my hand. With a sigh, I put them in my locker before heading to class. It would be hard to convince her to change, but Mom said that Dad had asked her out five times before she said yes. I'd be stubborn.

I didn't see her again until later. The plan was to meet at the vacant electrical room so we could get some time alone together before anyone caught us.

"There you are," she said, finally smiling at me before pulling me into a kiss. I knew she was about to drag me through the wooden door into the dark, but I wanted to ask this before she did anything else.

"Wait, we should talk first."

"Since when do we talk?" she asked as she shook her head. "Don't worry about that. Let's just have fun."

"Hang on a second." My grip on her tightened. "About this morning . . ."

"Oh, *that*."

"Yeah, I still have the flowers for you. I kept them in a paper towel so they would be fresh."

Julie sighed. "I don't need flowers. Just this."

"Just me, or . . ."

"I mean, you're kind of a part of it. I mean the whole sneaking around thing. It's fun." She leaned in and her voice lowered into a purr. "You're fun."

"I can be more than just fun."

Now she frowned. "What are you saying?"

"I wanna go steady. With you, I mean."

She blinked, her cheeks turning red. "Wait, really?"

"Yeah."

"But I'm about to go to college."

"I'm going too."

"I thought you were doing something else."

"Trade school. I wanna be an electrician. But it's still school."

She laughed, but I hadn't said anything funny. "That's not . . . That's like a different kind of school. Not the good kind."

There was a sinking feeling in my gut. This wasn't going how I'd imagined. None of today had, but I ignored it and tried to keep moving forward.

"It's still something. In two years, I'll have a good job, and you're going to school in Nashville, so—"

"Whoa," she said. "We don't need to be thinking that far ahead. And besides, once I get to Nashville, things are changing for me."

"Like what?"

"I'll finally be a part of something better. I'll be out of the small-town life."

"I'll be there too. We can both be out of it together."

"Yeah, but . . . my vision for this doesn't involve a guy like you."

Her words hit me right in the center of my chest.

"What does that mean?" I asked slowly.

She sighed as if I were the dumbest kid in the world. "I can't date the guy from Shady Acres who's going to *trade* school. I need someone . . . who's like what I want to be. You're good in bed, Dean. Or closets, I should say. But that's about it."

"I can be more than just good in bed."

She looked me up and down. "You're hot and all, but trust me, no one else wants anything more than sex from you. Stick to what you're good at. *Very* good at."

Julie bit her lip, and I knew she was trying to steer me back to focusing on her. I'd spent weeks focusing on her, in all the ways.

I had a feeling she'd told everyone exactly what I was good at doing. My stomach churned as I saw the last few weeks in a new light.

Some girls were giving me double takes. A few had smiled in my direction, but I thought they were pitying smiles like they always had been.

Maybe they were flirty ones.

How many people knew of me as the fun guy? How many thought this was all I was good for?

That was the thing about a town like this. Once you were labeled, your fate was sealed. No one changed their minds.

I was suddenly the fun guy who was good in bed.

"Now that we've cleared things up—" She stepped closer and I smelled her perfume. "Can we continue?"

I wasn't sure what I wanted to say because my mind was

still reeling. My heart hammered in my chest and it felt like I couldn't breathe.

That's what all of these people thought of me. I didn't care about the gossip, but this one hurt. Everyone here knew about Mom and Dad. They knew that they had raised me right. Most of my classmates had been at Dad's funeral, awkwardly offering their condolences. How could they see what I came from and still gotten it wrong?

A few things happened all at once. I tried to pull away from Julie as the door to the closet she was reaching for sprang open.

A man stepped out. He was sporting a tool belt and a thinning hairline. His eyes went between us, and I had no doubts in my mind that he had heard the whole thing.

"Aren't you a little young for this?"

Julie whirled around, her entire body tensed. "Oh my God. Sir, I'm sorry. I didn't know anyone was here."

"Always in the shadows I am." He crossed his arms. "Now, you might wanna scram before someone else catches you."

Julie didn't have to be told twice. She darted down the hallway. The guy didn't sound all that nice and I knew that I needed to make a break for it too.

My entire world had been pulled out from under me like a rug. I was moving slower than I should have been.

"You," the man looked at me. "Hang on a sec. I wanna talk to you."

"Technically, I didn't break any rules." Yet.

"I ain't a teacher or a snitch, but that was a level of awkwardness that I didn't wanna deal with."

Great. My mortification was heard by a random stranger. "So I'm guessing the whole town will know by tomorrow . . ."

"Don't worry, kid. I'm only a visitor."

Despite everything, I let out a chuckle. "That's one good thing, at least."

He looked in the direction that Julie had run off in and sighed. "You know . . . she's wrong. You're a good kid . . . probably."

"It's okay. You don't have to try and make me feel better. I'll get out of your way." My vision went blurry with tears I didn't want to shed as I tried to get the hell out of there.

"Now, hang on a second." His hand landed on my shoulder. It reminded me of how Dad would stop me before I ran out the door. "Look, I don't have any kids of my own so I'm shit at this, but you seem like you need a little pep talk."

"I think I'd rather crawl into a hole and die, actually."

"You're young. Things'll change. And you sound like you've got a whole life ahead of you."

"You'd think I was throwing it away with going to trade school with the way *she* acted."

"Don't worry about the opinions of some girl. People need the trades and there's good money in it."

"I know. Everyone here is so worried about how they're viewed. I hate it."

I was starting to hate everyone here, actually. I didn't realize how much I had started to resent this place until I was hurt by it. The selling of all the land and all of the change had caused micro cuts in my soul.

Julie had just broken it open.

"So, you said you're wanting to be an electrician?" the man asked.

"Yeah," I said.

"That's a good trade. I can't do electrical myself because I find it way too complicated. You must be pretty smart."

Despite myself, I smiled. Mom had never said anything bad about my career choice, mostly because I didn't choose to go into firefighting like Dad had. I considered it, but I knew that Mom wouldn't be able to handle the stress of it, especially after how Dad died.

Still, I wanted to do something that was tied to him. The fire that killed him was an electrical one. It was some kind of old wiring that should have been replaced a long time ago. If I went into this field, at least I could help people not make the same mistake.

"I hope you like electrical work, kid. Where are you going to school?"

"Nashville." I thought I'd been excited before, but I knew now that I would be counting down the days.

"There's a lot of good work there. It's always growing. What's your name?"

"Dean."

"Well, Dean, I'll give you my card, and if you make it through electrical school and need some work, give me a call."

I slowly took it and read his name. Mom had taught me not to turn my nose up at honest work. I didn't know this guy, but it couldn't have been a bad idea to have connections.

"Thanks, Clyde. I'll see you around."

"Keep your head on straight, kid, and I'll see you in a few years." He nodded and walked away.

I was starting to think he was right.

I stood there for a long time thinking over everything that had just happened to me. The mixture of devastation and anger that was swirling low in my stomach was something I never wanted to feel again. I wasn't sure if I could.

Things had been more fun when I was just messing around with Julie. It was the second I opened up and asked for more when it all went wrong.

Maybe things were better when I just had fun. Not because Julie was right, but because I didn't have to feel *this* when someone turned me down.

I always thought I would have a love story like Mom and Dad did. But if this was what it felt like, then it wasn't for me. Being something else sounded better. I could protect myself from pain, disappointment, and embarrassment.

The news of me asking Julie out would probably spread fast. People would be laughing for a long while, but they didn't know that I had bigger plans. Plans outside of here. Once I was in Nashville, I would have a new chance to be who I wanted to be.

And that guy was someone who would never get rejected like that again.

1

GRACE

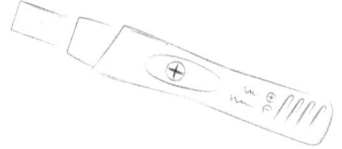

Strawberry Springs Neighborhood Watch

Kerry Winsor: Guys, it's getting a little quiet around here. Does anyone have any news for me?

Comments:
Kerry Winsor: Uh, hello? **@everyone**
Mollie Wilson: What do you want us to say? We JUST had a TV crew here and got our library renovated. It's gonna be a little quiet . . .
Kerry Winsor: I'm just used to the constant news! It kept me alive!
Kerry Winsor: So, when are you having another baby?
Mollie Wilson: When I'm not covered in spit up . . .
Hu Gh: I have a few questions for Goggle. I can just put them in here.
Jade Clark: NO. Please. The last time was bad enough.

I WAS ABOUT to take a bite of the best burrito I'd ever made when my front door opened.

"Come in," I said to the only other person who had the key. "I wasn't in the middle of anything."

My sister stormed into the living room. Her light, wavy hair was a mess, and she looked like she'd just woken up. I was used to random drop-ins from her ever since she'd moved to Nashville, but this was early for her.

"I *hate* them. I hate them so much!"

I set down my burrito with a sigh. Only my sister would drive three hours to complain about roommates, but I was the only one who would listen, and she liked to do things in person so no one could hang up on her.

When she moved to Nashville two months ago to pursue her dream of singing, I thought this would stop. But she'd been having issues with both her waitressing job and her two roommates. She'd switched jobs many times, but was stuck with the women.

Few people could tolerate Brooke like I could. When she lived here, she was the bane of the town's existence. Not once in her life had she been able to take no for an answer. She was rude, callous, and unkind to pretty much everyone she met. Many people had told me that it felt like she thought she was above all of them simply because she had big dreams to move out of this small town.

People wondered how I was able to deal with her. Hell, even I wondered how I did it, but Brooke was my only family, and I loved her.

Even if she interrupted my delicious breakfast.

She would be here to bitch about her roommates, get some home-cooked food from me, and then return to Nashville.

"What happened?" I asked.

"They all think that I should do everything around the

apartment to 'pull my weight.' As if they pull their own! No one does the dishes. Why do I have to do them for everyone?"

That was . . . actually a reasonable reason to be angry.

"I'm sorry," I said. "That's a lot to put on someone. Why don't I make you some tea to calm down?"

"I don't need to calm down. I need them to respect me." She stomped to the kitchen and I let out a long breath.

I checked the clock. I didn't have the time to spare for a tirade from Brooke, but I heard from her so rarely that I knew I needed to be here for her.

"So, that's a no on the tea?"

She scoffed and shoved a mug at me. That answered my question.

"I can't wait until I'm famous and have my own place," she said as I heated some water.

Despite her unannounced arrival, it was nice to have a second person in the kitchen. When Mom left the house to me, I thought Brooke and I would be sharing it for a long time. The two of us, even with how loud she was, still never felt like it truly filled the space. We'd grown up in a split-level family home. The kitchen flowed into a den that was made for hosting parties, and there were more than enough bedrooms.

It was too much for me.

In many ways.

As I grabbed the mug to add a tea bag, I ignored the stain that had been on the countertops for years. The house had a lot of cosmetic things wrong with it. It needed work that I didn't have the time or money to do. Mom must have been a super-woman to find time to work and keep up on this place.

Still, I'd never get rid of it. The wood-toned cabinets were familiar in the most comforting way. I knew every creak of the floor, every noise that the home made.

Brooke sat at the dining room table, which was right off the kitchen. The table was uneven and nearly tipped over. "Jesus, are you ever gonna fix this thing?"

It was on my list, but I knew the truth. I was way too overwhelmed to ever get to it.

People in the town would probably help, but I made a name for myself helping them and *not* the other way around. I couldn't imagine ever letting them return the favor. Mom had been the same way, always self-sustaining.

Brooke was not.

"Eventually," I said slowly as I poured the hot water and then made my way to where she was sitting. "Here you go."

She immediately took a sip. "It's way too hot, but it'll do."

That was as close to a thank-you as I'd get.

"How's fame coming along?"

That perked her up. I was wary of her chances becoming famous in a big town like Nashville. I wouldn't ever say it out loud, but she wasn't the kind of person to put in the work for anything. She wanted it to just happen. And judging by the talent that I had heard in the shower, she would need to work in order to become a singer like she wanted to be.

But I still supported her. I was her sister, after all.

"I have a few auditions for some bands. One of them could really be it for me."

"Good. I hope it goes well."

"You're using that voice again," she said as she rolled her eyes. "The fake Grace voice."

"I'm not being fake. I do hope it goes well."

"You think I can't sing."

"I just said that lessons might be good for you," I hedged gently. I *had* said that after a night of talking to my friends. They'd all told me to try to reason with Brooke and warn her about how hard getting a singing career would be. Needless to say, it didn't go well. "But all singers need them."

Brooke crossed her arms. "You're terrible at making me feel better."

"I recorded the Kardashians just in case this happened," I said, instead of taking her bait. She always felt better when she got to see her favorite reality TV family. "Watch that and feel better, then go back to Nashville."

"Fine."

I patted her shoulder before going to my room. My brain was still foggy from dealing with her, as it always was when Brooke was angling for a fight, but I pushed it away and focused on my outfit for the day.

I opened my closet and ran my hands over all of the clothes. I had a collection way too big for just one person, but I always put effort into my outfit. It was the one thing that always made me feel better.

I had all kinds of different patterns: floral, stripes, and even leopard print. It took me a while to picture what I wanted to look like that day, but eventually, I landed on a skirt that I had just gotten the week before. It had cherries all over it and went with a graphic tee with a lime that I'd had forever and never wore.

I loved finding the perfect match, for both me and others, and my mood was instantly lifted. Once I was dressed, I put on a little bit of makeup before taking in my entire self.

A long time ago, I would've refused to look at myself in the mirror before leaving for the day. I had always been curvier than Brooke, but my weight fluctuated over the years and I hated the way my reflection would change. Now that I was an adult, I was determined to grow to love my body exactly as it was.

A small smile made it to my face. My curly hair was laying perfectly and the two pieces went together just as I expected them to.

Brooke might have arrived and messed with my routine, but after getting it right today, I felt exactly as I should.

When I got to the square, the spots in front of my clothing shop, Treasure Trove, were taken. With the town's recent popularity, parking was sometimes hard to come by.

I didn't mind the walk, especially when the weather was nice.

The Tennessee October air was always a gamble. Sometimes, it felt like fall. Other times, the heat held on with an iron grip. This morning was cool, and just the feeling I needed.

"A little late today?" Marjorie asked as she walked by. She used to be retired with her wife, Henrietta, but recently, she went back to work at the town library and I got used to seeing more of her. "Bad girl, Grace."

I laughed. "When have you ever known me to be bad, Marjorie?"

"Good point. This is about as wild as you get."

"Shouldn't you also be at work?"

"Henrietta wanted a warm drink on a cold day. Sue me."

"Tell Tammy hi for me!"

"I hear they're building a coffee shop." She leaned in like it was massive news, and to be fair, it was. "I'll be the first in line. Tammy's coffee kinda sucks."

"Shh," I said. "Don't let her hear you say that. It's the one thing she can't find a good supplier for."

"I tell the truth," Marjorie said. "Don't lie to me, Grace. You're as excited as the rest of us."

"I might wind up being second in line," I said with a laugh.

"I knew it." She smiled. "I better see you there."

She waved before continuing on with her walk. As I did the

same, Hugh was walking by slowly. He looked like he always did, angry at the world and everyone in it. I smiled and waved anyway.

"Good morning, Hugh."

He paused and gave me a ghost of a smile. "Morning. It's getting cold, ain't it? This weather change is killing me." He rubbed his hands together, then blew a puff of warm breath onto them.

Most people saw him as a hindrance, but I knew he was a lonely old man who didn't have many people to talk to. I tried my best to be friendly.

"I'm excited for the cold," I replied. "You should go to Jade's shop and get some of the CBD cream she sells."

"I haven't seen that."

"It's a bit under the table since her dad thinks it's illegal."

Hugh frowned. "Are you trying to sell me drugs?"

I laughed. "You know me better than that."

"I do. I was just messin' with ya." He motioned in the direction of Jade's store. "I just might have to stop in."

"Need me to get some for you?"

"I can get my own drugs, thank you very much." He waved me off, looking annoyed at my suggestion, but it was our secret that if he truly needed it, he would take me up on the offer.

I was about to say something else when a vehicle pulled into the square, one I'd heard about but hadn't seen in action yet. People were talking because it was older than anything they'd seen around town. Not many of us had a classic truck.

As it got closer, it was obvious that it was well taken care of. The paint was pristine, and it looked like it jumped through time to be here. Whoever owned it cared for it a lot.

"Damn," Hugh said from beside me. "I haven't seen a truck like that in such good shape in a long time."

The window was rolled down and revealed a man with

dirty blond hair wearing sunglasses. On the dashboard sat a cowboy hat unlike anything I'd seen before. It was well-worn and sun drenched. It was a working hat.

I dragged my gaze to his face and the first thing I noticed was his facial hair. It was a touch darker than his hair and lined his jaw. Above his lip was a thicker mustache.

He wasn't from around here. Mostly because every woman in town would be clamoring for a man like *that*. I'd heard rumors over the last few days that Wren had brought someone new to town, but I didn't know he was so *hot*.

I could have sworn he was looking back, though his eyes were hidden by his sunglasses. My heart skipped a beat. It had been too long since a man looked at me. I was sure I had cobwebs in my vagina from the lack of romance in my life.

But all of my thoughts came to an abrupt stop when he neared a corner. Whether he was staring at me or not, he wasn't paying enough attention to the upcoming turn.

And he went over the curb and right into a stop sign.

The truck lurched and stopped suddenly. Next to me, Hugh gasped.

"The truck! He wrecked that beautiful truck! I swear, these youngins don't know respect."

I was less worried about the vehicle and more worried about the man inside.

"Let me check on him." As I ran over to him, I asked, "Are you okay?"

He took off his sunglasses, blinking as if he were shocked by his own actions. "Yeah. Must have gotten distracted at the wheel." His eyes flicked to me and stayed there.

"Why? See something you liked?"

He looked me up and down. "Definitely."

Oh, *shit*. He was into me. And he was hot.

Was I finally about to break my streak?

I blinked out of it as people started to gawk. Tammy was watching us out of the window of the diner. Jackie was doing the same from her hair salon.

What was I doing being horny in front of the whole town? I needed to get it together.

"Is your truck okay?" I asked.

"It better be!" Hugh called.

"That's something I should probably focus on." The man got out and glanced at the bumper, then he looked back at me. "It's just hard to look away from you."

"You might want to. I think it might actually do Hugh in if you ruin this thing." I nodded to Hugh, who was glaring at us.

His brow tightened as he thought about it. "I've heard that name before."

"Hugh's famous around here."

"The term is *infamous*," Hugh called. He had started making his way over as the man and I flirted. Now he was beside me. "Even I know that."

"I was trying to be nice, Hugh."

Hugh harrumphed, but I swore I saw a tinge of red on his cheeks. "Whatever. Check on the damn truck, kid, and stop staring at Grace."

"Right. Sorry, sir."

"Who the hell calls me sir?" Hugh muttered.

"People who have respect for you," I said.

"Don't flatter me."

"I always have respect for my elders," the man said.

"Did you call me old?" Hugh asked with another glare.

"Not as an insult. As a fact."

"Damn, he didn't even shrink away." Hugh crossed his arms. "Am I losing my edge?"

"Definitely not," I replied. I threw my thumb over my

shoulder at the man, adding, "He's new in town. He doesn't yet know how grumpy you can be."

"I'm not easily bothered," the man added with a smile. "And I'm happy to say I didn't just mess up my truck. I'm sure that's all you cared about."

"You're damn right. Keep your eyes on the road, kid. Or I'll take it off your hands." Hugh walked away, clearly going for a dramatic exit.

It was too bad he moved with the pace of a snail.

"Nice moves with Hugh there. You know cranky old men well."

"I work with them a lot," he said, a fond smile on his face. Then he must have remembered that we had been flirting before. "So, Hugh's the town grump. What are *you* known for?"

"Why do I have to be known for anything?"

"This is a small town. Doesn't everyone know everything?"

He wasn't wrong, but I wasn't sure how to answer. I was known for being kind. So kind to everyone in hopes I could make up for Brooke.

But that wasn't an answer a guy like this was expecting.

"Makeovers. And cute outfits."

"Definitely agree on that one. I think that skirt will be imprinted in my memory forever."

"I could give you more to remember than a skirt."

"Please do," he said lowly.

I was pretty sure my heart would explode if I didn't take a second to breathe. I stepped back and eyed him.

"How about a whole makeover? Just for you. The jeans and tight shirt can go—" *But what a tragedy that would be.* "And I could put you in . . . the new frilly pink dress I just got in stock."

He raised an eyebrow, a smile on his face. "Think I could pull it off?"

"Probably. You should show the whole town to be sure, though."

"Set the time and I'll be there."

I was hoping to make him blush as much as he was making me blush. I could see I was dealing with an expert.

"Where's your manly pride?"

"I know who I am. Don't need anything else."

"I like the confidence. More men should take after you."

"I don't think the world could handle that."

"I could," I replied. "I could handle anything you give me."

His eyebrows crept up. I could tell he liked that I was flirting back, and I wanted nothing more than for people to like me.

He opened his mouth to say something else, but we were interrupted by a loud voice. "Dean! I told you not to—" Wren looked at me. "Ignore him!"

Wren was a former reality TV star turned resident of Strawberry Springs. I hadn't gotten many chances to talk to her, but we were friendly. She was currently working with Theo, the town's former handyman, on the new coffee shop that everyone was excited about.

"She's everywhere," he muttered before turning to Wren. "For the record, she was making sure I was alive after a harrowing accident." He gestured to the curb he'd hit.

Wren wasn't moved. "Yeah, yeah. You're alive, all right. Remember what I said?"

Dean let out a long sigh before turning to me. "Sorry to cut this short, but scary boss lady calls, and she says I need to make sure my reputation doesn't reflect badly on her."

"You're known for having a reputation?"

"You could say that. Nice to meet you, Grace." He gave me a heart-stopping smile before walking toward Wren.

I stared the whole way.

2

DEAN

Strawberry Springs Neighborhood Watch

Jackie Anne: Did you see that truck that hit the stop sign on the square? That driver was YUMMY!

Comments:
Mollie Wilson: Um, Jacks, he's Cain's age.
Jackie Anne: I can look! I think Grace agrees. She talked to him right after.
Dale Garrett: I'm straight as a needle, but saw him yesterday. WHEW! I didn't know they made them like that anymore!
Kerry Winsor: He's practically a baby! What is wrong with you all!
Kerry Winsor: Wait, is he the guy with the cowboy hat??? THAT GUY?
Wren Hackett: He's my electrician and he's not gonna date any of you! Why are you all talking about him and not the wreck?
Jackie Anne: It's been a while for me, okay? I can look if I want!!!

I was craving cherry limeade, and it had everything to do with Grace's unreal outfit this morning.

It had been a long time since I was this excited to flirt with a woman, but I'd been good for a few days. It was time to ruin that.

"Are you daydreaming again?" Wren asked in the middle of her lecture. I hadn't been listening.

"Who, me? Of course not. I never daydream during important conversations."

"You're a terrible liar." She crossed her arms. "Is this thing you have with Grace gonna be a problem?"

Wren was *not* happy with me, and I didn't blame her. I'd been here two weeks and gotten distracted by Grace Day over a dozen times. Wren had told me not to talk to her, and I had kept that promise up until this morning.

This wasn't normal for me. Sure, I had flings on jobs, but they never took away from what I was trying to get done.

"Is a beautiful woman ever a problem?"

"Normally, no. But you're acting weird about her. Weirder than usual."

The difference was that I was stuck in a small town again. I'd come here as a favor to Wren, but I hated these kinds of places. Grace had been the only thing making it tolerable. And to find out she was even more fun to talk to?

Yeah, this was going to be a problem.

I'd dealt with attraction. A lot. But there was something about *this* attraction. I needed her. And being told no only made me want her more.

"Technically, she talked to me first . . . after I wrecked my truck staring at her."

"And you used that as an opportunity to flirt?"

"What? Am I supposed to just be rude?"

Wren considered it. "No, but flirting isn't a good option. Seriously, I asked Mollie, who asked Jade—"

"I don't know who any of those people are."

"Yet you figured out Grace's name pretty quickly." Wren rolled her eyes. "The point is, Jade is close to Grace, and is pretty sure that Grace would *not* be into a one-night stand. It's been a bit, but she always does things the usual way. Dating, and then sex. I don't think this would work. She would get attached."

Attachment was the bane of my existence. I'd managed not to have that issue ever since high school, ever since Julie. I had Mom. And then I had work. It was fine.

And if I had one thing to thank Julie for, it was teaching me to protect myself early. To everyone, I was the lighthearted, fun guy. The guy to sleep with and move on.

Some got attached and I had to turn them down, but I made it clear who I was from the get-go.

There would be no relationship. It was just fun.

That's what kept me from getting my ass hurt, after all.

Some tried to fight it. Some heard no and thought it meant yes if they pushed hard enough. I knew I was just a game. A challenge.

Wren had seen a perfect example of it when the director of the show she used to work on tried to get me to date her. I'd said no, and drama had ensued. Wren didn't want that here, and I didn't blame her.

I fucking *hated* being a part of the small-town rumor mill.

But dammit, I wanted Grace. I saw her, and every logical thought I had flew out the window.

"I've got it," I said with a laugh. "Contrary to popular belief, I can listen."

"I'm waiting for confirmation on that one. Now get your

truck off the curb before it gets stolen. A beauty like that is catching eyes."

"Is there even crime around here?"

"Most of it is committed by Hugh. But don't test the waters."

"I get it. No testing waters." I put my hands up in mock defense. "I can be good."

"Your truck, Dean."

I turned, hoping that Grace would still be there, but she must have gone on with her day. I wouldn't have been able to do anything anyway. I was being good.

After getting the truck into a parking spot, I was ready to get started for the day.

But I kept seeing Grace's dark curls in my mind. They hung down her back, and I had a feeling they would look even better splayed across my hotel pillow.

When I got out of the truck, someone was waiting for me.

"Hugh?" I asked. "How the hell did you sneak up on me?"

"Your damn head was in the clouds. I was gonna ask you where you got the truck, but I don't think you're capable of thinking straight."

I could've gotten offended, but I didn't. He was right.

"Well, there's no good coffee shop out here, so I'm running on empty."

"We have all the main brands."

Yeah, big brands that tasted like battery acid.

I knew better than to argue with Hugh. Though he looked frail, guys like him packed a punch. It took staying calm when they were cranky and listening to them when they talked.

Surprisingly, that was quite hard for some people.

"To answer your question, my mom passed the truck down to me. She got it a long time ago and kept it in good shape."

His eyes narrowed. "I bet it needs a lot of work."

"It does, but I do it myself. It's what I'm up to on the weekends." Even though people looked down on it, I loved working with my hands.

"Well, at least it's not something you blew a lot of money on. It's better than some of the yahoos that come through here."

I'd heard the town had been getting tourists ever since Wren's show had aired. Some loved the idyllic, small-town feel. I had a feeling it was played up for the cameras. A reality show had to have something fake.

"I'll try not to make too many waves. Wren has me on a tight leash."

"What, you usually make waves?"

"You could say that."

Hugh squinted. "Then you'll wanna stay away from Grace. She's the town angel. Everyone likes her and no one likes *waves* near her."

My shoulders tensed. Of course they all cared about her. Of course they didn't want a guy like *me* touching her.

"Got it. She won't have any issues from me."

He nodded and walked off. I had to take a breath.

It was clear that this town was tight-knit. They all knew each other and any mistakes would be known by everyone.

Which was the exact thing I hated about small towns.

"That went well," Wren said.

"Did you seriously follow me?"

She shrugged. "I was making sure you didn't ask for more info about Grace and then get your shins kicked. Usually, he's meaner."

I gave myself one beat to grit my teeth together. I was annoyed, but I wouldn't let it show.

"You know me." I said it with a laugh I didn't feel. "I'm charming all the ladies *and* grumps."

"You're doing something." She rolled her eyes. "But I'd

really love it if you would finish up the wiring in the back today."

"Consider it done." I gave her a smile before heading inside the shop to get to work, ignoring the way just being here made me more tense than I'd ever felt in my life.

———

Usually when I worked on a project with Wren, she kept us going until late into the night. I was one of the few who would keep up with her, mostly because Clyde was the same way. The two of us were always booked because of how hard we worked and how we got the job done right the first time.

I figured this would be no different, but hours later, I was proven wrong.

"All right," Wren said as she came around the corner, "time to leave."

"It's only been eight hours," I replied as I shook my head. *Just who was she?*

"And I'm under doctor's orders to not work myself to death. And considering he's my boyfriend, I listen to him."

I'd heard about Wren and Henry when they'd gotten together on *Renovating with Love*. I'd even worked on the first season, until the director banned me from season two. When I saw the location, I hadn't minded being left out.

I had a suspicion Henry and Wren were simply a way to get her out of dating her costar, Jude, who was as shallow as a thimble, but then she'd permanently moved here. I thought she wouldn't enjoy it, but one look told me I was wrong. She practically glowed.

"Can I stay?" I asked. "I could get a lot done."

"No, you need rest too."

"I thought you wouldn't want me getting up to anything."

"Just don't break hearts," she said with a roll of her eyes. "You're allowed to have fun."

"Having fun gets me into trouble. I thought you didn't want me in the Facebook group."

"You already are," she said. "But it's for wrecking your truck, and most people found it . . . funny."

"I like to make a name for myself." I shrugged, but I had a feeling people were doing more than finding it funny.

"Go to Bell's Brews. It's down the road." She pointed to one of the buildings on the square with neon signs advertising beer. The sun was getting low in the sky, and I knew I could either go do nothing in my hotel room or I could have a drink.

The second sounded less awful.

"All right, but don't get on me if you regret this."

"Yeah, yeah. At least you're not working on electrical while tired." She waved before she left the worksite.

I put on my hat and a smile, nodding at the random people who passed by. When I entered the bar, a few people were scattered around. Hugh was in a corner with a pint glass, watching something on his phone. A lone bartender was behind the counter cleaning a cup. I approached him.

"Hey, man."

"Hey," he said. "You're new here. Welcome in."

I ignored the ripple of tension that tried to make its way into my chest. The bars in Nashville were so busy that no one could keep track of anyone. Sometimes, that was nice.

"Yeah, I am. I'm working with Wren on the coffee shop."

"I heard about that." He leaned in. "Can you hurry it up? We've been waiting for good coffee for what feels like ages."

Despite myself, I laughed. "I tried. Wren is the one who called it for the night. She said we need 'rest.'" I put air quotes around it.

"Well, none of us are gonna stop her. She nearly killed

herself getting that library done." He sighed. "Naming it after her wasn't enough."

My eyebrows rose. I hadn't been over to it yet since my thoughts had been on work and Grace. "That wasn't in the show."

"Screw the damn show. We did it to be nice. We love Wren."

I slowly nodded. "Well, she's pretty awesome."

"Her boyfriend thinks the same." I wasn't sure if he meant it as a gentle reminder or not. I hated not knowing what had gotten out about me. I knew that I hadn't hit on anyone in town, but I wouldn't put it above Wren to warn people that I didn't stick around.

"I just work for her," I rushed to say. If word had gotten out, most people were going to assume I slept with anything that breathed. That had certainly happened in Shady Acres.

But I only slept with people who were single and wanted a fun time.

"I'm not a fool. No one's getting her away from Henry." He put the glass down. "What are you having?"

"Whatever you have."

The bartender laughed. "We have everything those big bars in Nashville have. Gotta be a bit more specific."

I spouted off a local beer brand from right outside of Knoxville. He nodded and grabbed me a bottle.

"Thanks, uh . . ." I looked for a name tag.

"Mark," he said. "I keep forgetting we have people around here who don't know me. So many newbies. It's weird."

I was about to take a sip, but then I remembered I would need to pay. "Let me go ahead and open a tab."

"A tab? How much are you having?"

"Probably just the one."

He waved his hand. "It's on the house."

I blinked in shock. "What? Why?"

"Welcome to Strawberry Springs." He said it like it was an explanation.

"But I have to pay. You're offering me a service."

"We're lucky here," he said. "Between the show and other things, we aren't hurting for money. And hell, if I'm lucky, you'll come back while you're here."

He started to walk off, and I remembered my manners.

"Thanks, Mark!" I called, to which he nodded and got a drink for the man who'd sat next to me.

Huh. He'd been shockingly nice.

Was it because I knew Wren?

I didn't get a chance to think too hard on it because the door opened. Mark looked up to welcome whoever it was who walked in.

But then he glared.

I knew I could learn a lot about the town from how they treated their least-liked residents. I turned too, certain I was gonna see their true colors.

The woman who walked in was probably my age with wavy hair dyed bright blonde. She was dressed to the nines in a short skirt and cowboy boots that had never seen a hard day of work in their existence. As she flicked her hair over her shoulder, she looked at everything as if it were beneath her.

And I immediately decided I didn't like her either.

Was she one of the new people in town? Was she like all the invaders of Shady Acres who'd come in and taken it over?

God, I hoped she didn't talk to me. I didn't want my dick to shrivel up and fall off.

"Mark!" the woman called. "Can you get me one of those martinis?"

"I'll need your card to open a tab, Brooke." Mark's voice was flat.

Brooke crossed her arms. "You don't ask anyone else that."

"I haven't had an issue with anyone else not paying," Mark replied. "And I'm not asking Grace to cover you again. Lord knows she's done that too many times."

At the mention of Grace, my eyes shot up. Did Brooke know her?

I realized my mistake the second Brooke's eyes met mine. Now she was smiling at me, and I hadn't meant to let her know I even existed. I gave her a wave and went back to my beer. She wasn't deterred.

"I haven't seen you around," she said. "And I've seen everyone."

"I'm just passing through, ma'am."

"Hopefully you're staying long enough to buy a girl a drink?" She tilted her head to the side.

"Not really. Sorry." Her eyes narrowed.

"Brooke," Mark cut in, "you need to pay for your own this time. Don't make me call Grace."

"Are you seriously being a tattletale right now?" Brooke rolled her eyes. "Not everyone has to call my perfect big sister to watch me."

Big sister. So Brooke was from here. They'd turned against one of their own. I didn't blame them from what I'd seen so far. But how was a person like Grace related to a woman like this?

"Brooke. Your card." Mark held out his hand. She slammed her card down.

Jesus. She was definitely over twenty-one, but she sure didn't act like it.

"And just so you know," she said to me, her tone now harder than I'd heard it, "if a girl out of your league is hitting on you, you don't say no."

"Someone in town already has my eye, sorry." I said it without thinking, but it worked.

"I bet it's fucking Jade. That weirdo gets all the guys." Brooke emphatically rolled her eyes again and went to a table.

"Well then," I muttered.

"Is she right?"

I jumped. "Shit. Mark, I didn't know you'd come back."

"I wasn't sure if I needed to save you or not. If you'd been into her, I definitely would've. But now I need to know who you've got your eye on. Brooke mentioned Jade."

"I . . . haven't met Jade, so no." I wasn't sure how to get out of his interested stare. Damn small-town gossip. "You probably shouldn't keep Brooke waiting for long."

Mark shook his head. "She needs to learn some patience anyway."

"I just said that to get her away from me," I replied with a shake of my head. "I haven't talked to anyone."

"I know you've met Grace."

I sighed. "You heard that in the Facebook group, didn't you?"

He smiled. "You know how small towns work, don't you?"

"All too well. And I won't be talking to Grace again."

His eyes narrowed. "Why's that? Don't let her sister scare you off. Grace got all the kindness from her mother."

"Grace is very nice," I said. "But I've been banned from talking to her."

"Who would've done that? Oh, Wren? She doesn't seem like the type."

Did they ever stop? Did I need to tell them my life story while I was at it?

"The point is you have nothing to worry about."

Mark hummed before I was saved by the ticking time bomb in the bar.

"Mark!" Brooke yelled. "Stop yapping and get me my drink."

"Fuck," Mark said. "She got worse when she went to Nashville."

He stalked over to work on Brooke's drink. I let out a sigh and went back to my beer. Thank God I was out of the hot seat.

I sipped on my beer, loosely watching the bar. Brooke got what she was waiting on. A few other people slipped in, greeting Mark like old friends. Thankfully, he seemed to stay busy and forgot about what he was asking me.

Out of habit, I scanned the bar for someone to go home with. I'd been banned from breaking hearts, but not from everything. Other than Brooke, there wasn't anyone here who was close to my age and looking twice at me. I shouldn't have been surprised that a bar like this was quiet on a weeknight.

But even if I did have my eye on someone, I had a feeling they wouldn't hold a candle to Grace.

Which meant I was going back to my hotel alone.

"So, you're the guy everyone's been talking about?" A man with close-cropped hair sat in the seat next to me. "I'll admit, I'm curious."

I knew they'd been talking. I wasn't a fool. I grinned like one anyway. "I like to make a good first impression. This time it was by hitting a stop sign. I'm Dean."

I offered my hand, which he shook. "Atticus. I'm the local vet."

"Careful with that one, man!" Mark called over. "He's a heartbreaker!"

I suppressed the urge to glare. Were they not even going to hide it? Damn. "Says who?" I asked.

"You turned down Brooke, of all people," Mark said. "That takes balls."

I sipped the beer. So, Wren hadn't warned anyone yet.

"You're a hot topic around here," Atticus said. "Watch out for cougars, though."

It was either the annoyance, or this beer was stronger than I thought, because I had no clue what he was talking about.

"How long are you in town for?" Atticus asked.

"Until I'm done with the coffee shop," I said. "Then I'm back in Nashville."

"Damn, you don't look like you're from there." Mark nodded to my hat. "Those usually look fake."

"This I use for the sun. I hate it in my eyes." I shook my head. "I did get it from one of those tourist shops, though. I figured I could put it to work, like a real cowboy hat."

Both men laughed.

"I wear them too," Atticus said. "My daughter and stepson think I look like a fool, but I think it's nice to see when a horse is about to kick me. It's bright here in the summer."

"Exactly. But for me, it's either a car about to run me over or some electrical line I'm dealing with."

"We're getting some of that stupid Nashville traffic out here." Mark shook his head. "And I thought Hugh was bad."

I laughed, but nothing I'd seen here was as bad as the city. "I'm a part of it, considering my wreck this morning."

"Speaking of that, we were talking about—" Mark began, but stopped. "Wait a second, did Brooke leave?"

We all turned. Lo and behold, the blonde was nowhere to be found.

"I knew it was too peaceful in here," Atticus said.

"This is why I always get her card." Mark stepped away to run the card. That was when his jaw dropped and his face went red.

"Is everything okay?" I asked when he returned.

"Got a call to make," he muttered.

"Did her card decline again?" Atticus asked.

"Yep. And I have a feeling she won't answer the phone."

"Don't tell me you're calling Grace."

"I don't have a choice," he said with a sigh. "I hate bothering the poor girl, but I can't leave an open tab."

"I'll pay it," I said immediately.

They both turned to me. I had a feeling Grace cleaned up a lot of Brooke's messes. I couldn't sleep with her, but I could do this.

"Seriously?" Mark asked. "You know, doing nice things for Brooke doesn't go that well."

"I'm not doing it for Brooke. I'm doing it for Grace."

Atticus's brow furrowed. "Are you and her . . ."

"She's the one you're into!" Mark said.

Well, shit. I'd been found out. "I'm banned from talking to her," I reiterated. "So you don't have to worry about that."

"Why?"

"I . . . don't really stick around."

Both men stiffened. "Oh," Mark said.

"You're one of those playboys then?" Atticus's tone was cooler than it had been earlier. "We don't really . . . do that around here. We all like connection."

Of fucking course they did. "That's why I'm staying away from her."

"Good. You have some sense."

"The point is, I just wanna do something nice." I needed to get them back on track and not lose my mind.

Mark seemed to consider it.

"You know getting involved in the young people's drama isn't gonna do any good," Atticus said to him. "I stay out of it."

"Yeah, Atticus, and I watch Jade in here trying to forget Gabriel exists." Mark gave him a flat look.

Atticus rolled his eyes. "Not this again."

"Do you guys have this conversation a lot?" I asked. "Seems like an old wound."

Dammit. Was I wanting to know what had happened? Yes. I did.

I was from a small town, after all.

"Every time he comes in here," Mark said with a sigh. "Welcome to Strawberry Springs. We have a lot of drama."

"Then let me take one away." I handed over my card. "Don't even tell her I did this."

Mark took the card with one pensive look and then disappeared. "And put my beer on there!"

"Absolutely fucking not!"

"Damn," I muttered. "What's a guy gotta do to pay a bill?"

"Mark does that for people he likes."

I nearly broke my neck looking at Atticus.

"Seriously?"

"You seem like a cool guy," he said with a shrug. "Other than the sleeping around thing."

And there it was.

Now that I'd been honest about my intentions, they'd see me differently. Normally, that wouldn't bother me, but being in a small town made me feel off-kilter, and them knowing me as a playboy didn't feel as comforting as it normally did.

At least I wouldn't be here long enough to care.

My card appeared in front of me. "Well, that's one less call to make. Thanks, Dean."

I took it. "No problem. I'm gonna get out of here and we'll all pretend this never happened."

Mark nodded and Atticus waved. I gave them one last smile before walking out the door.

I didn't make it one step before I ran right into someone.

Curly hair. Curves. And wide hazel eyes.

Grace.

3

GRACE

Strawberry Springs Neighborhood Watch

Hu Gh: Grace and Dean. Calling it now. Something is gonna happen between those two.

Comments:
Jackie Anne: You mean MY cowboy?
Mollie Wilson: What happened to only looking???
Atticus Thompson: Hugh, you need to get your eyes checked. As much as I love betting, Grace isn't gonna be into what he's offering.
Dale Garrett: I'm determined to continue my streak. Placing bets that Hugh is wrong.
Tammy Jane: I'll take that bet.
Hu Gh: Fools! All of ya!
Wren Hackett: Guys, when I say he's not gonna date any of you, I really mean it. He doesn't . . . do relationships. Ever. He's a one-time guy.
Tammy Jane: A breed 'em and leave 'em type? What a jerk!
Mollie Wilson: Did you have to use the word breed?

Jade Clark: Sometimes I wish I didn't know how to read.

DAMMIT. Shit. Fuck.

Cursing wouldn't solve my problems, but it was better than screaming at my sister, who wouldn't give a single shit that she'd just essentially stolen from Mark. When she'd come home smelling like a martini, I knew she'd been to the bar. And when I questioned her, that's when she admitted her little trick that she'd picked up in Nashville.

Give the bartender a card with just enough money on it to cover the initial check the POS system did, and then dip after racking up a bill.

What the hell was wrong with her?

Brooke had a reputation, one that she kept adding to, even when she was in town for only one night. I didn't want this for her, but she didn't seem to care.

Mark was a good man. He'd been patient with her, but if she kept doing shit like this, she would get herself banned from Bell's Brews.

God, I owed him his favorite whiskey for this, which meant I needed to drive out of town to get it, and then come back another day to drop it off when he wasn't around so he would actually accept the damn thing.

But first, I needed to pay this tab.

Did I have the money for it? Not really. But I could eat ramen for a few days and deal.

I parked in front of the bar and nearly ran for the door. I threw it open, planning to hurry in and out, but instead, I ran into a hard chest.

Hands steadied me, and I had to pull myself out of my thoughts to lay my eyes on who I'd nearly bowled over.

And it was Dean. Tall, well-muscled, and very good-smelling Dean. God, he was in the hat too. My breath caught, but I shook it off. I had a mission.

"Excuse me," I said. "I just need to—"

"Get a drink?" he asked.

"Talk to Mark."

His eyes narrowed, and I had no idea why he even cared. "About what?"

There was something about his light tone that gave me pause. To anyone else, it would be him simply making conversation.

But I saw more. I always saw more.

"You already know, don't you?"

His mouth partially opened at my observation, but then closed. "I know that you have nothing to worry about."

"I do have something to worry about, unless you know something I don't about an unpaid tab."

Dean huffed out a laugh. "You're quick."

"I tend to be, and as much as I enjoyed our little conversation earlier, I do need to handle this. Unless . . . something else happened." There were many things that could have gone down. Mark could have decided to clear it out, or some poor idiot charmed by her smile and boobs had paid it for her.

"The tab's paid," he said.

Oh, no. *No.* "Please tell me you weren't the one to do it."

"Damn, Grace. Are you a mind reader or something?"

I had to be if I were going to keep Brooke in check.

"Listen, don't do nice things for Brooke. Even if you think she's hot, it's not worth it."

"First of all," he said slowly, "I think she's a little too whiny to be hot."

Despite how tonight had gone, I laughed. I needed to hear that. "At least you're not totally dumb."

"And second, I didn't do it to be nice to her. Mark was gonna call you, so I stopped him."

"Wha—you paid it for *me*?"

"Yep. So go home and relax."

My brain couldn't comprehend this. People were always kind to me, but they never jumped in to save me. I always had to do that myself. "I can pay you back."

"Pay me back by having a nice night, Grace."

Damn. He'd done something nice for me and didn't expect anything in return? How could a man like this get even hotter?

"I owe you one," I replied. "Let's go in and get a drink."

I could tell he didn't expect me to invite him in by the way his eyebrows rose, but I *did* owe him. And even though I didn't have the money, I was already willing to pay for my sister, so two $5 beers wouldn't break the bank any more than Brooke's bill would have.

And it wouldn't be hard to look at him for a few hours. His vibe alone told me he was a fun guy, but there was something else I'd love to figure out. Maybe it was his confidence. Maybe it was how kind he could *really* be.

It wouldn't take me long to crack him open like an egg.

"I'd love to take you up on that," he replied. "But I can't."

"Let me guess, you have to get up early for work?" He did a physical job. Maybe we could take a rain check.

"Trust me, Grace, I know how to handle a late night." My cheeks darkened at the implication. "But I've been told not to do anything with you. And that includes having drinks."

"Would you *want* to do more with me?"

A slow smirk made its way across his face. "Baby, if I told you the answer to that question, I'd get in huge trouble."

"Get in trouble then." My voice was breathless and I felt like I had run a marathon. Then I processed his words. "Wait, who told you not to talk to me? Why would they do that?"

"Wren did. And it's because of me. I don't do relationships. Ever. If we did anything, it'd be a one-time thing and then I'd move on."

He said it like he'd rehearsed it, and I wondered how many other women he'd given this speech to before.

"O-oh," I said. Too much had happened in the last hour, and I was struggling to keep up.

Dean was a playboy. He was into someone for one night.

Years ago, I would have said no to a guy like this. I'd had big dreams of a romance that resulted in kids and a great, loud life.

And now I was over thirty. The last guy I was with was from out of town and thought my left butt cheek was my clit.

And since then, my options hadn't been great.

But now, I wanted to enjoy *something*. Vibrators only did so much. I wasn't desperate enough to ruin my reputation with anyone here. But a visitor? Someone who didn't want commitment? Someone who'd be gone soon?

Yeah, I could do that.

"Your information was wrong," I said.

"And what information is that?"

"Whoever told you I wanted a relationship."

"Really?" he asked slowly. "You sure?"

I nodded. "I love the idea of a one-night stand. Especially if you're still offering."

"I'd offer any time of the day, but I'm serious about the no-relationship thing. And I also don't think anyone should know."

"Because you're being a little bad?" I asked. I understood way too well.

"That, and I'd prefer to keep my balls attached to my body, thank you."

I laughed. It was too easy to talk to Dean, and I found myself wishing we could do it more. I genuinely did want to figure him out. But I had a feeling he didn't want to be.

If he wanted sex, then sex would be all he would get. And if no one knew? That was even better.

"I'm with you on the no one knowing thing. I don't really do things like this, and with how Brooke is, I'd prefer to remain the good sister."

"And the relationship thing?"

"I agree to your terms. I promise I won't be chasing you down after this is over." Slowly, he nodded and a smile crossed over his face. *Perfect.* I'd said exactly what he wanted me to. "So, wanna get outta here before anyone sees us? People will start coming out of the bar here soon."

"My hotel is twenty minutes away."

"Folks might see me get into your truck. Not ideal. I have the perfect place."

"This is *your* shop?"

My eyes roamed over the racks of clothes. Not much was visible since I hadn't turned the lights on. But I knew styles of all kinds were on display. "Yep. I bought it a few years ago."

I'd saved every dollar from all the jobs I'd ever had. It also helped that I bought the place when everything seemed to be falling apart. I put my heart and soul into this and the rest of the town.

"That's very impressive." His eyes trailed every wall. "A one-night stand in a clothing shop is a new one for me."

I shook myself out of it at the reminder. This was a one-night stand. Nothing else.

"The blinds are closed, and as long as we don't turn the lights on, no one will know we're here."

"So I can't even see you? Seems a little unfair."

"It's the price to pay to stay out of the town news," I said.

"The fucking town news," he muttered. That raised a flag in my mind. His words were coated with a bitterness that I wanted to understand. Had he been the subject of gossip before?

But Dean instead captured my lips in a kiss, which immediately silenced my thoughts. He was a good kisser. Actually, one of the best. His lips were soft even as his hands kept a tight hold on me. He smelled clean, like a man's soap that I couldn't place. It was the kind of thing I could come home to.

No. Nope. I pushed the thought out. This was just sex. No relationship would come of it.

Dean's hands moved from my hips to the small of my back, slipping under my shirt. It had been too long since I slept with anyone, and I tried to resist making a sound at the first skin-on-skin contact I'd had in a while. But it slipped out in the form of a quiet moan.

"S-sorry," I said, pulling away for a second. "We should probably be quiet. These walls aren't soundproof."

"Nah," he said. "I *love* hearing when I make a woman feel good. And these old buildings are better built than you think."

"I'm guessing you know from the coffee shop?"

"I do, and everyone's at the bar. So let loose, baby. Tell me if I make you feel good."

"Does that mean you actually know how to make me feel good?"

"I'll show you how good I can make you feel."

My breath hitched as I watched his silhouette get on his knees. This was all so new to me, yet it felt dangerous in a way I wasn't familiar with. I'd always done things the right way to keep myself in line.

Breaking that was both terrifying and thrilling.

Dean went under my skirt and moved my panties down. I hoped he gave as good as he talked. If I finally stepped out of line and he was terrible at sex, then I might lose my mind.

But then he picked me up and placed me on the counter before his mouth covered my core, his tongue going right for my clit. He didn't fumble around. He didn't struggle. He knew right where to go.

He gave it one long lick, which I felt all the way in my toes. If he could manage to keep that up, I'd come in a few minutes, which was a record for me.

I should have known he was just getting started. When Dean went in the second time, he painted a *mural* with his mouth, tongue dancing over my core in an expert way. I let out a shocked gasp and had to brace myself on the counter to keep from falling over. He wasn't a playboy just because of his charm.

He also knew what he was doing.

I'd never been given oral like this. And I let him know with my moans whenever he hit my clit just right. I didn't hold back any sound, just as he asked. I'd never built up so quickly, and if I wasn't careful, I could get addicted to it.

I didn't know a man could eat me out like this. If I had, I would have been looking for a one-night stand a long time ago.

"Fuck, Dean, I'm gonna . . ." I trailed off, warmth taking over. My orgasm pushed out every other thought and my head rolled back as my vision whited out.

I pushed away, ready to offer to return the favor, but he pulled me back.

"No. We're staying right here until you come as many times as you want." His voice was rough and he sounded like a man starved.

And now I saw why women wanted him. Why they wanted him to stick around.

I wasn't sure how he knew that I was the kind of person who could come multiple times, but no one ever had the patience to get me there. It was always one for me, if that, and one for him.

Dean returned to my pussy, and even though I was sensitive, it still felt incredible.

Ripples erupted from my core. This time, he added his fingers, finding my G-spot in a matter of seconds.

"*God*," I managed to say as I put more weight on my palms. I bet he made women feel like this all the time, and I wasn't sure if it made me feel better or worse that his talents didn't go to waste.

I was a mess when I came again. My body shook with the heat coursing through me. I figured he would let up after that, but he kept going and the pleasure never truly left. It kept increasing until it overtook me, and I was in space for a few blissful moments.

My life had irrevocably changed. That was for sure.

When it faded, he finally looked up at me. "Want more?"

When had I gotten so out of breath? Was it the never-ending orgasm? "I think I'll pass out if you keep going. Besides, when is it gonna be your turn?"

"I'm a patient man."

I could see that, but I wasn't sure *I* was all that patient.

"Good. It's time to reward all that patience." I coaxed him away and he stood. I brushed my hand over his cock. Just by the feel of it alone, I knew this was going to continue to be life-changing for me, but then I tugged his pants down and ran my hand from the base to the head, and I felt metal.

"Is that a . . . piercing?" I asked slowly. I'd heard of them, sure. But I didn't think anyone went through with it.

And certainly not anyone I'd slept with.

"It is. Like it?"

"I've never been with anyone who had one."

"This is the kind that makes it better for both of us." Could this be any better? Was it even possible?

"Did it hurt when you got it?"

He laughed. "Don't worry about me. Worry about how you'll be feeling."

I felt like a virgin again with no idea how this worked. He pulled out a condom from his pocket and ripped it open with his teeth. He was so hot like this, and I couldn't help but wonder what was underneath the fun-guy exterior he put out for everyone else. There had to be more to him, things that he hid. I wanted to know his whole story.

What was I doing? Wasn't the whole point of this that it was supposed to be just fun? I needed to turn my brain off and focus on *him*. Just how this felt. Nothing else.

"Are you good?"

I nodded, forcing myself back into the moment. He'd gotten the condom on and was watching me like I watched other people. "Never better."

"If you change your mind, you can let me know at any time. I might do this a lot, but I'll never take it further than the person is willing to go."

"That's sweet of you," I said, and it was. I didn't expect this one-time thing to include so much kindness. "But I'm ready to keep going."

I needed it. No more thoughts. Just feelings.

And that's exactly what I got when he bracketed me with his arms as he leaned over the counter.

Dean pressed inside of me slightly and I knew he was bigger than anyone I'd been with in the past. I regretted not turning the lights on. At least I would know what I was working with.

My body tensed, trying not to let him in. He paused.

"Ah, sorry." My cheeks burned. "It's been a while."

"Shh, it's fine."

"Just keep going. I'll relax eventually."

We'd already made it this far. He may as well get what he wanted. I was sure I'd enjoy it by the end.

"We're gonna take all the time we need."

"But—"

"Grace, breathe for me, baby."

"You should—"

"I'm not doing anything until you relax. I've got all night." He leaned down and brushed a kiss on my cheek. "Now, take a deep breath." I didn't understand why he didn't keep going, but I sucked in air anyway. "That's right," he said gently as his lips brushed my jaw. "You're doing so good."

My heart skipped a beat. Was that . . . doing something for me?

Dean was able to press in farther. The metal of his piercing brushed against my inner walls, and *fuck*, it felt good.

His lips found my neck as he pulled out and pressed inside of me again.

"You like to be complimented, don't you?" I could feel his words on my skin.

"I guess I do," I replied. "I've never had anyone do it before, though."

"I'll happily be the first."

"There's probably a limit to how many you can find." I was just sitting here as he slowly made his way into me.

"I can find plenty," he whispered. "Now shut up and let me compliment you."

I closed my mouth as he placed another open-mouthed kiss on my neck and followed it up with light pressure from his teeth.

"God, you feel even better than I imagined." His hands roamed from my hips to my breasts and he pressed in an inch deeper. I thought I was seeing stars. "You take my cock so well."

I was glad the lights were off. I had a feeling my whole body was flushing.

"I-I don't think I am, considering how slow we're going."

"You're not feeling what I do. I'm barely inside of you, and this is the best I've ever felt."

They were empty compliments. They had to be, but *oh*, how they worked. I was slowly opening up to him and he was able to advance with each word.

"Halfway, baby."

"Only halfway?" I let out a moan. "There's no way—"

He cut me off with another kiss. "Oh, it'll fit. With how perfect you are? There's no way it *won't*."

"Ah—I don't think—"

"Breathe," he stressed again.

I shut my eyes and took in a breath. Then one more.

"You look beautiful like this."

"You can't even see me."

"I don't need to. You're always so fucking beautiful. I can't stop looking at you."

I let out a gasp as I finally, *finally*, felt him push fully into me. I'd never been filled like this, and I knew that once this was over, I would need a new dildo. Mine wouldn't cut it anymore.

I was at a loss for words as he started fucking me. I could only let out broken sounds. The angle he had me at made the piercing hit me in all the right areas, and I had to screw my eyes shut as another orgasm grew.

"I'm gonna—"

"Come on my cock, baby." Dean's voice was rough in my ear. "Let it happen."

Coming three times in one session had to be some record for me, but it happened anyway. I heard him mutter a curse before he thrust into me one last time. He pulsed as he filled the condom.

Holy *shit*. He was a gift to women everywhere.

I wished he was a gift to only me, though. The thought made the post-orgasmic glow fade. I was plummeting back down to Earth, and fast. I thought I could do this, but the thoughts of attachment were already creeping in.

We sat in silence as both of us caught our breaths. The last bit of pleasure was gone from my body as I faced the fact that I had no idea what to do next.

"T-thanks," I said awkwardly as he pulled out of me. "That was good."

"Hopefully better than good."

"It was," I said as I tried to figure out what he wanted from me. Did I smack his ass and say "good game"? Did I simply tell him to leave? "Um, should we clean up?"

"Y-yeah, definitely."

At least he sounded as awkward as I felt. He disposed of the condom as I struggled to figure out what to say. There was only silence in the room as he walked over to where both of our clothes had been thrown around. I figured he would tug his on and then make a run for it, but he went through it all and handed me mine too.

"You okay?" he asked. His voice was steady and back to normal. Whatever I'd heard earlier was a blip.

"Yeah, definitely."

"You don't seem okay. Was it too much? Do you need anything?"

I would be sore, but I didn't mind that. "No, I'm good. I promise. I just don't know what to do at this part."

"This part?" he asked.

"When the one-night stand is over."

"Well, this is the part where I say you were amazing and I really enjoyed that."

"And then it's goodbye," I finished.

"Yeah. Then goodbye."

"Okay," I said as I took a breath. "Then I should say I really enjoyed that too. Thank you for the fun night."

There was a moment where he paused before saying something else. I wished more than anything that I could see his expression. Was he confused? Worried? Did he look like he wanted to do this again?

"Thank you too. See you around, Grace."

And then he walked out of my shop. When he was gone, I let out a sigh that turned into a groan.

I was a *terrible* one-night stand. It seemed that attachment was what I did best.

It was just my luck that the best sex of my life was with a guy who would never want to see me again.

4

DEAN

Strawberry Springs Neighborhood Watch

Marjorie Brown: Does anyone know if Dale has any more of those lime sodas?

Comments:
Jade Clark: I was there last night and I didn't see any.
Kerry Winsor: Wait a second, a serious post from you two? The world must be coming to an end . . .
Marjorie Brown: I would never joke about something so amazing to me.
Dale Garrett: Sorry, guys, that was a one-time thing. Someone came in and bought them all.
Marjorie Brown: Who could be so selfish? I should have bought them all first!

———

"Damn, Dean, that wall looks good."
I was still focused on making sure it was totally smooth

before I turned to Wren. I took pride in my work, and that included putting things back together when I tore them apart. Most people didn't worry about the details. I did.

And I was able to finish up early too.

But my mind hadn't been here, even as I forced myself to work on projects. It was in the Treasure Trove with Grace, reliving the night before.

The sounds she made. The way she felt. It was addicting in a way that I couldn't describe.

I hadn't gotten her out of my system, which was new for me. Usually, I was able to move on.

But I pulled myself out of those thoughts and focused on Wren, who was still staring at me.

"Hopefully Theo likes it," I replied. "He seems a little nervous about this being done."

"This is a dream of his. Now that he just has to paint, I bet he's realizing how close he is to being done."

I took a look around the coffee shop. Other than the joint compound I'd put on the drywall, it was put together. The walls were mostly white, with the exception of the one that was original brick.

"You'll have to let me know what he does with the place." Usually, I wouldn't care, but this was a man's dreams being realized.

"You could see it yourself. I might have more work for you."

"How much could you possibly have?" I knew how towns like this were.

"This isn't your average small town," Wren replied. "You'd be surprised."

I had a feeling she was wrong. Other than Grace, this place had mostly been what I'd expected.

My answer should have been no, but she had the same tone

as when she'd called me the first time. I'd never heard her sound so happy. I didn't want to turn her down.

"Let me know, but it depends on how my next few jobs go." Once I was out of here, I had a feeling I wouldn't think about this place ever again.

"All right, all right. I know you're in high demand. Thank you for coming to this one, though. It was good to catch up after *Renovating with Love* ended."

"It was," I said. "But small towns just aren't my scene."

"Fair enough," she said, and I was glad she wasn't pushing me. "Let's go get Theo. I can't wait to show him the whole thing."

Wren walked outside. As usual, Theo wasn't far. He'd been asked to help with something at the diner, which was the only way we'd gotten to finish it all to show him.

"Is it ready?" he asked the second we came outside.

"Yep. Are *you* ready?"

He took a breath. I could tell this coffee shop was his passion, and I knew he was going to put his all into it. Theo followed us back and his eyes traced over everything we'd done.

"How is it?"

"Perfect," he said, his voice low. "I can't wait to make it mine."

"How long will you need to open?" Wren asked. "I'll need my coffee fix soon."

"A few weeks."

She would enjoy it. Theo had told Wren what he had planned for the shop, and I knew it would be different than the sister store he was working with, even though the sister shop was already incredible. He knew what he was doing, and I hoped Strawberry Springs treated him right.

"I'll be here. And so will Mollie. She needs caffeine now that she's gonna have a newborn."

Wren talked so much about her life ever since she moved, and I knew it was a good thing. But I'd never seen her like this in all the years I'd worked with her. She was more confident and happier. It was all to do with Henry and the community she'd found here.

I was happy for her, and happy for her friend Mollie too. I hoped they didn't get hurt like I had.

"Do you need anything else?" I asked Theo. "If not, I should head out."

"No, I'm good. Excited to get to work."

I nodded and left. I assumed Wren was saying her goodbyes as I headed to my truck. She then followed me.

"Hey, wait up."

I paused and turned. "Yeah?"

"Do you wanna stay for dinner?" she asked. "Henry just texted and said he's feeling up for the diner tonight. And I owe you for staying a little longer to perfect the drywall."

"I shouldn't," I replied. "I need to get back."

"Really? I bet you'd like the diner."

"I seriously doubt that. And I bet everyone here is waiting for me to be gone."

I knew the second I said it that I shouldn't have.

"Was someone rude to you?" She crossed her arms. "Tell me and I'll beat them up."

No one had been rude, but I knew they didn't like playboys here.

"Of course not," I said with a laugh. "I'm just an outsider. Seriously, I just have a few things I need to get back to."

"All right. Don't be a stranger, though. I do like working with you."

"Uh, yeah. You too."

"I know that was hard for you considering how you hate being seen as liking someone."

This was teetering on a topic I didn't want to talk about. "It's not about attachment. I just like to not be tied down."

"Okay, okay. I'll leave you alone about it," she said. "Have a safe drive home."

I watched Wren walk away before my eyes turned to the Treasure Trove.

Was she inside? Would she want to see me?

I didn't go back for more. I'd learned a long time ago it wasn't good for me. We'd agreed to do it once and I was due to leave.

My feet carried me to Grace's shop anyway.

A bell announced my entry, and I saw her on top of a ladder changing a mannequin.

"One second," she called.

"Take your time."

Her head jerked toward me when she heard my voice, and she immediately lost her footing on the ladder. I was there in an instant and caught her right before she hit the ground.

"Oh my—thank you," she said breathlessly. "I'm surprised you were able to catch me."

"Why's that?"

"I'm not exactly thin."

I rolled my eyes. "Baby, any man who can't lift you should go back to the gym."

Her shocked laugh was beautiful, and I slowly put her back on her feet. She tucked a strand of curly hair behind her ear. She was wearing yet another perfect outfit. Instead of a skirt, she wore cheetah print pants that hugged every inch of her, and a crop top that showed the slightest bit of stomach.

"You should have used that panty-melting line a few days ago. It would have instantly worked."

Would it work again? I had to stop myself from saying it and a loud silence took its place.

Grace cleared her throat and looked away. "So, are you here for your makeover? I have a pink dress with your name on it."

I crossed my arms, feeling unusually tense talking to her. I hadn't felt like this since high school. "I was heading out, actually."

Grace's eyes went wide. "Is the coffee shop done already?"

"It is. The rest is just painting and decorating, which Theo insists on doing himself."

"Wow. It feels like you just got here."

"I've been here for a while. I spent most of it staring at you, though."

"If you weren't so hot, that would be creepy."

"You'll have to give me a little . . . grace."

She rolled her eyes. "Oh, *wow*. Never heard that one before."

I held my hands up. "I didn't mean it as a pun . . . unless you're into that."

She laughed once more before her gaze landed on me. "So, why are you here then, Dean?"

I considered it. Should I tell her I couldn't stop thinking about her? Should it be that I wanted her again? Or should I say I just wanted to talk to her once more?

Because all of it was true.

Instead, I took one step forward and pressed my lips to hers. She made the most adorable little squeak I'd ever heard.

But then she pulled away. "Dean?"

"One more time?" I asked. "For the road."

"I thought you didn't do things again."

I didn't. This alone was out of character for me, but I was leaving anyway. I'd never see her again. Once more couldn't hurt. "Once just isn't enough for a woman like you."

Her mouth popped open and I wondered if she was going to ask me why I'd done this. I wouldn't have an answer for her.

I kissed her instead.

"You're doing a great job of convincing me," she murmured against my mouth.

"Please say yes," I said. "I have more compliments to give you."

She gasped as I nipped at her neck. "Y-yes. Fuck yes, actually."

Relief flooded me.

"We should lock the front door," I said. "And close the blinds."

"I have a way better idea."

Grace led me to the fitting room and locked that door instead. I couldn't see much since the lights weren't on.

"Baby, you gotta let me see you." I would beg. I wasn't above it.

Grace laughed and the lights flipped on. "Impatient. You just have to give me a second."

The dressing room was massive, with a full-size chair and three mirrors in one of the corners. Grace obviously spoiled everyone who tried on clothes in here. I would be enjoying this for a different reason.

"Plenty of women don't want me seeing all of them."

"I'm not shy. I just don't wanna get caught."

When she kissed me again, she led me to the chair in the corner where she landed in my lap. I cupped my hand under her ass and tugged her closer.

"Your ass is so fucking perfect." I gave it one smack. "Just like the rest of you."

"The mirror's behind me. You can see it too."

My eyes followed her direction. The sight was obscene. "You know how to torture a man, don't you?"

"More like I know how to give him what he wants." She

reached for the hem of her shirt and tugged both it and her bra off.

"Fuck," I muttered as I saw her tits for the first time. They were a handful, maybe more, and they looked better than they felt.

"I can already feel you," she said as she pressed her hips down.

"When I have a view like this? It takes seconds."

Grace let out a gasp as I angled my hips up to give her more friction. Her pants, as hot as they were, now were in the way.

"I need these off," I said.

"God, yes." She was off of me, and a moment later, I had the best view of my life. She was in a thong of all things, and it reflected three times in the mirror.

I whimpered as I bit my knuckles.

"What? Too much?"

"This is the greatest view I've ever had in my life."

"Let's make it better," she said as she climbed on my lap and pressed her lips into mine. The sight alone of her ass in a thong had me on the edge like I was a fucking teenager, and then I felt how wet she was through the thin fabric and I thought I was going to lose it.

"The piercing makes it so good," she said. "Even just like this."

"We need to pause," I said through gritted teeth.

She froze. "Did I do something wrong?"

"No, you're too fucking good, Grace. I need a second before this is over way too soon."

Her eyes went wide. "Oh."

She had no clue what she did to me. And if I were being honest, I didn't want to think too hard about it either.

"Get on the chair," I said. "Let me eat you out while I wait."

She let out a giggle. "Who am I to say no to that?"

We swapped positions and I moved the thong out of the way, licking her cunt like it was my last meal on Earth. I loved eating women out, but she was a whole other story. Usually it took me time to figure out what they liked, to get them to be loud and let me know where they were.

But with Grace, it clicked immediately.

It was like I knew her even though I didn't. When I tried something, it pushed her closer to the edge. When she was getting tired, I knew.

Her thick thighs wrapped around my head as she ground against me. I matched her movements, ignoring the way she could easily pop me like a watermelon. If I went out, I went out in the best place on Earth.

"Fuck, Dean." Her voice was so breathy I almost couldn't understand her. "I'm about to come already."

That was the best compliment I could ever receive, so I renewed my efforts.

I felt the rush of liquid that told me Grace had come, but I also heard it too. She let out a cry as she tumbled through her orgasm, her entire body arching.

My little break had done nothing to slow me down. Just her sounds were about to take me apart.

"You're so fucking incredible," I muttered.

"Are you saying that to me or my pussy?"

"Fucking both at this point." I was about to go in for more and make her come again, but she pushed me away.

"I need you to fuck me," she said.

"I need you to let me make you feel good. Many times."

"Who says I won't do that on your cock?"

Fuck. She would be the death of me. I knew it. I kissed my way up her, stopping to pull her nipple into my mouth just so I could hear her gasp, and then brought her mouth to mine. She got off the chair and flipped us so I was sitting and pressing just inside of her.

I was lost in it all, so that was the only explanation for what I did next.

I kept going.

Grace was as tight and hot as she had been the night before, but this was better. Probably because I knew this would be the last time.

"Yes," she said, head tilted back. Her cheeks were red and she looked just as wrecked as I felt. This felt like reverence, like a version of heaven I didn't think I would ever see. Then she tensed just as she had last night.

"Grace, what did I say about breathing?"

"I don't care," she said as she shook her head. "There's no way I can."

"Yes, you—"

She leveled her eyes with mine. "Make it hurt, Dean. I want it to."

"You want it to, or you want it because you think I do?"

"That's a very astute observation." She tried to sink deeper. "Fuck. But this time I promise I want it."

"Why?"

"I have a feeling that'll be how this ends anyway."

I paused. Was she sore last night? Or did she mean something else?

"Dean, please." Her hands were tight on my shoulders, bringing me out of my thoughts. "Fuck me. I'm not above begging."

"You're not begging for anything with me. I'll give you what you want." My hands tightened on her hips as I prepared.

"Really? Because—*ah!*" I shoved inside of her. All the way to the hilt. "Ohmygod. *Ohmygod.*"

I worried for all of one second that I'd hurt her. "You okay?"

"So fucking good," she said. "Keep moving."

I bit my cheek as I fucked her. Behind us, I could see her ass jiggle in three torturous angles. I had to look away or I would be coming in seconds.

Grace bounced on me. Still lost in pleasure, I put one of my hands between us, hoping she would come one more time before I lost it.

"Dean!" she nearly yelled. "Yes. Yes, just like that!"

She was pulsing around my cock, and I could now hear her pussy along with her voice, and it propelled me over the edge.

I was gonna come. It was gonna be life-changing and—

Shit, I wasn't wearing a condom.

Right before my balls made the biggest mistake of both of our lives, I pulled out, letting my come explode between us and not inside of her.

I had to catch my breath as logic returned.

Had I fucked her without a condom?

I looked up at Grace and her mouth was open in horror. She was realizing the same thing.

"D-did we—" Her voice was quiet. "Tell me we didn't just do that."

"I pulled out," I said immediately. "It was definitely in time."

"I know that, but there're other risks and . . ." She trailed off, shaking her head. "I can't believe . . ."

"Me either," I said, but then I took her words in. "I get tested, though. The last one was a week ago, actually. And I have nothing. And I use a condom, always."

"Always?" she said slowly.

"Yes," I said firmly. "This was . . . a blip."

She gulped in a deep breath. "Okay, all right. Well, that's good. I got tested after the last time I did anything, and there wasn't anything for me either. So we're good there." Grace looked down at the mess between us. "Are you sure you did it at the right time?"

"Y-yeah. Mostly."

"Mostly. Awesome." Grace screwed her eyes shut. "It's fine."

"It is?"

"Yeah, it really is. I have a thing . . . I don't ovulate regularly anyway. My last period was ages ago, and I doubt I ovulated this late."

"That's called PCOS, isn't it?"

She blinked. "You know the term?"

"Yeah, my mom has it. It's why she only had me, actually. It was hard enough doing that."

"Then we're lucky, I guess. This might be the first time I'm saying this, but thank God I have PCOS."

"Yeah, and that I pulled out."

"It'll be fine." She waved it off. "Or it will be *after* I clean up."

She was gone in an instant, and I immediately missed her warmth.

I didn't need to. What was I going to do, ask her out? After I'd acted like an idiot and didn't use a condom?

"I should go," I said.

She eyed my stomach, which still had come on it. "You can stay for—"

"No, I should really go." I threw my shirt on. I was too numb to feel anything else. "This was . . . yeah. Goodbye."

"Bye," she said quietly as I threw my pants on and ran for the door.

But this was for the best. I would never see her again and life would go on. I would find someone else and resume being the fun guy. That's what I was supposed to do, after all.

This was the first time I ever wished things were different.

5

GRACE

THREE AND A HALF MONTHS LATER

Strawberry Springs Neighborhood Watch

Kerry Winsor: When is the power coming back on? I'm so bored.

Comments:
Jade Clark: We didn't do enough. She can still post.
Marjorie Brown: Dammit, there goes my quiet time.
Kerry Winsor: Do you really think I don't have cell service out at my house? I refuse to be silenced!!!
Jade Clark: How much battery does that thing have left and are you on the roof of your house to get signal? Be honest.
Kerry Winsor: 5% and shut up.
SherriffMike Finch: @**Kerry Winsor**, get your ass down before I call the fire department.

I WAS flat down on my bed, fighting for my life.

"Just . . . fucking *button*." My favorite leopard print pants were up on my waist, but for some reason, they were tighter than usual. I was used to my weight fluctuating because of PCOS, but I refused to lose my favorite pants because of it.

My period was going to start any day now. It was very late, but I'd had a small one after Dean and my . . . mishap that told me I was safe. Then I moved on, trying to forget about the sex that had changed my life.

I did wind up getting a new vibrator. And a monster dildo.

It wasn't enough.

But he was gone and it would stay that way.

And I would be fine, if I could only button my fucking pants.

With a sigh, I gave up. I stared in the mirror at my protruding belly and glared.

"You choose today to be bloated?" I muttered. The weather was nice and I wanted to look hot. Was that too much to ask?

Going back to my closet, I found one of my favorite, and looser, dresses. Once the pants were off and that was on, I took a second to admire myself again.

In all the years that I'd gained and lost weight, I knew the best way to feel better was simply wearing the right size. And in my coral dress, I looked hot as hell.

"A win is a win," I said to myself before going to the bathroom to put on my makeup.

When I was ready for the day, I headed to my car when one of the steps came loose and I fell right on my ass with a loud *thunk*. For a second, I stared at the baby-blue morning sky and wondered if I was cursed.

I wasn't. As with everything else with my house, I was letting things go. And this step had been loose for four months.

I really needed to fix that.

I really needed to fix a lot of things.

It must have been the abrupt ending to Dean and me,

because I'd been tired ever since he left. So tired that I was even behind at the store, which was new for me. Well, it wasn't all that new. I'd felt similarly when Mom died.

I shook it off as the cool air hit me. I almost wished I'd worn a jacket, but it would have ruined the outfit. My car took a while to heat up, but as I pulled into the square, my eyes drifted to the newest shop in town out of habit. Theo's had opened with an explosion of business, and while the coffee was great, I thought about the man who'd helped bring it to life.

Dean was never coming back, yet I kept looking, hoping he'd come to town to try the coffee.

It was ridiculous. Our little affair was over, yet there was something about the second time that lingered in my mind, like a puzzle waiting to be figured out. It kept me up at night, and it only added to my bone-deep exhaustion.

Hopefully, I was hiding it well. No one knew that I sometimes took naps in the stockroom, and they didn't need to.

When I got to the front door of the Treasure Trove, Jade walked up behind me.

"Are you about to open up for the day?" she asked.

"Nah, I was just gonna go inside and hang out for no reason."

She rolled her eyes as I smirked, but I would let her in even if I wasn't open. She and I had known each other since we were kids. We'd been friends, but it really solidified after Gabriel left. She'd needed someone, and I wanted to help.

"Come in," I said. "What do you need?"

I had a feeling I knew what it was, considering she was in her Converse instead of her usual combat boots.

"The soles ripped again," she said with a sigh.

"Seriously? What the *hell* are you doing with your boots?"

"Going through forests, kicking men when they piss me off." She shrugged. "They work hard."

"I have another pair I could sell you," I said. "Let me go grab them."

"You're the best," she called as I walked to the stockroom. "And who let your tits look so good today?"

I laughed, but I enjoyed the compliment.

Then my mind drifted to all the ones Dean had left me with.

"Grace, get it together," I muttered to myself. "He probably hasn't thought about you once."

I'd say this, and then think about him again. It was a brutal cycle, and I knew I was never allowed to have a one-night stand again.

I grabbed the shoes and brought them out to Jade. She walked right up to the checkout counter and handed me her card, knowing that I had her sizes memorized after all the years of being friends.

"What is it with men not being able to find the clitoris?" she asked.

I blinked at the abrupt topic change, but this wasn't unusual for her.

Besides, the last man I'd been with had no trouble with that, but I didn't need to be thinking of him.

"It might be too early in the morning to talk about this."

She rolled her eyes. "Come on, you love it when I complain about men. You say it's your time to live vicariously through someone."

She was right, but I'd been off for months. I didn't want her to notice that, though.

"Fine," I said with a laugh.

She immediately dug in. "Do they purposefully miss it?"

"You just have to find the right guy," I replied.

"Those are in short supply. I knew I should've found that hot electrician when he was here."

My gaze shot up. "You were into him?"

"Uh, *yeah*." She said it like it was obvious. "Who wasn't? I'd give anything to know the size of that man and—wait, you're blushing."

"I'm not." It was a lie. My cheeks were red.

"I should have brought him up sooner," she said. "I was too busy sulking over Gabe."

"No, you don't need to bring him up."

"Why? Are you trying to hide that you were into him too?"

"No," I said with a roll of my eyes. "I definitely wasn't."

"You're definitely lying. You can admit it. We all were into him."

This was not how I wanted this to go. I needed to forget the whole thing, not talk about it.

"Hang on," she said. "You're acting super weird about him."

"I'm really not."

She gasped. "You are. Did you sleep with him?"

I hated it when she read me. She was one of the few who was sometimes right.

"You did!" She jumped up and down. "Please tell me he fucked hard."

"Why do you need to know?" I nearly groaned.

"Because it's time for you to contribute to our clit talks."

"Clit talk?" I repeated and then shook my head. "We're not naming our conversations about your sexual disappointments *clit talk*."

"What about clit conversations? There's some alliteration there."

I laughed. "Still no."

"You're changing the subject." She put her hands out in front of her. "Stop me when I get to the length."

She started small and then got bigger. Her eyes did too.

"There," I said eventually.

"Holy hell, Grace!" She was nearly yelling. "You should have told me!"

"It was your moody time of the year."

"So? I wanna hear about you getting fucked by a monster cock. Was it good?"

"Of course it was."

"Then why do you look so bummed?" she asked.

I winced and looked down. "It was a one-night stand."

"Right, and?"

"And I got attached," I muttered.

Her face fell. "Oh. Yeah, that's a problem."

I shrugged. "It's nothing. I felt something and he didn't. He warned me he would want nothing more."

"I could still cut him."

"He didn't do anything wrong. I'll be fine. Once I get over all of this . . . weirdness I'm feeling."

"Weirdness?" she asked slowly.

"I can call my feelings what I want, Jade."

"No, no. It's not that. I'm just thinking . . ." She trailed off. "You feel weird after a one-night stand?"

"Well, yeah, but it's because of how it ended."

"But you used protection, right?"

"We did." And then I remembered the dressing room. "The first time. The second time, he pulled out."

"Um . . ." She tilted her head to the side.

"And I had a period after."

That should have stopped all of her curiosity, but even I couldn't deny the bubble of uncertainty that was growing deep in my gut.

"How soon after?"

"Right after."

"Was it normal?"

"It was . . . light."

"Oh, boy. I can't believe I'm saying this, but have you heard of implantation bleeding?"

"No," I said. I tried to keep my breathing even. "But I don't like how it sounds."

"You know, we should evaluate all options here."

"I'm not pregnant," I said firmly as I took a step back. "There are so many ways I shouldn't be pregnant."

"Precum can still get you pregnant, you know. It's always a risk when getting dicked down without a condom."

I made a sound that was a cross between a whimper and a scream. Then I shook my head. "No way. I'm not pregnant. I can't be."

"A test would confirm or deny."

"I don't have one because I never—" I ran my hand through my curls, not even caring if I messed them up. "I can't even buy one because people will know!"

"I'll buy it," she said gently. "I'm used to it. I take them all the time."

"Wha—why do you take them all the time?"

"Past trauma? Being a ho? There're many reasons." She shrugged as if it were nothing. "The point is, lock the door, crash out, and I'll be back."

I slowly nodded, trying to catch my breath.

"You're not going to Food 'n' Things, right?" Our local shop was run by only one man, and he knew us all.

"Of course not. What, do you think I'm a rookie? I'll go to the Walmart in the town over. No one'll know. And if they do, this is on-brand for me."

But it wasn't on-brand *for me*.

And that was the whole problem.

Jade was silent as we waited for the results. So far, it had been three minutes, and those three minutes were the longest of my life.

Even though I didn't have an answer, I couldn't help but wonder what life would be like with a baby. I'd always wanted kids, but I wanted them with a partner that I was in love with who'd make the decision with me to have a family together. The idea of tiny little feet running on my hardwood floors was always in my future, and even now I wanted it.

But I wasn't sure if I wanted it like this.

And what was worse, I didn't have my life together enough. There was no way I could have a baby.

The timer went off and both of us grabbed at the test. Jade got it first and flipped it over. In the seconds she stared at it, it felt like my life was at a tipping point. If there were two lines, *everything* would be changing.

"It's nothing, right?" I asked, still clinging to the hope that things were still going to be normal. "I don't know why we did this. Let's just throw it away and—"

"That is the most positive test I've ever seen, Grace."

I froze for all of one second before I clambered to get the test in my own hands. *Two* pink lines stared at me.

I could only stare back. The line *glowed*. I was pregnant. Very pregnant.

And it was Dean's.

My ears rang. I could've passed out.

What had I done? *Why* had I said yes to that second time? Why had I said yes at all? I should have known better. Hell, I *had*.

I'd stepped out of line, and this was what I got.

"Wow, so . . . congratulations? Condolences? What are we feeling here?"

"I'm pregnant," I said slowly.

"Yeah, very. Dean was in town like over three months ago too."

"Oh my God. I'm in my second trimester!" What all had I missed? There had to be tests and ultrasounds. Fuck, was the baby even okay?

"That narrows down options."

I turned to her. "Options?"

"If you don't want this . . . we should talk about *those* options."

I immediately knew what she was talking about. It wasn't a terrible thing to consider, especially with my financial status, but the second I did, I was shaking my head.

"No," I said. "That's not for me."

"All right," Jade replied. "Now we figure out the rest."

The rest. She said those two words like they were easy.

They were not.

Did Dean even want kids? Would he be pissed when I reached out to him? Would I be doing this alone? God, this was *so* bad.

I'd spent my whole adult life telling Brooke to use protection and stay safe. And now I was the one pregnant?

No one would ever let me live it down.

But Jade had caught on to my panic and her hands landed on my shoulders.

"Grace, you need to breathe."

I couldn't. How had this happened?

"Whatever you're thinking isn't important," she said. "The last thing you or the baby needs is you having a panic attack."

That snapped me out of it. My eyes locked on hers. She exaggerated her breaths to make sure I could hear them. Compared to my choppy breathing, they were at a snail's pace. But I followed her. My heart rate didn't return to normal, but at least I wasn't teetering on the edge.

"It's gonna be okay," she said. She didn't usually sound like this. Jade had always been sharp edges and cutting words. If *she* was being soft and kind, I must have really needed it. "We can figure this out. No one will know, if that's what you want."

"I think they'll have to know eventually."

"For now, Grace. They don't have to know for now."

I hung my head, feeling like a weight was crushing me.

"Everyone is gonna freak out." I drew out every word.

"Who gives a fuck about them?"

"I do. You know I do."

She huffed. "I get it. And you can't just turn it off. But there are higher priorities right now."

Yeah, like doctor's appointments. Telling Dean.

Ugh.

"So, what kind of daddy is Dean? Daddy . . . or *Daddy*?"

I wished I could have laughed at her sentence, but there was no humor in me while I was under the weight of this. "I have no clue. He doesn't *do* relationships. He made that very clear." I'd even promised him he wouldn't hear from me after our tryst.

What a fool I was.

"Well, a baby is different than a relationship. Maybe he'll surprise you?" She said it as a question.

"You don't have to sugarcoat it. This is bad."

"It's not ideal, but we'll figure it out. One thing at a time."

"I need to call my doctor to confirm this."

"Henry could—"

I glared.

Jade's eyes went wide. "Nope. Not anyone in town. Your gyno is somewhere else, right?"

"Knoxville."

"So, this appointment. Want me to close my shop?"

"No, both of ours being closed will only make it worse. You

know how people talk around here. I'll go by myself. Then once I know things are . . . more real, I'll find Dean to tell him."

I had a headache blooming behind my eyes, and all I wanted to do was sleep.

Jade picked up on it. "All right, you have a plan. So now you need to go home and rest. I'll put a message in the Facebook group that you pooped yourself and you'll be out for the day."

"Does it have to be *that* reason?"

"Do you want me to say the real one?"

That was worse. "No, but make it classy."

"Oh, you know me." She adjusted her fishnets to remove what I could only assume was a wedgie. "I'm the epitome of class."

I told myself I wouldn't look into Dean until after my appointment, but it was a lie. I didn't do well with sitting idle while my life changed. I wanted to have some sort of way to contact him if the time eventually came.

It took me far too many Google searches to find Dean's business. I'd had to dig deep into Wren's show that she worked on to find him, and when I did, that relaxed, carefree smile stared back at me in one of his pictures on his website.

And I was terrified.

He'd said no relationships, but we would always have one now. Whether he wanted me or not.

And I didn't know how to tell him.

In the strangest way, it felt like I failed. I wanted to be the easygoing woman who could match his energy. I wanted to have one night and then move on.

But that wasn't me. I didn't do well with surface-level talk, and things ended. I wanted them to last. I wanted to get to know someone fully.

Dean didn't, though. And I respected that. I let him leave.

And now I had to find him again.

"Are you looking that guy up?" a voice asked. "God, you're a terrible one-night stand."

I jumped. "Brooke? I thought you were back in Nashville."

"My roomie kicked me out." She looked at her nails. "I figured I would crash here."

"You got kicked out *again*?"

"It's fine. She'll get over it. She always does."

I opened my mouth to tell her she needed to try to make it work the best she could. But I was pregnant by a playboy. Was I in any position to tell her how to live her life?

Brooke had figured that I'd had a one-night stand when I came home with messy hair after she extended her stay by a day.

She'd been baffled that he'd even gone for me, especially after turning someone like *her* down. I'd told her it was rude to judge someone else's interests before she grilled me on the details, but I couldn't deny that she knew me well, and she at least congratulated me in the end for breaking my record and doing something for myself for once.

If only I had known how it would end up.

"So," Brooke said. "Are you ignoring the one cardinal rule about hookups?"

"I was just getting some information."

"Sure. I bet you wanna see him again, don't you?"

I *had* wanted to see him again. I'd thought about the sex a lot. Now I dreaded the idea of talking to him.

"You should watch some TV and relax." It was a desperate play to get her off my back. I hated letting her have the TV when I was home since I hated the shows she loved, but I'd suffer.

For a second, it worked. Her eyes widened. But then they narrowed.

"What don't you want me to know?"

"Nothing," I said, turning away from her and closing the tab.

"You haven't mentioned him since he left." Brooke tapped her chin. "And you look like you gained weight again."

"*Really?*" I asked. "You know I hate it when you mention my weight."

"It's just an observation." Brooke rolled her eyes and then zeroed in on me again. "When did you get your last period?"

I should have said it was recent. A lie was better than her knowing, but it must have read plain as day on my face, because she picked up on it.

"Did you never get it?" She gasped. "Are you pregnant? Is Dean the dad?"

I sighed and then nodded.

"Oh my *God.*" She pushed me out of the way and brought Dean's profile back up. "He's popular."

"I could see that when he made friends with everyone his few weeks here."

"He's younger too. He graduated eight years ago. That makes him twenty-six. No way he's ready to settle down."

"You're doing a great job of making me feel better before I have to tell him the news."

"No. No way. You can't tell him."

I blinked. "Why not?"

"Have you learned *nothing* from me?"

"From you? As far as I know, you never got pregnant by a playboy."

Brooke rolled her eyes. "No, but Mom did."

I sucked in a breath. We never talked about Dad. He'd been a playboy too. A man never tied down. He came to town twice. Stuck around for a bit, but when having kids lost its luster, he was gone.

"Do you really think he would do that?"

"First of all, he's a man. *Yes*, I think he would. He's also younger and sleeps around. Jude warned me about him after I mentioned he was in town. He's a heartbreaker."

"Jude knew about him?"

"He broke the director's heart in season one. She'd begged him to give her a chance and all he wanted was a night of fun."

My mouth went dry. He'd been nice to me, but our relationship had been short and he'd left just like he said he would.

"Listen, the baby is *yours*." Brooke shook her head. "You're the one growing it. He just shot right once and got you pregnant."

"Do you *have* to say it like that?"

"Am I wrong?"

She wasn't. "No. I just don't wanna think about it."

"You'll have to when you have it."

Just like Jade, she already knew my decision. "You think I'm keeping it?"

"You're a mom anyway. It may as well be to your own kid."

I felt a pocket of warmth for my sister. So much of our relationship was strained, but there were times I knew she cared about me.

"How do you think the town is gonna react when they find out?" I asked.

She laughed. "Oh, I don't wanna be you right now. Have fun with that. They're gonna be so in your ass, but at least it's not me this time."

All the warm feelings cooled. "That's helpful."

"It's the truth," she said with a shrug. "Sorry, Grace, but you've totally ruined your good girl reputation."

I shut my laptop. "You're so great at pep talks."

She didn't sense my sarcasm. "Thanks. I love giving them."

6

DEAN

Strawberry Springs Neighborhood Watch

SherriffMike Finch: Jackie, are you still keeping those raccoons as pets?

Comments:
Marjorie Brown: Plead the Fifth, Jackie. You ain't gotta tell him shit!
Mollie Wilson: But she's admitted it before. Can you use group comments as evidence?
Marjorie Brown: I've broken plenty of laws in my youth. They can and will do whatever it takes! Delete those posts, Jackie!
SherriffMike Finch: Dammit, Marjorie. This wasn't your attitude when I helped you change your tire.
Marjorie Brown: You weren't sniffing out arrests then.
SherriffMike Finch: A few months ago, Hugh was telling people to run over tourists and he's free. I just wanted pictures!
Jackie Anne: OH, in that case, yes!

THE BEER in my hands was barely cold and tasted terrible. Clyde had said this place was one of the best in town, but both of us felt like we'd been scammed.

Clearly this place was trying to be like all the other popular bars. I normally didn't mind that, but they had a limited stock, and the bartender clearly didn't know what they were doing.

"Well, it's at least some kind of beer," Clyde said with a sigh. "You try to give a new place a shot and this is what you get."

I could barely hear him and had to stare to make out what he was saying, but I nodded anyway.

Clyde had lost the remainder of his hair over the years, but he still had the same personality. After graduating, I wound up reaching out to him for freelance work. He'd taken me under his wing ever since.

I'd learned a lot from him over the years, including how to make connections. He'd been the one to tell me to shoot my shot at working with Wren, and that had gone well for me. After Dad was gone, he was the closest thing I had to a father, and I valued that more than anything.

I still worked with him a lot. Between the two of us, we'd garnered a respected reputation among anyone looking to build or renovate. When an office complex was announced out in Knoxville, he'd called me to ask if I would be willing to travel. I said yes, and here I was.

"At least the job went well," I said. I was having a hard time cutting up like I usually did, and I had for months.

Ever since leaving Strawberry Springs, I'd been in a rut with everything, it seemed. I thought it would wear off over the weeks, but it didn't. Clyde had noticed and grown worried. Mom had too on our weekly calls.

I had half a mind to think that Clyde invited me out to try to get me out of it. I didn't know how it was going to go.

"You know," Clyde said, taking another swig of his beer, "if something is . . . changing with your body, you can tell me. No matter how embarrassing."

I blinked. "I'm not a teenager, Clyde. What kind of question is that?"

"Your mom wanted me to ask." Mom had called Clyde? She must have been really worried. "And plenty of things can change even when you're young. It might be a receding hairline. Maybe . . . things don't stay up anymore."

I'd jerked off. I knew *that* wasn't an issue.

"No, none of that is happening. I swear I'm fine. What about work? What's coming up?"

"Oh, yeah. Get me talking about *work*. That's normal for you." He rolled his eyes, but considered it. "Fine, we have a few more jobs in the future."

That, at the very least, made me feel something. What I did earned me good money. I was lucky enough to never have to worry about paying rent, and I usually found a way to give any extras to Mom. She never complained to me about her finances after I moved out, but she had her own bills, and I wanted to help her.

She usually said no, so I found sneaky ways to do it.

The last time I'd helped her out, she'd threatened to hit me with a mop if I did it again. I'd have to figure out some way to pass on the luck.

"I'm your guy."

"I know, kid. But you can't live off of work. You need fun. Usually you always find that for yourself, but lately you come in and go home. That ain't normal."

He was right. The main way I had fun was finding a beautiful woman to spend the night with, but I also dabbled in other things, like hanging out at bars or playing poker whenever I got the chance. I hadn't done any of that, choosing to distract myself with work more than anything else.

That ended tonight.

This wasn't the kind of bar that had people playing cards in the corner. Nor was it the kind of place that had a pool table. It was all for dancing, and most people here were looking to meet someone else.

I surveyed everyone in the bar and my eyes immediately found a bachelorette party attendee staring in my direction. She had light blonde hair and blue eyes so bright I could see them from across the room. I'd had a lot of good luck with women at these kinds of parties, as they were always down to have a good time. Never with the bride-to-be, though. That would always be off-limits.

"And that's my cue to leave," Clyde said.

I was broken out of my trance. "I don't mean to cut our night short."

"It's fine. I brought you here to talk about how you were doing, and you seem to be back to normal. Enjoy your night with her."

That was one of the things that I enjoyed about Clyde. He never told me how I should live my life. Mom expected me to have some amazing love story just like she did with Dad. Clyde cared that I was happy.

"I'll make it up to you."

"Make it up to me by being yourself next time I see you." He rapped his knuckles on the table before finishing his beer and heading out.

I took a breath and looked back at the woman that I had been eyeing. She was still looking at me and giggled when my eyes met hers again.

Usually I would try to strike up some kind of conversation

before heading in to do anything else. Tonight, I wasn't in the mood for talking. Obviously, that hadn't gone well for me. I tilted my head, gesturing toward the hallway where the restrooms were, hoping she would get the hint.

She turned and said something to her friends before heading in that very direction.

I didn't waste time. The second I was near her, I pulled her in for a kiss. I wouldn't mind going pretty far in this bar, and then I could take her back to the hotel and enjoy the rest of my night.

I didn't need to know her name or anything else about her.

But as my lips slid over hers, my mind went somewhere else. Suddenly, I wasn't in a bar anymore. I was back in the Treasure Trove with Grace.

This woman didn't kiss like her, and her breathy moans were over the top. They didn't feel real like Grace's had. Normally, my body would be responding the instant that I laid my hands on someone else, especially when it had been this long.

But there was nothing. No part of me was interested in her.

And that was when I pulled away.

The woman in front of me got the wrong idea. "Please tell me you have an apartment or a hotel."

I tried to think about it. I tried imagining her light-colored hair spilled over my pillow. Tried to imagine going further with anyone other than Grace.

And my dick somehow got softer.

"I need to go." I couldn't believe the words that were coming out of my mouth.

Her bottom lip stuck out in a pout. "But—"

"Sorry, you're very beautiful, but I'm not into it."

She wasn't deterred. "I can make you be into it." She pulled me back in for a kiss, her hand drifting downward.

This time, I pushed her away. "No, I don't think you will."

Her brow furrowed and I could tell she was starting to get offended. I needed to get out of here before I broke another one's heart.

"Have a nice night, ma'am."

I left the bar in a rush. I told Clyde that I would try to have fun tonight, but obviously that wasn't happening. Instead of going somewhere else where I might be able to play pool or some cards, I drove straight to the hotel.

Mom had wanted me to call her to catch up, more than likely because she was so worried. I could try to placate her while ignoring my actual problems.

"Dean?" Mom asked when I called. "You're calling me at a decent hour?"

"Don't sound so shocked," I said.

"You haven't called me before ten since you discovered the other sex."

"Shouldn't you be happy? You hate it when I go out to the bars."

"You have me there. I just worry."

"You have nothing to worry about." That was a lie, but I tried to make sure she knew I was all right ever since we'd gotten the call that Dad was gone.

"How is the job?"

"Good. Busy. I got out late and was too tired to hang out with anyone."

She hummed. "Usually you always have energy."

"Maybe I'm getting old."

"Save it. You're under thirty. Are you sure—"

"Did you watch the last *Love Island* episode?" I changed the subject to something I knew she would love to talk about. "Who cheated on who?"

Mom sighed and I knew she wouldn't be deterred. "Is something wrong with you? Did Clyde talk to you?"

"I can't believe you called him. Yes, he did. Well, he tried to."

"I know how it can be with boys. I thought maybe you'd talk to a fellow guy about it."

"Seriously, there are no changes. I'm good."

"You do know that I can tell when you're lying, right?"

"Yes, I do. Can you please let me get away with it for a little bit?"

She went silent. "It's not hurting you?"

"No."

"Then, fine." She heaved out a long sigh. "Let's talk about *Love Island* then. You know I have thoughts about it."

As I listened to her talk about all the people who were fighting for love on that show, I wound up on Instagram.

And I found myself typing in "Grace Day" into the bar. It wasn't an incredibly uncommon name, but I was able to find her just from the profile picture alone.

Her account was private, which made me almost curse.

I half listened to Mom, but I also stared at Grace's profile. I didn't know what was wrong with me. I'd never been like this over a woman before.

I shook myself out of it. This would end the longer I was away from her. As long as it stayed that way, I would be fine.

Nothing good would come of reaching out.

7

GRACE

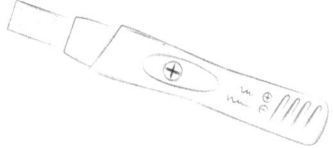

Strawberry Springs Neighborhood Watch

Jackie Anne: Great coffee and nice customer service. Will come back soon.

Comments:
Jade Clark: Huh???
Wren Hackett: Were you trying to review the coffee shop?
Hu Gh: Facebook isn't as easy as it seems, huh? Let me break it down for you. This group and Goggle are two different things
. . .
Jackie Anne: I was trying to do something nice! How do I delete a post?

THE HOUR DRIVE to Knoxville was already rough, but the additional feeling of worry made it worse. I'd barely slept after making the mistake of Googling all the tests I'd missed while not knowing I was pregnant.

My doctor was going to have questions. Lots of them. And I'd been going over every choice I'd ever made the last few months. Had I eaten healthy enough? Did I have a sip of wine? Had I slept on my stomach ever?

When I'd called, the nurse stumbled over her words when I told her how far along I suspected I was. When she went to talk to the doctor and came back with an appointment for the very next day, I knew they were worried.

I was a dangerous mix of emotions, all of which felt amplified. All I could do was put one foot in front of the other and make it to the next thing I needed to do. Dean was still on my mind, but I didn't know where to begin with him.

After parking in a lot, I had to walk farther than I wanted to get into the office. I had skipped breakfast and was regretting it. I'd need to eat immediately after the appointment.

I sat at the back of the waiting room after checking in and opened my phone. I needed something to occupy my hands with while I waited.

Without thinking, I opened Dean's website again. Brooke's words rang loudly in my mind, but I knew I wasn't the kind of person who could do that to someone. Dean had a right to know. He might hate me, but he should still know.

Biting my lip, I opened a message box, but I had no clue what to say.

Hey, sorry to bother you, but I'm pregnant.

No. That wasn't enough.

Hey, it's Grace Day. Can we talk?

God, would he even answer that?

I had no idea how to tell him about this. I didn't know him well enough to deliver the news in a way that wouldn't make him mad. This was why I always got to know people. So when things went wrong, I could say it the right way.

My fingers hovered over the keys, and the longer I tried to figure out what to say, the more they shook.

"Grace Day?" a voice called. I jumped up.

"That was quick," I said to the nurse. I'd come here for years. They were the ones who'd diagnosed me with PCOS when I kept missing periods.

"We can move fast when we need to." She smiled and then looked at my chart. "Now, you've had some changes."

I swallowed. "Yes, I have."

"We'll get it figured out," she said. "First things first, we want a urine sample to confirm, though I have a feeling it'll be a quick answer."

"It will be," I muttered.

She gave me another comforting smile. "Then we'll do some bloodwork and talk to you about your lifestyle and what to do from here on out. We might also do an ultrasound."

"I'll see the baby now?"

"Hopefully, yes."

Hopefully? God, what if there was nothing there?

As my heart kicked up in speed, I wished things had gone a different way. I was terrified to do this alone. Would it have been easier with a partner I'd been planning this with?

Hell, would *life* be easier with that?

I used the bathroom, they lined me up for bloodwork, and I was shuffled back to the waiting room. It somehow felt worse than when Jade and I had done this in the back of the shop.

Maybe I should have had her come.

I'd been brave since Mom died, but I wasn't sure I was built for doing things alone. Considering my dating history, I was pretty sure I'd have to get used to it.

My name was called again, this time by a woman I didn't know. She introduced herself as April, the ultrasound technician, and led me to the back.

I'd had one ultrasound in my life, but it was never to see a baby. It was to check on one of my ovaries when I'd been in pain that wouldn't stop.

This was more nerve-racking.

"So, you said your last period was in October," she said as she read my chart. "But it may not have been a period?"

"Yes."

"I think we can try not doing an internal ultrasound, but we may have to. Sorry if we do."

"It's fine," I said. "Whatever you need to do."

She took another look at me. "Are you okay?"

"Um, no." At least I answered honestly.

"Honest. I like that. Did you want kids?"

"Yeah, I did. Not like this, but life doesn't always go the way we think it should, does it?"

"Not at all, but take some time if you need it. I can come back."

This was why I loved this practice. Everyone treated me like a person.

I shook my head. "No, it's fine. Let's get this over with."

Lying on the bed, I lifted my shirt and let her put cool jelly on the exposed skin. She pressed the wand against my stomach, and within seconds, the side profile of a baby appeared on the monitor.

Holy shit. This was real. That was a real baby.

"Yep, you're definitely pregnant."

"How far along? Are they okay? Do I need to get the anatomy scan now?"

April only smiled. "All good questions, but the doctor will be the one to answer most of them. I'll just get a few pictures and we'll get you in an exam room. We might be able to know the gender today, if you want to."

I let out a laugh. "I . . . seriously, today?"

"Yep. You're far enough along."

I didn't even know this was happening until twenty-four hours ago. I shook my head. "I can't . . . I mean, not yet. I might wanna know after I can accept things."

She nodded. "I understand. This is a lot."

April pressed buttons, moved things around, and eventually, pulled up a new window.

The sound of a heartbeat filled the room. I'd known this was happening, but hearing that made it feel even more real.

Tears gathered in my eyes.

"Oh, shoot," April said. "I should have given you a warning."

I blinked them away. "Can you at least tell me if it's good?"

She paused and then nodded. "Yeah, it's looking good."

"Thank you."

A few minutes later, I was in an exam room and Dr. Anderson was already walking in. I hadn't seen her since my last pap smear. She was a great doctor, but it felt a little like coming home to tell my parents I'd fucked up. I clutched the sonogram printout that the tech had given me like a lifeline.

"Well, this is unexpected."

"Tell me about it," I said with a laugh. "But it's good. Hopefully."

"It's okay to be nervous," she said with a nod. "But your sonogram looks great."

I closed my eyes as my shoulders slumped. *Thank God.* "How far along am I?"

"Well, I'm hoping you can help me with that. I noticed you didn't put a last period down in your chart, but that's pretty normal, considering your PCOS."

"I have no recollection of an actual period. I did have some bleeding right after, um—" I squirmed in my seat. This woman had practically put her entire hand up my vagina, but somehow talking to her about my sex life still felt awkward. "Right when I probably got pregnant."

"I would say that was implantation bleeding then. So, you remember the last time you had sex?"

"I do." *Vividly.* "And it was the only time I'd had it in . . . a while."

I couldn't look her in the eye. This was actually my worst nightmare.

But Dr. Anderson didn't seem bothered. "Tell me the date, please." I did so, and she wrote it down. "All right then, I'd say you're sixteen weeks. That matches what we saw on your ultrasound."

"Sixteen weeks. That's . . . a lot of time not to know."

"We've seen it go longer, but we can make up for lost time." She gave me a smile. "Is the father here?"

The only thing I could do was shrug. "Not today. He doesn't even know. I should be telling him soon, but I have no idea how he'll react."

"Well, we can make it work either way." Her voice was level and calm. It was exactly what I needed. "Let's talk about what you've been up to the last three months and what we need to do now."

"Yes, please."

I listened intently, trying my best not to get overwhelmed. There was *so* much I couldn't do now, like eat deli meat or sushi. I had to limit my caffeine and make sure I took care of myself.

That one worried me. Taking care of others was easy. But me? I sometimes felt like I didn't know how to do that.

"That should be all," Dr. Anderson said. "Now we just need to schedule your glucose test."

I blinked as I tried to remember when that was supposed to be done. "Isn't it a little early?"

"Yes, but there's a risk that you can develop gestational diabetes with PCOS. We just want to make sure we catch anything early. We'll have you come back next week for that."

I nodded my head meekly, trying not to panic. How the absolute hell was I going to manage all of this on my own? How was I supposed to deal with the words "gestational diabetes" by myself?

Jade would help, even if I refused to ask her, but I wasn't the only one who had conceived this baby.

What was Dean going to do?

If I'd thought I was overwhelmed before, I was more so now. And I had less time than most to accept this. Three and a half months had come and gone while I had no idea what was going on.

But I would do it, even if I only had Jade.

The rest of the appointment went by in a blur. I barely remembered to take the appointment card for my glucose test before I was heading to my car.

There were so many things I needed to plan. I needed to tell Dean. I needed to figure out the right words to make sure this was done right. It was a mess I'd found myself in, and I wasn't sure how to present it without him thinking I'd baby trapped him.

I was so lost in my thoughts that I didn't see someone walking right toward me. I would have walked right into them if their hands didn't land on my shoulders. I was brought out of my thoughts by dirty blond hair and a tall figure in a cowboy hat.

I knew those hands. I knew them before I even saw his face.

"It's you," he said. "Grace."

I blinked back into myself only to be faced with Dean. My stomach did a flip and my body heated. Even now, when everything was so messed up, I still had a reaction to him.

But it was drowned out by sheer terror. It looked like I was facing one of my fears early.

Shit.

8

DEAN

Strawberry Springs Neighborhood Watch

Kerry Winsor: @Wren Hackett, do you work with any other men that might come into town? Asking for a friend . . .

Comments:
Jackie Anne: Following . . .
Wren Hackett: Sorry. Dean was the only one who I care to keep in contact with. I highly doubt he'll be back. You'll have to go back to getting your entertainment somewhere else.
Tammy Jane: Y'all need to read. I didn't need the eye candy when I was deep in a book about Bigfoot.
Mollie Wilson: Like a history book about him?
Tammy Jane: No.
Mollie Wilson: Wait, what kind of book?
Mollie Wilson: TAMMY PLEASE ANSWER

GRACE WAS as beautiful now as she had been all those months ago.

Just one look and I knew why she was stuck in my mind. She was ethereal, even in a T-shirt and leggings.

It wasn't my plan to see her. It seemed fate had different plans.

"Y-you're here." Her voice sounded distant, cheeks pink as she tucked a curl behind her ear. "Why are you here? I thought you lived in Nashville."

"What? Are you not happy to see me?" I was determined to seem normal in front of her. It didn't matter that it felt like I'd been hit by a train just at the sight of her.

"I—well, it's just unexpected." She took a breath. "But maybe it's not a bad thing."

She seemed different this time. I couldn't place it, but something was off.

"I'm here for a job. I travel sometimes."

"Wow. Lucky me."

"What are you doing here?" I parroted. "Do you often leave Strawberry Springs?"

"Oh, that." Her voice was low. "I'm here for a d—"

"A date?" The idea of her being with anyone else didn't sound like something I wanted to know, but it would be good for me to hear.

"Not really." She bit her lip and looked at me. "But I'm really glad you're here. I need to talk to you about something."

Now her voice was tight. Her insistence made me pause.

"What do we have to talk about?"

"Um, well . . ." Her skin paled as she fidgeted with her hands. I'd never seen her be so nervous. "Could we maybe not do this on the street? We could go for lunch, or something."

Oh no. I'd seen this before. She was happy to see me and nervous to talk to me about something?

She wanted to ask me out, didn't she?

"I don't really do lunch with women I . . ." I trailed off. This was always the worst part of it. I hated when a woman caught feelings and I had to find a way to gently turn them down.

This time was going to feel worse than others.

I *did* think about her, though. If there was one woman that I ever could consider saying yes to, it was Grace Day.

I wouldn't, though. That wasn't what I did.

"Can you make an exception this once?" she asked.

Dammit. "I don't make exceptions. I'm sorry, Grace."

Her jaw tightened. "I promise, I—"

"Grace, I said it would just be for fun." My chest ached at the words, but I needed to say it anyway. "I won't go to lunch with you. And I won't be anything more with you."

She blinked as my words hit her. "I'm not . . . I'm not asking you out."

"It's okay if you were. It happens to the best of us."

Her cheeks darkened. "I'm seriously not."

"Then what else could you be doing? You're nervous and won't meet me in the eye. It's like you know you're breaking a rule. This isn't the first time a woman was with me and—"

"I'm trying to tell you I'm *pregnant*, Dean."

My breath caught in my throat, all of my words forgotten. "What did you just say?"

She took a breath before repeating the very words I'd hoped to never hear. "I'm pregnant."

No. No way.

I stepped back from her, squeezing my eyes shut. I could remember every second from our two times. They played back in my mind like they'd happened just the day before.

But they weren't the day before. It was three and a half months ago.

A lot could happen in that time.

"It's not mine, is it?"

Grace's lips pressed together. "That's your first thought?"

"It's a fair question."

"I hadn't been with anyone in months before you, and I haven't been with anyone since. The baby is yours, Dean."

"Shit." The words came out before I could stop them and I paced around the street. "*Shit.*"

She didn't say anything for a good minute before she finally sighed. "Are you done?"

I paused and looked at her. Now that I knew she was pregnant, I could see the differences. Her cheeks were rounder, and her figure fuller. I didn't know much about pregnancy, but I could see her stomach poking out from her T-shirt more than it had when I first met her.

What the fuck had I gotten myself into?

Grace was the one woman I couldn't forget. I was trying, but it wasn't working. And she was pregnant? With my baby?

How the fuck was I supposed to stay away from her now?

What the fuck was I supposed to do at all?

"S-so, what do you want from me?" I asked. And how did I figure out how to give it to her without losing all I was? I *couldn't* step away from who I was.

And she was the one person who made me want to.

But my question made Grace's eyes narrow. I replayed what I'd said in my mind and knew I'd gone about this the wrong way.

I didn't have time to correct it, though.

"I don't want anything from you," she said. "You deserved to know, so I'm telling you."

"And you waited over three months?" I asked.

"I just found out yesterday myself, actually," she hissed. "So my last twenty-four hours has been filled with more stress and panic then I've ever felt in my *life*. And you're not—" She stopped herself, but I had a feeling I knew what she was going to say.

You're not helping.

Grace took a breath. "If you don't want this, I understand. I can do this as a single mom. I know that my community will help, and I can do this."

"Your community?" I couldn't help but huff out a humorless laugh. "You mean the ones who think of you as the good girl who never does anything wrong?"

"Well, it's at least someone!" she snapped and then shook her head. "I'll figure it out. You just figure out if you want to be a father or not."

"I didn't mean it like that, I—"

But she was done listening to me. She pulled out a napkin and a pen from her purse and scribbled down her number.

"When you do, call me. Or don't. I'll be fine either way."

She left so fast that I barely had time to catch the napkin she threw my way, but something else fell out of her purse. It was a long piece of photo paper. Slowly, I knelt and picked it up with shaky hands.

When I turned it over to look at it, it was a side profile of a baby.

Grace's name was at the top of it, and there was an estimated date of sixteen weeks listed.

A quick Google search told me that sixteen weeks was exactly where she should be if she'd gotten pregnant by me.

And as I looked at the outline of a head and upturned nose, I knew I was looking at *my* baby.

Fuck.

9

GRACE

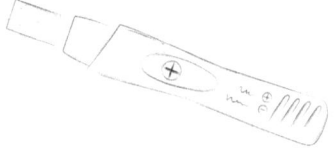

Strawberry Springs Neighborhood Watch

Kerry Winsor: @Hu Gh, why is your tractor parked at the square? It's taking up two spots!

Comments:
Hu Gh: Car wouldn't start and I drove it in. Where else am I supposed to park it?
Kerry Winsor: Fix your car!
Hu Gh: And trust some new-age mechanic with my baby? Nah. I'll get to it when my knee stops hurting.
Tammy Jane: I don't trust those mechanics either. Good on you, Hugh.
Kerry Winsor: What is the world coming to right now? Since when do Hugh and Tammy agree???

"Damn, it's not even seven and there's a line," Jade muttered. "Can't these people find something else to do?"

"It's moving fast today," I said. "Looks like hiring Kelsey was the right thing for Theo to do."

Strawberry Springs's new coffee shop, The Reserved Bean, opened up with an explosion of business. At first, I'd thought it had been because of the newness of it, but after trying the coffee, I knew the truth. It was the best drink I'd ever had, and all the business was well earned.

It was also more than one person could handle.

He'd been stubborn about it, but one complaint from Kerry was enough to get him in line. So far, Kelsey was helping keep the lines down and people were happier.

But Theo was still busy.

I'd asked Jade to meet up to talk about the disaster that was yesterday. We'd both made a silent agreement not to talk about anything involving the baby in public. She was doing a great job at pretending to be normal.

I was losing my mind. I hadn't been this angry since Brooke nearly started a fire in the bathroom with a hair dryer. I didn't do well when I was mad, and it showed when I walked away from Dean instead of figuring out a *plan*.

It was hard not to check my phone every five seconds to see if Dean messaged. I wasn't sure if I wanted him to or not.

Brooke had almost been right. A lot of guys weren't good people. It was easy for a man to pretend to be nice to get in my pants. But I bet he didn't stick around places for a reason.

It took everything I had to focus on the line, which was slowly leading us into the building.

Theo was taking orders while Kelsey made them. The two of them seemed to get along well and had quickly become friends, but there was too much going on for either of them to talk.

Still, Kelsey waved at us when she saw us. We all were friends by proxy since we grew up together, but she hadn't seemed to want to get attached to Strawberry Springs again. Jade had tried to invite her to hang out with all of us, but she turned it down.

The only person she talked to was Wren, but that was only because Wren was close to her mom, Tammy.

"You're busy," Jade said to Theo once we were at the front.

"Yeah, no kidding. What can I get you?"

This was how he was with me. Friendly enough, but distant. Everyone had their theories on why he didn't date around, but we had no real idea why he was by himself so much.

"Iced coffee for me," Jade said. "Grace, are you in the mood for any caffeine?"

I knew what she was hinting at. I dimly remembered the instructions Dr. Anderson had given me. I could have up to a certain amount a day.

"Just a regular, please. It's not too strong, is it? On the caffeine, I mean."

"No, it has the normal amount."

"Which is?"

Kelsey was eyeing us from behind the counter and I wondered what she would say.

"I just get jittery," I rushed to add.

Theo didn't seem like he cared. "I think it's around eighty milligrams, less if you leave room for milk and cream."

"I'll do that then. And please leave room."

He nodded and entered in our order.

Jade put her card down, giving me a glare that told me not to fight her on this. Deep down, I knew I wouldn't. I needed this.

"Thanks," I said as we walked to the pickup counter.

"You look like you need it," she whispered.

"One iced coffee and one hot," Kelsey said with a smile. "Having one of those hot girl walks?"

"Definitely," I replied.

"It's a nice day for it," she said. "It feels like spring is coming early."

"Definitely," Jade said. "Thanks, Kelsey."

She gave us a wave as we walked out of The Reserved Bean.

Instead of going near the busy side of the square, we went down a side street where no one usually walked. The end goal would be the Treasure Trove, where I would open the shop and go back to pretending that everything was fine.

"Have an update for me?" Jade asked when we were finally alone.

"You know I do," I said, and then took a sip of coffee. As usual, it was the best thing I'd ever had, and I let myself have one moment to enjoy it. "I talked to Dean yesterday."

"Damn, already?"

"I ran into him in Knoxville after my appointment."

"I knew I should have gone with you."

I shrugged, but deep down, I agreed.

"How did he react?"

I winced. "Not . . . well."

Her eyes narrowed. "What do you mean not well? Do I need to hunt him down? Wren has sledgehammers I can borrow."

I sighed as I remembered it. "He reacted like any playboy being told he has a responsibility, I guess. He didn't think he was the father, and then he asked what I wanted from him."

"I fucking *hate* men." Her grip on her coffee cup was tight. "As usual, they're glad to get some, and when real life comes in, they can't handle it. Well, fuck him. You have me. And the town, eventually."

I thought about what he'd said about the town, about what they thought of me.

It made my heart sink.

"Y-yeah. I know. I just wanted it to go better. I wanted him to either step up or it to be a clean break."

"Grace, you live off of trying to do everything right, but this is messy. It's okay to be messy."

The idea made me sick to my stomach. "Well, it'll certainly be messy now. I have a feeling Dean'll never talk to me again."

"Does he have a way to contact you?"

"He does. I just don't expect him to use it."

"You could fight him for child support."

I let out a long sigh. "You know I'm not gonna do that."

"You *deserve* any support, and he doesn't get off free from everything."

"I'll have enough on my plate once everyone knows. God, I'll be raising a fucking child. I don't wanna deal with all of that."

"It'll be okay. Maybe telling everyone won't be so bad."

I gave her a flat look. "Kerry will be so far up my ass that she'll get to meet my baby before me."

Jade blinked. "You do know that's not where babies come from, right? It's important to me that you know you don't give birth from your ass."

"Oh my *God.* Of course I know that. It's a figure of speech."

"Hey, the education system failed us." She shrugged. "A girl has to check."

I rubbed my forehead. "The point is, everyone will wanna know why I fucked up so badly, or if I'm more like Brooke than they assumed I was."

"Okay, *some* of that is realistic. We can put it off, though."

I was on a limited timeline. I could *see* that I was pregnant. Soon enough, everyone else would too.

The clock tower over the library chimed, and I was now two hours late to the shop. So was Jade.

"We should get to work. Who knows, maybe giving someone a makeover will make me feel better?"

"Boo," she said. "But you're right. At least I have this coffee to keep me happy. Oh, and show me the sonogram. I wanna see my mini-Grace."

I laughed as I reached for my purse. "Your mini-Grace?"

"Um, yeah. I bet they're gonna be freaking adorable. And I get aunt rights."

"Technically, Brooke—"

"I get them because I'll be here."

"Okay, you have me there." I'd gone through all my pockets only to come up empty. "Shit, where is it? Don't tell me I dropped it."

"Can you get another one?"

"I don't think so."

I was going through my bag with renewed vigor when we turned the corner to my shop. Jade came to an abrupt stop and I ran right into her.

"Ow, why did you—"

"Grace, be honest with me, do I need to murder him?"

I had no idea what she was talking about, but I followed her line of sight and nearly dropped my coffee when I saw a cowboy hat, black shirt, and tight jeans.

Because there, in all his glory, was Dean.

And in his hands was the printout of my ultrasound.

Dad Company (But Good Advice)

Dean Briggs: Hey, guys. I'm new here. Just found out I'm gonna be a dad and it's a huge surprise. I already bought a bunch of books to read, but those only go so far. Any tips for me from real dads?

Comments:
Robert Colt: Buckle up, get used to poop, and for God's sake, be there for your partner.
Oliver Brian: Get used to putting your partner first. She's the one going through it. Help her. Make sure she eats. Be supportive.
Dean Briggs: What if we're not partners?
Oliver Brian: Do it anyway. You can be friends, but help her out. She's growing a child, after all.
Dean Briggs: I'll just . . . try to do that. Thanks, everyone.

WHEN GRACE SAW ME, her cheeks went so brilliantly red that I could see it from across the road.

Then she *tore* over to me.

"Give me that," she hissed. I let her pull the pictures out of my hand. "Why are you holding those out in public?" She looked around wildly as if trying to make sure no one saw.

Shit. I should have known people in town didn't know, and there I was, holding evidence like a fucking idiot.

Normally, I would have had the brain space to consider that, but I wanted to return what she'd dropped and try to talk to her again now that I wasn't in pure shock.

It was a possibility that I would only make things worse, but I had to try.

Grace had been with another woman with brightly colored hair. She didn't walk up, but she glared at me so strongly I thought something might fall out of the sky and crush me.

And then she pointed at me and dragged her thumb across her throat.

Her message was clear.

"What are you doing here?" Grace asked.

I pulled my thoughts away from the death threat I'd just received and turned to her. "We need to talk."

"You could have just texted me."

"Is this really the kind of thing we talk about over text?"

"With your reaction yesterday, I wasn't expecting for us to talk at all."

I frowned. "You really thought I wouldn't reach out?"

"Yes, I did." She said it so forcefully that it knocked the wind out of me. I wasn't perfect, but surely, she didn't expect that. "But you're right. We should talk."

Grace turned and opened the door to the Treasure Trove and walked inside. I tried to let go of any frustration and followed her. Obviously, I hadn't taken things well. I needed to be better.

"What did you want to talk to me about?"

"You're pregnant," I said slowly. "Is there anything else *to* talk about?"

"Well, no. But I meant more like, what about it?"

"Everything, Grace. How did you find out? Is it a problem that you didn't know until this far in? What's the due date?"

The words came out before I could stop them. When I'd come here, I'd told myself to play cool and figure out a plan. But I knew more was on my mind.

Grace paused. "You *want* to know those things?"

"Yes, I do. You're having *my* baby. Did you really think I would run?"

She shrugged. "It's what you did after sex. That's the only frame of reference I have."

My molars clenched, but she wasn't wrong. "We agreed it would just be a one-time thing. Did you *want* me to stay?"

"Two-time," she reminded. "And I didn't expect you to stay or anything. But you have to admit, it didn't give me time to judge what you'd do when you found out. All I know is that you don't want to be tied down."

"That's gone out the window. I'm the father, right? That means I'm a part of this."

Grace stared at me for a long time, so long that it made me want to go over everything I'd said and done to her and try to figure out just what she had been thinking I'd do.

I had a feeling it wouldn't make me feel any better.

"I took a test because my friend picked up on me saying I felt weird. It was positive, obviously."

I blinked, unsure of what she meant for a moment. Then I realized she was answering one of my questions.

"And how did you feel?"

"Tired and more emotional than usual. And it had been a while since . . . you know, my time of the month."

"You can say period in front of me, you know."

Grace's eyes darted to mine and her brow furrowed. "You're not bothered by that?"

"I'm not a child."

She did a double take, and it hit me that she'd probably thought I was exactly that.

My choice to stay away from people had always seemed like a good one, but now, staring at Grace, it hit me just how much that had backfired. *Terribly.*

"A-anyway," she said. "I have more testing to go through. It's definitely not normal to find out at sixteen weeks, but so far, everything looks normal."

My shoulders lost some of the tension I'd carried ever since I'd found out. "That's good, right?"

"Yes, it is. But that means this is really happening." An awkward silence settled over both of us. "I have a lot to figure out, obviously."

"What do you need from me?"

"I need you to figure out what you're willing to do. I know you said you're a part of this, but I know plenty of guys who changed their minds halfway through when things got hard. My dad was one of them."

I opened my mouth. And then closed it. "I . . . didn't know that," is what I eventually settled on.

"You have time to make sure this is what you want. But if you think that at some point you'd prefer your current way of life, then walk away now. That would be easier."

Grace met my eyes and looked at me with the same flat expression she'd had the day before. I'd only ever seen it when she was thinking about Brooke.

And what did that say about me?

"I know what I'm gonna do. I want to be a father." I wasn't sure why, but I needed her to believe me. I needed her to know that I wasn't just a playboy she'd met. It was my choice not to have relationships, but that didn't mean I was an irresponsible person.

"You might think that's what you want, but I don't know if you realize all that it means." Her voice was soft as if that alone could pad the words. "So take some time to think on that. I do need to open my shop for the day, but you have my number if you need anything, right?"

"Yeah, I have it."

"Feel free to use it," she said, and then gestured to the door.

It was a clear dismissal. Usually, I wouldn't mind those, but this felt unfinished.

She still didn't believe me.

I gave her a tense nod before leaving to head back to my hotel in Knoxville.

The first time I left Strawberry Springs, I wanted to be done with the place, yet I still thought about Grace. This time, the unfinished feeling tempted me to turn the truck around and go right back. I didn't like Grace thinking I was the kind of man who would leave her to handle this alone. I wasn't.

I just didn't want to get hurt again.

Still, I had to figure things out with my life before I could even consider dropping everything.

Clyde had only given me a day off since I'd told him I wasn't feeling well after Grace dropped the news on me. He expected me to be there tomorrow, and I wasn't sure if he would believe an excuse.

As I neared my hotel, I tried to parse through all the emotions in my body, but I was spinning my own wheels. I was so out of it that I didn't notice a familiar car in the parking lot.

Nor did I notice the woman waiting at my hotel door.

"There you are," she said. "I thought I'd have to wait here forever."

I jumped, finally pulling myself out of my thoughts. "Mom? What are you doing here?"

"Is it not obvious?" She held out her hand and began counting off reasons. "I've known you're off. Your friend, Clyde, knows you're off. You call out of work, which you never do, and then you're not at your hotel, which is where you told Clyde you would be. Do I need more?"

I winced. "No, but this is a long drive for you."

"And I have my own room, but I'm not leaving until I know what the hell is happening." She crossed her arms. Her hair had grayed over the years, but it was in the same ponytail it always had been. I rarely got to see her since I moved to Nashville, and it was nice to have her in front of me.

Her worry would quickly be replaced by anger, though.

"Come in," I said. "We have a lot to talk about."

When I let her in and she turned to me, I could see the dark circles under her eyes. She'd been *very* worried.

I wasn't about to make it any better.

Running a hand over my face, I thought about all the times she told me to be safe. All the times she told me I couldn't let this happen. It was tempting to hide it from her, but Mom knew me best. She was my oldest friend, the person I looked to when I messed up.

"Someone's pregnant."

At first, her jaw dropped, but then her whole face hardened as I braced for her to unleash on me.

"By you?" I winced and nodded. "Dammit. I told you this would—" She stopped herself, but I wasn't sure why. "This is what you've been upset about for months? Wait a minute, you knew for *months* and didn't tell me?" Mom's voice was shrill, and I knew anyone in our vicinity would hear us.

I put up my hands in defense. "No, no! I just found out yesterday! The other part was . . . Well, it doesn't matter now, does it? This is bigger."

"No kidding, Dean. A baby? *You?*" She paced around the room. "Of all the things," she muttered to herself, "it had to be a baby?"

"What, because I can't handle that or something?" I said it before I could stop myself. I didn't get defensive with Mom. Normally, she was right.

But not this time.

Her eyes went wide at my harsh tone. "I didn't say that."

"But you're thinking it."

"Well, based on your actions, yes. It's what I have to go off of."

That sent me back to the Treasure Trove when Grace had insinuated something similar.

"Goddammit," I muttered. "Seriously?"

"Even you can admit they've not been great."

"Wha—I'm not a bad person, Mom."

She crossed her arms. "Let's ask the women who've been heartbroken by you. I'm sure they'll have a different story."

"Hey, I always tell them what to expect. They knew!"

"Humans don't just run from connection, Dean." She narrowed her eyes. "Or most of them don't. You can't either. I know you're a kind person. I raised you to be. But then sometimes you do things . . ." She shook her head. "Sometimes you act cold. And I wonder what you do when you're in the mindset. Who you've *hurt.*"

"I've tried not to hurt anyone."

"Has it worked?"

I blew out a breath, thinking about how I tried to end it with

Grace, only for us to be tied together forever. "Obviously not. I'm working on it."

"Working on it, huh? While the woman you got pregnant is dealing with it alone?"

"She's not alone."

"Oh, so her friends and family will handle it?"

"I'm handling it," I snapped. "Me. I will."

"You can't do that *and* run."

"Who said I was running? I have things to figure out and then . . ." I trailed off. I'd told myself Strawberry Springs was in the rearview mirror. I'd never stay there again once I got that job done with Wren. "I'll go back for a while."

"Back to where?"

"Back to where she is. That's the right thing to do. I'm not completely incompetent."

Mom stared at me, obviously trying to sniff out a lie. When she didn't find one, she let out a breath of relief. "Oh. Thank *God*. I was worried I'd have to fix this for you."

"You don't. I'm an adult. And contrary to popular belief, I *do* know how to do the right thing."

"I hope so. I raised you to be responsible and caring. Which is why I've been so confused these last few years. All you've cared about is sex and work."

That's what I *wanted* to care about, but it was a front. It was easy for me to care about someone. That was why I made the choice to leave before it happened. I wasn't an idiot. I knew myself and how I was.

It was the pain I couldn't take.

"Now I have more to care about," I muttered. "I'll handle it right after I make sure Clyde won't kill me for missing more work."

"I'll handle Clyde," she said. "You handle . . . everything else."

"Thank you."

"And you're sure you'll be able to deal with this?"

I was sure that I was doing the right thing. I was sure I could figure out how to be a dad.

There was only one thing that could go wrong.

And it had all to do with spending far too much time with the one person I couldn't get out of my mind.

11

GRACE

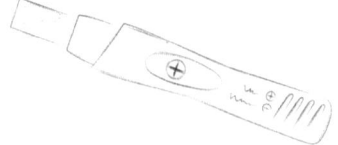

Strawberry Springs Neighborhood Watch

Kerry Winsor: Tree down on Highway 67! **@Sherriff-Mike Finch**, any news when it'll be cleared up?

Comments:
SherriffMike Finch: I'm cutting it up right now. You're distracting me, woman!
Marjorie Brown: Sorry, everyone, the wife was trying pole dancing again and knocked it over.
Jade Clark: I'm better than this. I won't laugh, I won't laugh.
Henrietta Brown: It's better than when you fell and your ass made the watering hole at Bennie Grove farms.
Jade Clark: oh my god SHE'S FIGHTING BACK.
Mollie Wilson: I'm sat and watching. Anyone want popcorn?

———

THE LAST THING I needed was something else to go wrong, but life didn't work that way. It had already been a long day. I'd had to go to Knoxville to get my glucose test done and came back to a frigid house.

"Dammit," I said as I held a flashlight. I had no idea how my heating unit worked, just that it was supposed to turn on when I needed it to. It had trucked along all winter, but this February cold snap finally did it in.

Why did Kelsey have to say spring was here? It was never truly here until it was summer.

The unit was a mess of wires, parts, and dust. I didn't know why I even tried to go down to the basement to look at it. There wasn't anything I could do.

Theo was the town handyman, but he'd told us all that he was taking a step back from his work to focus on the coffee shop. The town had come to depend on him, so the news was met with a lot of grumbling, but we were happy for him to do what he wanted to.

That just meant I had no idea who to call.

I didn't have money for this on any day, but I *especially* didn't have money for it now. Going back upstairs, I put a jacket on and got my phone out.

> Do we have a new person who can do handyman things?

JADE
> Do you mean handywoman things? Wren's your girl for that.

> Do you think she knows HVAC systems?

> Only one way to find out. (If you don't call her, I will.)

Attached was Wren's number.

The only thing that sounded worse than calling her was

having Jade do it, so I mentally put on my big-girl panties and dialed her.

"This is Wren speaking."

"Hey," I said. "Are you busy tonight?"

"Grace? No, I'm not. It's just a night in with Henry."

"Oh, if you're with Henry, I can—"

"What's going on?" she asked. "You sound a little stressed."

Stressed was my middle name at this point. "My heat's busted."

"Oh, shit. I can come take a look."

"Thank you," I said. "I can't pay much, but I can try to compensate you for your time."

"I am *not* charging you," she said. "This is a friend's call. What's your address?"

I hated the relief I felt when she said she wouldn't charge, and I told her my address. She promised she would be here in thirty minutes.

I *had* to make it up to her somehow, but I didn't know her well enough to. I spent the entire time of her drive trying to figure something out and came up empty.

Wren's red truck pulled up next to my car, and I took a breath to pretend like I was fine. Only Jade knew I was pregnant, and I was keeping it that way for as long as possible.

"Thanks for meeting me out here," I said.

"No problem at all. I love helping out my friends and Mollie never lets me do it. Besides, I didn't even know there was a house back here!"

No one did. Mom had bought a big plot of land and the house was far back on it. It was a pain for her to mow and take care of, but Brooke and I spent countless hours in the fields here.

"It's a work in progress," I said. "I wasn't prepared to be a homeowner when she passed, so it's . . . not all put together."

"I've seen it all. What's more important is that you don't freeze tonight."

I laughed humorlessly. "Yeah. What bad timing."

"Come on, show me where the HVAC is."

I took Wren inside and down to the basement. I'd figured out how to open the thing, but knew nothing else.

"Well, it's not that old," she said as she looked at it. "Honestly, it's in good shape."

"It's just not turning on at all."

"Did you reset the breaker?"

"Um, should I have?"

"It's always a good first option," she said patiently. "Where's your electrical box?"

I took Wren to the other side of the basement where it sat. I rarely came over here, which was obvious since there was dust all over it.

Wren didn't seem bothered. She cleaned off what she could and then opened it up.

"It's tripped," she said. "Which means it's just off. And everything on here is labeled. That's another good thing."

"Mom took good care of this place," I said. "I'm . . . trying."

"It's a lot for one person," she said as she flicked the switch to the left. There was a buzzing sound, then it returned to the center. "I think it's busted," she said.

"Can you fix that?"

She winced. "I probably could, but I don't know electrical all that well."

"Fuck," I muttered. "Well, I guess I should find the blankets that I stashed down here."

I went to an old cardboard box. They would need a wash, but it would still be helpful.

"Hang on, you're not entirely out of luck. There happens to be an electrician in town tonight. Dean just arrived."

I dropped the box onto my foot. "What? I thought he—"

I paused as Wren turned to me. "You thought he left months ago?" she finished.

"Y-yeah. Definitely."

"Apparently, he wanted more. He called and asked to work with me again. Want me to help with that box?"

I shook my head and bent down to get it. I didn't need her looking at my face anyway.

It had to be red. I didn't think Dean would even call again, but now he was working here? I thought he hated Strawberry Springs.

"So, should I call him?"

Did I even want to see him again? The way he stared at me like I was a bomb ready to go off didn't feel great.

"He's really expensive, though, isn't he?"

"I can call him in for a favor. As long as you can handle some light flirting."

Light flirting had gotten me pregnant.

At least I couldn't get more pregnant.

And I doubted he was looking twice at me anyway.

"Okay, let's call him." It felt like pulling teeth, but as I picked up the box and saw how dusty the blankets were, I knew these would need more than a wash.

And I was freezing.

Wren stepped outside to call him, and I tried to prepare myself for the fact that I would be seeing Dean *again*.

Wren walked back in. "All right, he'll be here in a few."

"So, how long is he staying?"

"No idea. He asked how much work I had, which is always promising. I know all the ladies missed him." Wren laughed, but I was processing.

None of this made sense with how he'd acted. Just what was about to happen?

"Do you have any warm drinks?" Wren asked, rubbing her hands together. "That might help us both."

"You don't have to stay," I offered. "I can handle Dean."

"Dean constantly flirts. If you don't want that, then I'll help you out. I know how to keep him in line."

I highly doubted he would flirt with me *now*. Our one, well, two-time thing, was over. This wasn't a fun little escapade anymore. This was real life.

"But you were off for the night. I'm sure Henry wants to spend time with you."

"He does, but making sure someone doesn't freeze is also important. And I could fix that step out front. Did you know it was loose?"

"I'll get to it," I lied.

"Will you?"

"Seriously, I can't ask you for anything else. This is enough."

"Fine, I get it. Mollie doesn't want me snooping around her place either. But let me at least make you a hot drink."

"That's a good idea, but this is my house and you're my guest, so I'll make something for the both of us," I said. I led Wren to the kitchen.

"Wait, does this fireplace work?" she asked as I got water started. "I could light it for you."

"Oh, um. I don't think it does." My cheeks burned. In reality, it probably did. But I hadn't tried to light it since a bird made its nest in the chimney. I wasn't sure why, but sweeps were expensive as hell, and I'd nearly passed out when I got an estimate.

Wren raised her eyebrows and I knew what she was going to offer.

"Here, have some tea." I gave her a warm cup to distract her. "I feel like we haven't gotten to talk all that much since you moved here."

That was enough. Wren loved to fix things, but I had a feeling that deep down, she liked people more.

And thank fuck for that.

"Thanks," she said. "And you're right. I wanna try to get to know people around here more."

"Well, you know my house is a bit of a mess. But I do know most of the people in town. So I can exchange some details if you keep this between us."

"Deal," she said, and then leaned over. "What's the deal with Hugh? Does he hate me?"

"He probably doesn't. He's just like that."

"Dean seemed to get along with him."

"Dean has one of those personalities."

Wren raised an eyebrow. "But you do too, don't you?"

"I like to know people and I'm good at it. I know that Hugh seems like a dick, but he just wants someone to listen to him. Kerry wants to know everything she can because she's bored during the day when her son's at school."

"That's definitely deeper than Dean goes. I've worked with him for years and I barely know anything about his personal life."

"He's shallow. It's . . . pretty typical for a playboy."

Wren nodded with a sigh. "Luckily for me, I don't need to know him too well to work with him. It's just so different to how people are here. I like that they all wanna get to know me."

It was one of the things I liked too. Sure, people could be annoying, but they cared.

Sometimes I forgot other people *weren't* like that.

"Speaking of the devil," she said. "He got here fast."

Headlights came down the driveway and his older truck pulled in next to Wren's.

Would this be a sight I saw often as we traded our kid back and forth?

I shook myself out of my thoughts and went to meet him by the door. That was . . . way ahead of things.

Dean was heading up my porch and tripped right where everyone else did.

"Sorry," I rushed to say. "That plank is loose."

"Yeah, no kidding."

"I'm working on it."

Dean met my gaze, eyebrow raised. I had no idea what that expression meant. I hated that I didn't know.

"We're here for one thing," Wren reminded him as our eyes remained locked for far too long. "You need to look at this electrical panel."

"Right," he said, shifting his focus away from me. "Where is it?"

Wren took over, showing him what she'd found. From how they talked, I knew Dean was an expert. He muttered things about the wiring of the whole house and something about the brand of the breakers.

I both loved and hated experts. Usually their experience came with a price.

"It looks like it just needs a new switch," Dean informed me.

"Okay, how much will it run me?" I asked.

"I told you not to worry about that," Wren said.

"I still have to pay something."

Dean watched our exchange. I had a feeling he was about to tell me a number that would put me in debt.

"One dinner."

"Oh, for the love of—" Wren groaned. "Really?"

"Dinner, seriously?" I asked.

"Just one."

"That's not usually how this works."

"Save your money, Grace," Dean said. "Take this deal instead."

I'd been so sure Dean was only around me because he had to be. After all, this was his worst nightmare.

But if I'd had it my way, I would have liked to get to know him. We didn't have to be best friends, but something was better than nothing when we'd be sharing a child.

Had he figured out what he was able to offer? Was this dinner to discuss that?

I knew my answer immediately.

"Fine. Dinner."

"Grace, you really don't have to do this." Wren turned to Dean. "And you should really know how to ask people out better."

"I'm not asking her out. I'm asking for one dinner."

"Right, because you don't date." Wren crossed her arms. "I know where this leads."

"It won't go there," I said, because it already had. "It's a good deal. What other electrician is gonna offer this?"

"Whatever. If he hurts you, I'll kick him in the balls for you."

"Scary," Dean said. "Thank you for your business, Grace. I have the stuff in my truck. Give me a few minutes."

He walked away.

"Seriously, dinner?" Wren muttered. "The nerve of that guy."

"You did warn me about flirting." Though, I doubted it was true flirting. "It's fine. I'd rather make him food than deal with how much he would charge."

"You just know his whole thing, right?" she asked. "He only sleeps with people. He doesn't commit."

"Trust me, I know."

"And he doesn't change his mind."

She was making sure I knew what I was getting into. And I

had, back when I thought it would just be a one-night stand. Now, we were something else.

What? I wasn't sure. But we certainly weren't together.

"I've got it," I said gently. "I know what I'm getting into."

"Good. Now let me clean up some of this dust so Dean isn't here longer than he needs to be."

My allergies were going to hate that. There was a reason I avoided the basement.

"I'll do it," I said. "I have a duster I brought down here and forgot about." Wren sighed and let me get it. But then she stole it when I walked past her. "Hey!"

"Too late! It's mine now." She got to work with a smirk sent in my direction.

My body went tight, and I wanted to find a way to steal the duster back so I could do this myself. Every cell in my body demanded me to move, to not need the help in the first place, but I did. I already felt sneezing fits coming on, and I wasn't sure if I could even take allergy medicine if I pushed myself.

I was still struggling with it when Dean finally came down the stairs to work on the problem.

"Did you get lost?" Wren asked. "I had time to dust the whole basement."

"A little, but it's good now." He held up a toolbox. "Now let me get to work. And you . . ." He turned to me just as I was about to sneeze again. "Get out of the dust. It's killing you."

My cheeks burned, but he was right. Since when did he care if I was sneezing? I was so shocked about what he'd said that I didn't fight it. I slowly went upstairs and let them do what they needed to.

I wound up washing up before Dean came back up the stairs and told me everything was done. Wren said she would leave to get a shower and thanked *me* for letting her help. It felt wrong to even accept it, but at least I had working heat.

I went to bed, promising myself that I would get it together and not need it again.

I didn't even realize the loose step was fixed until the next morning.

12

DEAN

Dad Company (But Sometimes Good Advice)

Dean Briggs: Hey, guys, it's me again. While the mother of my child is pregnant and I'm helping her, how do I prevent attachment? I don't do that kind of thing.

Comments:

Robert Colt: ??? You don't do attachment? You're gonna be a dad. That comes with some element of attachment.

Dean Briggs: Yeah, I know. I'll deal with that later. One day at a time, right?

Ryan Kim: You might wanna look inward on this one. Attachment isn't inherently a bad thing.

Graham Hamilton: Hey, maybe he's been hurt before. Just help from a distance and watch out for her hinting at child support and wanting money from you.

Ryan Kim: Child support is very common, Graham.

Graham Hamilton: Some women are only in it for the money.

Robert Colt: And he broke rule one again. Can someone delete that?

"You're not slick, you know that, right?" Wren said it to me the second I walked into our next job. She'd given me work on the apartment above the coffee shop. I was looking forward to starting on it.

"I promise I won't start drama with dinner."

"That was your normal thing." She waved her hand. "I mean, what you did outside."

I shrugged, choosing to play dumb. "I didn't do anything."

"You fixed that loose plank."

"What loose plank? I don't think there's one there now."

"You're ridiculous." She rolled her eyes, but then smiled. "But that was the right thing to do. I'm sure she'll thank you, if she doesn't kill you first."

"I like to ask for forgiveness. Not permission. And I knew that look. She's overwhelmed. I might as well take something off her plate."

I didn't mention the fact that I was the reason she was overwhelmed. I didn't know when I could.

Grace and I had a lot to talk about, which was why dinner was a good idea. I needed to make it clear that she could ask anything she needed of me. I wished she'd called me and not Wren first. I needed to fix what I'd messed up.

"That was actually sweet. Who knew you had it in you?"

My shoulders tensed. I still didn't want to be seen as what I wasn't. Maybe I should've worked out the deal when Grace and I were alone.

"Now, our job," I reminded Wren. "We're working in the apartment above Theo's coffee shop, right?"

She blinked at the topic change, but nodded. "Yep. I have all the permits and just need to rewire it."

"What's the plan here? Is Theo gonna live here?"

"No, he has his own place. This is for someone else to move into."

"Is Theo okay with that?"

"He doesn't own it," Wren said. "He rents it from the grant, and they approved me to fix up all the apartments I want to."

"*All* of them?"

"Yep. So you can join. They're even paying the full rates."

I turned to her. "A *grant* agreed to the rates we usually charge the big businesses?"

"Yep. Didn't even bat an eye."

"I . . . what grant is this?"

"You're asking the same questions I am." She only shrugged. "But it does pay, and I wanna use it while it's here. Besides, I have to be competitive to keep you here."

"I thought you didn't want me here to cause problems." It was supposed to come out light, like a joke. But bitterness had crept in.

"I only meant don't break hearts," she said. "But I figured you would do what you wanted. And then you surprised me."

I hadn't surprised her. She just didn't know what I'd done.

The fact of the matter was, Wren was right to try and warn me. I didn't listen, and look at where I got. I did hope that when the news came out, it didn't reflect badly on her. That would only make me feel worse.

"Yeah, I surprised you."

"Anyway, I'm sorry if I came off rude. I just really like it here."

And she didn't want me messing it up.

"I know," I said. "I'll be on my best behavior."

"Even if you're not—"

"The apartment," I said. "Can you show me around? I don't wanna keep you too late."

"Right, the apartment. You're always very on topic when you're avoiding things." She smirked at me and led me inside.

I was glad when I knew what I needed to do and was able to get to work. I had a lot on my mind. I needed to figure out how long I could stay before I ruined what I had with Clyde. Mom had talked to him, and he told me to take the time I needed, but I hated having to use that. I'd never left him high and dry before like this.

There were too many things to figure out, including how to not mess things up with Grace *again*. It had been a long time since I was anyone other than the playboy. I didn't know if I knew how to connect at all.

Much less connect and not get attached.

The air was cold and the square was dark when Wren called it for the day and kicked me out of the apartment. When I got outside, I realized that the square was lit again. The first time I'd been here, I was struck by how much someone cared about this place. Most small towns were run-down, but this one felt like it was up-and-coming.

I had a feeling it would be short-lived. But it was still nice to see for now. Back when I was young, everything had this glow. That had faded over the years.

When I got to my truck, I paused. The plan had been to go back to my hotel, but being alone would make all the thoughts of my future come back, and I was exhausted from ruminating on everything I'd fucked up over the last few days.

Bell's Brews was fun the first time I went, and I couldn't say no to a beer. When I walked in, it was slower than it was the last time. There was just Mark and Hugh, who were playing cards at a table alone.

"Oh, look who it is. I heard you were back in town," Mark said.

"Just for a short while," I replied. "Wren has more things for me to rewire."

"It's good to see you."

I nodded before turning to Hugh. "Hey, Hugh."

He huffed. "You remembered my name? You must like me or something."

"I remembered to take care of my truck. I fixed the dent a while ago."

"Good. Don't go hitting any more stop signs."

"I'll do my best, sir."

He didn't grace me with a response, and I walked up to the bar.

"Want what you got last time?"

I blinked in shock. "There's no way you remember that."

"Kid, this ain't one of those big bars in the city. I remember everything. Too much, even." He shuddered.

I almost asked, but it wasn't my business.

"Yes, please."

He disappeared and brought back my beer. "How've you been?"

"Busy," I said. "Uh, you?"

Mark laughed. "You're not the best at small talk, huh? If you prefer your beer in private, I can leave you alone."

"I'm trying not to be rude."

"We have city people come in here all the time. They all are a little different."

I opened my mouth to say I wasn't from the city, that I used to be just like everyone else here, but I was cut off.

"He could come sit with me," Hugh said.

"You want someone to sit with you?" I asked.

"You better not offer to play poker with him," Mark said. "I can't watch you swindle someone else."

"Now hang on a second." I shook my head. "Who said he'd win?"

"You could put money on it, if you want." Hugh gave me a rare smile.

"Ten bucks."

"That's baby money, but sure."

"It's your loss," Mark said with a shrug. "Come see me if you need to wallow in another beer."

"You know Texas Hold'em?" he asked.

"I do."

"Spend a lot of time in bars, don't ya?"

"That's also true. Oldest goes first."

"You'll regret that." Hugh was either lucky or knew what he was doing. I knew better than to underestimate a man like him. Clyde always gave me a run for my money too.

Hugh wound up winning the first round. And the second one.

But I was close to winning both times.

"I see I finally have a challenge," Hugh said. "None of the idiots here play like you do."

"I was worried no one here would measure up."

Hugh made a sound that was close to a laugh as he dealt the next round. Eventually, he came out on top again.

"Dammit," I muttered.

"I shoulda made you bet more."

"We can have a rematch next time."

"Come in when there isn't one of those sissy concerts, and you're on."

I laughed and handed him his money.

"So, why are you back?" he asked, eyeing me. "Something here catch your attention?"

"Just good work. I never turn it down." I thanked every god I knew that my voice sounded normal.

"Really? That's it? You kept looking at someone last time."

My shoulders tensed. "I get over those things quickly."

Hugh hummed, still watching me as I stood to get another drink. "We'll see about that."

"Well, that could have gone worse," Mark said. He handed me a second beer. "He almost tolerated you."

"At least he's good at poker."

"He smokes anyone else who's dumb enough to play him. Maybe one day you'll break his streak."

"He got lucky this time."

"So, that means there'll be a next time?" Mark asked. "I can stock more of your beer if so."

I wanted to say yes. Even if this bar was a bright spot in a town I didn't like, I'd always be tied to here.

But the idea of promising anything to a small town sounded wrong.

"We'll see," I said. "Who knows where life will take us?"

"That's a cop-out answer." Mark shook his head. "But I'll hold out hope."

13

GRACE

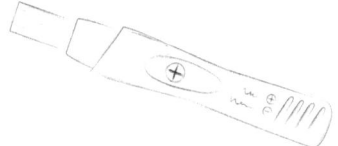

Strawberry Springs Neighborhood Watch

Tammy Jane: @Henrietta Brown, y'all have gotta get your website updated. I need to request a book.

Comments:
Henrietta Brown: Just request it here for now.
Tammy Jane: Well, I was trying not to offend sensitive ears here . . . but here we go. It's the romance book about the woman who gets lost on a spider planet.
Mollie Wilson: I—did I just read the last original sentence on the internet?
Wren Hackett: Wait, a romance book??? Who does the woman end up with??? Please say it's another man who got lost too.
Jade Clark: Oh, I know that book! It's so good. No, it's not a human man.
Wren Hackett: But how does that even WORK?
Tammy Jane: It's a popular genre, Wren. And after being

married to a human man for far too long, I need a little fantasy in my life.

Marjorie Brown: I TOLD you to stock a monster romance section, Henrietta! Now look at what you've done.

Henrietta Brown: I'm gonna hire someone to update the website.

WHEN I WALKED down the steps, *not* falling on my ass was the biggest shock of my life.

After safely making it to the ground, I saw that the loose wooden step had been screwed in, leaving it secure and stable.

My first thought was that Wren had to have done it, but she was with me most of the time. The only one who had disappeared was . . . Dean.

But that didn't make sense.

I knew Dean's type. He was emotionally insecure. The only time he'd been nice since finding out I was pregnant was when he'd fixed my heat in exchange for dinner. But he was getting something from that.

Had he seen the step and simply . . . fixed it?

If he did, then I *had* to do something in return. I couldn't simply accept help and not return the favor.

I was early for the day, and I'd heard he was working on the apartment above Theo's coffee shop, so I had time to get a hot drink and see if it had been his doing.

Coffee wasn't enough, but it was a start.

Of course, when I got in line, I knew it was rude of me to get something for me and nothing for him. And I did really owe him.

"Morning," I greeted Theo when I got to the front. "Good day today?"

"It's been all right."

Kelsey turned around. "Speak for yourself. My shirt's been ruined and I think I permanently smell like peppermint."

"I knew I should have taken that off the menu, but Kerry insisted," Theo muttered.

"You did that to stay on her good side, right?" I asked with a laugh.

He shrugged. "You want the same thing you got last time?"

"Yes, and I'd also like . . ." I trailed off. What would Dean like? Did he even drink coffee?

"Are you ordering for someone else?" he asked.

"No. Why would you ask that?" My voice rose in pitch.

"Write down who." He said it so lowly I almost couldn't hear him. He stared at me, and then handed me a pen.

"What do you . . . oh. Good idea."

Theo was the kind of guy who knew the town drama, but never added to it. If anyone would know I was buying a coffee for Dean, it could be him.

I passed the notebook back and Theo nodded.

"Coffee with cream and sugar," he said.

"You knew it off the top of your head?"

"Coffee orders are easy to guess," he said. "By the way, you should try the hazelnut cappuccino. I think you'd like it more."

"But the—"

"Caffeine? It's got about the same. It shouldn't make you jittery."

I blinked and then nodded. "You know what? I'll do both. Thanks, Theo."

I paid for my order and walked to the pickup counter.

"So, can I know who this is for?" Kelsey asked.

"Will you tell people?" I replied.

"Maybe if it's interesting."

"Then no."

Her bottom lip poked out. "Rude, but fair."

She started to make the two drinks, which still kept her near me, and my eyes drifted back to Theo. I wondered how long he would wind up staying out of the news or if he would find his way into it.

"Don't even, girl." Kelsey set my drinks down. "You're barking up the wrong tree."

"I wasn't barking up any tree. He doesn't date."

"And thank God for that," she said. "At least for me. It keeps people off my ass about working here. But I know a few people are bummed about it."

"Why aren't you?" I asked.

"He's not my type. I like them nerdier."

I laughed. "Are you sure you and Wren aren't related?"

"We're starting to question it," she said with a shrug. "And anyway, it's sorta nice having a boss who isn't in my business like Mom was."

"So, it's working out?"

"I haven't pissed anyone off."

"Hugh still doesn't come here."

"Another gift from fate," she said as she slid my drinks to me. "Have fun with whatever you're getting into. Though, it's you, so I doubt it's anything too wild."

"Yeah, you know me." I tried to sound convincing, but I wasn't sure it landed when Kelsey tilted her head at me. "Anyway, gotta go!" I grabbed both drinks and nearly ran.

As I turned the corner, I saw Dean at his truck. He was balanced on one of the wheel wells, grabbing wiring out of the bed.

I got the pleasure of seeing his thick arm flex, and my body immediately responded. Suddenly, I was grateful for the cool air.

"Hey," I said as I got close.

He saw me and did a double take. "Grace?"

"Yep. It's me. I'm trying to solve a mystery this morning and I'm hoping you can help me."

Dean hopped down and put the wiring on the ground. "What kind of mystery?"

"You see, I had this stair that was loose. And suddenly it's not, and I'm trying to find the very kind fairy who did it." I held up the extra cup. "Whoever did it gets free coffee."

"Whoever did it doesn't need a thank-you. It was just the right thing to do. You don't need to be falling over." He sounded so different. Instead of the emotionally stunted playboy I'd talked to just the day before, he seemed more real.

I handed over the cup. "I owe you one."

"You're not here to yell at me?"

"Do you want me to?"

"Usually when I help someone who insists on doing things herself, it doesn't go well for me."

"How many people do you help?" I asked. "I didn't think you stuck around long enough to."

He looked to the ground and then back at me. "Not many, admittedly. But my mom is one of them."

"And she yells at you?"

"Sometimes. It's usually when she gets money in the mail." He looked at the coffee and then to me. "I wanted to try Theo's shop, but I didn't think I'd get the chance. What did you get me?"

"I actually let him guess." Now I wondered if I shouldn't have. "He said you'd like coffee with cream and sugar. Hopefully that's not too boring."

"That is my actual order," he said slowly. "How the hell did he know?"

"He also gave me a recommendation," I said, holding my

own up. "Let's see if he was right." I took a sip and had to bite back a moan. "Dammit. He was."

"Is it really that good?" he asked. "I've been to his sister shop, so I have high expectations."

"Try it and you tell me."

He lifted the cup to his mouth. The second he got a drink, his eyes rolled back. "Fuck, that's good."

And I was blushing again. I really couldn't handle him saying anything like that around me. I also couldn't handle him being *nice* either.

Clearing my throat, I smiled. "Glad you like it. And that I could pay you back for the step."

"You don't owe me anything for helping you out."

"I thought I owed you dinner?" I asked.

"All right, you have me there. We should figure out the details of that." He straightened and took a breath. "I was thinking the diner. Or maybe we go out of town to not raise suspicion yet?"

"Neither. Come to my house."

Dean paused with the cup halfway to his mouth. "I'm sorry, what?"

"My house. Whenever you want to."

"I . . . really meant dinner. We should probably talk about things."

What was with this guy and thinking I was asking him out? I wasn't a fool. I knew he didn't date. "I really mean dinner too. I'm cooking."

"You're cooking?" he asked. "And I don't mean this in a rude way, but do you know how?"

I crossed my arms. "Do I know how? Of course I do. Haven't you heard—" I paused. "I forgot you're not from here. Yes, I definitely know how. I'm second only to Tammy's husband in my skills."

"Thank God. I've had a lot of bad experiences with home cooking."

"Your mom?" I asked.

"Yeah, she can burn water." He shook his head.

I was so curious about his family. I was curious about a lot with him. Why didn't he settle down? Did his mom have anything to do with it?

But that wasn't for me to know. Even though we shared a kid, some rules were still in place.

"Hopefully I can turn that streak around," I said. "Tomorrow? Are you free?"

"What else am I gonna do? Go get beat by Hugh at poker again?"

"That's what you get for playing with him in the first place," I said. "He does that to everyone."

"I almost had him," Dean said. "I'm not bad at poker, you know."

I shook my head. "It's your money, buddy."

He laughed and took another sip from his cup. Then he stared at me.

"I really didn't mean to be rude about . . . everything, by the way," he said. "I feel like I owe you a lot of apologies."

I blinked again. "I-I mean, it was a shock to both of us. But you seem . . . like you've accepted it now?"

"More than accepted it. I'm doing this right, Grace Day. And dinner is just the start of that."

Oh. *Oh.* This was better than I imagined.

Were things finally looking up for once?

"I mean the father thing," he quickly clarified. "Not . . ."

I rolled my eyes. "I know. I guess I'll see you tomorrow then."

Dad Company (But Sometimes Good Advice)

Jett Nelson: Hey, guys. My wife is calling me "Daddy" while talking to our kids and I think I want her to do it in . . . other places. Should I bring this up to her?

Comments:
Oliver Brian: Is this a joke post?
Ryan Kim: Communication, man. Also, have some decorum.
Robert Colt: Ack, I don't wanna know this. Admins, delete please!
Robert Colt: But also, just communicate it. Plenty of us have our things in the bedroom. Even weirder things than being a daddy.

In the light of day, I could see more of Grace's split-level home as I drove up. It was a good family home with plenty of space. Even with the minor work it needed, I liked the idea of our kid being raised here.

Our kid. I would never get used to that.

As I walked up to the door, my repair on the step was holding up. I was proud of myself for getting that done without her noticing it. And I'd liked her response even more.

My eyes traced over the house. One gutter was leaning, but that was easily fixable, and her porch could use railings to make it safer.

The front door opened as I stared.

"Eyes on me," she said. "You're not sneakily repairing anything else."

"You say that now, but I don't need your permission."

Her eyes were narrow. "It's my house."

"You know I'm good at sneaking around."

Her cheeks went pink. "I . . . do know that."

I replayed what I'd said and knew I needed to clarify. "I mean with repairs. And fixing things."

"Right, *that.*" She nodded and opened the door wider. "Come on in. Hopefully the food will distract you."

Grace turned to let me follow her.

As I did, I couldn't help but let my eyes trail downward. God, she looked incredible. The feeling I'd been missing when looking at others was back full force in her presence.

It didn't help that there was more of her to look at now. I knew better than to ever comment on a woman's weight, but the sight of her ass these days would easily put me into an early grave.

There was only one other thing that could have distracted me, and it hit when I got halfway to the kitchen.

Food. Delicious, home-cooked food.

Was there anything she couldn't do?

"Holy shit, what is that smell?"

"That better be a compliment," she said.

"Oh, it is." I looked into a pan where there was a meat sauce simmering. At first glance, I was thinking we would be having some sort of pasta, but the smell was different. A mix of spices hit my nose. I wasn't good enough at cooking to be able to tell them apart.

"It might not be Tuesday, but I figured we could have tacos. I'm about to start the tortillas."

"Is this sauce for them?"

"No, it's just the meat. I simmer it in a sauce to make it taste better."

My mouth was already watering, but then I caught what she said. "Wait, *start* the tortillas?"

"Yep. I make them from scratch."

"You do all of this yourself?"

"It's one of my favorite pastimes. Usually, I just don't have others to cook for, but I make enough to feed an army."

"Where did you learn this?"

"From my mom."

"Is she here?"

"No," she said softly. "She passed away about three years ago."

"Shit, I'm sorry."

"It's okay. It's part of life."

I didn't know how she could talk about it so calmly. Some days, I still felt like the kid who came home to his mom sobbing on her knees on the living room floor.

All I could do was stare, and she caught on to that.

"Have you lost someone?"

It was tempting to answer. But also dangerous to.

"Some days, I think I've lost my mind," I said. "Does that count?"

She laughed. "Not really."

"I *am* sorry about your mom, though." It was easier to say it as she was focused on flipping a tortilla. "I shouldn't have brought it up."

"It's okay," she said. "It was a fair question. And I'm doing okay. Other than . . . you know, managing a house. She made it look easy."

"The best moms are good at that," I replied.

"I don't know how I'll manage to make it happen, but I'll get there somehow."

"You'll be great. Certainly better than I'm gonna be at being a dad."

"You're not all bad. You did fix my step instead of running like I thought you would."

I huffed out a humorless laugh. "That was never an option. Even when I was acting like a jerk."

"Really? But you seemed so . . ." She trailed off, wincing.

"Sometimes how I sound doesn't match up with what I mean," I said. "I'm used to a one-and-done thing, so I don't have to rethink things when I mess them up."

Grace paused in her work and looked up at me. "So, are you willing to rethink things?"

"Not about dating," I said quickly.

She rolled her eyes. "I'm not gonna ask about that. Trust me, I remember that you don't date."

"Then, what is it?"

"I wanna know what went through your head when I told you."

"You mean other than pure shock?"

She nodded. "On my end, it felt like you were looking for any reason to get out of it."

"No," I said immediately. "That's not what I was thinking. I was making sure the timing was right, and then figuring out what I should do. In bad words, of course."

Grace hummed, eyeing me for one more second and then looking back down at the food. "You know, I keep thinking I have your whole personality pinned down. And then you do nice things and I realize I'm wrong."

"What did you think about me? Before, I mean."

"That you were a playboy running from responsibility."

"I can handle responsibilities."

"It's attachment you can't," she said.

"*Now* you get it."

"I want you to know that I respect that you don't do attachment, but you also need to know that that's the opposite of how I am. We don't have to be together, but we have to be *something* here. We'll have to get to know each other."

"Right," I said. "I'll . . . work on that."

"We can start with the basics," she said. "Just general things, and work our way up."

I knew she was right, but the uncomfortable pressure in my chest told me this was a bad idea. I knew I would be tempted to let her get deeper than anyone else had been before.

"Just basics. That's a good start." That was the best answer I could give, even if it wasn't entirely truthful.

She smiled and continued flipping tortillas. A few minutes later, the last one was done.

"We're ready to eat," she said as she turned to grab plates. "What would you like on yours? I have salsa, sour cream, cheese, and a bunch of other things."

"I'll have all of it, but I'm making my own plate."

She turned and frowned at me like she'd never heard that before. "You're my guest."

"And I'm a grown-ass man," I said. "I don't need you to serve me."

She blinked, her cheeks darkening as if she didn't expect that kind of answer from me. But it was the truth. I didn't want anyone to serve me, nor did I want her bending over backward to make sure I got what I wanted.

I had a feeling she would try.

I went to the fridge and got out all of the toppings. Grace had an iron grip on the plates, but I got my own and made it.

There was a dining room right off the kitchen. It had at least six seats. It could fit more.

"This is a good house for raising a kid," I said.

"I'm lucky," she replied. "Mom left it to me. It felt fuller when Brooke and I were kids here, though."

"You'll get there."

"Yeah, I imagine it won't be as quiet when there's a kid running around."

She looked over the house as if she were imagining it. I was tempted to do the same thing. Instead, I took a bite of my food. Flavor like I'd never known exploded on my tongue. It was spicy with a hint of sweetness. The meat was perfectly seasoned, and the tortilla tasted different than any I'd ever had from a store.

"Holy *shit*," I said. "This is fucking incredible. I should marry you right now over this."

"Marriage again? You're gonna have to get your priorities straight. You just told me you didn't do relationships." I froze. I'd said it as a joke. But then she laughed. "I know what you meant, Dean. And I take it as the highest compliment. It's not every day that I meet someone that doesn't know that I can cook."

"I'm bad at this for a reason." My cheeks were still burning.

"We can't all be the best at everything. Trust me, I'm a pretty forgiving person." She gave me a smile and then bit into her own dinner.

She had to be if she was still talking to me after how I'd acted when I first found out. That also had to extend to Brooke. I had tried not to think much about the person I met when I first came into town, but the information I did have stuck out hard. I remembered meeting her and being so shocked that she was related to Grace. I remembered how Grace rushed to fix her sister's problems.

And I internally vowed never to be one of those problems.

I could do it too. If only I could keep my mouth shut.

This dinner was proving that it was harder than it seemed.

15

GRACE

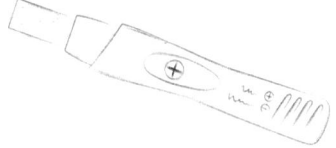

Strawberry Springs Neighborhood Watch

Tammy Jane: Our cowboy man is back. Spotted him today.

Comments:
Atticus Thompson: So not a lot is going on in town news, I guess.
Jackie Anne: Speak for yourself! I need eye candy. My garden is in BLOOM, if you know what I mean.
Mollie Wilson: I'm showing this to Cain IMMEDIATELY.
Jackie Anne: Please don't show my son my thirst. I'm begging.
Jade Clark: Jackie, how the hell do you know anything about thirsting?
Jackie Anne: I'm not a regular old lady. I'm hip with the times.

DEAN GREW quiet as we ate. I could see him glancing at me as he took bites. For a while, I let him sit in the silence, but I wouldn't let it go on forever.

"You're having thoughts over there," I said. "You can share them, you know."

Dean looked up at me like a deer in headlights. I could tell he didn't love being read by me, but that didn't mean that I wasn't going to enjoy it. This whole time he'd been like a brick wall, one that I wouldn't allow myself to break through. Now I had a chance.

"I was letting you eat."

"What fun is a silent dinner?" I asked. "We can talk. We're supposed to be getting to know each other, aren't we?"

"We . . . are."

I waited for him to say something, but he looked like he was struggling with it. "Dean, seriously. Ask me anything."

I knew that he never stuck around with women. So having a conversation with one that he'd slept with couldn't have been easy. I decided to break and throw him a bone instead.

"Did you ever see yourself doing any of this? Being a dad?" I asked.

"No." The answer was so immediate that I knew it was the truth. My shoulders slumped even though I didn't want them to.

"I thought you didn't. I knew I would have kids someday, so while it was a shock, I was able to adjust. But I guess it's not the same for you."

He shrugged. "I'll get used to it eventually."

"I want you to know that I'm not trying to mess up your life. I seriously would have left you alone if that's what you wanted." I would have been pissed, but I would have done it.

"That's not how things work. We both took part in it, and good *will* come of it. Some of my best memories are of my dad. It'll be cool to give that to someone else."

That was the first time he'd mentioned his dad. For a second, I thought over every single detail he'd given me about his family. That was when I knew what to say. "I bet your dad was a good person."

"He wa—wait, how did you know to use the word *was*?"

There I went again, pushing. I told him I would keep it in check, but it was too tempting. "You tried to hide it, but you did lose someone. People usually do that when it was someone very important to them. And you mention your mom all the time, but not your dad."

"Yeah, well. It sucked. But I'll try my best not to die in an electrical fire."

"That would be nice," I said. I thought about what that must have been like and quickly decided I needed to change the topic or else I'd feel emotions I was sure he wouldn't want to deal with. "Though, you might have your work cut out for you with my house, considering it just had an electrical problem."

"No, all that work was done well. I'm not worried about it." He said it with complete confidence.

"You would have told me if you were worried, wouldn't you?"

"I would have fixed it if I was. There is no way I'm letting anything . . ." He trailed off, but I knew where he was going with it.

"You don't want anything like that ever happening again. I get it."

His eyes met mine and he swallowed.

I was continuing to push things and I knew it. I decided to give him a reprieve from all of my questions and went back to eating. As I finished up my food, I promised myself that I wouldn't go any further. This was enough.

But it was addicting to be able to get a read on him. I liked knowing more about the person I was spending time with, and he *had* opened up, if only slightly.

I was about to start dishes when my phone rang. Pulling it out, I saw it was my OB-GYN's office. It was late in the day, but they usually called after office hours with lab results. They had when my PCOS results came back too.

But I knew that whenever they called, something was wrong. My office had a policy of not reaching out when everything was normal.

So that meant something with my *pregnancy* wasn't normal.

My heart stuttered in my chest as I looked back at Dean.

"I-I need to take this." I didn't care if my voice was shaky. All I could think about was what could be said to me on this phone call. "Hello?" I answered as I walked into the kitchen.

"Hi, is this Grace Day?"

"This is she."

"I'm calling about some lab results from a few days ago. Can you discuss those?"

I had to take a breath before answering. "Yes, of course."

"You failed your first glucose screening, meaning we need you in for another, more in-depth test. When can you come in?"

"I—what?" I asked. My mind ground to a halt is I tried to process all the words she just said to me.

"Your lab results, they're—"

"No, I heard that." I honestly didn't want to hear it again. I curled in tighter on myself, as if this would somehow protect me from this unexpected news. "I'm sorry, I'm just shocked about it. The baby is okay, right?"

"The baby is probably fine. It's pretty common," she said, and I could imagine her shrugging. She seemed so unbothered, and yet, to me, this was terrifying. My heart rate had already kicked up, and I was scared that by me not knowing that I was pregnant for so long, I had somehow messed this up.

"Of course. I can come in to the office for that test tomorrow."

She offered up a time and I took it without hesitation. When she hung up, I squeezed my eyes shut and tried to remain calm. Dean was out there. I didn't want to worry him.

"What was that about?"

I jumped, not expecting him to have followed me.

"How much of that did you hear?"

"All of it. It seemed like a doctor. Is everything okay?"

The right thing to do would be to slowly explain to him everything that I had just been told. That would have been logical. I could have also said something about not following me next time. However, my pregnancy brain didn't work on logic. It worked with feelings, it seemed.

I knew I'd been lucky that more hadn't gone wrong. I knew that I'd been lucky to skate past the first trimester and not notice that I was pregnant at all. Plenty of people didn't.

But *this?*

This was scary.

And all I could do was burst into tears.

16

DEAN

Dad Company (But Sometimes Good Advice)

James Marson: How to keep from feeling the crushing fear of something going wrong?

Comments:
Robert Colt: You don't. Hope this helps.
Oliver Brian: It happens, but worrying about it won't change anything. Try some meditation and deep breathing.
Dean Briggs: You could also take a step away and get your head on straight.
Robert Colt: Don't know if that's a good idea, Mr. Insecure Attachment.

WHEN GRACE BURST INTO TEARS, all I could do was stare. This entire time, she had been taking every shock with ease. Or at least it seemed that way. I had a feeling she wouldn't show me if she was struggling.

Until now.

I didn't usually do well with women crying. A few had shed tears when I'd reminded them that I didn't do relationships. And I would leave before anything got messier.

But this wasn't because of me; Grace was crying because of our *baby*. And something was wrong.

Walking away wasn't an option here. It hadn't been since I found out. So, my normal reaction was out the window. I had to do what felt right.

My legs carried me to her before I could stop myself.

Instead of keeping my distance and trying to stay friendly with her, I immediately pulled her into my arms. She let me do it willingly. And if she wasn't fighting me and trying to keep distance as well, then this wasn't good news.

I despised more than anything that I didn't know everything that was going on with her. I hadn't had a chance to ask her about her appointments or what tests she had gotten. I knew nothing, and I hated that. She was growing my child, and what was I doing?

I held her in my arms and let her cry. I worked through my own pounding heart and tense shoulders, and I gave her time. But the second she told me what was going on, I wasn't going to let it go. Whatever it was, it was getting fixed. Either by me or by some doctor that I would find.

There were reasons I shouldn't be thinking this way, but as she was crying into my shirt, I couldn't remember them. In fact, I didn't care about them.

"I-I'm sorry," she said.

"Don't be sorry," I replied softly. "Just tell me what happened."

"Glucose test. I failed it."

I went through all of the information that I'd learned since finding out she was carrying my baby. I'd spent every single night since staring at my phone, trying to memorize everything about pregnancy. The glucose test was to make sure that she didn't have gestational diabetes. But wasn't it later in pregnancy? I knew that they added two weeks before implantation, so she should only be about sixteen weeks. Maybe closer to seventeen.

Was I going to ask her any of that? Absolutely not. The last thing she needed was for me to be mansplaining how her own pregnancy worked.

"Was it the one hour or the three hour?" I asked.

"Since when do you know anything about pregnancy and glucose tests?"

"Since the beginning. I've been doing some reading." Then she pulled away, eyes wide. "I'm doing the bare minimum a father should do," I reminded her. "I know I didn't give you a good first impression, which is why I'm here trying to make it better."

"You are." She wiped at her eyes. "It's still more than I'm used to, though."

"Raise your expectations, Grace."

"I will once I figure out if I have gestational diabetes or not." She let out a huff of laughter that didn't sound very humorous. "And to answer your question, it was just the one hour. But the way the receptionist made it sound, it just . . . terrified me. I didn't know for sixteen weeks. There were so many things I could have messed up."

"Gestational diabetes is mostly genetic, just like PCOS is. I highly doubt you did anything to cause this."

She blinked at me. "How much research did you do?"

"I like to be prepared."

For a second, all she could do was stare at me. "Well, I can't say it's a bad thing because you're saying exactly what I need to hear."

"So, what's the next step?"

"The three-hour test. I go tomorrow morning." She let out a sigh that turned into a groan. "That means the shop will once again be closed, which will raise questions. I can't eat breakfast, and I have to make an hour-long drive to Knoxville where I'll drink a disgustingly sweet drink and then sit for three hours. It's going to be *so* fun."

I knew what I was going to do before she was finished talking. Wren was going to be pissed. Mostly because I couldn't work tomorrow.

"I'll take you."

"Why would you do that? Don't you have work?"

"Yeah, but my boss is also your friend, so I might as well take advantage of that a little, don't you think?"

"She doesn't know."

"I could just say it's something else involving you. That I'm working on your house or something."

She bit her lip and I hoped that meant she was considering it. "It's gonna be so boring, and we're not even gonna get the answers tomorrow."

"I'll pack fun things to do."

"But—"

"Grace, if you can look me in the eye and say that you would prefer to do this alone, I'll drop it." Something told me that she would not be able to do that. I had a feeling I knew exactly the kind of person she was, and with that knowledge, I needed to make sure that I could help her.

"I'd prefer to go alone," she said as her eyes met mine. Her voice betrayed her. It wasn't steady like it usually was, and each word sounded like it hurt coming out.

"I'll pick you up at eight tomorrow."

Grace let out a long sigh. "Can't you at least try to believe me?"

"Put on a better act next time. Sorry, but you're not meant to be an actress."

Her cheeks were pink. "That's rude."

"I call it like I see it. So, does eight work?"

Grace crossed her arms. "We can actually leave closer to nine."

"Thank you for seeing sense."

"I think I hate you." She muttered it, but there was a ghost of a smile on her face.

"You can hate me and be well taken care of. I'm sure you're great at multitasking."

Grace was waiting on the porch, sitting on the fixed step, staring out into the distance.

She was dressed for comfort, and yet, even from where I parked the truck, I could tell she put thought into her outfit. The gamble of a Tennessee February was on, and some days were warm and incredible while others were cold and frigid. This was one of the cooler days, and even though Grace was in leggings, she had on a hat that covered her curly black hair, boots, and leg warmers that were . . . kind of cute.

At first glance, anyone would think that she was completely fine. But as she got in the truck, I could see that her eyes were still tinged red, just as they were yesterday when she'd been crying.

"Rough night?" I knew I should have called her. I had a feeling that she wasn't okay after I left yesterday.

"It's not the worst I've ever had, but admittedly, I didn't sleep very well."

"You need your rest," I said, even though sleep had been hard for me too.

"I would have slept if I could." She sighed, not even attempting to convince me I didn't need to go today. When I was still in denial about how she was doing, I figured I would have to fight her on every step of this journey. If she was giving in, then things weren't great.

"We can get coffee after. I'll make sure it's under three hundred milligrams."

"Stop talking dirty to me."

I let out a chuckle before her words sank in. I tried to push them out of my mind as I backed out of the driveway, but I had to turn to make sure that there was nothing behind me, and that gave me the perfect view of Grace.

After months of trying to hunt down a woman that would interest me, I'd wondered if my dick was dead. But looking at her, even when I was worried to death and she was half asleep in my passenger seat, my mouth went dry.

I wanted to memorize the planes of her face, the colors her skin turned with each emotion she felt.

I'd gone so many years not needing anyone romantically. I never even had the urge. That part of me had been locked away so tightly that he would never escape, and it was good for both him and me.

Now he was fighting back.

Turning my eyes away from her, I focused on the road. Eventually, this spell would be broken. Either by me or by her.

The drive went by mostly in silence. I thought Grace was asleep and I wasn't about to wake her up. If she indeed was, then she needed it. And I needed the silence. I had a feeling we would be spending most of the day together. We'd get to know each other pretty quickly.

She only stirred when we hit Knoxville, the stop-and-go traffic causing the engine to grumble in protest.

"Sorry, the truck's a little loud."

"No, I don't mind it. Sometimes things feel a little too quiet."

I'd felt that before, back when I still lived in Mom's house. Thankfully, that emptiness had been filled by the city. Even if they weren't noises I liked and cared about, they were still there. I had a feeling, though, that Grace wouldn't follow in my footsteps.

"Many people have asked me why I've never upgraded. The truth is, I like the noise too."

She smiled over at me, and it was very tempting to take my eyes off the road and stare right back. I was glad I didn't, though, because somebody cut me off and I had to slam on the brakes.

"I could do without that." Grace's voice was flat.

"I'm used to it. Everyone here has somewhere to be. And some of them don't care about who they step on to get there."

Grace's lips pursed. "It's fine if I'm visiting, but it gets old when I have to spend a lot of time in the city. This kind of stuff doesn't happen in Strawberry Springs."

I had to press my lips together to keep from saying something stupid. Because I was pretty sure that this thing definitely happened in Strawberry Springs.

"I hear what you're trying not to say," Grace said with a laugh. "And I need to amend my statement. This type of thing does happen in Strawberry Springs, but usually you can complain about it in the Facebook group or to their face and they'll apologize."

"Even Hugh?"

"Not to most people. But he would to me. I think."

"He's a funny guy."

"Do you mean funny or mean? It's okay, you can be honest with me."

I had a feeling most people would say the second one. "He's mean, but in kind of a funny way. Most people would just see him as an annoyance, but I have a lot of experience with gruff men who put up walls for everyone else."

Grace's eyebrows raised. "You're good at reading people."

"Sometimes. When I get my head out of my ass."

"I'm glad you did."

We were pulling into the parking garage, and I had to figure out where to park. It took a little bit longer than I wanted it to, but that was the nature of city driving.

"Thank you for handling this, by the way," Grace added as I finally found a spot. "It wasn't fun the first time I came out here and I would have hated doing it again."

"It's not a problem. Cities don't bother me."

"At least one of us is unbothered."

That was only partly true. I *was* bothered by all of this. Not because of her, though, but because if I didn't keep my distance, she could mean something more to me than being the mother of my child, and I didn't want that.

Finally, we were in a parking spot and I could tell she was eager to get to the doctor. Grace got out of the truck and grabbed her jacket, me following closely behind. I gave her space and she took the lead on getting into the doctor's office and checking in. Right after we sat, she was given a brightly colored liquid and told to drink it all within thirty minutes.

Grace looked a little green halfway through it. "I think I'd rather eat straight sugar cubes," she muttered as she finished it.

After it was done, she threw the bottle away and let the receptionist know that she had finished the drink before slowly making her way back to me.

"So now is the fun part. We have to sit here for three hours. You can be honest and let me know when you regret coming."

"Like I would just sit here for three hours with nothing to do." I reached into my pocket and grabbed something that I had brought from the hotel. "Do you know poker?"

"You brought a deck of cards with you?"

"Not any cards. They're pink princess cards."

She had to cover her mouth to keep from laughing. "Why would you have pink princess cards?"

"Why not? It was either these or basic ones."

"You're something else," she said with a laugh. "But I do know poker, so I would appreciate any distraction I can get."

I had her move to a seat that had a table next to it and I moved a chair. I could feel the receptionist's eyes on me, but if we were going to be here for three hours, we might as well get comfortable.

I tried to let Grace win a few games. I really did. But after the third one, my instincts kicked in. I wasn't the kind of person to let other people win naturally. I enjoyed a challenge and I enjoyed winning them. It was one of the reasons why I wouldn't mind a rematch with Hugh in the bar.

It also might be the reason Grace murdered me.

When I showed my hand, which was a flush, she narrowed her eyes suspiciously. "You're counting cards, aren't you?"

"Who? Me? How would I even know how to count cards?"

"You're smarter than you let on."

"I'm *luckier* than I let on. There's a difference."

Her stare-down continued, and I was sure I was going to burst into flames at any second.

"Grace?" Both of us looked up. A nurse had walked out to where we were sitting. "It's time for the blood draw."

We glanced at each other. The three hours had slipped by. I'd been so lost in the game and her irritated glare that I hadn't kept track of time. Neither had she, apparently.

"I'll handle this." She said it like she knew I was going to offer to follow her. "Thank you for making time fly."

Any other time, I would have argued, but it felt like a rock had settled in my chest. Some time to myself would be good. As

Grace disappeared into the back, I returned the chair to its original spot.

"She's one lucky woman," a woman behind me said. She was older, sitting with her hands crossed and a small smile on her face.

"I think that game proved she's very unlucky."

"That's not what I meant."

I tensed. I was hoping she *wouldn't* go there. "We're not like that."

She slowly nodded. "Interesting." She went back to her book.

Sitting back down, I thought over everything with Grace. I thought about how she'd warned me this would be boring, yet it wasn't, simply because she had been here. Instead of me sitting with her awkwardly, waiting for her to be called back, we had connected.

And that was the most dangerous thing that could have happened.

My phone went off, pulling me out of my thoughts, and I cursed when I read the message.

MOM

You said she owned a clothing shop in
Strawberry Springs?

What are you planning?

When Mom sent back only a shrugging emoji, I sighed. She wanted to meet Grace and wouldn't be held back for much longer.

If Mom came into town and saw how I was with Grace, nothing would stop her from trying to get us together, and that *wasn't* happening.

And if the town got a whiff of this? We were *fucked*.

17

GRACE

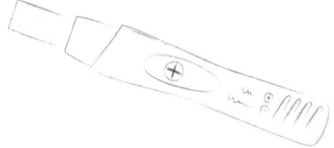

Strawberry Springs Neighborhood Watch

Dale Garrett: Listen, I know everyone is enjoying the early flowers since it's warmed up so quickly, but there's this tall one behind my house that's suspicious. I can't tell if it's a hidden camera, but it's pointed right at my house.

Comments:
Tammy Jane: Who would even spy on you!? You don't do anything that interesting.
Dale Garrett: HEY!!! I'M INTERESTING.
Marjorie Brown: Not gonna lie, I thought this was from Hugh.
Hu Gh: Even I know they don't use no damn flowers. They spy on us using these damn phones!!!
Dale Garrett: Oh God, don't compare me to Hugh again. I was just worried about my privacy!!!
Jade Clark: When are you gonna show your entire ass like Hugh did in here? I'll just need a bit of a warning before I'm scarred again.

SATURDAYS WERE ALWAYS DECENTLY BUSY, but this one kept me moving the whole time. By the end of the day, when an older woman walked in, I felt like I was dragging my feet. I did my best to ignore it.

It didn't help that I was anxious as I waited to hear back about the test. I wouldn't know until Monday, and that made everything feel worse.

The woman looked familiar in a way I couldn't place. It was possible she'd come in years ago and I'd forgotten. I wouldn't admit it, but pregnancy was making me forget simple things. I wasn't sure if it was the exhaustion or the stress.

"Hi! Welcome to the Treasure Trove. I'm Grace. Can I help you find anything today?"

The woman's eyes found mine immediately and she perked up. "Hello! I'm Virginia. How are you?"

This wasn't that unusual. Usually, people from the town cared more about me than the clothes, and it was nice to see someone not from here do the same.

"Oh, just a little tired, but it's been a day. I'm happy to help you find whatever you need, though."

Virginia's mouth twisted. "I'm not sure what I want, honestly. I just figured I'd see what you have."

She was wearing a T-shirt and jeans, which told me she probably worked on her feet. I tried to cater to how people lived their lives. There was no point in telling them to buy clothes they wouldn't like.

"You know, I have a few new pairs of jeans in. One of them holds the record for the most pockets."

"In women's jeans? How many pockets do they have, four?"

I laughed. "About ten, actually."

"Now that's interesting. But I also want something . . .

nicer." She sighed. "Over the years, I've gotten into a bad habit of not ever dressing up. Do you have anything that'll look nice on me?"

Now I had energy. A makeover? Oh, I was lucky today.

"I've got a lot of things that would look nice on you. Hang on just a second."

I piled dresses of all shapes and sizes onto my arm.

"Oh, hon, I'll carry that. You just said you were tired."

"Absolutely not." I gripped the pile tighter. "You've made my day by asking for new outfits. I have all the energy in the world for this."

"Feisty," she said with a laugh. "All right, I'll back off."

I resumed my hunt before putting everything in the fitting room. "First things first, it's a rule here that I get to see what you like on yourself."

"Are you making sure it truly looks good?"

"No, I just like to see people's faces when they feel amazing."

Her cheeks turned red. "That's so sweet, Grace."

I waved her off. "I try. Now, rule two is the most important to me."

"And what's that?"

"Have fun."

"I'll do my best," she said when she went to the back.

Virginia shuffled around and I waited patiently for her to find something she liked. I heard her gasp when she put one thing on.

"Okay, I might need an opinion on this." Her voice was unsteady.

"Show me," I said.

"I like this," she said as she opened the door. "But I feel like I can't pull it off."

It was a linen spaghetti strap dress in a light blue. At first glance, it complemented her figure beautifully and the color was perfect for her skin tone.

But she picked at the fabric and shuffled it around, eyes on the mirror I kept outside of the dressing room.

"I think it's beautiful, but what do you think?"

"Sometimes people say I can be a little hard on myself. It's just that things change over the years and . . ." Her eyes were stuck on her arms, and she poked the loose skin there. "Well, I don't always like it. I should just get over it and buy the dress, right?"

"No," I said. "You don't have to do that."

"B-but I like the dress. And I want to feel beautiful."

"Then let's find one similar that you actually feel beautiful in," I offered. "I have a few ideas." I went to the back and got dresses in a similar shape with sleeves. "Here, try these."

Virginia looked at them and then me. "I'm sorry to make you run around like this."

"Hey, remember rule two. You're supposed to have fun. I sure am."

"Okay, sorry." She finally took the dresses. A minute later, she came out in another one.

And her smile was blinding.

"It has pockets!" she said with joy. "Oh, and it's so comfortable and cute."

That one was made with a softer material that I was planning on putting out in the spring.

Virginia could get it early.

"I think that's the one."

"You're so right." She twirled around. "I haven't felt like this since before I had my son."

"You deserve to feel like this every day."

"Do you have this in any other colors? Would pink look okay?"

"I have something very similar in pink."

"Perfect. I wanna try that one."

"It's the fifth in the pile," I said with a wink. She laughed and went back in. When she came back out, her smile was just as bright.

"These colors look so good on you. I think you'll have to even get T-shirts too."

"I bet I could wear them at work." When she mentioned her work, her smile faltered. "But on second thought, I think I should just focus on the dresses."

"What do you do for work?" I asked.

"I'm a house cleaner," she said. "It's not glamorous or anything, but it pays the bills. Or it used to."

"Not everything has to be glamorous," I said with a shake of my head. "But you said it used to pay the bills. Did something happen?"

"No, not entirely. But a lot of my clients left recently, so I'm not sure what's gonna happen." She sighed. "I live in what used to be a small town. But Nashville's growth swallowed it up and it's more of a suburb now. A new company extended their services and they're far cheaper."

"I'm sorry," I said.

"I lowered my rates to get my old clients back, but they didn't want to go through the hassle of changing cleaners again. People there used to care about each other, but it's changed, and as much as I wanna deny it, I can't anymore."

"Change like that is so hard."

"I just miss the town it used to be. Honestly, being here is the closest I've felt in years."

"Are you in a position to move?" I asked. "Hell, we'd be happy to keep you."

"That's sweet," she said. "Before recently, I never would have considered it. My husband and I met there. Hell, he came into this world and left it there." Her eyes grew wet. "I never thought I'd ever wanna leave."

It was like looking in a mirror. I would never want to sell Mom's house, not with all the history there.

"Take your time with something like that," I said softly. "If you can, just think on it. Something might pop up that'll tell you what you should do."

"Yeah," she said. "It just might." I smiled and gave her a moment to feel her emotions. Then she let out a laugh and wiped at her eyes. "Oh, look at me, crying on a stranger."

"It's pretty normal for around here. Don't worry about it."

"I at least need to get cleaned up before my son sees me like this. He's such a worrywart, I swear."

She went back into the fitting room, and gears turned in my mind. She'd mentioned her son twice, and the more I looked at her, the more I realized *she* wasn't familiar.

Her facial structure was.

"All put together now," she said when she was done. "I'll help you put this back."

"Oh, I've got it."

"Honey, please let me help."

"It's nearing five, and Dean's done working around now."

"Yeah, he is. I'm sure he—" She paused. "Wait a minute, why did you mention Dean?"

"He's your son, isn't he?"

Virginia's jaw went slack. "How the hell did you figure that out?"

"You look alike," I replied. "And I'm good at reading people."

"No kidding. I didn't mean to lie or anything. I just had to meet you, considering . . ." She looked at my stomach.

So she knew.

"I'm not easily scared off." I shook my head. "It's great to meet you. We would have to get to know each other eventually."

"Just know that if you need anything, I'm here. Well, for now I am, until I go home. But I'll answer the phone. Or drive. Just ask Dean."

I had a feeling Dean wouldn't tell me if I did.

"That's very sweet of you, and I'll definitely take you up on that. I'm still figuring things out."

"As you should, I can't believe you found out so far in!"

"Yeah. That's what I get for having an irregular cycle."

"Tell me about it. Mine was terrible and it took me years to get pregnant with Dean. I don't know if you have that issue, though."

I let out a laugh. "No, obviously I don't. Let me at least ring you up."

"Don't you dare give me any discounts."

I sighed. That was exactly what I was going to do.

"Fine. Full price for my . . . mother in . . . accident?"

She had to smother a laugh. "We're gonna have to come up with a better title than that."

"I'll add it to the pile of all the other things to figure out," I said. "It only grows now. Hey, maybe you could ask Dean."

"Oh, he doesn't know I'm here. And he won't."

I blinked. "Really?"

"He has a habit of stopping me from doing what I wanna do. And I wasn't letting him this time."

I laughed. "You seem to have it all figured out."

"Sometimes I do, but I do need to get back to my house. It's quite a long drive and I have one of my last remaining clients tomorrow. I can't be late for that."

"So you drove all this way just to see me?"

"I did, and it was a great decision."

Now I had to work not to tear up. Thankfully, I managed to keep it together while we finished.

Virginia paid and left me her number before heading out. When she was gone, I played over our time together, hoping I'd made a good first impression.

That was when my phone when off.

DEAN
How is your day going?

I didn't expect him to check in . . . but then again, I didn't know what I expected from him anymore. He was younger. He was a playboy. Yet he'd handled parts of this with more maturity than I'd expected.

I met your mom.

DEAN
Did she seriously come into town? I should have known she would do something like that.

She did. She's sweet.

She is until you get on her bad side. But that's more of a me thing. Is she still in town?

She just left. I think she has a client tomorrow so she can't stay.

She's probably admiring the town square. I'm gonna try to shove some money in her car. If you hear screaming, I got caught.

I laughed and put my phone away. I liked this side of him. He was both playful and nice. It was a far cry from the man I'd run into on the streets of Knoxville.

A moment later, I had another text from him.

DEAN

Mission accomplished. I'm so glad she takes
forever to do things.

Have you eaten anything?

> I had breakfast AND lunch. Thanks a lot for
> checking, Dad.

I realized my mistake just after I hit sent.

> I meant Dean. Sorry. Maybe I should wait to
> call you that until our child is born.

DEAN

You can call me Dad when I'm being
overbearing. Daddy is better overall, though.

My face was flaming.

> Any chance you'll forget that happened?

Nope.

"Are you sure you're still up to this?"

I was in Jade's car and we had just pulled up to Mollie's farm-
house. As the owner of Bennie Grove Farm, she had one of the
nicest houses in town. And a couple of weeks ago, she had invited
us to a girls' night, the first one since she'd had her baby. At the
time, I didn't know my life was going to blow apart, so I said yes.

Now I was regretting it.

"No idea," I said. "I have no clue if I can even pretend
things are fine."

"Still no word on the glucose test?" she asked.

I blew out a breath. "Nope. It feels like this is the only thing that's on my mind. I have no idea if I'll be any fun today."

"I could make up something for you and drive you home," she offered.

I immediately knew I didn't want to do that. I wanted to see my friends. I wanted to have fun.

I also wanted to see Mollie in action. She'd just had a baby a few weeks ago. Would watching her be a peek into my own future?

"No, I wanna stay." I looked at the house, which had the lights on. Inside, I could see two figures setting things up. "Would it be the end of the world if they knew?"

Jade's eyebrows raised, but she didn't immediately turn it down. "It's your secret. You can tell who you want."

"Mollie just had a baby," I said. "And Wren knows Dean better than the rest of us."

"You don't have to justify it to me. I think it makes sense. I know next to nothing about all of this. Expanding your support group is never a bad thing as long as you trust them."

I bit my lip, but nodded. "Will you defend me if they get weird?"

"To the death, girl."

I let out a sigh of relief and got out of the car. The door opened as we got to the porch.

"You got Grace to come!" Mollie looked great for someone who just had a baby. She was glowing *still*. I wanted to be like her when I had mine.

"I did. Now, where's Jasmine?" Jade wiggled her fingers. "I haven't gotten to hold her yet and I'm dying to."

"Cain took her to give me a break," Mollie replied. "Which was very sweet, considering no one would have been upset if she were here, but he said he wanted baby time."

"Has he been helpful?" I asked as we walked in.

"Cain's been the best," she said. "But don't worry about him. I won't bore you all with baby talk. I promise I still have a life."

"She never stops," Wren said. "It's making *me* tired."

"What? I also have berries to think about! I doubled my fields."

"And had a baby?" I asked.

"It's what I used my nesting energy for."

Would I get nesting energy? It sounded nice. I was still tired all the time.

"Oh, I should get the lemonade." Mollie had sat on the couch and then shot back up.

"You literally gave birth a few weeks ago. Sit down." Wren got up.

"I could help too," I offered.

"You're a guest." Mollie waved me off. "Just relax."

I was *not* good at that. My leg bounced as I resisted the urge to get up and help anyway.

Wren was already walking out of the room. "And sorry if either of you wanted alcohol, this girls' night is gonna be sober since Mollie is breastfeeding."

"No problem," Jade said. "It was like that the last time too."

I'd come to that one. Back when my problems felt smaller.

"I can't have it anyway." I said it without thinking.

"Do you have one of those allergies?" Mollie asked. "Because if you do, I'll make sure we never have it."

"I didn't agree to that," Jade said.

"Let's just say it's a temporary thing," I replied. "For a few months."

Mollie raised her eyebrows and glanced at Wren as she returned with the lemonade. She opened her mouth and then shut it just as fast. I could tell both of them had questions, but neither wanted to pry. At least they weren't trying to drag it out of me.

I gave Jade one glance and she responded with a smile and a nod. This was terrifying, but it was only a taste of what things would be like when I told the town.

"I'm pregnant," I said, ignoring the way my fists tightened.

Wren ran straight into a wall and Mollie's jaw dropped.

"I'm sorry, what?" Mollie asked.

"It's a secret!" I rushed to say. "I'm trying to figure out how to tell the town. But, yeah. No alcohol for a while."

A silence stretched out between us as both of them processed. I thought of all the things they could say.

You, of all people?

How did you mess up this badly?

You know this is gonna ruin your reputation, right?

All of those might have broken me.

But then Mollie slammed her hands down on the table. "Finally! Someone to talk about this with! Oh, I thought I was gonna be the only new mom forever."

"There're a lot of moms in town," Wren reminded her.

"Not fresh ones! They're all too old to remember the struggle." Mollie turned to me. "Please tell me you're throwing up everywhere."

"Don't wish that on her," Wren said with a shake of her head.

"Wait, not like that! I just need to know I wasn't alone."

Finally, I loosened. This was going better than I thought it would. "Will you hate me if I said I didn't know I was pregnant the whole first trimester?"

Mollie's jaw dropped. "Seriously? So, it was just normal?"

"I was a little tired."

"I'm . . . so happy for you," Mollie said through clenched

teeth. Then she shook her head and smiled. "I mean, really, I'm happy for you."

"Is there anyone else in the picture?" Wren asked. "Or is it just you?"

I looked at Jade again. I hadn't told her that things were going tentatively well with Dean. She didn't know that he was slowly opening up, or that he'd held me while I cried about the glucose test.

"You know," Mollie said, "if anyone can raise a baby on their own, it's you."

"Yeah, definitely," Wren said. "And if you need help, I can build whatever. Cribs, toys. Ooh, what about a rocking chair?"

"Thank you," I said. "I'm not . . . entirely alone."

"The jury's still out on that," Jade muttered. "Can I tell them about your lovely baby daddy who I might murder?"

"I love a good murder," Wren replied.

"Things aren't that bad," I said. "It was rough for a bit, but we're working things out."

"Or *you're* working things out. Grace here has a terrible habit of doing whatever she can to make others feel comfortable."

"We can also add that she doesn't love accepting help from others," Wren added. "It took Dean sneaking off to fix a step because she kept insisting she would do it."

Jade blinked and turned to me. "Dean was at your house?"

"My heat didn't work and it turned out to be an electrical problem."

"You can't forget the part where he asked you out," Wren added. I stared at her, silently begging her to shut her mouth.

"He *what*?" Jade nearly yelled.

"Is that a bad thing?" Mollie asked. "Being pregnant doesn't mean you can't live."

Jade pressed her lips together. She wouldn't reveal who he was, but it was clear we would be having a *long* talk about this.

"It was just to get to know me," I rushed to say.

"Oh, I bet he does want to get to know you." Wren laughed. "But not in the way you expect. He's been into her for four months."

I winced when she said it. Neither Mollie nor Wren were dumb, and after the words were out, I could see Mollie's gears turning.

"Wait, how pregnant are you?" she asked.

"A-about four months."

Wren gasped. "Wait a minute. *No.* Tell me you didn't."

"I could but . . . I'd be lying."

"So, is Dean the dad?"

I opened my mouth to answer, but Wren made a distressed whine.

"No, *no.* Dean is *not*—he told me he stayed away from you!"

"We kept it a secret."

She groaned. "But he's not dad material! He's all charm and sleeping around."

"We know," Jade said flatly. "Hence the threats."

"He told me he was sick yesterday!" she snapped. "Was he really? Or was he running from his responsibilities?"

"No," I said. "He drove me to redo my glucose test because I was worried about it. I told him he didn't have to, but he was there when I got the call and I cried and—" I paused when I realized I was rambling, and my cheeks grew hot. "Yeah, that's it."

"Hang on a second." Jade's voice was calm, but it shook in the way that told me she was *not* happy. "You mean to tell me he did all of that and I didn't know?"

"I'm still processing it." I shrugged. "It's not every day that I think I have a read on a guy and then he flip-flops out from under me. He's been . . . surprisingly mature lately."

"Mature?" Jade scoffed. "I love you, but you and I have very different opinions on mature."

"Why don't you tell us what he's done?" Mollie offered. "We can give some third-party advice."

I nodded and told them about our dinner, where we'd agreed we were different but could meet in the middle. Then I mentioned all the things he'd done for me while I was worried about the glucose test, even mentioning when he'd snuck money into his mom's car.

The three women in front of me all listened intently, but their eyes went wide the longer they did so.

"That's . . . actually kind of mature," Mollie said.

"Some of it's the bare minimum," Jade muttered. "But some's more."

"Wren, what do you think?" I asked. "You've known him the longest."

She blinked and shook her head. "I mean, I've known him a long time, but only ever in a work capacity. I can say that he's good at his job. He cares about it and goes above and beyond. That *might* extend to his personality, but he's never let me get close enough to find out."

"Things could change," Mollie suggested. "Maybe this is the start of something new."

"Not a relationship, though." I shook my head. "That's never gonna happen."

"I mean, never say never. Henry and I did fall for each other while pretending to date."

"Hang on," Jade cut in. "Pretending to *what*?"

"Our relationship was fake for the cameras. Did you not know?"

Jade and I looked between each other.

"*No!*" Jade's jaw was on the floor. "You mean the whole time, you were acting?"

"Not all of it," she said. "It became real before the library renovation ended."

She leaned back, hands running through her colorful hair. "I need to reevaluate everything. But you were so cute!"

"And you kissed!" I added.

"Yep. All fake. Until a few weeks after I fell. We hooked up on the exam table in the clinic."

Jade and I gasped.

"The clinic? *Where he does exams?*" I was scandalized, yet I was no better. I'd done it in the dressing room and on the counter of the Treasure Trove.

"That's his precious space!" Jade said. Even her face was red. "You two are freaky."

"They are," Mollie said. "I've heard too much."

"So have I, Mrs. Breeding Kink."

"Whoa!" Jade said. "Grace gets a bedazzled cock, you get a breeding fetish, and Wren gets to do things in public places?"

"And I get tied up," Wren added.

"This isn't fair! When will it be my turn?"

"Hang on," Mollie said, putting up a finger. "I think we need to circle back to the bedazzled cock."

"I think Grace would too if it hadn't gotten her pregnant."

"Jade!" I hissed. "You are the worst."

"But you love me!"

18

DEAN

Dad Company (But Sometimes Good Advice)

G. Singh: What do you do when the kids you're watching start to throw bees at people?

Comments:
Robert Colt: Please remember rule one. Only real advice is needed here.
G. Singh: It's real. Pic for proof. They're scooping them up. With their hands.
Ryan Kim: OH.
Dean Briggs: Kids throw bees???? Like throw them? Is this what I have to look forward to?
Oliver Brian: I am a dad to three kids and this might be a first for me.
Robert Colt: Calmly tell them the risk associated.
G. Singh: Tried that. They told me to eat rocks and now I have a bee sting on my eyebrow.
G. Singh: Kids still have zero bee stings.

"Holy shit." Wren's eyes went wide when she walked in. "Did you finish the electrical?"

I stepped back from the wall I'd been working on. I'd not been able to sleep much over the weekend while waiting for Grace's test results. I'd felt bad for calling out sick on Wren, so I'd come in during the night.

"Yeah, I did."

"How the hell—" She crossed her arms. "Did you sneak in here?"

I only shrugged. "I wanted it done. And I felt bad for calling out on Friday."

Wren hummed. "You had a good reason."

I hadn't given her much of one at all, but she'd still let me have the time off. It only made me feel worse.

Plus, my time here was wearing on me. I'd never tell Grace, but I hated that people were starting to recognize me and wave. I didn't want to be a part of things here, but I didn't want to leave her while she needed me either.

"You should be good to go now," I said.

"Hang on," she said as I walked past her. "You know you can talk to me about anything, right? Any . . . life changes?"

I stared at her like she'd grown a second head. She was sounding like Clyde.

"Good to know," I said. "But I'm good."

She sighed. "Okay, I see trying to be subtle isn't working."

"Subtle about what?"

"Dean, I *know*. About you and Grace."

I froze. "You . . . know? Shit, does everyone? What the hell happened?"

"Calm down." She put a hand up. "We had a girls' night last night and Grace told us. We're not gonna tell anyone else."

"Oh," I said. "Great. Are you here to yell at me for being with her?"

"I'm tempted," she said. "But no. I just wanted to say that I thought it was nice that you took her to a doctor's appointment that she was worried about. Something about a glucose test? She didn't explain it to us, but I had a feeling she didn't wanna talk about it."

"She failed her first glucose screening, which means she could have gestational diabetes. She did a second one with a longer interval to see if she may have it."

"Wow, you know a lot of detail."

"I'm not half-assing this, you know."

"You never half-ass work, so I figured. But I also know all of this isn't for you. Sharing something with someone. Being tied down."

She was right, this wasn't normal for me. And yet talking to Grace was easy. I'd told her we were starting with the basics, but ever since she failed her first glucose screening, it felt like we'd snuck right past that and were heading toward actually getting to know each other, something I *should* be struggling with.

Yet we were almost . . . friends.

I hadn't made a new one of those since I met Clyde.

"Yeah, I'm working on that."

"You do have support here," she said, giving me a small smile. "I know we've always only talked about work, but if you need anything, I can help. I offered the same thing to Grace."

It was nice of her to offer, it really was. But I didn't see myself taking her up on that. I liked Wren, but I couldn't shake the feeling that she didn't want me messing up things in her precious town.

And I would, once people found out.

"Thank you, but I'll mostly be focusing on work."

"I might have some more," she said. "Are you interested?"

I had an out. I could say no and leave and get a break from this town.

That would also mean leaving Grace when she needed me. Hell, even if this test came back okay, what else could come up?

I'd seen her house. It needed work, and she had a lot to do before the baby arrived. I wanted to find a way to get her to let me help with that.

"Yeah, I think I'm up for that."

Wren perked up. "Really? So it's not so bad here?"

"I didn't say that. I have a reason to be here, remember?"

"Yeah, yeah. We'll charm you."

I highly doubted that, but I only shrugged. There was no reason to crush her hopes.

After I said my goodbyes, I was eager to be alone so I could get my head on straight. Wren's conversation had me off kilter. Hell, the entire town did.

When I was alone in my truck, I finally checked my phone and saw I had a message from Clyde.

CLYDE

You near Knoxville? I could take you out to eat.

I was immediately glad that I'd gotten my work done for the day.

I can be there in a little over an hour. Where do you wanna meet up?

Clyde told me to meet him at a deli, and I couldn't deny that I was excited. It would be nice to get out of Strawberry Springs for a bit and feel more like myself.

He was waiting for me outside the door, foot tapping. When

he saw me, he stilled and acted like nothing was wrong, but as we got our order, he glanced at me like I was a bomb waiting to go off.

"So," he said before taking the first bite of his sandwich. "You gonna tell me what happened?"

"Yeah," I said with a sigh. "But I should also apologize first for being vague."

"Must be something big."

"Yeah, it's very big."

"Please don't say cancer. If it's something like that, you're gonna have me crying in the middle of this deli."

"No, I'm not sick, and no one I know is either. But . . . someone is pregnant. Someone I . . ."

He paused in his eating, eyes wide. My heart hammered as I waited for his response.

"Oh. That certainly is big."

"You and Mom both taught me to be safe. I wasn't." My eyes fell to the table. "I'm handling it. I know it's mine and I'm trying to be there for her as much as possible, but she's in Strawberry Springs, which is three hours away from Nashville."

"Ah. That is quite a ways out."

"You can yell at me if you want. I fucked up. Now I'll have to adjust my schedule and figure out how the hell to be a father to someone when I live this far away."

Clyde put his sandwich down and sighed. "What good is yelling gonna do?"

"I feel like it's kinda what I deserve and it might make you feel better."

"You know, I've done some reading, and when a kid fucks up, it's better to be supportive than yell. This is shocking, and it's gonna change a lot, but you seem to have a decent handle on it."

"Now. I fucked up in the beginning, but I think I smoothed

it over." I sighed. "I just . . . My responsibilities are changing and I feel terrible about it. I enjoy our time together."

"Yeah, but I'm not a selfish dick. I don't keep you around just to go out to dinner after we work together. I also don't keep you around because you're always available. I keep you around because you're a decent kid."

"Can you still call me a kid when I'm gonna be a father soon?"

"Okay, slow down a little bit. I've called you 'kid' for almost a decade, so you're gonna have to give me that one. Can't handle too much change."

Despite everything, I laughed. "I'll let it slide."

"So, what does this mean for you and this woman? Are you—"

I cut him off before he could suggest something I didn't want him to. "Friends. I think we're becoming friends."

"You're friends with a woman you slept with. That's new for you."

"A lot of this is, but it can't be a bad thing to be friends with the person I'm sharing a child with."

"I don't disagree," he replied, taking a sip of his drink. "A lot of things are changing here."

"Are you still gonna keep me around?"

Clyde rolled his eyes. "You're smart enough for electrical, but you're still dumb as hell sometimes. Yeah, I'm keeping you around. I may not really know how to help you out because I never had kids of my own, but I can still be here. You need a friend, don't you?"

"Oh, thank God."

He reached across the table and patted me on the shoulder. "Everything's gonna be fine. Now eat. I'm worried you forgot to take care of yourself while out in the middle of nowhere."

I huffed out a laugh. "It's not the city, I'll say that much."

"So, why are you staying there?"

"I need to get to know Grace, and pregnancy can be a little scary."

Clyde slowly nodded, and I wondered what he was thinking. "So, the mom's name is Grace? Got it. You got work out there?"

"For now, yeah."

"A good place to stay?"

The hotel was basic, but it wasn't great. I dreaded going back there, but I would make it work.

"Yep."

"Then call me if you need me. I have a few things out here, and it sounds like that's not too out of the way for you." He eyed me again. "I was serious about eating. I've got a long day of work still and I'm *starving*."

19

GRACE

Strawberry Springs Neighborhood Watch

SherriffMike Finch: I was just coming back into town and got into traffic in the middle of nowhere! What the hell is going on?

Comments:
Kerry Winsor: Shouldn't you know?
SherriffMike Finch: What, you think because I have a badge I can see everything?
Marjorie Brown: I cursed the town after getting these witch books. I told Jade it was a bad idea to order them.
Jade Clark: No regrets.
Mollie Wilson: I'm sorry! It was me! Some of the cows got out and we had to herd them in.
Marjorie Brown: Hey, Mike, would you say you were stuck in traffic until the cows came home?
SherriffMike Finch: I fucking hate this group.

"Is THAT PANTSUIT NEW? I don't think I've seen you in it before."

At Kerry's question, I looked down at my baggy outfit. As a confident curvy woman, I usually went for things that accentuated my figure. Now, I had to find things that hid it.

The longer I looked, the more I realized I was seeing a bump. It could have been bloat, but I didn't want there to be any questions.

"I'm trying out a new style. Do you like it?"

"Yes," she said. "It looks so *comfy*."

In some circles, "comfy" didn't mean anything nice. But I'd long ago learned not to think too hard about the things Kerry said. Most of the time, she was being nice. And if she wasn't . . . then I'd see about it on the Facebook group when she tried to vague post. She'd been better since things blew up over a year ago when Mollie moved into town and they got into it, but I didn't know how long it would last.

The jumpsuit, though loose, was cute as hell. I wouldn't let her stop me from enjoying it.

"Thanks, Kerry," I said. "I have a few more of them if you wanna try one on."

"Oh, I think that's a thing only you could pull off." She waved me away.

Yeah, she hated it. Oh well.

"Of course. What else can I help you with then?"

"I saw something on the internet that I wanted to show you." She pulled her phone out and showed me a woman clad head to toe in leopard print.

Kerry was the *worst* about following fake internet trends. I was pretty sure this entire photo wasn't even real.

"I might have a shirt in this style, but I'd really recommend against pairing both together—"

"I'm bold enough for it. I want people to stare when I walk by."

This had happened with a hat before. I'd told her it was a terrible idea, and she told me my fashion sense was stuck in the past. This time, I knew better than to argue with her.

"In that case, let's get you glammed up."

As I pulled out the outfit for her, Kerry watched closely, as if hunting down something different about me.

I tensed. Things *were* changing, and I wasn't sure how I felt about it. I was still tired and my body was slowly growing. I could *feel* that I was pregnant, and for some reason, I thought everyone else could now see it. I needed to figure out how to tell the town eventually, but under Kerry's appraising stare, it felt impossible.

"Here you go," I said as I handed her the outfit. "Why don't you go try this on?"

"Oh! Right. Be right back."

I let out a breath when she disappeared into the fitting room.

Kerry came out looking like a leopard. While it wasn't my style, she practically bounced on her feet.

"How do you feel?" I asked, even though I knew the answer.

"Amazing!" she said. "I'm gonna be the talk of the town!"

That was the thing about fashion. It didn't matter how *I* felt about it. It was how they did. My own style was one thing, but others had different views on how they wanted to look, and I wanted everyone to leave happy.

Even if they would end up being made fun of in the Facebook group.

"You should get it then," I replied. "You look amazing."

"I knew I didn't have to get just one thing in leopard print! Don't you have some pants like these too? We could match!"

I wouldn't be fitting into those for a while, and all of my

current clothes budget was going toward things that would accommodate my growing belly. Did they even make patterned maternity jeans?

I bet I could find them if they did.

"I do, but they're retired for now. I'll have to get a new pair."

"Is it because you're gaining weight?" I crossed my arms. Kerry's eyes went wide and she rushed to explain. "I mean, not that you're not beautiful! I just meant it as an observation."

"Um, yeah. Sure. I *am* gaining weight. Which means a new wardrobe for me."

"I've already stepped in it again. Sorry, Grace. You really do look beautiful no matter what size you're at. I mean, your skin is glowing!"

That was one good thing about this whole no-period thing. My acne had really cleared up. It was nice to get a break from the ups and downs of PCOS, even if I was still waiting to hear back about my three-hour glucose test.

"Thanks," I said. "Why don't we get you checked out so you can go show off your new outfit?"

I tried not to think too hard about Kerry's words as I rang her up, but they stuck with me. If she was noticing my changing body, how long did I have before other people did? How long did I have before they asked questions?

Eventually, my pregnancy would be obvious. I was on a timer, one that may run out quickly, depending on how fast my body changed.

It would have been nice if I'd had time to accept my own pregnancy, but I'd only known for a little over a week.

As Kerry walked out the door, Dean walked in.

I saw her do a double take, and then look at me with a smile on her face.

Fuck.

"Hi," I said, trying to channel that he was just an average

customer while Kerry was still in earshot. "How can I help you today?"

The door shut before Dean answered.

"Is that how you greet all of your friends?" he asked.

We're friends? That was news to me, but I'd take it.

"I was trying to play normal in front of Kerry," I muttered. "She can sniff out a secret from a mile away."

"That's the infamous Kerry?" Dean turned back around. "I didn't think she would be so . . . into leopard print."

"I tried to talk her out of it." I sighed. "But she can't be stopped."

He looked out the window and then back to me. "A trap could work."

"Trust me, someone'll try it." I shook my head. "And not to be the fun police, but shouldn't you be working? Wren won't accept endless excuses."

"I finished my job," he said.

"That fast?"

He shrugged. "Yeah, and with a day off, I met someone for lunch and then figured I'd check in."

"You met someone? Like in town?"

"No, out of town. I didn't want anyone seeing."

That had . . . implications. Ones I didn't like.

I cleared my throat. Why was I feeling this way? I knew he was a playboy. Who knew how many women he'd been with since me?

"Are you here for a makeover?" I asked.

"Not really. I was hoping the doctor called. It's Monday, isn't it?"

I'd been doing a good job of not thinking about the call that should have been coming in at any moment. Sometimes the Treasure Trove did me well and I was so busy that I couldn't think of anything else. Today was one of those days.

But the second Dean said something, it all came rushing back.

"No, I haven't heard from them, but I should call them." I went behind the counter to grab my phone.

"Okay," Dean said. "Mind if I stay in case it's bad news?"

"Yes, of course you can stay." I would prefer not to be alone, even if I didn't tell him that. I hated dealing with big things on my own, which was ironic since that's all I'd been doing since Mom died. Sure, I had Brooke, but she wasn't here often. Having Dean here helped.

When I called, the same receptionist answered in a bored tone.

"Hi," I said, trying to sound like I wasn't panicking. "I came in for a three-hour glucose test on Friday, and I haven't heard anything back. Are my test results in?"

"I'll look them up. What's your name?"

I gave her all of my information and waited anxiously as she pulled up my file.

"Looks like everything is good."

"Everything's good," I repeated. "Does that mean I passed the second test?"

"Yep." That was all she said.

"I had no idea. I was really worried about it."

"We don't call if the results are normal. Is there anything else I can help you with?"

"No. Thanks." I blew out a breath when she hung up. All that panic and worry and they didn't even call me.

"Was that good news?" he asked.

"Yes. I just had to call and find out." I muttered it, my chest tightening. I was annoyed, a feeling I didn't deal with all that often. "I'm relieved, of course. Just . . . I thought they'd call. Especially because I failed the first one."

"They deal with this every day, I'm guessing. It must be easy to forget that, to you, this is all new."

"It's fine." I pushed away the annoyance. Dean raised an eyebrow. "No, it really is."

"You can be annoyed about it."

"I can also be happy that it was normal."

"Two things can be true at once, Grace."

I let out a sigh and nodded. "You're right, but the last thing I need with all these hormones running through me is to be mad. I don't feel as stable these days."

"I'll make sure to remember that when I'm planning on pissing you off," he said with a laugh, but it was broken off by a yawn.

"Tired?"

"I was worried about the test," he admitted softly. "I couldn't sleep."

Statements like that showed me how much he cared. I'd been so worried about how he would react, but he surprised me at every corner.

"Get some rest at your hotel," I said. "I'll be here tomorrow."

"Yeah, I think I'm gonna do that. This was too much fun in one day. I'll see you later." He gave me a tired grin that I forced myself to return.

At least one of us had fun.

I sure didn't have any when I heard him talk about it, though.

20

DEAN

Strawberry Springs Neighborhood Watch

Atticus Thompson: So, we all saw that bobcat on the loose, right?

Comments:
Jade Clark: That was a leopard, DEFINITELY. You don't have to be nice about it.
Kerry Winsor: So you DID all see my new threads?
Jade Clark: Threads? Dear God, Kerry. It's not Halloween yet.
Kerry Winsor: I looked AMAZING.
Atticus Thompson: People. Focus. I'm talking about an actual bobcat. Not the eyesore Kerry wore.
Kerry Winsor: EYESORE???

WHEN I PULLED up to the hotel, I let out a sigh of relief. This place wasn't home, but it was a bed that I could pass out in, and now that I knew everything was okay with Grace, that was exactly what I would be doing.

I parked next to a tractor that was pulled in sideways, thinking about how odd this town could be. Shady Acres used to have things like this when the town was full of farmers, but that had faded over the years.

I found myself letting out a laugh as I walked to my room. After putting in the keycard, I was about to fall face down on my bed and be dead to the world.

But then I heard the shower was on.

I paused, wondering if there could be a leak. The hotel was old, and it would be my luck that something broke while I was away.

It couldn't be a *person*. I was in the middle of nowhere. What would be the odds of a break-in?

If I hadn't been so tired, maybe I would have made a better decision, but I'd barely slept, so that was the only reason for me shuffling to the bathroom.

The entire room was full of steam, which meant this had to have been happening for a while. I pulled the white curtain back to see what was happening with the water. What I was met with would be burned into my memory for the rest of my life.

"Hey!" a rough voice said. "Don't you kids know how to knock?"

I saw far too many wrinkles, an entire ass, and a dick that wasn't my own.

A scream made its way out of my mouth and I shut the curtain. "Hugh!" I yelled as I squeezed my eyes shut. "What the absolute hell are you doing in my hotel room?"

"What are *you* doing in *my* hotel room?" The water shut off and the curtain opened.

I let out a yelp and stumbled out of the bathroom. I did *not* need to see that again.

"Put some clothes on, man!"

"What? You've never seen an ass before?" I heard shuffling, but Hugh didn't move fast. I wasn't opening my eyes until it was safe.

"Why are you in a hotel?" I asked. "Don't you live in town?"

"My hot water's been busted for years. Sometimes I want a hot shower."

"And you chose mine?"

"This room was given to me, you little shit. I checked in this morning!"

"I've been here for days, there's no way they gave you this room."

"The card worked!"

"We're going to the front desk." I finally opened my eyes, only to be scarred again. Hugh had his arms crossed, but hadn't done anything else. "You're still naked!"

"Yeah, what about it? You're young, but when you get to my age, you don't care about people seeing your junk."

———

The woman that worked at the front desk looked like she could be freshly out of high school. She nearly fell over when she saw Hugh and me coming.

"H-hi, how can I help you?"

I was exhausted and tired. But I wasn't rude. Before I spoke, I took a breath to calm down. "I think my room was accidentally double-booked. Can I get a new one?"

"O-oh, I'm so sorry." I expected her to look at her book and give one of us a new room, but she glanced at Hugh instead. "Um, we're fully booked."

"You're *what?*" I looked out at the parking lot. There was just my truck and the tractor. "How?"

"We're doing some remodeling," she said. "We only have a few rooms."

"I guess we're roomies then," Hugh said. "I'll warn you like I warned my first wife. I snore. And fart in my sleep."

I stared at him for all of one second before I looked back at the woman. "Please tell me this is a prank."

"I'm *so* sorry."

It was official. Life hated me. There was no explanation for this happening.

"Come on, roomie. I'll even let you have the side of the bed near the door."

"No, no. You can have the room. I'll figure out another hotel."

Hugh laughed. "Good luck with that. You're in the middle of nowhere, kid. Any other hotels all have bedbugs."

"I'm *not* rooming with you. No offense, but I need my alone time."

"I ain't thrilled about this either, but you've got no other options. It's not like you made any nice friends who would let you stay with them." He shrugged and slowly hobbled away.

"Do you really not have any friends?" the front desk lady asked.

"I—of course I have friends." Under her appraising gaze, I walked away and outside.

"Come on, boy! You gotta catch up." Hugh had only made it about ten feet.

"You've had your shower. Aren't you done with the room? You have to have a bed at your house, right?"

Hugh frowned. "I've got a bad back and the ones here are comfier."

"But—"

He glared. "I paid good, hard money on this room and I'm using every part of it. You'll just have to deal."

For fuck's sake. "You have a good night, I'll figure this out."

"What are you gonna do, sleep in your truck?"

That would be a better option.

"Like I said, I'll figure it out."

As Hugh considered me, I wondered if he had any kindness in his body. Maybe he would change his mind about going back to his house. But he shrugged and went back to the room.

My teeth gritted together as I gathered my things and set out. I checked for other hotels, but the only ones that were decent were over forty-five minutes away.

I cursed. Should I have even taken on the job with Wren? Things were fine with Grace, and I was sure I could leave if I wanted to.

But I knew I didn't want to. Leaving meant not being able to help her out. It also meant I would miss things.

Did I even have a choice?

I was dialing her number before I could think about anything else.

"Dean?" she asked on the second ring. "Is everything okay?"

"Not really," I said. "I might need to leave town."

"What? What happened? Did someone say something to you?" Her voice rose in pitch.

"No, there's a hotel issue. And since we're in the middle of nowhere, there's nowhere else to go."

"Oh," she said. "That's surprisingly easy to fix. Just stay with me."

I blinked, the idea bouncing around my head. Her house was nice, even if it did need some minor work. It certainly would be better than a hotel with a planning issue.

But that would be far too much time with her. I knew that

Grace's charm could be dangerous for me. I didn't need to make it any worse.

"No, it's okay."

"Seriously," she said. "I have a guest bed. I'll need to tidy up, but it's here for you. And it's free of charge!"

"Grace, I'm fine. I don't need anything. I just figured I'd let you know I would be gone for a while."

"I thought you took a job with Wren?"

I sighed, my shoulders slumping. "I'll have to cancel it."

"You don't have to do anything," she reminded. "I have a place for you to stay. Isn't this what *friends* do for each other?"

Yes, they did. But just the thought made my shoulders tense, though not because I didn't want to spend time with her—I did.

A little too much.

And where could that lead?

"It's a bad idea."

"If you stay here, you might find things to work on," she singsonged. "And I might let you."

My jaw fell open. She might have found the one thing that would get me to say yes. "You play dirty, Grace Day."

"That I do. So, will I see you soon?"

Should I say no? Yes.

Was I going to? Absolutely not.

21

GRACE

Strawberry Springs Neighborhood Watch

Marjorie Brown: Anyone lose their shoe in front of the library? I'll keep it warm until you come and claim it.

Comments:
Henry Connor: Just a friendly reminder to NOT wear random shoes you find on the street.
Marjorie Brown: I do it all the time. It's good for my immune system.
Kerry Winsor: PLEASE just throw that away! It looks gross!
Jade Clark: Marjorie, out of curiosity, can I see a pic of your feet? For science?
Marjorie Brown: I knew you had one of those fetishes.
Kerry Winsor: Jade has a foot fetish???
Jade Clark: I do NOT. I wanted to see if she had an infection!!!
Mollie Wilson: It's okay. We all support you.
Jade Clark: I DON'T LIKE FEET! THERE ARE WAY HOTTER BODY PARTS THAN THAT!!!

I was on my fifth sneezing fit when I heard a knock at the door.

"Shit," I muttered. When I'd told him to come stay, I'd forgotten about all the junk that had piled up in that room. I was rushing to get it all cleaned up, but my allergies were fighting me every step of the way.

I sent up a silent prayer that my nose would keep it together and brushed the dust off my clothes.

"Hey!" I said as I opened the door. Dean towered in the doorway, and he was wearing that damn hat. "You made it. Come in."

In the light of the house, I could see he was tired. His eyes had been half lidded when I'd seen him earlier, but this was an entirely new level. I'm not even sure how he'd driven here safely.

"Why don't you sit on the couch? I'm just finishing up the room."

"Aren't I supposed to be helping you?" he asked as he took his hat off and ran a hand through his hair.

"No, I—" I was cut off by a sneeze.

Dean's eyebrow crept up. "Been near dust?"

"Yes, but I'll be fine. You're tired and I can handle sneezing." I made my escape, determined to finish the room so he could get to sleep. I was sure he was far too out of it to fight me.

I let out a sigh when I was alone. I should have kept up on all this while it was happening. Then I wouldn't have a pile to organize.

"So, this is the junk room?"

I jumped. "You're supposed to be resting."

"And you're pregnant and worked all day, so you should be too. Looks like we're both breaking rules."

"But—"

"Why don't we make this easy and skip to the part where you tell me what you need me to do?"

"I kinda wanna fight more about it."

He only shook his head. "Okay, then I'll figure it out."

"No, I'll tell you, but I wanna help a little bit."

"Fine," he said. "But only a little."

I wanted to be mad that he was so pushy with helping me, but it was also a breath of fresh air. Ever since Mom died, it had been me taking care of either the house or Brooke. Sometimes both.

I didn't have much of a plan beyond shoving everything into the basement, but with Dean's help, we were able to get a donation pile made, as well as a somewhat-organized pile in the basement. The room wasn't totally clean, but the twin-sized daybed was visible, and I could reach the sheets to change them.

Once everything was put together, I surveyed the room with a nod.

"Not bad," I said. "And this makes it easier for when I turn this into a nursery."

"Why not use Brooke's room?" Dean asked. "It's closer to yours."

"Brooke would have a cow over that." I shook my head. "She randomly visits, so it's still hers."

"Is this her house?"

"Does it matter?" I asked.

"It can if you run out of space," he said.

"I have plenty of that. Almost *too* much." Dean opened his mouth to argue, but it was broken up with a yawn. "You should get rest," I said, patting him on the shoulder. "You need it as much as I do."

"As long as I don't see Hugh's wrinkly butt again in my

dreams." I was heading out the door when I heard it, and I paused, wondering if he was joking or if he'd had the misfortune of actually seeing Hugh's ass.

The sun was peeking over the horizon when I flipped the last pancake. I wasn't sure why, but I woke up before the sun had risen wanting to make sure Dean felt welcome.

When Brooke was here, she always wanted my homemade breakfast. I'd need a nap later in the day, but it was worth it for my guest.

As the coffee pot beeped that it was done, I heard footsteps.

"Perfect timing," I said, turning to him. "I made breakfast."

I wasn't sure how Dean woke up in the morning, but I figured I would see him in some kind of pajamas and messy hair.

Instead, he was fully dressed in a T-shirt with his work logo on it and jeans.

"Really?" he asked. "You didn't have to do that."

Of course I did. This is what I always did when Brooke was here. He deserved the same treatment.

"I do it for all guests," she said. "And I bet it's better than whatever the hotel gave you."

"The hotel didn't give me anything but trauma," he said and then glanced at the door. "I was gonna head out to work, though."

"Right," I said, trying to keep my voice level. I'd hoped he would eat with me, but I also knew he had a life. "I can make yours to go."

"No." He shook his head. "That would be fucking rude of me. You go sit down, I'll make plates."

"I can—"

"Grace," he warned. "You cooked. You did more than enough."

It hadn't seemed like much in the moment, but it was nice to have someone else finish things out. I sat at the dining room table, trying to resist a smile at getting him to eat with me. He was slowly giving in and letting us be *friends*.

What else would he give in on?

The second the thought entered my mind, I shook my head. What was I doing thinking like that? Sure, he was being friendly. Sure, he'd stayed in my house and I'd seen a tiny glimpse of him that no one else had, but that meant nothing.

I didn't need to get my hopes up.

"Butter and syrup?" he asked.

"Yes, please," I replied. "Thanks."

"Creamer in your coffee?"

"Yes, that too."

Dean nodded and was gone. When I was alone again, I thought over how domestic this all felt.

It had been a long time since I felt like I was a part of a team in my own home. That had to be why I was acting so weird.

I felt mostly normal when Dean set down a plate and mug in front of me. "Pancakes, bacon, and coffee, just for you, ma'am."

"Are you sure your calling isn't to be a server? You're good at this."

"I'm good at it with *you* because I like you. Give me one rude customer and I'd be fired." He walked back to the kitchen.

He likes me.

Oh, fuck. I needed to get it together.

I was planning on waiting for him to sit, but I started digging in to get my mind off his words. My pancake recipe had been from Mom, and the fluffy, light texture took me back to when she would make it for me. Closing my eyes, I enjoyed it.

"If that's the chef's reaction, then I'm about to have my life changed."

"You'll probably propose to me again." He laughed and sat. I watched as he took his first bite, and when his eyes rolled back in his head, I knew I'd done well. "I'm waiting for my proposal."

"Hang on, I'm still living in the moment." Dean went for another bite, and I couldn't help the swell of pride I felt in my chest.

We'd never be anything, but I liked it when we joked like we could be.

"Now don't think I made all of this for you for no reason."

His eyes opened. "Are you about to ask for *help*?"

"I'm about to ask for information. What the hell happened at the hotel?"

Dean's shoulders fell and he rolled his eyes. "Don't even get me started."

"That's the best hotel in the area."

"It's the *only* hotel in the area," he said flatly.

"It's not riddled with bedbugs, so that's pretty good. What happened?"

"They double-booked me with someone."

"Double-booked?" I laughed. "Are they ever full?"

"There was something about renovations temporarily closing a lot of the rooms." He shook his head. "All I know is that I came back to the room expecting to fall into bed and sleep, only to find Hugh naked in my shower."

I choked on my food. "Hugh? Why was he at a hotel?"

"He said he didn't have hot water."

"Him? Of all people? *Naked?*"

"It's gonna give me nightmares. He's wrinkly . . . everywhere. And not proportionate." Dean looked like a five-year-old who'd seen a horror movie. His eyes were wide and his lip curled with disgust. And I had to stifle a laugh. "Are you laughing at my trauma right now?" His jaw dropped.

"I'm not trying to, but it's a rite of passage around here to be traumatized by Hugh being naked."

He blinked. "What? Why?"

"Hugh makes poor choices. Like getting the Facebook group mixed up with one of those Google image searches. And another time, I offered to measure him to make sure he had the right pant size, and he thought he needed to strip down. I only saw the outline of things before I told him to pull his pants up, but yeah. He's like that."

"I don't know if I feel better or worse that I'm not the only one who has wrinkly-ass trauma."

I pressed my lips together to keep myself from laughing. I only spoke when I felt safe. "Welcome to Strawberry Springs, Dean."

"You guys are fucking weird."

"Oh, yeah. We are. It's part of the charm."

When I got home from the shop and saw someone with a massive pink cowboy hat on, I first wondered if Dean had decided to change up his look.

Then I realized the hat was on my sister.

"Brooke?" I asked. "H-hey. What are you doing here? Is everything okay?"

"Why do you automatically assume something's wrong when I come see you?" She crossed her arms, her bottom lip poking out.

"You're right. I just didn't expect to see you."

"Well, it's not like you do much. I figured I would spice things up." She shrugged.

"My life isn't all that boring. I have this—" I gestured to my stomach. "Remember?"

She looked me up and down. "Trust me, Grace. It's hard to miss."

I bit down on a snarky response. "So, is this just a visit, or are you staying?"

Brooke flipped her hair over her shoulder. "I'll be here for a few days. I have some big plans."

"Big plans, huh?" My gaze traveled in the direction of the hallway where I knew Dean would be staying. "Well, in that case, you should know we have another guest."

"What?" Brooke frowned. "Who?"

"Dean's here for a little while."

"*Dean?* You mean irresponsible baby daddy Dean?"

"He's not irresponsible," I said immediately.

"Oh, sure. Why is he here?"

"There was an issue with his hotel and—"

"Let me guess, you just swooped in and offered him a place to stay? God, you are *so* gonna get taken advantage of."

"How about you let me handle Dean, okay?" My voice came out harsh.

Brooke's eyes went wide. "Whoa, touchy. Don't come crying to me when this goes wrong. And *don't* give him my room."

He didn't want it anyway. "Trust me, I won't. And his hotel issue could be resolved by now. He may not even come back."

"You'll get used to that," she muttered.

I had to clench my molars to keep from snapping. I knew Brooke well enough to know that she would finish anything I started. This was how she'd always been.

"What's been going on with your singing?" I asked slowly. "I'd love an update."

That did it. She immediately perked up and gushed about her new life. Apparently, she'd been the lead singer on one of the busiest nights of the week, and she'd made decent tips too. It was strange to go from knowing everything about her to her having her own life, but I knew she would never truly leave.

Some days I wasn't sure if that was a good thing or not.

"All of that sounds great," I said. "I'm happy for you."

"It's all finally coming together for me." Her gaze turned to me. "Have you figured all your stuff out yet? How did the town react?"

"I haven't told them yet."

Her eyes widened. "People still don't know?"

I shook my head. "No."

"But you're like . . . *round*."

"I'm not—that's kinda rude to say."

She rolled her eyes. "I'm your sister. I'm allowed to be honest."

I wanted to let the words roll right off my back, but they stuck. A lot of the stuff she'd said tonight was sticking with me.

"I'm gonna go start on dinner." I stood before I started a fight I couldn't finish.

"Yay! I love it when you cook."

She was lucky I was planning to cook for Dean anyway. It wasn't anything fancy, but I had frozen soup that I wanted to use up before it got hot outside. My chili was one of my favorite dishes to have over and over again.

I'd wanted to show it off to him, but plans had changed.

While that heated, I pulled out my phone.

> Brooke is here. I know you don't wanna be around her, so I understand if you wanna try the hotel again or find somewhere else. I'm so sorry. She didn't give me any warning.

After that, I put my phone away to focus on getting everything ready. I had a tin of rolls, so I decided to make that as well.

"It's simple tonight," Brooke muttered. She must have come to check in on the progress of dinner.

"I'm tired."

"You're only gonna get more tired. Might as well do things while you have the energy."

I only stirred the soup, refusing to give in to her. Obviously, she wanted something different. She could always go find something else if she felt that strongly about it.

She waited for a long moment before scoffing and going back to the living room.

The soup was almost reheated when the front door opened. I peered around the corner and saw that Dean was walking in.

"Did you get my text?" I asked as I abandoned my station to get to him. He was taking his boots off on the mat.

"Hello to you too," he said.

"Dean, Brooke's here."

"I know."

"Did you check with the hotel?" I asked. "Maybe they fixed whatever was happening."

"No, I didn't. I'm here for backup. And whatever you're cooking."

I blinked. "I don't understand."

"Brooke stresses you out, and that's the last thing you need right now. So, I'm here."

"But you don't like her."

"I don't only do what's easy, Grace." He put a hand on my shoulder and then walked into the kitchen.

I had to process what the hell he'd said to me.

Everyone took the easier path. It was human nature. I didn't, of course. I always wanted to help other people as much as I could.

Had I finally met someone the same way?

I followed Dean to the kitchen and found him leaning on

the countertop. As I stirred the soup, Brooke poked her head into the room and glared when she saw him. When she was gone, I grabbed Dean's arm.

"She's pissed. Beware."

"I've already seen her mad. She didn't like that I turned her down when she hit on me."

"She hit on you?" I hissed.

"Watch the grip, Mama. I ended up with you anyway."

He walked away to get bowls, but I stood frozen. My body was hot at the memory of the two of us being something. Him bringing it up was dangerous for me.

The nickname made the feeling worse.

"Is everything done?" he asked.

"Yeah." I shook off my thoughts and held out my hand for a bowl. "I'll get Brooke's—"

"Food's ready!" he called out.

"I usually make her plate."

"How old is she again?" he asked, and I knew what he was getting at.

"I'll take some sour cream!" Brooke said as she walked into the kitchen.

This would be when I broke and did what she wanted. Dean was undeterred. "It's right here when you're ready," he said.

Brooke's jaw dropped for a second before I saw fire blaze in her eyes as she moved in on Dean. "You don't get to come around and change things in *my* house."

"Things didn't just change because of me. You're gonna act like an adult and not make your pregnant sister serve you. Got it?"

I'd never heard him sound like this. His deep voice and narrow eyes left no room for arguing. He wasn't angry. He was calm, and somehow that made it all the more intense.

I thought Brooke was going to either slap him or storm out. Instead, her jaw clenched and she got her own bowl.

My eyebrows raised. That . . . worked? I should have brought Dean around a long time ago.

After we served ourselves, we sat at the dining room table. I thought she was going to continue pouting, but she must have had an ounce of maturity in her body because she brought something else up while we ate.

"Are you going to Mark's birthday party?" she asked.

Mark always held a birthday bash at Bell's Brews. He usually brought something fun out of storage and invited the whole town. Not everyone could always make it, but a lot tried to, and I regularly went.

"Are you?" I asked back. "I thought you'd have better things to do in Nashville."

"I do, but I also wanna show these people how far I've come. I'm gonna perform."

Last year, he'd bought a karaoke machine, telling us all that the best gift would be to watch us make fools of ourselves. The town delivered what he asked for, and then some. With how much he'd laughed, I wouldn't be surprised if he brought it out again.

"I didn't know Mark had a birthday party," Dean added.

"It's for people who live here," Brooke said sharply.

"I'm sure Dean would be invited," I said, an edge to my voice that I usually didn't have. Brooke's eyes went wide, but she kept her mouth shut. "I could just bring him as my plus one."

"Because no one would notice *that*." She rolled her eyes.

For the first time, I wished people knew about Dean and me. It would have been easier if they did. We could say we weren't dating, but we had a reason to hang around one another.

"I'll just ask him," Dean said. "He and I get along."

"Yeah, yeah. You do whatever." She waved her hand. "At least everyone will finally get to see me perform."

Dean glanced at me and rolled his eyes. Brooke was too busy daydreaming to notice. I couldn't resist the smile that made its way to my face. Usually, I took on Brooke alone, but this time, I had someone to help me make it through her visit.

A girl could easily get used to this.

22

DEAN

Strawberry Springs Neighborhood Watch

Jackie Anne: So sorry to anyone who saw me run out into the alley in my robe screaming for Chaos. Dang racoon took my donut and ran with it.

Comments:
Mark Bell: That was real? I thought I was having one of those nightmares again . . .
Mollie Wilson: Jackie, do I need to do a welfare check on you?
Marjorie Brown: HA! They're turnin' on ya!
Marjorie Brown: Did anyone get any pics?
Jackie Anne: They better not have! I didn't have anything on under the robe.
Jade Clark: WHOA. Of all the people to halfway streak through the square . . . Jackie? Wow, I didn't recognize your game.

THE FIRST NIGHT I'd stayed at Grace's house, I slept surprisingly well. The second night, I was half expecting to get stabbed by Brooke, so sleep mostly evaded me.

I managed a few hours before getting up in search of caffeine. I would need all the help I could get, and I had a feeling Brooke wasn't an early riser.

When I heard footsteps creaking on the old hardwood floor, I started the pot of coffee. My shoulders tensed, and I wondered if my gamble had blown up in my face.

And then I saw Grace with her hair tied into a messy bun coming around the corner.

She blinked when she saw me, and her eyes trailed my form, no doubt taking in my old, gingham pajama bottoms and messy hair. The day before, I'd left the guest room ready for the day. Today hadn't gone as well.

"Morning." It came out awkwardly. I'd never let a woman see me like this, and I wasn't sure if I wanted to.

It was too late now.

"Hi." Grace's voice was slow and still full of sleep.

I chuckled. "Not a morning person?"

"Not this early."

The coffee pot beeped as she leaned on a nearby countertop and rubbed her face. I grabbed two mugs for us.

"Oh, you don't have to—"

"You made breakfast yesterday," I reminded. "It's the least I can do."

Her lips pressed together the same way they always did when she didn't want to accept help, but thankfully, she didn't stop me.

The previous night had been tense and awkward, but when it was just Grace and me, things felt . . . natural. Like it was too easy to be around her.

"Why are you awake?" she asked.

"I could ask you the same thing."

She winced. "Hip pain. I hear it's pretty normal."

"Oh," I said. "Can I help?"

"You already did by starting the coffee pot. Now, are you gonna answer or do you want me to guess?"

That was the last thing I wanted. "It feels weird with Brooke here," I said. Grace slowly nodded, lips pressing into a thin line. "I'm not complaining or anything. She can stay when she wants."

"No, it's okay. I can also admit that it's not fun." She shrugged. "She'll leave after the party, though. I think she just wants to show off."

I wanted to ask her why she did all of this for her sister, but then I imagined that my only family—Mom—was like Brooke was. Would I have walked away?

In theory, yes. In practice? I wasn't so sure.

Mom was one of the best people in my life, and while she deserved it, I did feel like I owed her for raising me. We were tied by bonds that I couldn't have easily shaken.

"You're wanting to tell me I shouldn't deal with all of this, aren't you?" she asked. When I finally looked back at her, I saw her shoulders had crept up near her ears.

"It's tempting to, but it isn't that simple, is it? Not when she's your last family."

Grace blinked. "You're exactly right."

"I don't like Brooke, and I really don't like how she treats you. But I get why it's hard to fully let her go. So, I respect that."

"That's really mature of you, Dean."

"This younger guy can be mature. Who knew?" I shrugged and finished off my coffee. "I'll see if Mark will have me at the birthday party tonight. I'll go after work."

I washed my mug and walked past her to get ready for the day. It was way too early to go to work, but I didn't want to be around Brooke more than I had to be. I could easily go hang out at the library when it opened, if need be.

As I did so, Grace's knowing eyes were on me, and I wondered if she was seeing past all the walls that I'd put up. I should have been terrified of it.

The thought didn't scare me as much as it should've.

It wasn't hard to find Mark. He was outside of his bar, washing the panes of glass on the door. When he saw me, he immediately told me about his party and asked if I wanted to come. I didn't even have to bring it up.

And just like that, I had plans for the evening.

I almost wished they were truly for fun. But I knew how Brooke was and that nothing good could come of her attending the party. I could be there for Grace in case she needed backup. And for Mark too.

Watching the time closely, I arrived at work. Wren was in and out as she managed other projects, but I knew she would come by near the eight-hour mark to make sure I didn't overwork myself.

Sure enough, right at five, the front door to the apartment opened.

"You better be—" She paused when she saw me. "Oh, you're actually wrapping up. Are you finally listening?"

"Mostly. I also happen to have plans for tonight."

Her eyebrows raised. "Oh, hot date?"

"Just going to Mark's big birthday thing. Are you going too?"

She winced. "As much as I'd love to try one of Tammy's drinks, I'll be at home with Henry. We aren't big on the party scene."

"You might miss out on some drama. Brooke is in town."

Wren frowned. "I haven't heard good things about her. How did you know she was in town?"

"I pissed her off. It's a talent of mine." When Wren went to ask again, I added, "And it has nothing to do with me breaking her heart."

"I wasn't gonna say that." She rolled her eyes. "I was gonna say I've heard it's easy to do that."

"Very easy," I muttered. "And I'll probably do it again."

"Why?"

"I'm not letting her walk all over Grace. She has a bad habit of doing that."

"That's really sweet of you. It's good how you and Grace—"

"Grace and I aren't anything."

"I know. I'm just glad you're getting along. Take a breath, Dean. I'm on your side here."

I forced myself to relax. "Sorry. I just don't want these people getting any ideas."

"You feel really strongly about it."

"Grace and I are doing well. I don't need fucking gossip to ruin it."

Wren only stared at me, no doubt curious about why I hated gossip so much. But unlike Grace, who would dig in without a second thought, Wren let stuff go.

"I shouldn't keep you," she said with a smile. "You have a party to enjoy. And a Brooke to piss off."

"Wish me luck."

"I will." She walked toward the door. "And have fun with Grace. You know, there's a bet on you two."

Normally, I'd ignore a comment like that. Plenty of people had taken my interest in a woman and tried to make it something it wasn't.

But *this* hit me in a different way. I wanted to chase Wren down and make sure she knew that it wouldn't be happening. I was defensive. My hands were clammy. And I needed, more than anything, to shut this down.

The last thing I needed was a small town fucking up the tentative good thing I had with Grace.

And if they found out, that was exactly what they'd do.

23

GRACE

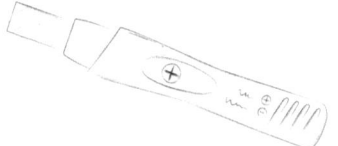

Strawberry Springs Neighborhood Watch

Henrietta Brown: Single and ready to mingle, folks! I will not be taking questions unless it's asking me out on a date!

Comments:
Jade Clark: Wait, seriously? Are you and Marjorie done?
Tammy Jane: Well, things will finally be quieter.
Dale Garrett: I always thought she could do better.
Henrietta Brown: I am NOT single! Marj took my phone because I said she was getting soft since we went back to work. Ignore everything from her!
Marjorie Brown: Wait, what do you mean she could do better???

"You BETTER BE HEADING to Bell's Brews!" Tammy called when she saw me. I'd parked next to Dean's truck on the opposite side of the square. He must have been waiting because he fell into step beside me.

I was trying to play it cool—people were everywhere. I shouldn't have been surprised Tammy said anything.

She had on her cowboy boots and sparkly eyeshadow, which meant she was bartending. I'd partaken once or twice. Obviously, I couldn't tonight.

"I am. Don't worry."

"You too, Cowboy?" Tammy's eyes flicked to Dean and she raised an eyebrow.

"Yes, ma'am. I was invited."

"I'm sure you were. Mark has a habit of inviting everyone he sees to this thing." She rolled her eyes and shoved her hand at him. "I'm Tammy. I'll be getting you drunk tonight."

"Dean," he said slowly. His voice was slower than I was used to hearing it, and I wondered if he was unsure about her. "Cowboy kinda works, but I only wear the hat. I don't do the work."

"Well, at least you're honest." Tammy laughed and then her gaze flicked between the two of us. "You two know each other?"

"I just happened to be next to her." Dean was quick on the draw with an explanation.

"I do know his name, though."

Tammy hummed and Dean took the chance to go on ahead of us. I had to resist the urge to sigh.

"So, what do you think of him?" Tammy asked.

"Of Dean? Nothing. Why would I think anything about him?"

"It seems like every woman in town has thoughts about him." She looked between the door—which Dean had disappeared through—and me. "You know, I'd be careful if I were you."

My heart skipped a beat. "About what?"

"I heard he's one of *those* guys. A use 'em and leave 'em kind of thing. None of us want that for any of the women here. But especially not you."

"Who said that?" I asked, my voice harsher than usual. When Tammy's brow lowered, I corrected. "I mean, was he really here long enough for anyone to pass judgment?"

"He told people how he was the first time he went to the bar, and Wren confirmed it. He's not the kind of guy you should be spending time with. Not romantically, at least. I hear he does good work, though."

"Right," I said. "At least there's that."

"Just take care of yourself, kid. I wouldn't want any of you gals to get your heart broken."

And then she was gone into Bell's Brews. I took a deep breath, hoping it would calm me down. But I was quickly learning that I didn't like people bringing up Dean's reputation. Especially when I knew there was more to him.

A headache brewed behind my eyes, and Brooke hadn't even gotten here yet.

That didn't mean anything good.

When I walked in, I expected the makeshift stage to be set up from the year before and to hear someone I knew ruining a song they loved.

Instead, there was no singing. Only a crowd in the center of the room.

"Oh, you outdid yourself, Mark!" Tammy's voice was the loudest as she approached him. "Where did you even find this?"

"Facebook Marketplace." Mark sounded proud of himself, and I ventured closer to see what everyone was having a cow about.

In the middle of the dance floor, a mechanical bull was waiting to break someone's face.

Who in their right mind was stupid enough to ride that thing?

"I haven't seen one of these in years!" Dean said with a laugh. He was across the room looking like a kid at Christmas. I'd never seen him like this. The only person with a wider smile was Mark.

I rubbed my temple. Of course there would be a bull. Of course my baby daddy was going to wind up in the hospital. And if I stepped in, it would look suspicious.

I needed a damn drink. But I couldn't fucking have one.

Instead of completely losing my mind, I walked to the bar, ordered a Shirley Temple, and found a corner to wallow in. I had to get my mood in check before Brooke got here.

But things seemed to *want* to go wrong.

Once Mark promised to get the bull going, people filtered to the bar. Atticus spilled his drink next to me, and the smell of alcohol hit my nose like a train. I turned away, trying not to seem obviously grossed out by it.

I was always the designated driver. I dealt with my drunk friends all the time, but I hadn't done that while pregnant.

Thankfully, I managed to keep it together until the smell of beer hit my nose and I turned to glare at whoever was stupid enough to bring that in my presence.

That was when I was met with Dean.

"Everything okay?" His voice was low, and he sounded like the man from my house who cared enough to check on me.

"I'm fine. Don't worry about me." It came out sharp, but I meant it. We didn't need to get caught, and I needed to get my shit together.

"You say that as if it's possible for me to not worry about you." He stepped closer and I took one step back.

"Can you not . . ." I trailed off and took a breath. I only smelled more.

"Can I not what?"

"The beer," I managed. "It fucking—"

"Grace, are you okay?"

Dean took a healthy step away from me as we both looked up to see Mark looking in between us suspiciously. He must have seen me shying away from Dean, but it wasn't him that was the problem. It was what was in his hand.

"S-sorry," I stuttered. "I'm just a little . . . overwhelmed."

My excuse was weak to my own ears, but Mark seemed to take it. "Kinda like Henry gets sometimes?"

"Yeah, exactly."

His eyes darted between Dean and me. "And you . . . Why were you getting in her space?"

Dean's eyes went wide. "I-I was just trying to talk to her."

"She didn't seem interested."

"Mark, he's fine." I said it before I could think. "Seriously. I just didn't like the smell of his beer."

Dean nodded. "The beer. Shit, that would do it. Could I get a water instead?"

"Only if you give Grace some space," Mark said. "Head to the bar and don't distract Tammy. I'll get you water in a second."

Dean looked at me, but I knew that it would look worse if he insisted on staying with me.

"Yeah, of course."

"Now for *you*," Mark said. "You can use my BBC if you need it."

My eyes widened. Had I heard him right? "Your *what*?"

"The Bell's Brews Closet."

"Oh," I said. "That makes a lot more sense."

"And I know *you* won't violate it. Let me tell you the code."

As much as I didn't want to need it, I had no idea how the

night would go. Being the good girl had its benefits. I would use them as long as it lasted. "That would be great."

Mark told me the number and I committed it to memory. Then Mark went to meet Dean at the bar.

I moved to a different spot, one that didn't smell offensive, and texted Dean.

> I really am fine. I just discovered I hate the smell of alcohol. Who knew?

> That looked bad, though. I'll get it together.

DEAN

Don't worry about how it looked. Take Mark up on his offer if you need to. I'm sorry for getting in your space. I should have seen you were trying to get away from me.

> It was just the beer. I promise. Enjoy the party.

I'll be enjoying the bull.

> Just don't die before you meet our baby.

Promise I won't.

I was tempted to text him even more, but I was tackled into a tight hug.

"You're here! You made it!" Jade clung to me like an octopus. I could smell one of Tammy's cocktails on her, but it wasn't as offensive as Dean's beer or Atticus's spilled drink.

"I did make it. Are you having fun?"

"I love it when Tammy bartends. I got here early to scope out the crowd, but it's all locals."

"It's Mark's birthday. It's always locals."

She groaned. "I need a hot man to stick his wang in me."

"Jade," I whispered with a laugh. "Mark will pass out if he hears you talk like that."

"You do know I'm the reason he's so protective of his closet, right? He caught me in it and couldn't look me in the eye."

"He caught you? Did he give you the lecture about waiting for the *one*?" Many had tried. It was why she kept her affairs out of the news.

"He knows I'm too fucked up and will do it anyway. He just doesn't want it in his BBC."

"So, you heard the name too?"

"Oh, I heard it. And I told him to announce it to the Facebook group."

I snickered. "You're evil."

"Don't blow this for me."

"You know I'd never." I looked around the bar, which was filling up. Atticus was at the bar talking to Dean and Mark. One of the guys we'd grown up with, Lucas, was here, which was a rare sighting since his move to Nashville.

"So, be real with me." Jade leaned in. "Should I ride the bull?"

"No," I said. "God, you're as bad as Dean."

"Well, it's the only thing I can ride," she said with a sigh. "It'll be *some* action."

"Don't ride a bull just because you need dick, okay?"

"I'm riding for the thrill of it."

I shook my head and caught Dean glancing at me. I could see he was still worried, so I gave him a thumbs-up.

"Speaking of a good ride, have you gotten any lately?"

I gave Jade a flat look. "You know the answer to that."

"Do I? Because you went super quiet and Dean keeps looking over here."

I *wished* I'd gone quiet for that reason. There was something about him being in pajamas that made heat rise within me. I'd had to go back to my room and take care of things.

And it still lingered.

I needed to Google pierced vibrators when I got home. That was what I was craving.

"Nothing's happening," I said. "I would tell you if it was."

"Just like you'd tell me if you had a new *roommate*?"

"What?" I asked. "How did you—"

"I have a habit of checking on your house when I go in and out of town. I saw his truck."

"He just had a hotel problem." I rubbed my forehead. "Please don't tell anyone. I can't have people knowing yet."

"You know I won't. And if anyone else mentions it, I'll make up a reason he's there."

"What would I do without you?"

She shrugged. "Develop a stress disorder?"

I laughed and scanned back over the crowd. Kerry was by the bar, which meant I needed to be on my best behavior.

And that was when Brooke walked in.

She looked for the karaoke machine, which was the only reason she was here. When she didn't find it, I saw her smile turn into a frown and then a sharp glare.

"Shit, sorry. I need to go."

"Oh God." Jade gagged. "Good luck."

I made my way over to Brooke, who was already seething. "No karaoke?" she asked when I got over to her. "Seriously?"

"Mark wanted to do something else," I soothed. "You can still have fun."

"I want to *sing*."

"It's Mark's birthday. He can do what he wants."

She rolled her eyes. "I should just leave."

I didn't want to say it out loud, but that was a great idea.

"But I'm sure Mark wants that," she continued. "I'm getting a drink and hoping someone hot climbs on the bull. I need eye candy."

Brooke was gone before I could say anything else. I groaned. Leave it to her to do the worst thing possible.

I made my way back to Jade as Brooke ordered a drink.

"Everything good?"

"No, but what else is new?"

"She wanted to show off, didn't she?"

"Yep," I replied. "How did you know?"

"Brooke hates it when anyone else has *fun*." Jade rolled her eyes. "Oh, shit. Tammy's getting on the bull. Time to get in line!"

I turned. Just like Jade said, Tammy was climbing on. She was lucky that neither Wren nor Kelsey were here to talk her down.

Or maybe they'd join her. I had no idea.

"Feast your eyes!" she called. "I'm gonna win this thing!"

"There's nothing to win!" Mark called back.

"I'll win my pride!" she snapped. "Hit it, old man."

"We're the same age!"

"Do you listen or do you complain?"

Mark sighed, but turned on the bull. Tammy jerked once. Then twice. Then she was ejected.

"I hope Henry doesn't have any plans," I said to myself as I shook my head.

A few more people tried, all lasting about the same time as Tammy. The bull was brutal, and I had no idea how people were laughing as they got off. Jade was even cackling as she hit the ground, claiming it was the best ride of her life.

After she was helped up, she limped over to me. "That was awesome. It threw me around like I want a man to."

"You're something else."

"At least I'm fun. But I think you'll like who's going after me."

That was when I saw Dean climbing on.

I gasped. "No. You should have convinced him out of it!"

"Do you see those muscles? Watching him hang onto anything is a view for us all."

"He could get hurt."

"And then you get to kiss it better. This is for *you*."

I shook my head, tempted to go demand that he get off, but that was when the bull started.

Dean was more controlled than most of the people. He watched the mechanical bull's movements carefully, even as he put his hat on his head.

He looked every part the cowboy as he rode the thing, even down to his muscles. I could have sworn I saw abs underneath his tight shirt.

And suddenly, the room felt ten degrees warmer.

I'd tried to put Dean in a box ever since I'd been with him. It would never be able to happen again.

But God, did I want it. Especially after seeing his forearms flex.

"Go, Dean!" Mark called.

Dean was in a risky mood because he only held onto the mechanical bull with one arm and waved his hat with the other.

"Fuck, he should be on a magazine," I said.

"Are you drooling?" Jade asked with a laugh. I shook my head at her. I was watching Dean too closely to care about anything else.

Then his round ended without him getting thrown off. The entire bar cheered as if he'd won something. Just like that, he'd charmed the crowd. It was probably the abs.

No, it was *definitely* the abs.

Jade cheered too, and I joined in. I was physically attracted to him, yes, but as I watched him laugh, I could see how bright he could be. He was smiling wide, high-fiving people as he walked by. I wondered if this was the kind of dad he would be. Fun. Energetic.

Everything a kid needed.

I hadn't thought much about what parenting would be like with him, mostly because I was terrified it would be difficult to do with a near stranger.

But this eased some of my worries. Maybe it would be fine.

Maybe it would all work out.

"Uh, Grace?" Jade grabbed my arm. "You might wanna go watch that."

She pointed to Brooke, who had a half-empty drink in her hand. She was heading right for Dean.

"Yep. Bye." I made my way across the room and intercepted her. "Hey, what are you doing?"

"Going after the eye candy," she said. "He turned me down once, but I'm willing to try again. Even if he's grumpy sometimes."

Her words pierced me. "Brooke, come on. You know what he is to me."

"You're not together, though. And unlike you, I know how to use a condom and won't get pregnant."

"Shh!" I hissed. We were in the middle of town at the biggest party of the year. Why the hell would she say that?

"What?"

There was a pit in my stomach, and I turned around to see if anyone heard. That was when I came face-to-face with Kerry.

And she was smiling. She had *the* smile. The one she always got when she'd heard some good gossip.

"What did I just hear?" Kerry asked.

"Nothing. You heard nothing."

"No, I heard something."

"Kerry, *please.*" I wasn't above begging. In fact, I was very, *very* below it.

"Oh, come on." Brooke climbed onto a table. "Everyone! Grace is knocked up! By Dean, by the way!"

The entire bar went *silent*.

I could only stare at Brooke. She'd done a lot of stupid things while drunk, but this took the cake.

"Are you kidding me right now?" Jade snapped. "You selfish little *bitch*."

I turned to Jade. I needed to diffuse that. I needed to get Brooke off the table. I also needed to figure out some sort of lie to get myself out of this. Or figure out some way to minimize the damage of Brooke's actions.

I needed to do it all.

And I was only one person.

I hadn't noticed it, but my breaths came out faster. This was my worst nightmare, brought on by my own sister.

Everyone's eyes were on me and the whispers had started.

"Grace is pregnant?" Atticus asked. The *of all people* was heavily implied.

"By the playboy?" Mark asked.

Oh *God*. I couldn't do this. I couldn't face them.

All I could do was break into a run. As much as I wanted to go outside, there were more eyes trained on *me* in that direction, and I couldn't face that.

Mark's closet was the better option. I stumbled inside, and as I pulled it shut, an arm blocked my way.

"Leave me alone," I begged. My voice was thick with emotion, and I knew I was seconds away from crying.

That was when Dean opened the door. "Grace, are you—"

"Oh my God," I said as I dragged him into the closet. "I can't believe she—why would she—"

"I know, I know." His hands landed on my shoulders. "I need you to breathe, though."

"I can't breathe right now. The whole town knows, I need to fix this!"

"No," he insisted. "Right now, their opinions don't fucking matter, okay? All that matters is that you take care of yourself. If you can't do it for you, then do it for the baby."

That got me out of it. It always did. I didn't want them to know a ton of stress before they were even in the world.

I sucked in oxygen, hating that tears pricked my eyes as I tried to calm down. I wondered what they were saying about me. If they were thinking I was as bad as Brooke, or if they were disappointed.

"Grace, stop thinking about them. I know you're doing it."

Dean had me there.

"How do you do it? How do you just . . . not care?"

"I do care," he replied. "But I also know that I'm a human being. And they're not gonna like me sometimes."

"I *want* them to like me."

"And how much of yourself have you given up to achieve that?"

A lot. And I knew it. I was exhausted every day from it.

I'd put my all into being perfect. And I still couldn't. I'd done so much for my sister. I'd put myself second to help her. I'd made her dinner when I was too tired to. I'd listened to her rants about how no one else wanted her around.

And look at what she'd done.

I was so angry with her. I didn't think I'd ever been this angry at her in my life. She'd betrayed me. And I'd let her.

Dean's hands migrated from my shoulders up to my neck and cheeks. "Right now, it's you and me. Don't think about anyone else."

It was impossible not to.

But I needed to try.

My hands met his and we breathed together. Every time my mind wandered, I emptied it again.

And eventually, I calmed down.

"Good," he said. "That's my girl."

"I still need to—"

"Take a minute to yourself. I'll be right back."

I didn't want him to go, but I nodded anyway. When he was gone, my skin felt cold.

24

DEAN

Strawberry Springs Neighborhood Watch

Kerry Winsor: GUYS! Grace!! Pregnant! Dean!!!

Comments:
Marjorie Brown: Is this a puzzle or something?
Wren Hackett: @Jade Clark @Mollie Wilson
Mollie Wilson: Kerry, this is one of those things you should NOT be posting about. Admins, delete this. We're not doing this again.
Kerry Winsor: You sound like Dean.
Mollie Wilson: Whatever Dean said, I agree with.
Wren Hackett: Same.
Jade Clark: If y'all gossip about my girl, it WILL be over for you all. Leave her ALONE. Admins, please get this trash out of the group.

My first thought was yelling at Brooke for what she'd done. I didn't know how a person couldn't care less about how they affected others, but she somehow did. When I got back into the bar area, I didn't see her. Maybe it was better that way.

All eyes were on me the second I came into view of others, though.

Kerry tried to sneak past me, probably to find out more information, but I held my hand out.

"Nope. Grace isn't available for questions."

"So, are you then?" she asked.

Goddammit. "Back to the bar." The words were forced out, my voice deeper than I ever let it get.

Kerry's eyes widened and she scurried away.

I hated these kinds of people. I hated that they were always trying to get information. I hated that this kind of thing was huge news. I hated that I had to do this.

But I would for Grace.

"So, what's the plan?" a woman whispered to me. She was the one who I'd seen Grace talk to many times. They were close. "We probably need to get Grace outta here and then we figure out how to minimize . . . damage."

Damage. That word irritated me. We were grown fucking people. Grace could do what she wanted, be with who she wanted. She shouldn't be terrified of what they all thought.

I pulled a chair out and stood on it before thinking.

"Hey! People!" I didn't need to yell. All of them were watching me anyway, but it felt nice to raise my voice.

"Are you finally ready to tell us what happened?" Kerry asked, pushing her way to the front of the crowd. "Because I have plenty of—"

"This isn't about gossip," I snapped. "This is about Grace."

"We just want the story!"

"You all do realize she's a real fucking person, right? She's not a story."

Her face slowly paled, but someone else took over. It was Tammy, the woman I'd met outside. I'd seen her in the diner and she'd barely given me a second look. I had a feeling she didn't like me all that much.

"Hang on, you come to our town and tell us how to take care of our own? We've known Grace longer than you, buddy!"

Now I *knew* she didn't like me.

"Oh, yeah," I snapped back. "You know her. And she knows you well enough to hide from you because she's terrified of what you'll think. You've clearly done a real good job of making her feel safe."

"And how do you know that?"

"Uh, Tammy?" Mark spoke this time. "He was the first one to go after her."

Tammy's jaw dropped and her questions stopped.

Kerry took over. "You can't blame us for having questions. We're owed an explanation."

"We don't owe you shit."

"This town's like a family," Tammy said. She must have processed what Mark had said and was right back to it. "Not that you'd know much about that, city boy."

I was already on my last straw. This sent me over the edge. "First of all, I grew up in a town like this. You all think you're family, but then don't give a flying fuck when someone's hurting. It's all about the gossip. All about some info *you* need. The second someone doesn't do what you want, they're ousted. You're not fucking doing that to Grace."

"You think we're gonna oust her because she's pregnant?" Kerry asked, her voice growing high. "God, no! This might be a shock, but she needs extra help right now!"

"I would've given her extra food at the diner!" Tammy said.

"I need to stock more sizes of diapers at the store!" Dale yelled.

"And I would've guessed she had an aversion to the smell of alcohol." Mark shook his head. "No wonder she kept avoiding it."

I paused. "You're not gonna ostracize her for having a baby with *me* of all people?"

There were some whispers, most of which I couldn't tell who they were from.

Well, it's not the best idea.

How do we know he's actually gonna stay?

What if she gets hurt?

And that was when I saw it. The issue wasn't with her. They all cared about her. Genuinely.

I was the issue.

It shouldn't have annoyed me as much as it did. I could play the bad guy, and I would.

"All right, here's what we're gonna do. If you actually care about Grace's well-being, then leave her the fuck alone about this. She needs space. Do *not* pester her."

"But how will I know how far along she is?" Kerry whined.

"You don't get to make that choice!" Tammy yelled.

"I'm saying for you all to pester *me*. I'll answer your questions."

"But you just said you don't owe us shit!"

"I don't," I said firmly. "I'm not telling you because I owe you. I'm telling you because you all seem to care about her. There's a difference. If you wanna know how to help out, I'm your guy."

"Thank *God!*" Kerry exclaimed, and then she unleashed her barrage. "How far along is she? When did you find out?"

"Are you gonna stick around this time?" Mark asked.

"He better not be an absent dad!" Tammy snapped. "If you do a breed 'em and leave 'em, I *swear*—"

"She's eighteen weeks. We found out two weeks ago. I'm gonna stick around for *her*, and then we'll figure out custody once the baby's here. And for your information, Tammy, breeding was *not* the intended goal, and I'm gonna do the right thing."

She crossed her arms and I doubted she believed me.

I already regretted giving them permission to do this. I was so tense that I wondered if I'd be sore the next day.

"Oh, also—"

"That's enough questions for now. I need to get Grace home and make sure none of you bother her."

"Just who do you think you are, talking to us like this?" Tammy asked.

"There's only one thing you need to know about me. I don't play when it comes to my woman. I don't care if you hate me. She's not getting hurt or stressed out by you."

For once, the bar was shocked into silence.

"Hang on, hang on." Hugh slowly stood. I saw him when we first got here, but I still couldn't look him in the eye since I'd seen him naked. "So, does this mean I win my money?"

"Why are you winning money?" I asked.

"He bet you two would get together," Dale muttered. "And he obviously won."

My stomach churned and I grimaced. "Oh, absolutely not. We're *not* together."

Even the *thought* made fear ripple through my body.

"Excuse me?" Tammy snapped. "Is there something wrong with the beautiful angel that is Grace?"

"N-no! She's great. Just not for . . . me." Tammy narrowed her eyes so much that I thought she might throw something at me. "The point is," I said, "just leave her alone."

"Yeah, leave your woman alone that you're not dating." Dale scoffed. "That makes sense."

"Friend. I meant *friend*."

A wave of whispers made its way through the crowd. I wanted to yell.

"Is everyone fucking clear on not bothering her?"

"Don't worry, friend-of-Grace," Mark said, clapping me on the shoulder. "We all hear your message loud and clear."

I had a feeling he was talking about multiple things, but I didn't care. I was done with these people and I needed to make sure Grace was okay.

"Back to business then. I'm getting her home. Continue with questions tomorrow."

Grace didn't say anything on the way home. It was only when we pulled into the driveway that she finally spoke.

"This is my worst nightmare." Her voice was slow, and broke halfway through her sentence.

"Brooke telling everyone?"

"Everyone knowing. I've made it my life mission never to get in trouble like this."

"Are you in trouble?"

She shook her head. "Not with you, I guess. But I don't do things like this. I don't sleep with someone and get pregnant. I don't step a foot out of line because Brooke always does it for me. I can only imagine what they're thinking."

"Don't imagine it."

"I can't help it. I bet they think I'm as bad as Brooke is. Or that I'm a complete idiot."

"They're not thinking that," I said softly.

"Then what are they thinking?"

"That it's a shock. But they wanna help."

"Really?"

"The people in this town care about you. Even if they don't understand *how* this happened, they'll adjust. And it's gonna be okay."

Grace's eyes were wet and she let out a long breath. "That's . . . incredible. It'll be hard to deal with them adjusting, but at least they're not thinking I'm a failure."

"You have nothing to worry about." And I meant it.

I *was* happy that the town had reacted like they had. Even if they weren't happy with *me*, they'd showed that they wanted the best for her. That was a good thing.

But for me, it felt a little like being punched in the stomach. This was the best-case scenario, but it still brought me back to being a teenager, where I was an outsider in the place I spent all my time.

"Were they hard on you?" she asked.

"Don't worry about me. You just spent a night in a bar while you have a smell aversion to alcohol, and your sister did the most selfish thing I've ever seen. You need some rest."

Grace side-eyed her home with a wary expression. "When I get in there, Brooke's gonna act like she did nothing wrong. I don't think I can deal with that."

"I'll handle Brooke."

"You don't even like her."

"I don't like most of the people here," I said. "I'll be okay."

I didn't give her a chance to argue. I cut the engine, got out, and walked over to her door to open it.

"Thank you, Dean. You've really helped me and I don't know how to repay you."

"Repay me by getting some rest," I said.

I helped Grace out of the truck and we went inside. Just as she expected, Brooke was waiting for us, and she opened her mouth to say something that was probably going to piss me off.

Brooke was met with the iciest stare I could muster. And considering I wanted to throttle her, it was easy to glare. Her jaw dropped when she saw me, and the shock of how I looked at her had her quiet just long enough for me to get Grace to her room.

Brooke met me at the end of the hallway. "I need to speak with my sister."

"The fuck you're not."

"I don't know where you get the balls, buddy, but—"

"I don't wanna hear it. You ruined Grace's night and told everyone something she wasn't ready for them to know."

Brooke scoffed. "I did her a favor. She would never tell everyone from the way she was going."

"So what? You don't get to make a decision like that for her just because you think that you know what's best."

"But you sure try to."

"I'm not a selfish bitch, so I can get away with it."

"Fuck you." She took a step toward me and raised her hand. "How *dare* you—"

"Do you *want* to lose your sister?" I spoke slowly, hoping she would understand.

Brooke paused in her tirade. "What?"

"Do you want to lose your sister? Because with the way you're going, it's very likely she's never gonna talk to you again."

That finally got through to her. I wasn't sure if it were possible for Brooke to truly care about someone, but she wanted Grace in her life, whether that was to use her or to get a free place to stay.

"She wouldn't do that. I'm her family."

"Keep testing the boundaries then and we'll both see what happens." I went to go to my own room, eager to get over the pressing anger that had entered every part of my body, but then I paused. "Make her breakfast or something tomorrow. But leave her the fuck alone tonight. I already heard her lock her door just so you couldn't bother her."

"Grace never locks doors."

"Things are changing around here. You're gonna have to grow up, Brooke. Or get left behind."

25

GRACE

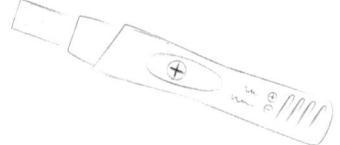

Strawberry Springs Neighborhood Watch

Mark Bell: The BBC made it through the night untouched, guys!

Comments:
Kelsey Marie: I—you know what. I'm better than this. I'm happy for you and your BBC.
Atticus Thompson: Are we really not talking about the . . . other thing?
Mark Bell: SHH! They're watching.
Jade Clark: You're on thin ice, Atticus.
Atticus Thompson: I just want to make sure she's okay.
Wren Hackett: She's all good. She's gonna have a normal day.
Mark Bell: Good. Can we talk about how this might make Kerry explode?
Jade Clark: Approved.
Kerry Winsor: Why does everyone assume the WORST of me?

Kerry Winsor: @Wren Hackett, is Dean working with you today?

WHEN I WOKE up the next morning, I wondered if the night before had been some sort of terrible dream.

But dreams made less and less sense as time went on . . . and Brooke having a meltdown about not getting to sing and telling everyone that I was pregnant? It did make sense. Because that was the kind of person she was.

Getting out of bed felt like I was getting ready for my funeral. I dreaded every step, but I couldn't avoid it forever.

Dean's words about the town caring helped, but I was *not* ready for all the questions. Deep down, I always knew that it would be coming from a place of care, but it would still be a lot.

I still had to face it.

When I came out of my bedroom, Brooke was in the living room.

Looked like I was facing this too.

"Finally," she muttered.

"Seriously?" I snapped. I couldn't help it. "That's what you have to say to me?"

I expected her to bite back, but instead, her eyes went wide. "So, you're mad."

"No kidding." I shook my head and brushed past her to go get a quick thing for breakfast and then leave.

"Wait, hang on."

"What could you possibly say to make what you did okay?" I snapped.

"I got you breakfast."

I paused. "You what?"

"It's on the table. I had to drive way too far because Tammy wouldn't serve me." She rolled her eyes. "But it's a few waffles and eggs."

"Why?" I asked.

She shrugged, looking away. "Dean said you were mad. I guess he was right."

I'd known she'd tried to follow me to my room and that he stopped her, but I'd gone to bed right after locking the door. I needed that time, and even with it, I hadn't looked forward to facing her.

This was nicer than I'd expected.

"That wasn't okay, Brooke. You have to know that."

"Well, were you going to ever tell them?" she asked, throwing her hands up. "I got it out of the way."

"That's still not—"

"I know, okay? Dean already said I was wrong. So, I got breakfast."

I stared at her. This was the closest I would get to an apology, and even this was more than I'd ever seen.

Just how had Dean gotten through to her?

"Thanks, Brooke."

"It's whatever. Enjoy it. I'm going back to Nashville." She muttered it and went to get her purse. She got to the stairs in front of the door before she paused and looked back at me. "Just remember. *I'm* family. He's not."

And then she was gone.

I was still angry, but she'd tried, which was something. With a sigh, I went to the dining room where there was food left out. There was even coffee in a Styrofoam cup.

I had no idea how to feel, but I ate breakfast, grateful that I didn't have to cook. Once I was finished, some of the anger had dissipated.

Now I had to deal with the town.

Slowly, I went to my closet and started to put together an

outfit for the day. This was one of the few times I wanted to dress in something to help me blend in, not stand out.

But I fought that urge. I'd feel better in something pretty, and after a few outfit changes, I landed on a pink dress with a jacket, and knew this was the right choice.

My heart hammered as I walked the streets. I had to face this, but it was terrifying.

I passed by Marjorie first. I expected some smart-ass comment about getting knocked up, or a poorly made joke about pregnancy, but she only waved.

Next was Jackie. She waved and asked, "It's getting warm, isn't it?" and moved on.

Okay. Neither of them were at the bar, so maybe news didn't spread too fast.

Then I saw Kerry. She was outside the diner, about to walk in. Her eyes met mine and she froze when she saw me. I figured she would run up and pepper me with questions. Instead, she squeezed her lips together and ran inside.

I paused on my walk. Kerry didn't have questions? Since when?

Mark was walking from Food 'n' Things and nodded when he saw me. "Like the dress. The jacket might make it too warm, though."

I looked down at my jacket. "Probably, but it makes it look better."

I waited for the comment about pregnancy not helping, but he only laughed and walked into Bell's Brews.

What the fuck was going on?

I knew this town and how they operated. There was *no* way they found out about me being pregnant and just let it go.

Collective amnesia was more possible than that.

I had barely opened the door before I heard fast, loud footsteps. Jade was *running* toward me, and in her combat boots, it was terrifying.

"Oh my God," I said. "Is everything okay? Did Gabriel come back into town?"

"Funny, but no. I'm here to talk about you." She looked around like she had contraband stuffed in her pockets. "Get inside. We need to talk."

"What? Me?" I was pushed inside my store. "What did I do?"

"You didn't do anything. It's your baby daddy we're talking about."

"Please don't call him that," I said. The only person who could use *daddy* to refer to him was . . . I wanted to say me, but could I?

"Defensive, are we? You should be. That man was hot enough on the mechanical bull last night, but then he goes and gets even hotter."

"Jade, are you about to ask me if you can sleep with him?" I rubbed my forehead. "Because I don't think I can take that."

"No." She rolled her eyes. "He's yours through and through. I'm telling you what he did at the bar."

"I was there. He rode the bull."

"I mean after Brooke told everyone you're pregnant."

"He helped you deal with Brooke, right? And fielded some questions?"

"He did way more than that. He basically whipped the whole town into shape so *no one* would bother you."

"Dean did? The same guy who's always smiling and would never hurt a fly?"

"Uh, yeah. He went toe-to-toe with Tammy of all people. And got Kerry in line!"

"Wh-what did he say?"

"He told everyone that they need to treat you like a person and not a story, and that neither of you owed them shit."

I blinked as I tried to picture it in my mind. "I'm sorry . . . Dean did all of that? Is *that* why no one's brought up the pregnancy?"

"Yeah. Not only did he go into hot and scary dad mode, but he did it for you. That's kinda romantic."

For a second, I agreed. *No one* had ever stepped up and done all of this before. It went beyond checking in. Dean had protected me.

"I . . . that's really sweet. But I'm not getting any romantic ideas. I can't."

She shrugged. "But think about all he's doing. He's been here and—"

"Jade, *no.* I can barely handle my own life, much less being turned down in the way he's turned down every other woman. I won't be like them. He told me what he is, even if I see things that . . . don't match up."

I was getting worked up, so I let out a long breath instead of continuing. It was hard admitting that he was a great guy, and it was even harder to admit that I was terrified of getting turned down.

"It's okay to admit you like him, though," she said. "And if you're serious about not pursuing anything, then there's someone better out there."

I flinched at the words. Was there someone better for me than Dean? I wasn't so sure.

"You're right," I forced myself to say. "One day I'll believe that."

"You know what?" Jade said. "We should go get some coffee and open our shops late."

"I've been late way too much," I said with a shake of my head.

"You can do whatever you want now that Dean yelled at everyone, so live a little. We can get coffee and catch up. The Reserved Bean is slower today, so we won't have to wait an hour."

"All right, fine. Only because it's incredible and I need a pick-me-up."

"Yes!" she said before linking her arm through mine.

The shop was left closed as we walked to the coffee shop. Even for a slower day, there was still a line and most of the tables were full. Theo was at the front and Kelsey was working too, and she waved when she saw us.

For a second, her eyes trailed down to my stomach, but her gaze snapped back up just as fast.

"She won't ask," Jade said.

"I know. I just know what everyone's thinking."

"And what's that?"

"That I fucked up."

"You didn't," she said. "This kind of thing happens, even to people who don't usually have one-night stands."

"I just feel I should have done better. After Brooke, I wanted to be normal."

"You don't owe anyone anything. Especially not Brooke." She left me to think about her words as she put in her order. "I'll also get a regular coffee for Grace."

I blinked out of my thoughts. "You don't have to get mine."

"I'm gonna do it anyway." She waved her hand.

"Got it," Theo replied. "But do you want the hazelnut cappuccino instead?"

"Definitely the hazelnut."

Jade turned to me. "You changed your order?"

"Theo made a guess and was right." I shrugged.

"Wait, you guess orders?" Jade asked. "What's your call on me?"

"Lavender latte."

"You have lavender?" she said with a gasp. "I'll be taking that then."

Theo nodded and changed both of our orders.

"How did I not know he worked magic?" Jade muttered as we walked to the pickup counter.

"He only told me because he guessed Dean's order."

"It's a waste of a man, isn't it?" Jade asked. "To be that hot and not date?"

"The same could be said for Dean," Kelsey said as she put our drinks down. "But it's true. Neither of them are my type, but I can appreciate the view. Someone recorded the bull riding last night."

Both Jade and I gasped. "Who?" I asked.

"No idea, but boy, is it beautiful. I should have been there, but I'm adjusting to the new early morning schedule and struggling. Should I send it to you, Grace?"

"Oh n—"

"She'd love it," Jade said. "You absolutely should."

I glared, but didn't disagree. It was the best reminder I had of the two times we'd slept together.

"I'll send it, don't you worry." Kelsey winked.

"And on that note, I'm gonna get to work." I took my coffee and sipped on it. "I'll talk to you both later."

"Enjoy your peace and quiet!" Jade said with a wave.

My walk back was both peaceful and quiet. A few people waved. A few people's eyes wandered, but I was left alone.

Dean was a miracle worker. I *so* owed him one.

When I got to the shop, I messaged him.

> Your next five coffees are on me. Thank you for what you said at the bar last night.

DEAN

People are leaving you alone?

Yep. They're all scared of Daddy Dean.

I didn't think hard about what I said until after I'd flipped the sign and opened the shop. Then I realized he hadn't answered, and I wondered if I pushed it too far.

Can't really call you daddy if you're younger than me. Ignore me.

DEAN

You can call me whatever you want.

I stared at the message. This was the first sign of flirting in forever.

But he couldn't mean it that way. Could he?

Then he messaged again.

DEAN

When is your next appointment, by the way?
That's the anatomy scan.

I want to be there for that.

Will you still be in town?

I'll make sure I am.

You could stay at the house. Brooke is gone.

I think I'll take you up on that. I still have things to find and fix.

My heart picked up speed as I read his messages. Maybe I was reading way too far into this, but this was close to how we'd been when we first met, before responsibility got to us.

And I liked it more than I could say.

26

DEAN

Dad Company (But Sometimes Good Advice)

Dean Briggs: How do you deal with people you hate asking a ton of questions about your kid?

Comments:
James Marson: In theory, you can tell them nothing. But that never works for me . . .
Dean Briggs: It won't work here either. I have to tell them SOMETHING.
Robert Colt: Keep it simple, but they don't need to know the details.
Robert Colt: I'll let you in on a secret—a lot of parenting is just dealing with people you hate. Sometimes it's teachers. Sometimes it's other parents. Learn it now.
Dean Briggs: Got it. I'll see it as practice. It'll keep these people off the baby's mom, and I'll do anything for that.
Ryan Kim: Isn't this the girl you said you didn't wanna get attached to? Got some updates for us, buddy?

"You GOT A LOTTA NERVE, you know that, right?"

I had barely gotten out of my truck when I heard her voice. I sighed and turned to Tammy.

"No one said I didn't."

"You better treat that girl right, you hear me? None of this playboy shit."

If only she knew I hadn't been interested in any woman other than Grace since I met her. "Grace and I have already talked about that. And I'm not the kind of person who would leave my *child*. Or her."

Tammy watched me with narrowed eyes, and I waited for her to argue more. I doubted she would let it go.

"You got any pictures?"

I paused. "Of what?"

"The kid, dummy. I wanna see little Grace."

"You're supposed to yell at me."

"Don't tell me what to do. I wanna know stuff now. And close your mouth. You'll catch flies."

I did so, remembering that she only wanted information. She probably still didn't like me.

After getting my phone out, I showed her the picture of Grace's first sonogram. It was the only one she'd gotten, and I was eager to get more.

"That's a whole baby!"

"Did you think we were having half of one?"

She shook her head. "I mean, she's far along. Eighteen weeks is a lot, huh? I guess I owe you a congratulations."

"Uh, thanks."

Tammy gave me a smile and then handed my phone back to me. After, she turned and walked away.

"Wait a second. Is that seriously it? Don't you have more for me?"

"You'll be getting plenty throughout the day. Don't you worry. I got to see the baby, and that's all I wanted."

"Still . . ."

"You have it in your head that you seem to know who we are." She paused and turned back. "Now we just need to prove you wrong."

I only had a moment to take in what she'd said before someone else found me.

"There you are. I finally found ya!"

"Hey, Dale." I gave him a wave. "I'm assuming you have questions for me?"

"A few. You know, this is a big adjustment for all of us. We see Grace one way and now . . . you know."

"People change."

"Yes, they do. You taking good care of her?"

"I'm trying to."

"And this whole playboy thing you got goin' on?"

I had to take a breath before answering. This was standard. I knew it was coming. "That's not an issue." I said it tightly.

"Just don't go sleeping around, yeah? We don't need that kind of drama."

He was gone and I rolled my eyes when I was alone. This would be a long day. Hopefully, I'd get a break when I started work.

But I didn't. Kerry *ran* for me the second I was alone.

"Oh, thank the Lord I found you!" She was bouncing on the balls of her feet as she pulled out her phone. "I have a few things I didn't get to ask last night . . ."

I scrubbed a hand over my face, but answered everything the best I could. She wanted to know Grace's due date, how she was feeling, and if I was moving into town. The woman didn't stop, and I was acutely aware that if *she* knew something, everyone would know.

Still, I was glad to take it for Grace.

I hadn't gotten to see her this morning, and I hoped Brooke had actually apologized and she was feeling better.

The thought of doing this for her got me through everything that Kerry asked. And when she was appeased, someone else now blocked my way into the apartment I was working on.

"Annoying, aren't they?" Hugh muttered.

"Always. Maybe one day I'll turn into you."

"You've probably got more going for you than I do. Speaking of which . . ." He trailed off.

"You got something to ask?"

His nose scrunched. "Nah. I just wanna know if they scared you off from the bar. I'm owed a poker rematch."

Despite everything, I laughed. "The only thing that scared me off was you in my hotel room."

"Eh." He shrugged. "You have the same parts."

They did *not* look like his. "I'm . . . I'm not sure that—"

"Get over seeing my balls and play poker with me again. Can you do that, Cowboy?"

I struggled for words for a moment, but Hugh's eyes slowly narrowed. I was sure he was planning my death.

"I'll get over it."

"Good," he said before hobbling away.

I was almost an hour late, and I knew it was only the beginning.

And it was still so fucking worth it.

27

GRACE

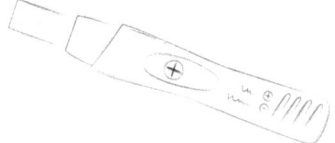

Strawberry Springs Neighborhood Watch

Tammy Jane: I'm speaking in code here. Our new Day is gonna be a cute one.

Comments:
Jade Clark: What did you do???
Kerry Winsor: WHAT DO YOU KNOW?!?!
Dale Garrett: Is anyone else confused?

MY DAY CONTINUED to be normal. No one broke down my door for information. No one gave me a second look.

I'd never seen a secret be revealed in Strawberry Springs that didn't blow up the entire town. I wasn't sure what kind of magic Dean had, but whatever it was, it worked.

I should have been feeling pure relief. I wanted to be, actually. But instead, there was an uneasiness in my stomach that grew as the day went on.

Was it from the town knowing? I had no idea. Was it guilt that Dean was inevitably dealing with everything while I had a peaceful day? Whatever it was, it refused to go away.

By the afternoon, I was worried that I was going to throw up at any given moment. I kept thinking about Mollie when she was pregnant and how often she got sick. Had I not made it out of pregnancy without morning sickness after all?

A quick Google search told me that while it was rare, morning sickness could develop in the second trimester. Was I seriously this cursed? That the very second I told people I was pregnant it would suddenly become extremely obvious because I'd be throwing up all the time?

It would be my luck.

I needed to tell Dean, but I could see the steady stream of people going in and out of the apartment he was working on. He had been doing it all for me, answering all of these questions and dealing with townspeople he didn't even like. I didn't want to worry him more than I had to.

I did, however, have a friend who had been through this. And it was time that I reached out.

> I feel like I could throw up. This is awful. I'm so sorry you had this.

MOLLIE

All of a sudden?

> Yeah. It's rare but possible.

Keep hydrated and take things slow.

> What do I do if I throw up?

> It feels like it could happen at any moment.

Once or twice isn't bad. Henry could help if it
doesn't stop. Or your OB-GYN, but I'm
guessing that's far away. You just don't need to
get dehydrated.

I'm sure this'll pass.

Hopefully.

I needed it to. The last thing I wanted was to be sick while Dean was staying with me. I didn't want anyone to see me while I was sick, but especially not him. He'd play nice, but no one wanted to deal with someone while they were throwing up.

Whenever I did get sick, I always tried to handle it myself. Being around Brooke, who never helped anyway, forced me to have to fend for myself. She was always the center of attention, and it was worse when someone else needed care. I was fine to melt into the shadows.

I wanted to do that today and pretend I was fine.

I wasn't getting any better. I'd had a few customers come in, but the shop had been mostly slow. So instead of suffering further, I decided to flip the sign and go home. Hopefully, I could sleep this off.

The house was quiet and I went straight to my room to lay down. My stomach turned, but I ignored it and closed my eyes, hoping sleep would make this better.

I was able to get a little bit of rest, but I never truly felt okay. Eventually, my stomach started to cramp and there was no more resting. I sat up and fought my own body for far too long. Then I heard sounds from the living room.

Dean was here and working on something. I had no idea what it was. I slowly made my way downstairs. He was on a ladder, working on one of the cracks in the doorway. I'd learned to ignore it since it popped up years ago.

"Hey," I said softly. "Thanks for working on that."

"You're up," he replied as he turned. "I figured it was time to make true on my promise to work on things. I was beginning to feel like a freeloader."

"You've been here three days."

"Which is three days too long." He eyed me up and down. "How are you feeling?"

I could only stare. How the hell did he know I wasn't feeling well? Was it obvious or something?

"W-why do you ask?"

"The whole town found out when you weren't ready, in case you forgot."

It was strange how a stomachache could make me completely forget about what was going on in my life. Yesterday had been my worst nightmare.

It was too bad today was hanging around the corner with a baseball bat.

"I've been fine."

His eyes narrowed as he looked me over, and I had a feeling that he knew I wasn't fine, even if he didn't know what was going on yet.

"You took on all of that for me," I said. "How are *you* doing?"

Normally, Dean would not let me get away with changing the subject. But obviously, the town had been rough today because he immediately rolled his eyes. "They're a typical small town. What else can I say?"

A slight stab of anxiety made its way through the unease in my stomach. "Did they do anything out of line?"

"That's not for you to worry about."

I blew out a breath. "I'm gonna worry about it anyway."

"I said I was taking this off your shoulders and I am. There wasn't anything that out of line. I just know how small towns can be and it's not my thing."

"You really don't like people in your business, do you?"

"Not really."

I wondered what he thought of me. I loved reading people and I enjoyed it when I could get a read on him. Did that bother him too?

"Let's figure out dinner. I would have gone to the diner, but I've had enough of Tammy for the day."

The idea of dinner brought back all of the nausea in my body. "You do whatever you wanna do. I'm not hungry."

His brow furrowed. "Did you already eat?"

"I had a big breakfast."

"Breakfast isn't enough. Something's wrong."

My jaw tightened. I could see why it would be annoying when I read him, because he was also good at doing the same thing to me. "I think I'm finally developing morning sickness."

"In the second trimester?"

"It's possible."

"I'm sure it is, but this could be something else."

Dean immediately strode to me, putting a hand on my forehead. "You don't feel hot. What did you eat this morning?"

"Brooke went out to get me something to eat. It was part of her apology."

"From the diner? I have a feeling Tammy cares a lot about her food being safe."

"No, not the diner. Brooke isn't allowed to go there because Tammy won't serve her. It was from somewhere else. I think it was from out near the interstate."

Dean got out his phone. It was obvious he was looking for the restaurant.

"I'm fine," I tried to tell him. "It'll pass. I'm sure it's just morning sickness hitting me late, like everything else has in this pregnancy."

"Was it a waffle place?" Dean asked as he looked at his phone.

"There were waffles, yes."

His lips pressed together. "Grace, if it was from there, they have terrible reviews of people getting sick after they eat there."

"No way." I took his phone from him and saw the reviews for myself. They were all absolutely disgusting. It did nothing for my nausea.

"I don't think it's very good to have food poisoning while pregnant."

I swallowed even as my nerves grew. "I'm sure it's not that. I can't be that unlucky."

But even as I said it, I felt my stomach turning more so now than it ever had before.

"Grace . . ."

"I'm gonna lie back down," I said. "That should help."

"Let me help—"

"I've got it." The words came out more forcefully than I meant them to. And Dean's eyes went wide. "I can handle this on my own."

"You don't have to handle anything on your own while I'm here."

The words sounded nice, but I still didn't want him to see me like this. I shook my head and made my way toward the stairs, hoping and praying that I would make it to my room and lay down before anything bad happened.

But my body betrayed me. The second I got up the first stair, a new wave of nausea hit me. My mouth watered and I immediately tried to stop it.

It did *not* work.

28

DEAN

Strawberry Springs Neighborhood Watch

Henry Connor: I don't usually do this, but I can't be the only one who heard Marjorie arguing with herself in the library, right? Should someone check on her?

Comments:
Jade Clark: Nah, I'm sure one side of her won the argument.
Mollie Wilson: Yeah, but that means she lost an argument with herself.
Henrietta Brown: She's just like that, guys.
Henry Connor: Does she have a family history of dementia or anything?
Henrietta Brown: Probably. Or she's just weird. I'd try to dig, but I realized a long time ago that you can't help a woman who doesn't want to be helped.
Marjorie Brown: Or I wanted Henry to be concerned about me. It's nice to be appreciated.
Henrietta Brown: Oh, for the love of GOD. We have full-time jobs and you're still a menace!

"I'M SO SORRY," Grace said from the toilet bowl. "I hate that I—"

She retched again, cutting off whatever she was about to say. I'd already cleaned up what had happened on the stairs while she ran to the bathroom, and now I needed to know she was okay.

Grace had looked pale when she'd gotten up from her nap. I'd told myself that it was because of what happened the day before.

I needed to trust my gut more often.

"It's okay," I said. "It really is."

"I must look so gross."

"It doesn't matter," I replied. "How are you feeling?"

"Terrible," she said. "Awful."

"Here, I can—"

"No, I'm fine. You don't need to come in here and see this."

My jaw clenched. "But—"

"Seriously, please don't."

That was the last thing she said before she went back to throwing up, but there was nothing *to* throw up. She was paler than I'd ever seen her and her skin looked clammy. And now she wouldn't let me get close enough to see anything else.

Grace seemed determined to handle this on her own, but I didn't know if I could take it. I wasn't the one going through it, but it felt like a part of me was. I'd been like this with Mom many times, and I knew I would need to ask for forgiveness, not permission, once again.

Grace *was* getting taken care of, whether she liked it or not.

"Be right back," I said. She only gave me a thumbs-up from the toilet bowl, but she was visibly shaking.

Hey, is your boyfriend working today?

I regretted the text as soon as I sent it. But Wren didn't waste time before answering.

WREN

Do I even wanna know?

Grace is sick.

Shit. Yeah, take her in like right now.

She attached Henry's number.

I'll keep you updated. Thanks.

Grace had made it clear she wanted to handle this on her own. I was going to make it clear that I wasn't that kind of man.

When I called the clinic, I expected a phone tree like most other doctors' offices I had been to. Instead, it was picked up on the third ring.

"This is Dr. Henry Connor."

The doctor answered the phone here? Well, that helped me not waste time.

"Uh, hi. I'm sure you've heard the news, so I'll get right to it. Grace is throwing up. A lot."

"How far along is she?"

"She's almost eighteen weeks."

"And how long has she been sick?"

"She's been feeling off all day, and she's been clutching her stomach. I don't think she's even had water. She never had morning sickness either, so this isn't normal."

"Bring her in," he said. "Are you in town, Mister . . ."

"I'm at her house."

There was silence on the line, and I wondered if one more

secret was about to come out. How good was this doctor at keeping quiet?

"I'll have an IV ready," he said in lieu of anything else. "I'll see you in a few minutes."

I took a shaky breath and went back to the bathroom.

"Grace," I said gently. "We need to go."

"I don't know *what* is happening right now, I'm not leaving this toilet. This is my emotional support toilet."

I would have laughed if she had been able to lift her head and look at me.

"I'm taking you to the clinic."

She finally met my gaze. "What? You're taking me to Henry?"

"He's the closest doctor."

"But I'm—"

"If you say fine, I'm carrying you to the doctor and letting him tell you you're not." I didn't let myself get this firm with her, but I was worried. More worried than I'd ever been.

And I needed her to let go and let me *in*.

"I'll drive."

"Grace." This woman. She would be the death of me.

"You don't need to deal with this. You had a long day at work and you had stuff you were in the middle of. I'll handle this on my own."

Oh, fuck everything. There was no way I was letting this happen. "Let's get one thing straight. You're not handling anything on your own, not as long as I'm here. This isn't a situation where you're left to fend for yourself when you need someone. When you need me, I am here. And when you think you don't need me, I'll be here anyway. You and me, we're a team. And you don't carry stuff on your own anymore."

In the back of my mind, I wondered if I would regret those words. This was getting very close to something I thought I would never say. But the words were true, and I needed her to understand that she was not going to handle this on her own.

Thankfully, it seemed to work. Her eyes grew wide as she stared at me and she finally nodded. "O-okay. Message received."

Dr. Henry Connor, in only one word, was professional.

Whatever questions he had for me, he kept to himself. He hooked Grace up to an IV and asked about what she ate. He also had an ancient fetal heartbeat monitor, and was able to pick up the baby's heartbeat.

I almost passed out when I heard it.

He also added pregnancy-safe anti-nausea medicine to Grace's IV, and her throwing up finally seemed to calm down. He was possibly the one person cooler than Wren was in an emergency, and I was sure both of us needed it.

After she finally seemed stable, I could see how exhausted Grace was. She wasn't as pale, but she nearly dozed off as Henry was talking to her, something she would never do in her right mind.

I could only stare at her. I was being as brave as possible, but seeing her like this was terrifying. It would have been like that even if she hadn't been pregnant, but her carrying our baby made that even scarier. This wasn't the most severe thing that could happen in pregnancy, but it was one of many things that could go wrong. So far, a lot of it was smooth sailing. Hell, half the time we didn't even know she was pregnant.

Henry also saw that she was tired, and he gave me a look and gestured for me to follow him. I did so reluctantly. I thought it wrong to leave her.

"Can we make this quick?" I asked.

"I'm just letting you know that I'll be typing up all the instructions so both of you can refer back to them."

"Is there anything else you wanna ask me?"

"Not really. Should there be?"

"I'm the man that everyone's going to with questions about what's happened. It's been a big shock to everyone, but I don't want her to deal with it, especially not now."

Henry slowly nodded. "I thought I'd heard something about that, but I don't have any questions for you. You seem like you've been through enough."

"What? The curiosity isn't gonna kill you?"

"I'm a little better than that. And I have a feeling that you're only half listening to me anyway. You'd rather be with her."

The discomfort hit me again, just like when I'd told her we were a team. "I'm just making sure she's okay."

"I would do the same for someone I cared about."

I'd spent my entire life trying to avoid caring about anyone but Mom. I told myself that it wasn't worth it, that I would get myself hurt, that I could live without caring.

And yet here I was, agreeing with a man who barely knew me.

I cared about Grace. I cared about her a lot.

It was one of the most terrifying realizations I'd ever had. Not because I didn't want to. I needed to care about her. I needed to care about her and her child. *Our child*. But usually, caring didn't involve me.

"I'm sorry. Did I step on some toes here?" Henry's cheeks colored.

"No, it's just been a long day."

He hummed and I wondered if he knew that I was lying to him. But I glanced toward the room that Grace was in, eager to get going, and that spurred him into action.

"Will you also let me pay her balance?"

Henry paused in his typing, but nodded.

I was doing a terrible job of hiding that I cared about her. That was the worst part of this all. I was better at staying away so I didn't get myself in this situation.

And yet here I was.

Henry finished up the notes and let me pay for Grace's treatment.

"You're gonna wanna keep that between us," I told him. "She hates it when I do things like this."

Henry chuckled. "I've known Grace since I moved here, and that tracks. She's always had her hands full with Brooke. And it seems like she still does, even though Brooke's moved out. It's a good thing she has someone now."

"It's not romantic or anything. You know that, right?" I had to say it, though every time I reminded someone of it, the words came out with less bite.

Henry smiled. "Sure, definitely not."

"Don't start. I'll tell you the same thing I've told everyone else. I don't date women."

"I didn't date either until I met Wren."

"The town was okay with that?"

"The town doesn't get to say what I do or don't do. Sure, they were excited for me when I finally showed interest in someone, but my life is my life, and the same goes for you."

"I don't think the town would respond well to me sleeping around."

"Have you been?"

The words hit me like a train. "Not here, of course. Or . . . anywhere, really."

"I'm not gonna pry because we barely know each other, but if it's not been here and it's not been anywhere else, then what's going on?"

"I . . . I'm not sure I wanna know."

Henry's eyebrows rose. "The world doesn't end when you fall for someone, you know, especially not someone like Grace. In fact, it's when it begins."

"I'm not falling for anyone. Grace is amazing, but that side of me is dead."

Henry only raised one eyebrow this time.

"It really is. Trust me, there's no chance."

"Sure, whatever you say."

I didn't know why the need to convince Henry was so strong. Normally, I wouldn't want anyone to be in my business because they would talk, but Henry had already told me that wasn't his style.

So, I wasn't sure if I needed to convince him or *myself*.

29

GRACE

Strawberry Springs Neighborhood Watch

Mollie Wilson: Have you guys SEEN the drama about the diner about an hour away? They've always been shady, but apparently they made a lot of people sick recently. I almost stopped there while visiting my mom!

Comments:
Tammy Jane: Anyone with sense knows my place is the only place to go! Never gotten under a 100 on my health score, thank you very much.
Marjorie Brown: What about the time I found a press-on fingernail in my soup?
Tammy Jane: HEY! That's supposed to be on the lowdown!!!
Mollie Wilson: Lowdown??? What???
Wren Hackett: I think she means the down-low. Don't worry, no more nails can be found in soup.
Kelsey Marie: My bad, y'all!
Mollie Wilson: Should we be worried about them being in coffee then?

Kelsey Marie: I've gotten my shit together!!! Just ask Theo. I cause WAY less problems now.

I DRIFTED in and out of sleep in the clinic chair, but one thing stayed with me through it all.

Mortification.

To some, accepting help was easy. To me, it felt like I'd failed.

I wore my independence like a badge of honor. I didn't need anyone. Even if I suffered, I'd be okay alone.

And after how today went, I wasn't so sure I would have been.

I heard the door open and Dean shuffled into the room. I peeked through one eye at him.

"You're awake?" he asked as he got close.

"That might be a strong term."

"All that matters is that you feel better." Instead of keeping the usual distance between the two of us, his hand held mine. In my sleep-heavy mind, the physical touch was just what I needed.

I nodded. "IVs do the trick. Thanks for bringing me in. It was the right call."

"Anytime," he said.

The door opened again and Henry walked in. Dean's hand loosened, but I gripped harder. If I were in my right mind, I'd know that Dean wouldn't want Henry to see anything. I'd let him pull away. But Dean's hand was warm and I wanted it there.

And when he didn't fight me, I felt like I'd won the lottery.

"Dean has notes just in case anything else happens, but I

will say to both of you that if this happens again, I recommend you go to a hospital."

Dean's eyes met mine. I had no doubts that if it did start again, he would be on top of getting me where I needed to go.

I nodded. "Will do, thank you, Henry."

"Feel better," he said. "And good luck with everything."

When Henry had moved into town, some people were put off by his professionalism. But in this moment, it was one of the greatest things I'd ever seen. He could have grilled me or Dean for a ton of information, but it seemed like he was most focused on making sure I was okay.

Wren had gotten so lucky. Mollie too. They'd paired off with perfect men. I didn't think it was possible for guys to have so many green flags. Dean had a lot too.

If only he were emotionally available.

Despite my mortification and despite me trying to fight him on all of his help, I enjoyed every second of having him around. I hadn't realized how much loneliness had crept up on me over the years.

I supposed I should have been happy that I had a friendship with Dean. That might be all it stayed, but it was nice.

But I was at that part of being sick where I only felt sad for myself. The exhaustion was hitting me full force, and even though I wasn't throwing up anymore, I didn't feel like myself. I felt like a little kid again, back before I realized I needed to handle things on my own. I used to crawl into bed with Mom every single time I got sick. I'd want someone to hold me and tell me that it would be okay. Eventually, I got over that need. Except in moments like these.

Dean helped me to the truck, and I let him carry some of my weight. Now that it was over, I realized just how bad that could have been. I'd been so worried about trying to appear like I was fine that I let something go that could have been very dangerous.

This independence mixed with people-pleasing was only hurting me.

"I'm sorry that I fought you on bringing me here." I said it when he'd gotten into the truck.

"It's okay."

"It's not. I should have listened. You have every right to be pissed at me, for that, and for making you hold my hand in front of Henry. I'm sure you didn't want him to see that."

Dean was quiet for a second and then I heard him huff out a breath of air. "Grace, you need to know that I'm never gonna stay mad at you for long. You're okay and the baby's okay. That's all I care about. And whatever Henry saw, Henry saw. You were sick. It's okay to want to hold someone's hand when you're sick." He reached over to brush a curl off of my cheek, and just that little touch almost sent me clinging to him. "Rest on the way home. I've got it from here."

All I could do was nod and lean against the window. What had I done to deserve a man like this?

As my eyes closed, I listened to the sound of his breathing. Just that was more comforting than being alone.

Was that what things around Dean had started to feel like? Comforting?

We would always be tied together in some way, and I could try to explain all of this as me feeling friendly toward him. But with the way that I hung on to every one of his breaths, I knew the truth. I knew it even while sick and exhausted.

I had feelings for Dean. They were terrible, useless, annoying feelings, and yet they were here. I was going to get my heart broken. I knew it, but in the moment when we drove back to my house, I could pretend that he would someday feel the same way.

When we got home, my plan was to rouse myself enough just to get up the stairs and get to my room. Dean had different plans because he opened the truck door for me and carried me all the way inside.

It once again would have been romantic if it hadn't been for the fact that he didn't believe in romance.

"Wait," I said as we walked to the hallway. "I want a shower."

"You're exhausted."

"I'm exhausted and stinky. I would like to only be exhausted."

Dean pressed his lips together and I could tell he didn't like the idea of me showering alone. If we were in a different scenario, I'd suggest for him to shower with me. Not for anything untoward, but just to have him around.

"Fine, but I'll stay next to the door just in case something goes wrong."

"I can live with that."

He slowly set me down and I shut myself in the bathroom. One look at myself told me that showering was definitely the right thing to do. My hair was a mess. I was pale. And the smell of myself almost made me throw up again.

I made it quick, knowing I was working with borrowed energy. When I was done, Dean was waiting with clothes.

"So you did leave me."

"Only for a second. I figured you'd want something clean to wear."

He was very right about that. I took them and slowly changed into them, and I was officially done with my shower.

The second my head hit the pillow, sleep tried to claim me. Dean was still in the doorway, looking at me as if I could fall apart at any second. Today was the reminder that I could.

But his lingering reminded me of something else that I wanted. I assumed nothing but time would fix how I felt.

Having him walk into my room and lay on my bed next to me sure would too.

Sleep made everything fuzzy. It seemed easier and easier to ask him.

"Stay," I muttered.

"What?"

There was a part of me that was still lucid enough to know that I was making a mistake by asking him this. This could ruin everything. But as much as that part of me tried to get my attention, the need to not be alone was so much louder.

"I don't wanna be by myself. I'm sad and sick, and I'm always alone."

He was silent for so long, I almost drifted entirely to sleep. "I don't do things like that, Grace."

And yet I was still awake enough for that to hurt. My eyes grew wet.

"Okay." I wouldn't push him, but I couldn't hide the crack in my voice.

I expected him to make his escape, and then tomorrow, we would pretend that this never happened.

"Dammit," he muttered. I had no idea what he was so frustrated with, but then the bed dipped with his weight. "I'll stay until you fall asleep."

The heat from his body was intoxicating. I could only blame my tiredness and sickness for what I did next. Instead of giving him space, like I always did when he was awake, I shuffled closer. He must have laid down because my cheek was pressing against his arm tightly. I wanted to touch more of him, so I wound my arms around him.

His breath stuttered, but he didn't push me away. I'd be mortified about this tomorrow, but for tonight, I drifted off, staying as close to him as I possibly could.

30

DEAN

Strawberry Springs Neighborhood Watch

Nicole Rudder: Is this anyone's dog? I found it on my property last night. He's cute but wary of people.

Comments:
Jade Clark: Not mine, but I want to pet it.
Nicole Rudder: He growls whenever I try.
Jackie Anne: I know I'm supposed to be the resident animal charmer, but that doesn't look like a dog . . . **@Atticus Thompson**, any thoughts?
Atticus Thompson: DO NOT ENGAGE. THAT IS A COYOTE.
Henry Connor: Did you say you tried to pet it???

WHEN I WAS A KID, I used to try to sneak into Mom and Dad's room all the time. They'd chalked it up to a fear of the dark, but in reality, I just hated sleeping by myself.

Then I found out what love was, and how much I wanted it. I used to daydream about what it would be like to wake up next to someone else.

But then that dream died when my heart had been broken. Ever since, it had been locked away in a vault, never to see the light of day.

And then Grace softly asked me to stay with her. I'd tried to say no, but the second her eyes watered, I knew that I had no choice but to. I should have left when she was asleep, but I didn't. I stayed, listening to the sounds of her sleeping, knowing that she was okay after everything that had happened today.

There was no hope for me.

And when I woke up, I knew it was even worse than I had previously thought.

Because when we'd fallen asleep, Grace was clinging to me. Now, in the light of day, I was clinging to her as if she could vanish at any given moment.

She was facing the window and I was pressed against her back. One of my arms was underneath her neck and the other one was around her rib cage, keeping her as close to me as I possibly could. If she woke up, there was no way for me to explain how I'd ended up in this position.

Other than to say that she must have rolled away from me throughout the night and I followed her.

I had to force myself away from where she slept. It went against every fiber of my being, but I did it. When I stood, a cold seeped through my bones unlike any other I'd ever felt. It had nothing to do with the weather outside.

This would end badly. I was going to get hurt. These were all reminders that I needed to tell myself. And yet all I wanted to do was go climb back into bed with Grace. And not for sex. Just so I was near her.

A knock on the door only added to my shit mood because I had a feeling it was Brooke returning from Nashville.

She just left. Could I not catch a break?

But when I opened the door, I saw it was much worse than that. Kerry stood with a plate in her hands. When she saw me, her eyes grew as wide as the moon. Mine probably did too.

"Dean?" she asked.

"Shit," I muttered.

"Are you—am I interrupting something? You can tell me if I am. I can vanish."

"No, you're not interrupting anything. Why are you here?"

"Well, I heard in the Facebook group that Grace was seen leaving Henry's clinic looking very sick. You were helping her to the truck, which makes sense why you'd be here. And here I was thinking you were staying here or something." She laughed. "You're not, right?"

I really wanted to go back to bed now.

"Yes, Grace was sick. She's still asleep and recovering."

Kerry hummed. "A nonanswer. Interesting. Will you please give her this? This is a bunch of toast made with special butter that doesn't upset stomachs. I was very sick when I was pregnant with my son, and it is a godsend."

I didn't want to admit it, but this was actually helpful. I was so bad in the kitchen that I wasn't sure that I could toast bread without burning it.

"That's very nice of you. Hopefully she'll be up to eating it."

Kerry stared at me, and I wondered if she was about to push for more information. "So, are you okay?"

"What?"

"Are you okay? If she was sick, it had to be pretty scary."

"It . . . was. But it turned out fine."

Kerry slowly nodded and her eyes started to my truck—which I should start parking farther back in Grace's driveway—

and then back to me. "You know, if you've been staying here with her . . ."

"Please don't." I would beg if I needed to.

"Then it's good that she's not alone, especially if she's sick."

That wasn't where I expected Kerry to go with this. "This is just while I'm in town."

"So, for the foreseeable future, I guess?"

"It's like I said yesterday. I have no idea."

Kerry hummed. "Well, I won't keep you. I know you have a lot of denial to be in, and I have gossip to find. Don't worry, though, I won't say anything about what I've learned here. I do have some decorum, even if it *is* newly learned. And if I did say anything, I have a feeling the girls and Hugh would cuss me out. They're rather protective of you two. It seems like you have a good support group here." She gave a little half wave, turned on her heel, and headed back to her car to leave.

I was sure she meant well, but her words did nothing for my rising anxiety.

It was only made worse when I heard footsteps and saw Grace slowly making her way down the stairs. I tried to shove it all away and focus on her.

"Hey, how are you feeling?"

When I spoke, she paused and looked me up and down. Her cheeks grew dark, and I wondered if she somehow knew what I'd done overnight.

"Better. Not one hundred percent, but I'm alive."

She sounded more like herself, not the version of her that needed me to stay with her last night. I would never admit it out loud, but I missed that.

"Kerry came by."

"Kerry?" Grace frowned. "And you answered the door?"

"I thought it might be Brooke."

"Brooke has a key and doesn't believe in ringing a doorbell. I'm guessing everyone's gonna know that you're staying here."

"She said she would keep it to herself, but they might."

"I suppose it's not the end of the world. I just wonder what they're gonna think about it."

"They can keep their damn thoughts to themselves."

"It wouldn't be anything bad. It would mostly be them wondering when we're gonna get together." Her cheeks were a delicate shade of pink. "That's probably not a good idea for us."

It wasn't, but I could certainly think about it, especially after what had happened the night before.

"Do you feel up to eating?" The topic change was all I could do. There was no way I could think about this for much longer and look her in the eye.

"The idea of food doesn't make me wanna run to the toilet, so I think that's a good sign."

I went to the kitchen and set a few pieces of Kerry's toast on a plate for Grace. We sat at the dining room table, and as she took slow bites of her food, I got a text.

WREN

Henry told me you might need a day off. Which is fine. I hope you're both okay.

> Grace seems to be on the mend. I have a feeling she's gonna try to work, which means she'll think that I'll also work. But I'm debating whether or not I'll let her win that one.

I'd love to see a battle of the wills between you two.

> It's always entertaining, but I usually win.

You better.

"Good conversation?" Grace asked, pulling me out of my thoughts.

"Sorry." I put my phone away. "How are you feeling?"

"I'm really fine. Going slow, but I'm keeping it down."

"That's good," I said with a sigh of relief.

"Don't let me keep you. I'll take the day off from the shop and you can get to whatever you need to get to."

"I'll take whatever time I need to." Especially now that Wren wouldn't kill me for it.

"Dean, I promise I'm okay. I finished my toast. I feel more like myself."

I was getting too protective. I was getting too . . . everything with her. I needed to be careful.

"You'll call me if you need anything?"

"Surprisingly, I think I learned my lesson. I know to always call you now."

I was sure she didn't mean it in any type of way, but the words hit me hard. I liked being the one that she called. I never wanted that to change.

I was in so much trouble.

31

GRACE

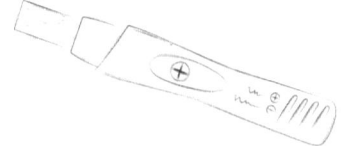

Strawberry Springs Neighborhood Watch

Kerry Winsor: @Dale Garrett, do you have something called a labubu? Tommy wants one for his birthday.

Comments:
Tammy Jane: Is that some sort of lab table?
Marjorie Brown: Is that a slang term for a lobotomy? If so, I need one too.
Jade Clark: Guys, it's a purse charm, but it was a trend that ended a while ago. I would order one online. I doubt Dale has them.
Marjorie Brown: A purse charm? That's dumb as hell. A name that good should be reserved for something that deserves it.

WHILE NOT OPENING up the shop was the right thing to do, it left me with far too much time to think. I was on the couch trying to watch a baking show, but my mind kept drifting to last night.

I wished I didn't, but I remembered it all. I remembered needing someone, and Dean turning me down before changing his mind.

And I was once again wondering what else he could change his mind on. I didn't want to think this way. This wouldn't do me any good. I was starting to think I didn't care about what good came from it.

Thankfully, my phone rang and I was pulled out of my thoughts. I thought it might be Dean checking in, but I saw his mom's face pop up on my screen. I'd told him to give her my number, and this was the first time she'd used it.

"Hi, Virginia," I said. "It's nice to hear from you."

"Sorry it took me so long to call. I was getting a few things in order around here. I won't keep you since I'm sure you're busy with the shop, but—"

"I'm free actually. I have a day off."

"Oh, really? I thought you were open during the week."

"I usually am. I was sick last night."

She gasped. "Sick? What happened? Are you okay?"

I could see where Dean got his concern from. "I'm okay, and so is the baby. I just ate something bad and took the day to recover."

"Does Dean know? He could've helped."

"He was here, actually. He's been around for a few days."

A second passed before Virginia answered. "Really? Normally it's hard to get him to leave the city."

"He said he wanted to help me with my house a little. I'm sure he misses Nashville a lot." As I said it, I wasn't so sure. He only mentioned Nashville when he talked about the things he didn't like about Strawberry Springs. I never heard about it on its own.

Was there a meaning there I hadn't realized?

"It's where he likes to stay, but I'm so happy he's been there with you for a little while. I'm sure it's good for both of you to get to know each other."

"It is. We're making it work."

"He talks highly of you."

My cheeks heated and I was glad this was only a phone call. "That's nice. It would be awkward if he didn't."

"I'd smack him into place if he didn't. And if he steps out of line, you let me know."

After all the stories I'd seen about nightmare mothers-in-law, it was nice that mine was so kind. Even if she wasn't my mother-in-law. She was . . . my baby daddy's mom?

Fuck. I still had to find a better name for that.

"Now, I did call for a reason, I promise. You'll have to bear with me, dear. I get distracted easily."

"It's not a problem." And it really wasn't. I'd spent most of the day alone. I didn't mind the company of someone else's ramblings.

"Do you have any ultrasound pictures you wouldn't mind sharing with me?"

"Yeah, I have one that I can text you. And there's the big ultrasound next week."

She gasped. "Already? Oh, please send me photos of that too. I wanna make a scrapbook, especially since I live so far away . . ." She trailed off.

"I have an extra room." I said it before I could stop myself. "You could always stay with me."

"You wouldn't mind?"

"Not at all."

It would have to be when Dean wasn't here, and he'd been staying more than I expected. I didn't mind it, but I also knew I couldn't give Brooke's room out either. I'd also have to make my third bedroom a nursery eventually.

"I might take you up on that. Have you offered Dean the same thing? I bet he would save money on a hotel."

"Yes, I did."

"Don't take it personally that he turned you down. He's a little finicky about attachment, but—"

"He didn't. Turn me down, I mean."

But Virginia seemed so sure, and I was already reading between the lines. Had he already stepped out of his usual for me?

Were things different?

"Really?" She sounded like she'd won the lottery. "This is great! Maybe he—" She stopped herself. "How has it been?"

I knew when someone was fishing for information. "He's a very good guest."

"Interesting."

"Is . . . there anything else you *want* to happen?"

"Boy, do I." She laughed. "I've been waiting for years for him to settle down, but he never wants to. Please tell me that streak's been broken."

I wished I could tell her that. I hated to be the one to break her hope. "Unfortunately not. I'm sorry, Virginia."

She let out a long sigh. "I suppose that's in character for him."

"Maybe it's for the best. He obviously enjoys his fun."

"He wasn't always like this, you know. Once upon a time, he was a little romantic! Can you believe that?"

"It's . . . hard to." And it was. I wondered what I would have thought of that version of him. I wondered where he went. I had the right to pry, and I couldn't help my curiosity. "When was he like that?"

"Back in high school. About a decade ago now. I don't

remember all the details, but he came home one day and told me he'd never date again. I thought he would give up eventually, but he's stubborn. And I suppose there are a lot of women his age who don't mind simply getting what they want, right?"

I winced. I was one of those women. It had been good. Amazing, even. But now I was tied to him and wanting more.

"Right. It's about the fun."

"He's not the kind of guy to only care about the fun, which is what I've never understood. Maybe I was just wanting grand-kids. And now I have one on the way! You're gonna be a great mom, Grace."

I wanted to ask her to tell me more about Dean so I could figure out what had happened. But I wasn't sure that was a good idea. I didn't need to pry into his life.

"Thank you, Virginia. And I bet you'll be an amazing grandma too."

We talked for a good hour about how the pregnancy was going and how it compared to hers. I told her how I was still struggling with hairs growing in places I didn't want them to, and she was thrilled to find another woman who'd gone through the same thing.

Despite my downtrodden mood about Dean, it was nice to talk to someone else and get my mind off of it.

But the second I said my goodbyes and hung up the phone, all the thoughts flooded back.

I was at an impasse, unsure of whether to stuff my feelings in a box or try to see if Dean could ever feel the way I did.

Whether I pulled back, jumped in, or did nothing, it all ended the same way.

And I was terrified.

32

DEAN

Strawberry Springs Neighborhood Watch

Kerry Winsor: Dean's at the diner, everyone! Line up if you have questions!

Comments:
Jackie Anne: I'm too shy to say hello . . . one day I will.
Jade Clark: He's gonna hate you all.
Kerry Winsor: He offered!
Jade Clark: Don't tell people to line up!

"Okay, but what if we all got together and threw a massive party to say we all support Grace? Then she'll know we only wanna help, and we can break the embargo!"

I wanted one meal to myself. Just one. And since Center Point Diner was the one place I could get decent food, I'd braved the chance that Tammy would corner me for questions and came in.

She wasn't my biggest problem. Kerry was.

"For God's sake. It's killing you, isn't it?" Tammy was back with my food. "Don't you know not to ruin a man's breakfast?"

"I just need to talk to him."

"Get to your own table, or so help me, I will ban you from the diner." Kerry whined, but slowly got up. "There. Now you owe me one."

I blew out a breath. "Thank you."

"Didn't have breakfast with Grace this morning?" Tammy asked.

"Why would I have breakfast with Grace?"

She paled, a common reaction whenever they hinted at me living with her—a detail none of them should've known. "Well, I just figured it would be . . . economical, if you were staying with the woman you're here for."

"Wow. What a conclusion. How long did Kerry last?"

"Two days."

"That's longer than I thought."

"She tried. Now are you gonna tell me or not?"

I sighed. "Grace makes eggs on toast every morning. I'm happy she has breakfast and it's nice of her to share, but if I ate it one more time, I might have started crying."

"Eggs on toast is pretty tame for a pregnant lady."

"She douses it in hot sauce and sour cream, which . . . makes no sense, but I know better than to say anything."

"You're smarter than you look." She gave me a half smile. "And it seems like you're treating her right. She hasn't kicked you out yet."

"Grace wouldn't do that, but I'm still gonna make sure I don't do anything to upset her."

"And I thought it was bad when you kept staring at her." Her smile was downright vicious as she walked off, and I had to resist the urge to groan.

I should have eaten the eggs on toast. Or hell, just the toast. Grace's company would have been preferred.

Still, the food was good, and I was able to get a reprieve from the same thing every morning. Once I was done, I'd get a little bit of work done before taking Grace to her appointment.

For the first time in a little while, I'd finally be back in a city. Strawberry Springs hadn't been terrible, but I looked forward to a dining experience where I didn't have to spill my life story.

I didn't know how many more questions about Grace I could take.

I hadn't been able to stop thinking about the night I slept in her bed. I had a feeling she hadn't either. I'd waited for her to ask me about it, but she never did. She only watched me with a furrowed brow, and I had no idea what she was looking for.

Did she want me to admit it? Did she want me to apologize?

Did she want me to do it again?

That might have been the worst of all the options because I knew that I wouldn't hesitate to do it if she asked. There wasn't a question she could pose that I would say no to.

She didn't know it yet, but I was wrapped around her finger. There was no getting out. She had me, even if she didn't want me. The time I spent in Strawberry Springs didn't help, but there was no way I could leave.

And that was fucking terrifying.

I didn't even want to leave for Clyde. I told him that things had been rough here with Grace being sick and I wasn't sure when I would be back. The more that I thought about leaving her, the less I wanted to make plans to return.

He understood and told me to take my time, but the fact that I had even said I didn't want to come back in the first place was alarming. He'd offered a few jobs in Knoxville that were coming up, where I could be closer to Strawberry Springs if I needed to be. I told him I'd find a way to work those. At least I would get to see him.

Grace opened the door only seconds after I turned off the engine and got out of the truck. She was in a skirt again, this time burnt orange, with a white shirt tucked in. I could see her belly openly now, and every time I did, it made my heart jump into my throat. There was no denying she was pregnant.

She looked beautiful. She seemed to glow a little bit more every single day. I was lucky that I had gotten to be here for so much of it. I might have been sleeping on a tiny twin bed and developing permanent back issues, but it was worth it.

"Do I look okay?" she asked as she brushed nonexistent crumbs off her skirt. "Now that everyone knows, I can go back to my normal wardrobe."

"You don't just look okay. You look fucking stunning. I missed those skirts."

Both of us had carefully avoided anything that could be considered flirting ever since I found out she was pregnant. This was the first time I'd let anything slip.

Grace's eyes grew wide as she stared at me. "R-really? I missed them too."

That was the best response she could have given considering the circumstances. It was almost professional the way she said it.

It reminded me of my place.

She began to walk to the truck, but stopped herself and turned back to me. "I would have thought that seeing me throw up would have completely ruined the vibes. Do you somehow still find me hot after that?"

"Nothing can ruin the vibes," I replied. "You're hot all the time."

She smiled the same way she did when she was leading me to the Treasure Trove to have sex with me.

"You should compliment me more often. I like how it sounds."

That was enough for me to continue.

"You're so beautiful all the time, but seeing you pregnant is really something. Your skin is literally glowing. Your smile is even more beautiful now that your cheeks are fuller. You catch my eye every time you walk by. You always did, but now I can't look away."

Her eyes grew wide and I realized my compliments weren't flirty, they were deeper, coming from the heart rather than anywhere else.

"Sometimes a girl needs to hear all of that," she said. "You're good at this."

"Not as much as you think." I led her to the truck, pushing away any other thoughts. "We should get going, though."

"Yeah, we should."

I needed to keep it together.

But the more I wanted to do for her, the harder it was keeping myself in check.

"So," she said as I started the truck, "there's a chance we might get to know the gender today."

My heart stuttered. "There's a lot of stuff we'll get to know today."

"Are you nervous?" she asked. I didn't know how she'd figured it out, but she always did.

"Terrified."

She blew out a breath. "Yeah, me too. A lot of people wait until after this point to tell family and friends, but I didn't get so lucky."

"Fucking Brooke."

She let out a sigh. "Yeah. Brooke is a piece of work."

"Have you heard from her?"

"Nope. Not at all. Is it bad that I'm grateful?"

"After what she did, no."

"I still *feel* bad, though. She's my only remaining family."

"That doesn't change the fact that she's a terrible person."

"I know," Grace said quietly. "I really wish she wasn't. It would be nice to be able to share all of this with her and have her care about it, but she's just not that kind of person. She never was."

"You can share it all with me."

"I know. It's good to have a friend who cares."

Friends was exactly what we should have been. It was what we'd stay.

But I fucking hated that word.

I was cracking at the seams. Living with her was a terrible idea, and yet I knew I'd never leave.

"Do you wanna find out the gender today?" I asked. All of this had been so vague in my mind. I knew that there was a baby coming. I was working hard because of it, yet I still hadn't wrapped my mind around it.

"That's what I wanna ask you. We're doing this as a team, right?"

"We are." Just the thought of being a team filled me with a feeling I couldn't describe. I'd been the one to start this and it still hit me hard. "I'm not sure, but it would help to figure out the gender so we have ideas for our nursery."

The room I'd been staying in would eventually be one. I hated the idea of not living with Grace anymore, but maybe it was a good thing for me to be forced out.

"Right, *that*." She let out a sigh. "I still haven't cleared the room out, and getting a crib? Baby furniture? That sounds over-whelming."

I turned to her. "I can—"

"Just in the last week, you cleaned out my gutters and

worked on the front porch. You've done enough. Don't make me lock you out of the house."

"Well, at least it would be safer than you leaving the door unlocked for me all the time."

"I left the door unlocked all the time before. It's not just you."

I blinked. "Do you not lock the front door?"

"I live in the country." She shrugged. "No one locks up their stuff."

"That's so unsafe."

"Did your mom lock up?"

"She did after all the city people moved in."

"Well, you're city people. So I guess I'll start."

This woman. Did she know what she did to me? I could see her smile from the corner of my eye.

"Lock the door, but not just because of me."

"Sure, sure."

"Grace—"

"*Anyway*, back to the baby." She changed the subject forcefully. I knew I'd be bringing this up later. "I've heard through the grapevine that Kerry's wondering if we're having a gender reveal party."

I glared. "Did she ask you? She better not have—"

"No, she asked Jade, and I happened to walk into the shop during the conversation. She played it off and ran away."

"Good."

"It's a fair question, though. I should say yes, right? I bet the town would be happy if I did."

"It doesn't matter what the town thinks. What do *you* think?"

She paused. "I wanna celebrate it once. But not yet. So maybe I should have a baby shower."

"Kerry will want to plan it then."

"I was thinking Mollie should."

I laughed. "You're gonna betray Kerry like that?"

"Kerry wouldn't know subtle if it smacked her in the face. Mollie would. And she's done all this recently. I bet she knows how to run one. If she has time. She's always up to something."

I hadn't met Mollie, but I'd heard of her through Wren. With how Grace talked about her, I almost wanted to.

We were heading out of Strawberry Springs, but my mind drifted back to the tiny little town. How would Kerry react to Mollie planning the baby shower? Would Tammy still play nice or was she harboring resentment for me over this entire situation? Would Hugh go to the baby shower? Would he try to gamble there?

Despite how much I didn't like small towns, I was curious about all of the things I'd seen in Strawberry Springs. It had to be because I was spending far too much time there.

Or I was starting to like the place, which possibly made me the biggest idiot in the world.

I was fine up until we checked in at the doctor. Mostly fine, at least. But then my nerves only got worse. Grace seemed to be suffering the same fate.

"Being nervous doesn't mean anything's wrong," I said as we waited.

"That actually helps," she replied. "I just don't want anything to go wrong."

"Me either. But you're not alone if it does."

She nodded, and my hand curled around hers. I hadn't done this since she was sick.

It felt right.

"Grace Day?" a nurse called. Grace shot up and pulled her hand out of mine.

"Here!" she said, and gestured for me to follow her.

"Brought a guest this time?" the nurse asked as she looked me up and down.

"Yep. He'll be here a lot."

"Hi, I'm April. Are you the dad?"

"Yeah," I replied. "I'm the dad."

It felt monumental to say that. It was a mere fact that I was the baby's father, but after what Grace had thought of me when she'd first found out, I'd worked hard to make sure she knew I was more than a sperm donor.

I'd done that, but I hadn't given myself credit for it.

"Well, it's great to meet you. I'll be taking you back for the ultrasound."

"We're getting started already?" I asked.

"We try to move as quickly as possible," April said, waving for us to follow her. We went into a dark room and Grace laid on the table. April got the machine started before she looked for something and sighed.

"Forgot the gel," she said. "Be right back."

She was gone before either of us could say anything.

"Feeling okay?" I asked.

"No," Grace muttered. "But I'll feel better once this starts. I'm just worried I'll get bad news again."

"Everything's been normal."

"I know. But ever since I was diagnosed with PCOS, it feels like my body wants things to go wrong. Out of everything I've been through, this is almost easy. Feels like the second shoe's gonna drop any moment now."

"Do I need to remind you that you were almost hospitalized because you were throwing up and the bad results from the first glucose test? It's not all been easy."

"Okay, you have me there, but considering how bad my PCOS used to be, this is still easy. Trust me."

Without thinking about it, I grabbed her hand. "The past doesn't affect the future. You may have PCOS, but as far as we know, things are developing normally. We're not completely out of the woods for things going wrong, but your body is doing something monumental here. Even if it's had issues in the past, it doesn't change how things are going now."

Grace squeezed my hand. "How do you always know what I need to hear?"

"I watch, I listen, and I want to be here for you."

She looked at me, and I swore that her eyes were glistening. She opened her mouth to say something else, but we were interrupted when April came back into the room.

"Sorry about that. I forgot to replace the bottle of gel. We can start now."

I spent a second trying to get back my bearings. Talking to Grace so openly had me teetering on the edge of something massive. But I should have known I would be hit once more when the ultrasound started.

My breath was knocked out of my body when I saw my baby flash on the screen. First, the tech checked their heartbeat, and it was a stark reminder that this was *real*. This was happening.

I was gonna be a dad.

I was terrified. But I was also *so* excited.

The tech showed us a profile of their face. Ten fingers and ten toes. I saw all of it.

We'd made that baby. Grace and me. They were ours.

"I can print some of these out for you," April said. "Do Mom and Dad both want one?"

I loved the sound of being referred to as a dad.

"Yes," I said.

"Two copies?"

Grace nodded. "One for my place and one for his."

My place was in the middle of the city, and it no longer felt like mine. I'd have to figure out how I felt about *that* later.

April glanced between us, and I had a feeling she was wondering what we were to each other. Her eyes lingered on me, and I saw the familiar double take ladies did before they would come and talk to me.

It used to fill me with excitement, but I didn't want that this time. Today was for *Grace*.

Every day was for Grace.

Still, I gave her a polite smile and April's cheeks darkened. I quickly averted my eyes back to Grace, hoping that she didn't notice anything.

"Can you see the gender?" I asked.

"Honestly, no." She stared at the screen and pressed a few buttons. "They're being stubborn in there. We can try to move them to get them to uncross their legs."

"It's okay," Grace said. "I don't have to know today. I don't know if I have to know at all."

"Not sure? Some parents don't find out." She laughed. "What about you, future daddy? Do you wanna know?" April's voice lowered when she spoke to me, and I knew there was no way Grace didn't catch that.

"I'm good with whatever Grace wants."

"Fair enough. We'll just get what we need here and get you to seeing the doctor."

April finished the exam in a few minutes. Then we were heading to the room to meet with Grace's doctor.

Thankfully, April didn't make any moves. I may not have been the boyfriend type, but I hoped I could play the part long enough to get out of here without having anyone hit on me.

I hadn't thought that Grace had noticed anything, but I should have known she saw everything.

"April's always been really nice."

"I bet she is."

"And she's cute."

My mind was still in the room, but not with the ultrasound tech. It was with the baby I'd seen. "Yeah, she was."

If I were in a different part of my life, I would have gone for her. I would have noticed her more. Nowadays, looking at another woman, it felt like looking at a piece of art. Yes, it might have been beautiful, and I could appreciate its beauty, but it didn't do anything for me.

Not in the way Grace did.

"She might ask you out."

That got me out of my thoughts and looking at her. "I-I don't—"

"You could say yes if you wanted to. It's not like we're together or anything."

The words gutted me, even though usually, they would be exactly what I wanted to hear.

"I'm not worrying about anyone else when I'm focused on you and the baby," I said.

"That's sweet, but I'm a grown woman. I know what we are. If you change your mind, I'm sure she'd be happy to get your number."

"I'll keep it in mind, but don't worry about it."

She opened her mouth to say something else, but the door opened and her doctor walked in. Her focus was broken as she introduced me and listened for the results of the test.

Everything was developing well. The baby seemed to be a bit large, but that was the only concern. It was a relief to hear.

Grace made her next appointment and had a few more

questions, so she sent me outside to get the truck. I had a feeling they were things she thought I'd be grossed out by, even though I'd told her I was fully prepared for all of it.

I picked her up from the front of the doctor's office. She still seemed tense, but I could tell most of her fear was gone.

"Do you have a lot to do when you get back?" Grace asked as she climbed into the truck.

I did have a lot to do, but she didn't need to know that. "Why do you ask?"

"I'm kind of having a craving for something and it won't leave me alone. I heard Knoxville is a good place to find it."

"You're having a craving? What is it? Please don't say hot sauce and sour cream."

"Gummy bears on ice cream."

Thank God. Somehow, that was far more tolerable than the other one.

"Then that's what we're having," I said. "Do you know a place?"

Grace told me the name of a local shop and I drove there. When she had vanilla ice cream piled high with both sour and regular gummy bears, she was bouncing on her feet as we walked to a table.

"Have you been craving this for a while?" I asked.

"It came out of nowhere last week and it's been sticking around. Dale doesn't stock the good kinds at Food 'n' Things, but I looked up the brand that this shop had." She took a bite. "Which might make me sound like I'm nuts."

"My mom apparently craved pickle and mustard sandwiches with me."

Grace frowned. "That's disgusting."

"Definitely, but my dad knew better than to tell her that."

"Smart man. And I see you took after him."

Did I? Dad had faded in my mind over the years. He was a warm, fuzzy glow in my childhood. But the main thing I remembered was what happened when he was gone. I would never tell Mom because I knew it would break her heart, but time did what it always does, and wore away at him in my mind.

"I guess I do."

Grace took another bite and moaned, unaware of my internal struggle. "*Yes*. A bite with both kinds."

"Is it everything you wanted?"

She paused and then slowly nodded. "It is. Thank you for coming here for me," she said. "We should probably head out, though. It's a long drive back."

I would have been content to stay longer, but I had a feeling she was tiring out.

Grace was quiet on the way back to her house, and I wondered if she was playing the day back in her head. When we pulled into the driveway, she finally spoke.

"I . . . have something for you."

I turned to her. "Really?"

"Yeah." Her voice shook, but she reached into her pocket. "I got that tech's number for you."

Grace handed me a card, but I tried to push it back. "I don't need this."

"I know you said you don't need it, but I also know that you're trying to be so focused on me that you might be missing out on . . . other things."

"I'm really not." My heart pounded as I realized I *needed* to convince her, but the only way to was to admit something . . . terrifying.

"Dean, come on. You've been more than a stand-up guy this entire time. You've put your entire life on hold because of this, and I know you haven't had the time to take care of other things. Let me do this for you."

"I-I haven't—"

I needed to get the words out: *I haven't thought of anyone else. I think you might be it for me.* But they were so weighed down with emotion that I couldn't. After all of these years running from any romance, protecting myself from it, I didn't know what to do.

Grace broke the silence. "You don't have to pretend to be anything else for me. I know the kind of guy you are, Dean. Just call her. Who knows where it'll go."

The words hit me like a train. For a second, I could only stare at her and replay the words over and over again. Grace put the card in my hand with a small smile. I was so dumbfounded that I let her.

"You know the kind of guy I am," I said quietly. "Right."

She nodded once, got out of the truck, and went into the house. The card burned a hole in my hand.

The only person I wanted was *her*. I'd tried to play it off as friendship and deny it until the feelings went away, but they never had.

And now she'd made her feelings on it clear.

The feeling that burned through me was so painful that I thought I'd been stabbed.

I'd done everything I could to prevent feeling like this again. I'd tried to keep my distance, to keep it platonic.

And yet here I was.

There was no way I could go inside and pretend to be okay. There was no way I could brush this off when I'd done the one thing I told myself I would never do again.

I was in love with Grace Day.

And she'd told me she wanted me to find someone else.

"Fuck," I muttered. I crumpled up the card and tossed it on the passenger seat. Later, I'd burn the damn thing. I'd burn it and then figure out how to burn these feelings too.

It was time to do what I should have done from the begin-ning. Leave. Get my head on straight, and then come back when these feelings were locked away like they should have been all along.

33

GRACE

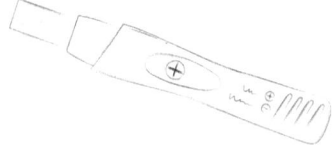

Strawberry Springs Neighborhood Watch

Jade Clark: Hypothetically, is it illegal to drive around the square forever?

Comments:
Marjorie Brown: Like in circles?
Tammy Jane: Technically, it would be in a square.
SherriffMike Finch: Jade, don't.
Jade Clark: I said hypothetically! It's not like I'm trying to set a record or anything . . .

DEAN LEFT THE NEXT MORNING.

He said that he needed to meet with someone back in the city. I had no idea if he meant Nashville or Knoxville.

I didn't like the idea of either one. I didn't like him being gone at all.

When April had flirted with him, it reminded me of all the other women he must have talked to before and during his time with me. How some of them may have even been after we'd met. He wasn't tied to me even though we were a team and I'd been going back and forth on what to do ever since that fateful night after I'd been sick.

He'd seemed so out of it when I mentioned that she was cute, and I knew that he'd been thinking of her.

So, I made my decision.

And I fucking regretted it.

The idea of him doing the things he'd done with me to anyone else made me feel ill. But I had no influence over him. I couldn't tell him not to see anyone else, and I knew that we weren't together. We would *never* be together.

That had been what he'd told me.

Why was I having such a hard time accepting that? People didn't change. They didn't get happily ever afters. I was under the impression that he would only ever see me as a woman he'd been with.

I had no right to be jealous, but I was.

I wallowed in it for two days. But the final straw came in the form of a familiar face walking in the shop.

After only meeting his mom once, I'd hoped I made a good first impression. But then we had our phone call, and had been texting ever since. So when she ran up to hug me, I nearly started crying. I only barely held it together.

"Hello," she said with a smile. "It's so good to see you. How do you feel?"

"I'm . . ." *Losing my mind?* No, not a good answer. "Mostly okay. There's a lot going on . . . obviously."

"No kidding. But look at you. I didn't know you were showing yet!"

"I feel huge," I said. "It's a bit of a habit to try and hide it, even though everyone knows."

"Don't worry about hiding a thing. You look beautiful."

"What did you come into town for?"

"After you sent me those ultrasound pictures, I just wanted to see you. It gets a little lonely living all by myself." I could relate. The house had been eerily silent ever since Dean left. "How did the most recent ultrasound go?"

"It went great." With the baby, at least. I didn't want to think about him not talking to even his mom. "Everything's normal, though the baby is a bit big."

"That can happen with PCOS. At least you passed your glucose test."

I blew out a breath. "Did he not tell you that I failed the first one?"

Her eyes widened. "No, he didn't. I almost wish I lived near him so I could easily track him down and get all this information from him."

"He was more worried about making sure that I wasn't losing my mind. That was terrifying, but everything was okay in the end."

"I'm so glad to hear that." She pulled me into another hug. "I do have an ulterior motive for being here. None of the pictures said if it was a boy or a girl. Did you mean for that to happen?"

I shook my head. "We still don't know, actually. Crossed legs."

"Dean did that to me. We didn't know until he popped out!" She laughed. "The mystery was kinda fun."

"That does seem fun," I replied as I thought about it. "How did you decorate his nursery?"

"A lot of gender-neutral things. We went with yellows and

grays, things like that. Yellow wound up being his favorite color for a while."

I hummed. Now that that room was free again, the idea of making it a nursery was back on my mind. If Dean was busy with another woman, then I might get started on making it for the baby.

"Have you not started on the baby's room yet?" she asked.

A sinking feeling pulled me out of my thoughts. I'd been putting this off for a while. "Oh, um. I'm getting to it."

Virginia's eyes narrowed, and it felt like she was reading me.

"And also, Dean stays in that room." If he ever came back to stay.

"Is it a two-bedroom house?"

I winced. "Three. One is reserved for my sister, unfortunately, so that one's not available."

"I see. He can always sleep on the couch or something. The baby needs a room."

"I'm sure he'd do it too, but I have a feeling his time staying here is done. He's back in the city busy with something."

"Oh." She frowned. "I was hoping to see him."

"Maybe he needs a break from me."

"It might just be the town. He's not a fan of close-knit communities like this."

"I've gathered that. Though I don't know why. People can be annoying here, but it's not all bad."

"Some of them can be more judgmental than helpful. Unfortunately, Shady Acres grew that way over time. I think he's a little scarred. He'll be back when he's feeling better."

"Or he'll be back when he's done with his flavor of the week." I muttered it, and I instantly felt some of the bitterness I'd been fighting creeping up on me. Virginia's eyebrows raised, and I turned to her with wide eyes. "Sorry, I shouldn't have said that."

"Are you—"

"I don't wanna talk about it," I said. And especially not with his mom of all people. "Dean's been clear, and he's been great with helping with pregnancy stuff."

"But if there *is* something he's doing, tell me."

It was tempting to. I hadn't had a mother figure in so long. And I hadn't talked with any of my friends in town about most of this. But this was his *mom*. She would be on Dean's side.

But I did need to vent. And I had a whole group of women who offered to be there for me.

It was time to take them up on that.

"What if I show you the new collection of sundresses that I got instead? That might make us both feel better."

"You drive a hard bargain, but I'll let you get away with it this once."

"Finally, a girl meeting," Mollie said as she sat. "I've been meaning to get coffee from here since forever."

I bit my lip as I followed. I'd texted them all, asking to meet up. I didn't immediately mention Dean in case he reached out and I realized I was simply in my own head. But the silence for two days? I was sure I was losing my mind.

It helped that Virginia was now staying in the guest room. She'd offered to get a hotel since she came into town as a surprise, but I refused to let her do that. At least my house wasn't silent again.

"Seriously," Jade added. "We should do this weekly or something. Oh! Or we could do one of those clubs at the library."

"Yes," Wren said. "I wanna try the crochet one that's tomorrow."

"You wanna learn how to crochet?" Mollie asked.

"I'd like to do something with my hands that I don't have to beat up my body for," she replied.

"Grace," Jade said gently. "Does that sound fun?"

"Um, yeah." I nodded. "Really fun."

Jade narrowed her eyes. "Okay, spill. Something's wrong."

"Oh, is this one of *those* girl meetups?" Mollie asked. "Is everything okay?"

"Did Dean do something?" Wren asked.

"Dean hasn't done anything. Not even reach out."

"I'll kill him," Jade said immediately. "No matter how much he's done for you."

"I think *I* did something," I said. "I tried to set him up with someone that was flirting with him." All three women stared at me like I was growing a second head. "So, bad move?"

"Honestly, yeah, considering I'm pretty sure you have feelings for him." I loved my best friend. Except when she called me out and was right about it.

"I'm trying to be cool. I do like him, but we're not together. And he turned down this one really nice girl just because he's with me. I don't have to like it but . . . he doesn't have to give anything up for me."

"And what did he do?" Wren asked slowly.

"I don't know. He got quiet, he left, and then hasn't reached out. Hell, he might be with her now."

"Where was this?"

"Knoxville," I replied.

Her lips pressed together in a thin line. "He *does* go out to jobs out there."

I let out a sigh. "Great. So that's probably where he is."

"Maybe. Maybe not." Wren shrugged. "The way he looks at you speaks for itself. He has feelings for you."

"Then why not tell me? Why keep his distance at every move?" My voice grew hard and my grip grew tighter on my tea. No. I didn't need to think this way. "I would love to think that, but he's just being friendly. Not romantic."

"It's obviously bothering you," Mollie said gently. "So why did you set him up with someone else?"

"I think I needed the reminder that he's not mine. And I know this is my fault. I'm not the kind of girl who can be friends with someone I'm attracted to and never fall for them. I was set on this path when I slept with him. And now I'm tied to him forever. It's almost better to . . . break my own heart than embarrass myself."

"Yeah, no." Jade shook her head. "No good comes from getting your heart broken, trust me."

She spoke gently again, which meant she was serious. I was about to spiral over my own decisions again when Wren interrupted.

"Maybe this distance is good," Wren said. "You can get your head on straight and then figure out what to do when he's back."

"I'm not telling him, that's for sure. I know how this ends."

I could say it all I wanted to, but there was this nagging feeling that I couldn't shake. I felt like I was missing something, that I *needed* to figure him out.

And I didn't know why I couldn't let it go.

"We should go to that crochet night," Mollie announced. "Because Grace needs a distraction."

"Yeah, girl time erases boys," Wren said. "We're here for you."

"Thank you," I said. "I'll take you up on that girl time. I need . . . any kind of distraction right now."

"Tomorrow. The library. The four of us are messing with yarn." Jade slammed her hand down on the table.

"Are you gonna try to murder someone with it?" Mollie asked. "Be honest."

"It depends on my mood for the day."

Despite myself, I smiled. "Do you even have the patience for this?"

"Who, me? I *love* having patience. I'll bring my calmness crystal and be fine."

"Can I use this hook to stab myself?" Jade muttered a day later.

"Is the crystal not working?" I asked.

"Shut up," she hissed.

I wasn't faring much better. I'd made one thing. I successfully cut a six-inch strand of yarn to create a worm. My brain couldn't comprehend how to hold the work, the yarn, *and* keep good tension. So a single-strand worm it was.

Marjorie, of all people, was in charge of the class. Trying to listen to her was a little like trying to track a drunk bird as it flew south for the winter. She was all over the place and fought with the yarn as much as I did.

"You have to make the yarn your bitch," Marjorie said. "Demand respect."

"I demanded respect and now I have a knot around my hand." Wren held up her mess.

"I think it's a bow. That's your first project right there."

Wren's brow creased and she stared at her yarn. "Um, is your teaching method working for anyone else?"

"No idea. I forgot my glasses today. You're all beautiful little fuzz balls."

Shaking my head, I pulled out my phone and played a YouTube video. Jade huddled in and watched it too.

The person speaking went nice and slow. I still didn't get it.

The door to the room opened, and Marjorie turned, ready to tell off another teen for coming into a reserved space, but instead, it was someone I knew.

"Hello? Am I too late?"

"Virginia?" I asked.

"Grace! Hi!"

"Are you here for the crochet class?"

"Yes. I just saw it on my walk to my car. I brought my own project." She pulled out a half-finished stuffed animal. Even from a distance, I could see each stitch was done well.

"Oh, hell. You're good at this." Marjorie threw her hands up. "Wanna teach the class?"

Virginia laughed. "I bet you're doing fine. I just figured I could work and listen. Maybe meet some people while I'm at it."

"I'm Jade and I want to murder right now." My best friend raised her hand. "And I'm guessing you met Grace at her shop?"

"I did, but I'm also Dean's mom."

Jade's eyes went wide. "Oh. That's awesome. We *love* your son. Never had a problem with him before or anything."

"I have a feeling he's being an idiot right now."

"Thank God. We can speak freely."

"We weren't saying anything that bad," Mollie added. "Most of us are trying and failing to crochet."

"All of us are failing," Wren said flatly.

"Miserably," I added.

"What yarn did you pick up?" Virginia asked as she came to me. In my hands was a beautiful red yarn. I didn't know anything about it other than it was a color I wanted to make a scarf out of.

"I have no idea," I replied. "The label is to my right."

I would have handed it to her if I wasn't tied up in my own mistakes.

"Oh, honey. You might want to try a new one. You're using a

wool blend, and that can be notoriously hard for some begin-ners." Virginia gave me a new yarn to try.

"Can you please help me untangle my hand?" Wren asked. "I think I'm losing circulation."

Virginia went right over and helped.

"All right, my job here is done. Say hello to your new teacher, everyone." Marjorie pointed to Virginia.

"I can't just take over a class."

"Please do. Our last teacher canceled and I don't know how to crochet."

"You don't?" Mollie asked, her jaw dropped. "You told us you were an expert!"

"Fake it till you make it." Marjorie shrugged. "Come to the front and I'll pay you for your time. Bye!" And she was out the door.

"What just happened?" Virginia asked.

"I think you just got a job."

She blinked and then slowly went back to untangling Wren.

"Hey, so could we start from scratch?" Mollie asked. "Mar-jorie told us to be one with the yarn and I think my brain exploded."

"Uh, sure. We'll start with a chain. Is everyone listening?"

We all agreed and Virginia continued on, teaching us how to do the basics. We followed along better, but Mollie got it far faster than we did.

"I think I'm making a scarf," Mollie said as she held up her own work. It looked more put together than mine or Jade's.

"Is there anything you're not good at?" Wren asked. She was nearly buried under yarn.

"Shutting up?" Mollie said with a shrug.

Wren let out a long sigh and went back to it. She made two moves before she said, "Hey, when does this get fun?"

"About three months in," Virginia said with a wince. "But I think you have potential."

"Potential means failure," Wren muttered. "I'm only good at breaking things."

Virginia's eyes went wide. "Oh, I'm sure—"

"She's not being negative," Mollie said. "She *is* good at breaking things. And she loves it."

34

DEAN

Dad Company (But Sometimes Good Advice)
Robert Colt: All right, @**Dean Briggs**, I need an update.
How is not getting attached going?

Comments:
Ryan Kim: You're really asking? We all know where this is
going. They'll be together any day now.
Dean Briggs: She actually tried to set me up with someone
else. Thanks for asking.
Ryan Kim: Oh, whoops.
Robert Colt: Sorry about that, kid. That's a sad update. Drink
the pain away?
Ryan Kim: That's terrible advice.
Robert Colt: Well, his kid isn't here yet, so he might as well!

I LOST my third hand in a row when Clyde let the cards hit the
table and stared me down.

"All right, kid, I've let you have some time to be emo over whatever the hell happened. But now it's time to talk about it."

His words were so out of character it finally knocked me out of my thoughts. "Emo? Really?"

"I'm hip with the times, and I'm also concerned about you. You told me you were busy in Strawberry Springs, but I knew that you were inseparable from that girl you got pregnant. Now all of a sudden you wanna be here, so something happened."

"Can we just keep playing cards?"

"This isn't playing cards. This is me mopping the floor with you. Usually, we're pretty evenly matched."

I sighed. "I don't wanna talk about it. It's better if I pretend it's not happening and move on."

"Yeah, that seems to be going well." Clyde said it flatly. "At what point of depression do I call your mom?"

My gaze shot up to his. "You wouldn't."

"If you stay in denial, nothing'll get better. You need to *talk* about it."

"There's nothing to say."

"Let me be the judge of that." He leaned back in his chair. "It's girl problems, right? You've only looked this sad when it was that."

I blew out a breath. "Yes, it's girl problems."

"You and Grace?" he asked.

I could only nod. "She . . . I—"

"You fell for her, didn't you?"

I swallowed. "How did you know that?"

"There aren't many words you would struggle that hard to say. Are you here to try to stay in denial about it, or did something else happen?"

"She tried to set me up with someone else."

"Oh."

"I tried to tell her what I felt, but I didn't get it out before she told me she knew what kind of guy I was and that I should call someone else."

He sighed. "Shit, kid."

"Yeah."

"What did she say when you told her about your feelings?"

"I didn't need to. She made her half clear."

Clyde only blinked in my direction. "Really? You're confident that you know?"

"How else do I take that?"

"Have you guys talked about what would happen if either of you had feelings for each other?"

"No."

"And what was the last thing you said about relationships?"

"That . . . I didn't do them." I said it slowly, teeth clenching as Clyde led me right to the point.

"Oh, interesting. So you're either assuming or you can somehow magically tell the future. Do you also happen to know this week's lottery numbers?"

"Well, what else am I supposed to do? Get hurt again? No. I refuse to feel . . . all of this all over again."

"Kid." Clyde's voice was low. "You're already feeling it now."

I gritted my teeth. If I thought about Grace, then the burning pain came right back. Clyde was fucking right and I wasn't thrilled about it.

"Can you at least kiss the brick before you throw it at me?"

He shook his head. "You need some tough love right now. And that means hearing it exactly like it is."

"I liked what we had before until emotions messed it up."

"Did emotions mess it up, or were they there the whole time?"

I thought back and then sighed. "The second one," I muttered.

"Right," he said. "You had some good ones and you now have some bad ones. But I promise you, hiding things and not dealing with feelings is why most of my girlfriends left me."

"I thought it was because you had an unhealthy obsession with trains."

He narrowed his eyes and pointed at me. "Don't change the subject. We're talking about *you* telling Grace how you feel."

"What happens when she says she doesn't want this?"

"When or if?"

"When."

"You're assuming again. You have no idea what she feels."

"I have a hint. She fucking set me up with someone else."

"You have no idea why she did that. Maybe she wasn't sure what you wanted. Maybe she made a mistake. This is where you talk to her."

"Still . . ."

"What? Are you scared?"

"Maybe I am. Maybe I want to be a little afraid for a bit. The idea of walking in and laying it all out on the line again is terrifying."

"That it is. And I'm not gonna sit here and say that you can't be scared. I'm also not gonna sit here and say that you can't take time to figure out exactly what you wanna say. But you have to do it, because more things are gonna pop up like this, and eventually, you're gonna have a kid together."

"I know. I just don't want to get my heart broken again."

"I haven't met the girl, so you'll have to tell me. Is she like the one who broke your heart in high school?"

"No, she's nothing like her." I said it quickly. "Other than this one blip, but . . . I think it was bad wording. She doesn't know about high school."

"Then is it fair of you to assume that she's gonna do the same thing?"

I blew out a breath. "No."

"Exactly. You know I'm right."

And I did know that he was right. Still, there was a fear simmering under my skin that I couldn't explain. I would need to tell her eventually. It would be better for both of us if I did, but it set me on edge.

It didn't make sense, because I knew she was different. Grace was kind and understanding. Even if she turned me down, it wouldn't be with such cruelty.

It was feelings like this that made me turn away from love in the first place. I hated feeling powerless. I hated feeling pain. And that's all it had done for me.

"How about this: You hide out until this job's done. Maybe I'll let you take one more on, but then you're gonna go back and you're gonna fix this."

"That's probably for the best."

"I'm gonna do one more thing that's probably gonna ruin your night too."

"If you call me out one more time, I think I'm gonna leave. There has to be a limit to how many times you can be right in one night."

He laughed and stood. "No, it's not that this time. Normally, I would pat your shoulder and move on, but I don't think that's enough for this."

Clyde opened his arms and I knew he wanted a hug. I didn't think I'd ever hugged him once.

But I couldn't deny that I needed it.

He didn't linger or make it weird, but it was nice to get support from him.

"Now I'll let you drown out your problems with some cards. But can you please kick my ass this time?"

"Shuffle the cards and you'll see."

"That's the kid I know."

We played for a good few hours, and now that my mind was clearer, I did kick Clyde's ass many times.

As we played, I told him some of the stories from Strawberry Springs. I told him about Tammy and how I was pretty sure she hated me. I told him about Hugh, who should have hated me, but didn't. And then I told him about Grace, finally giving him all the context as to why she was on my mind.

He listened to all of it, not judging me for halfway liking some of these people, and only interjecting to say that he'd like to meet them someday.

By the time it was midnight, I could tell he was tiring out. We'd had a long day at work and both of us needed rest. He said his goodbyes and headed out, and I went to the restroom.

When I was on the way out, I ran into a woman.

Actually, "ran into" was a strong phrase. I would have collided with her if she hadn't seen me first. The second she realized I was only inches from her, she *jerked* away from me like I was on fire.

"Sorry," I said holding my hands up in mock defense. "I wasn't watching where I was going."

"N-neither was I," she said, keeping her hands close to herself. "Um, having fun?"

"I was just heading out. Are *you* having fun?"

"Debatable," she said. "Actually, no. I'm not. I don't even know what I'm doing here."

"Bars aren't your scene?"

"Leaving my house isn't my scene . . . for reasons. Sorry for being weird, by the way."

"It's fine," I said. "I didn't think you were weird at all."

I turned to leave.

"U-um, wait," the woman said. "This is even weirder, but could you walk me out to my car?"

If it were anyone else, I would have thought she was hinting at something more. But one look at this woman told me she was terrified.

"Did someone bother you?"

"No, not really. I was just trying something new and it's not working. I think I need to be home."

I nodded. "I'll walk you out then."

She gave me a grateful smile and walked ahead. Then she paused. "Could you make sure no one touches me?"

Suddenly, her reaction to me being near her made sense. "Yeah, no problem."

The woman nodded and nearly darted out of the bar. She was quick, and it was so busy inside that it was hard to make sure she got out untouched. When we were in the cool night air, she let out a sigh of relief.

"Finally," she said. "Thank you."

"Not a problem. Are you okay?"

"I'll be fine," she said. "I've dealt with this for years."

"It's kinda hard to live in a big city if no one can touch you."

She laughed with no humor in her voice. "Yeah, you're right. It's why I never leave the house."

"That's not a life."

"Any idea on how to get one?" She laughed awkwardly. "Obviously, my most recent attempt failed. I'll be going home to rot in front of my TV where I try, and fail, to find a new show and then wind up rewatching *Supernatural*."

There was a ton of information there, and I had no idea where to start. I wasn't even sure if she meant to tell me all that she had. "I have a TV show rec for you if you need one."

"You know what, I'll take it."

"Check out *Renovating with Love*. Season one is good, mostly because I'm in it."

"Are you trying to brag?" she asked, a ghost of a smile on her face.

She was a gorgeous woman, and if I'd met her months ago, I'd have smiled back.

"Not really. Just warning you that this is a little bit of self-promo."

Her smile faded. "Noted. Thank you for your help. I'm Piper, by the way."

"Dean."

"Do you happen to be single, Dean?"

"It's complicated right now, but there *is* someone. I'm sorry."

"I get it, don't worry. I just figured I'd ask to see if something good could come from this night."

"Something good *did* come from this night."

"And what's that?"

"You now know most bars aren't your thing and you have a new show to watch."

"You know what?" she said, her smile returning. "That's one way to look at it."

"Have a good night, Piper." I waved as she turned to her car. After making sure she got into it safely, I walked to my own, glad I could help one more person.

But the feeling of missing someone else hit me before too long. I could see why Clyde had given me a time limit. Because even though everything had gone to shit, being away from Grace felt like I was missing a limb.

35

GRACE

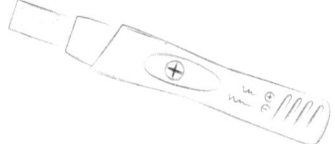

Strawberry Springs Neighborhood Watch

Kerry Winsor: @Mollie Wilson, look at this video of chickens on a trampoline! Do you think yours would like this?

Comments:
Mollie Wilson: Um, I've never seen chickens move like that. Idk if that's real . . .
Jade Clark: It's definitely not, lol.
Kerry Winsor: WHAT! But it's so cute! Who doesn't love a little bouncing???
Atticus Thompson: Most animals don't . . . Humans are the weird ones here.
Kerry Winsor: You could train them!
Mollie Wilson: How about YOU train them? You can train Hennifer. She's our most . . . opinionated chicken.
Jade Clark: You'll take a video of that, right?
Mollie Wilson: Absolutely.

"MOLLIE, I swear to *fuck*, if you're coming in to show off another baby onesie, I'll *scream*."

I loved the woman, but she'd taken to crochet way too well. Just a week later and she was miles ahead of me, even as I tried my hardest to figure it out. I even had yarn in my hands when the door opened, and I couldn't make a chain to save my life.

"I'm not Mollie," a deeper voice said. "And I feel like I missed out on some things."

My gaze snapped up, and standing in front of me was a too-familiar figure with a cowboy hat and unfairly buff arms. God, he looked good. And I missed him. "Dean. You're back."

"I am. Did you miss me?"

I had, but seeing him again twisted the knife that had been lodged in my chest ever since he'd gone. I hadn't known what he was up to or who he was with. I'd pushed the feeling away. I had no right to feel this way after I was the one who'd set them up. Of all the things I'd ever done, that might have been the dumbest one yet.

"A little. I've been busy losing my mind, though." I held up yarn.

"My mom crochets. Maybe she could—"

"Teach me? Yeah, she tried. I fear I'm incompetent."

"She's been here?"

"Yeah, she was here a few days ago. She said she wanted to hang out with someone."

He nodded, but his face fell. "I need to call her. I was pretty busy."

"Was it fun?"

"Was what fun?"

"Whatever you were up to." I tried to sound nonchalant, but it came out forced.

"Nothing to worry about. How are you feeling?"

I felt like I'd been stomped on. Mostly because of his vagueness about everything. I wanted—no, needed—to know what he was up to. But I didn't have the right to know.

"I'm fine. Mollie's a bit jealous that I'm not suffering more, but it's not a huge deal."

"It's going by fast," he said.

"It is. And we have a lot to figure out."

"That we do." He muttered it, eyes cast downward. He seemed to be lost in thought. He also barely looked me in the eye.

I needed to say something. I couldn't put it off.

"About that setup. If I offended you in any way or hurt your feelings, I'm really sorry about it."

His head shot up. "How the absolute hell did you figure that out?"

"You seem off, and sometimes I can read you. It's either that, or you think I'm ugly after being next to April for a while."

His eyes narrowed. "That second one is not likely."

"That's why I apologized first. I do have self-esteem, you know."

"It was the wording you used when you said you knew what kind of guy I was. Someone also said that a very long time ago, and it wasn't so nice."

My heart sank into my ass. "Oh, God, I didn't mean it in any type of way. Seriously, I don't care what you get up to when you're not around me. It didn't come from a place of judgment."

"I get it. But recently, I haven't loved the kind of guy I've been seen as."

That could mean two things. One, he didn't like the idea of being a father or the idea of being responsible. But I knew Dean. I knew that was highly unlikely.

And the other option? He didn't like being known as the playboy.

I wanted the second one *so* bad, but people didn't change. I wasn't this lucky.

"Fuck, I guess I'm doing this," he muttered to himself. He took a shaky breath before he spoke. "I like you. A lot. And that's terrifying because you could turn me down, and it would crush me. But I still want you to know that. I want you to know that it's you. It's been you since the day we met. Even when I didn't know what was happening."

I should have said something intelligent back, but he was saying the very thing that I thought would never happen. So my answer was, "Uh, bu—wha?"

"I know this is out of character for me, or at least the version that I've shown people. I used to want this, but someone told me that I would never have it, and that I wasn't the kind of guy for it, and I let that go. Mostly to protect myself. Somewhere along the way, protecting myself became less important than . . . you."

There was no way this was real. There was no way that Dean had walked into my shop and confessed that he liked me. This was supposed to be off the table. This was never supposed to happen.

Slowly, I reached my hand over to my forearm and pinched hard.

Dean watched and his eyebrows furrowed. "What are you doing?"

"I'm making sure that I'm actually awake right now."

"Because you wanna wake up or because . . ." He trailed off. Dean couldn't sit still. Since I'd lived with him, I learned to read him pretty well. But I was sure that even Hugh could see how nervous he was.

I shook myself out of it. "Because I feel the same way. And I thought I was ridiculous for feeling that way because you told me from the beginning that you didn't do relationships. So this has to be a dream. And if I wake up, I'm gonna be pissed."

He lit up like a kid on Christmas. "You feel the same way?"

I didn't give that an answer. Mostly because if this was a dream, then I was gonna take full advantage of every second I had. I darted out from behind the counter and strode to him, putting my lips on his before I could stop myself.

Dean let out a long breath before his hand cupped my cheek, and he pulled me closer.

"To be clear," he murmured against my lips, "if one of us was dreaming, it would be me."

"Nope. Me. Definitely me."

He laughed as I pulled him back to me.

"You taste better than I remember," he groaned. My hands tightened on his shirt just as he pulled away. "But we're stopping."

"What? Why?" I nearly whined. "If you instigate a no sex on the first date rule, I might cry."

"I . . . might be."

"Do you know how horny I am? Do you know what pregnancy is doing to me?" My voice rose in pitch as I spoke.

"I just don't wanna only focus on sex. Especially not after how we started things."

"It's not like I can get *more* pregnant."

"I know it's inconvenient, but I wanna see if I can remember how to be the guy I used to be."

I closed my eyes even though I wanted to argue further. I would need my dildo tonight. "That's a very good point, but I'm not happy about it."

"I may be terrible at this. You'll have to bear with me."

"I once dated a guy who fell asleep on the first date. Trust me, the bar is low."

Dean laughed and shook his head. "You need to raise it a little higher than that."

"I'm just saying. I'll be happy with your piercing and you paying attention to me."

He winced. "Don't say things like that to me right now. It's been almost four months without any, and I'm suffering."

"Orgasms. Cock. Inside me."

"*Grace*," he growled.

"I said you had a good point. I never said I would make it easy."

"A date. Tomorrow. Let's start there."

"Fine. I do owe you coffee, and the flowers are blooming. We can go on a walk."

"You don't owe me anything. I'll be paying for our date."

"You'll be paying when you have all the questions the next day. The town *will* see this."

He sighed. "Yeah, I know. You're worth it, though."

I couldn't stop the smile that made its way onto my face. It still didn't feel real. Sometimes things worked out exactly as they should.

Maybe this was one of those times.

36

DEAN

Strawberry Springs Neighborhood Watch

Marjorie Brown: The winds in the east . . . something's brewing. And YOU can tell us what it is after you've joined our weather-watching class!

Comments:
Hu Gh: I don't need no class. I have a rock. If it's wet, it's raining. If it's smoking, it's hot. If it's gone, then there's a 'nado!
Marjorie Brown: That's nice, buddy. This is for people who want to know about the tornado before it's coming for their ass!
Hu Gh: I'm used to things coming for my ass.
Jade Clark: !!! Is no one gonna say anything?
Marjorie Brown: Nah, that sentence speaks for itself.

STAYING AWAY from Grace was one of the most difficult things I'd ever done. My body craved hers. Not only for sex, but for everything.

I wanted to do this right, though. And I stuck to my guns throughout dinner and even as we watched a movie together. Grace kept glancing at me, as if still unsure if this were real, but it was.

The fear I felt told me it was.

I didn't understand why it still lingered. I'd done the hard thing. I told her that I liked her and she had said that she liked me back. I wanted this more than anything, and if I hadn't hidden from love for so long, I might have jumped into it with both feet.

Maybe there was something else holding me back.

I wasn't sure what it was, but there was a buzzing in the back of my head. It told me I was doing something wrong. Did I tell her my feelings in the wrong way? Was I expecting her to change her mind at any given moment? I wasn't sure, but it lingered even after I went to bed and got up the next morning.

I was determined to push past it. It made sense that my fears would stick around. I'd had my heart broken, after all. But I wouldn't let that ruin this.

Nothing would ruin this.

Grace always wore incredible outfits, but today, she had gone overboard. She was in a light blue dress that showed off both her curves and her growing belly. Her curls were in perfect ringlets around her face, and she traded the light makeup for a different look that accentuated her cheekbones.

I found her gorgeous every single day I was around her, but this was something else.

"Are you trying to give me a heart attack?"

She turned and hitched her purse onto her shoulder. "A little bit. Do you like it?"

"Like it? I feel like you're torturing me."

"You're the one who set the stupid rule. You even slept on a twin mattress instead of in my bed with me."

"You play dirty."

"I never claimed to be anything else."

When I was in front of her, my fears were quiet. This felt natural, just like so much had with her.

"You know, after this, everyone will know."

"Yeah, they will." Her smile dimmed a little. "Are you having second thoughts about that? We could go out of town, if you prefer."

"Even though they'll all be mad about losing the bet on us getting together, I'll deal with it." I walked toward her and grabbed her hand. "I'm not having second thoughts about you, though."

Her grin returned. "Let's do this. Consequences and all."

"You know, whoever turned you down a long time ago was an idiot. This side of you is great."

"I'm a little rusty. Hopefully, it'll get better from here."

She nodded and turned toward the door, and it was only when her back was to me that my smile faded.

The fear was back.

It didn't make sense. It wasn't like I had changed my feelings for Grace overnight. It wasn't like I regretted telling her how I felt.

But I was just terrified.

The ride into town was quiet, and I wondered if maybe my fears were because of telling the town. But when I thought about them seeing us together, it didn't bother me.

I had my issues with most people here, but I wouldn't lie and say that I didn't think about them while I was gone. Despite my hatred of small towns, I was curious about what they would say and think.

We pulled up to The Reserved Bean and I once again got Grace's door for her. There was a line down the sidewalk, as there usually was. Theo was now one of the most popular men in town.

While we stood in line, I grabbed her hand. There was no fanfare, no one calling us out . . . for all of two seconds.

Then I saw Jade walking across the square. She took one look at us and her jaw dropped.

And she walked straight into a potted plant.

"Oh, Henry's plants." Grace bit her lip. "Maybe I should have given her a warning."

I wondered if Jade would run over to ask us directly what was happening. Thankfully, she had some decorum, because instead, she pulled out her phone.

And Grace's buzzed a minute later.

"She's asking if we fucked. I get to say no."

"Please tell me you'll give her more context than that."

"I'll also add that I'm not single."

The second Grace sent the text message, I heard Jade call out "Yes!" and then she fist-pumped. That got a few other townspeople's attention.

At first, they seemed curious about Jade. That something happened with her. I didn't know her well enough to decide what it could even be for, but the town did.

Once I saw her shake her head, that was when eyes turned to us.

"Dammit!" Dale said from the front of Food 'n' Things. "This means Hugh won again!"

"He has to be swindling us!" Tammy yelled. "Did he inter-fere? I call foul!"

"Or you should all mind your business!" Grace yelled back.

I could have sworn that I saw Tammy's cheek's color from all the way across the square.

"You're mean to them."

"I've known them my whole life. I get to be." She shrugged

and it hit me how nice it was that she didn't try to preach to me all the benefits of small towns. She was realistic about it. While she obviously liked it enough to stay here, there were things that weren't perfect. People who weren't perfect. "Also, Kerry's not here. She gets to find out in the Facebook group for once."

"I'd kill to see her response."

"Don't worry, Jade'll send it to us."

My eyes found Grace's best friend and she gave us both a thumbs-up. It was a far cry from a death threat.

The first night that I spent with Grace should have been one of the best ones of my life. I had finally gotten what I wanted. I got to sleep next to the woman that I cared about, and I wasn't alone. Sure, we didn't have sex yet, but it was only because Grace crashed earlier than usual. She tried to convince me, but I knew her sleep was more important than anything else.

There was always tomorrow.

Or so I thought.

Getting to sleep was easy. I had her in my arms and everything was perfect.

But then I woke up with my chest heaving, memories dancing behind my eyelids that I swore I had forgotten. There was the sound of an endless heartbreak for person you were meant to be with forever.

I hadn't had a nightmare in years, not since I was a kid. I used to run to Mom and have her stay with me, but she wasn't here.

I should have woken up Grace, but I already felt guilty that she was so exhausted from her long walk. And I knew there was something about her that was the center of all of my fears.

Standing, I tried to walk through the house to work it off. When that didn't work, I walked up and down the driveway.

And then I knew I needed to bring out the big guns.

I left a note for Grace, saying I needed some space. And I drove off.

I didn't know where I was going, only that I needed time to think. Roads stretched out before me. They'd gone from interstates to highways. I didn't realize I was in Shady Acres until I was at the old stoplight I used to sit at when learning how to drive.

Mom would sit in the passenger's seat, yelling at me to stay in the lane and to hit the brakes way before I felt like I should. In the end, she would always apologize and say she wished Dad were here to teach me. He'd been calmer than her, apparently.

I wasn't sure how I ended up here, but there was something about the weight in my chest that made me continue on. I turned right, just like I always had when heading home from school.

Then, the roads became one lane each way with fields on either side. One parcel had been sold for the first strip mall.

Now all of it was developed.

Every bit of what I knew had been razed to the ground in favor of shops and manicured perfection.

Why the fuck had I come here? Was I a glutton for punishment?

I ended up in front of Mom's house. A lot had changed. The field where I picked flowers for Julie was even gone. Houses had inched closer to hers, and it wasn't the same place I grew up in.

It was the middle of the night, and the last thing I expected to see was the lights being on. Mom had never enjoyed late nights when I was a kid, but then again, I hadn't spent a lot of nights with her ever since I'd grown up either.

I avoided this place and, by proxy, her, like the plague.

I got out of the truck before I could drive away. What was she up to?

And before I could think twice about it, I walked up and knocked on her door.

"Dean?" she said as she opened it. "What the hell are you doing all the way out here in Shady Acres at this hour?"

Her shock made sense. I'd driven hours to be here.

"Just . . . checking in." My eyes roamed over all the walls, which for the first time in my life, were bare. "What are you doing? Are you painting?"

"Um, something like that," she said. "Come in."

When I did, my gaze traveled to the living room where I saw even more things were gone. "Why are there boxes everywhere?"

She swallowed. "You never answered my question, you know."

"Are you moving?" I asked.

Her lips pressed together. "Dean . . ."

"Mom . . ."

She sighed. "Not yet. But I want to."

My emotions were already at the edge, but this tipped it over. "Seriously? Did all this new shit finally price you out? I could help you with the taxes, or the higher bills. Just tell me what you need."

"I don't need anything, Dean. Except maybe a job, but that's not happening here."

"We can find you something."

"I don't want to stay here," she said slowly. "I'd rather move somewhere where I'm happy. Like Strawberry Springs."

"You like it there?"

"I do. It feels like this place did once upon a time."

"But you and Dad met here."

"We did."

"This is where you're from."

"It is."

"Why would you let all of that go?"

"Why would *you*?" she countered.

"Because it didn't . . ." I trailed off, but she knew where I was going.

"It didn't feel like home anymore," she finished with a sad smile. "And I wanna be near my grandbaby, Dean. Even if, God forbid, I live in an apartment."

I could see why she was doing it, but my teeth gritted anyway. She was letting go of everything in favor of a town that I wasn't sure deserved her.

"I hope it works out then. I wish I'd known sooner."

"I had a feeling you would take it hard. And you are. On top of that, something else is going on."

"That's the last thing I wanna talk about."

"Really? You drove all the way to your childhood home. It must have been big. Is it about the fight you and Grace had?"

"There wasn't a fight."

"Well, she certainly looked like a kicked puppy the last time I saw her."

"That's resolved."

"Is it?"

"Yes," I hissed. "Or, it should be. I don't know what's going on with me. I should be . . . thrilled right now. We decided to be together."

"A couple?" She gasped and then smiled. "This is great news! Unless . . . unless you're doing this because you feel like you have to."

I jerked back. "What? No, I would never do that to her."

"You come to a place that you've avoided for over a decade in the middle of the night. I'm gonna be convinced that it's the worst-case scenario."

"It's not. At least, it's not logically the worst-case scenario. Like I said, I don't know what's happening. I asked to be more and she said yes, and ever since then I've been feeling . . . off."

"Off. You finally ask a girl out and you're feeling off?" She rubbed her forehead. "Does this have to do with what happened in high school? You asked that one girl out, I can't remember her name, and then you suddenly hated love."

"It started out that way, but I worked through that. I don't know why I feel this way. It goes away when I'm around her, but then when I fall asleep, I . . ."

"What happens when you fall asleep?"

"I had a nightmare."

She jerked back, all signs of frustration vanishing from her body. Mom's voice was soft when she spoke again. "Is that why you're here?"

"I don't know."

"You haven't had nightmares since your dad died."

Just hearing her mention him made me flinch. "That was a long time ago."

"You've had a lot of life changes. And you're about to be a father. Is that maybe why?"

I shook my head. "It has to do with Grace. Definitely her."

"But you care about her, so what's the problem? This is your happily ever after!"

Those were the words that finally broke me. My chest tightened. "People don't get those, Mom."

"Yes, they do. You're almost there! God, Dean, what's the worst that could happen if you let yourself have love?"

"I could lose her!" I finally snapped.

Once the words were out there, they became real. Images flashed through my mind. Ones I tried not to think of. They were the ones I'd seen in my nightmare.

Her lying on the clinic bed, but this time she was far too

pale. I saw Mom falling to the floor when she got the news of Dad dying, but this time, I went with her.

And there it was. The real fear. The one that I'd been hiding from myself. I'd unlocked it, and I only felt worse. Fuck, she was pregnant. So much could go wrong.

Mom gasped at the words, eyes going wide. "That's what you're scared of?" she asked softly. "Dean . . ."

"I can't," I said, shaking my head. "Don't tell me I should push past it. Not when I saw what losing Dad did to you."

Her eyes shut and her head fell to her chest. I looked away, knowing I shouldn't have brought Dad into this. I didn't want to hurt her, so I always stayed away from the topic entirely. Mentioning him in passing was one thing, but that day, the worst day, was banned for me.

Until now.

"Dean, that was the hardest day of my life," she said. "But I lived. And I'm okay now."

"No one is okay after something like that."

"It doesn't feel like you ever will be. But it happens."

"You can't honestly tell me you would go through losing Dad again if you had the choice."

"But I would," she said. "I would do it a hundred times."

I shook my head, unable to believe her. "Why?"

Mom stepped forward and grabbed my hands. "Because loving him was better than losing him. If I hadn't, I would have always wondered what could have been. But now I don't. I *loved* my time with your father. I'd go through the day I found out he was gone a hundred times for the years I had with him."

"You would?"

"Yes, I would." Her gaze was steady. "We *lived*, honey. All those days were more important than the last one."

The words made my throat close up, and I had to turn away. Maybe I hadn't avoided this topic just for her.

Maybe it was for me too.

But Mom wasn't done. "He left early, before I could show him all the love I had for him. And you know what I wanna do now? I'm gonna take all that love that he left me with and give it to others. I'm gonna enjoy the time I have now rather than holding on to a past that isn't making me happy anymore." Her hand landed on my shoulder. "Are you happy, Dean? Do you truly love hiding the kind man you are underneath being a playboy?"

"No." I could barely say it, but I knew it was the truth.

"Then why are you wasting your time? Why spend it unhappy when you and I both know that we don't have a lot of it?"

"It's easier this way, Mom."

"Maybe it is easier. But it's not better. He left us with so many memories, so many lessons of how to live a good life."

"I don't remember them," I said. "I used to, but he's gone."

"Then let me remind you." Her hands returned to mine and she squeezed. "Let me *show* you how to live, even when you're sad. Even when you're scared."

I missed her. I always had, even when I said I was leaving Shady Acres.

"It's a good thing you're moving to Strawberry Springs then."

She nodded, eyes misty. "The distance isn't good for us. It makes us forget what's important."

Mom finally let go, but I wasn't ready. "Wait—"

"I just wanna grab one thing," she said. She walked away and dug through a box to grab something. She came back with a picture of Dad.

"Samuel Briggs," she said. "You look just like him."

It hurt to look at the picture. He was so important to me, and he was gone too soon.

"He would hate what I've become, wouldn't he?"

Mom laughed. "No. He could never hate you. He would just tell you to get your shit together and go after Grace. And he would want one other thing."

I slowly turned. "What's that?"

Her eyes were wet, but she still smiled. "He would give you the biggest hug."

A dim memory finally burst forth. He gave the best fucking hugs. He'd wrap us all into his huge arms and pull us to his solid, warm chest.

"I miss those."

"He's not here to give them, but I am." She held her arms out. "And I'd rather give you one, if that's okay."

I nodded and nearly fell into her arms. The tears that I'd been hiding for years, the ones for Dad, for Julie, for *me*, finally broke free.

And Mom and I sat in the weight of it. She held me while all the walls broke, leaving only me.

Just Dean.

I could only hope I would be better on the other side of it.

37

GRACE

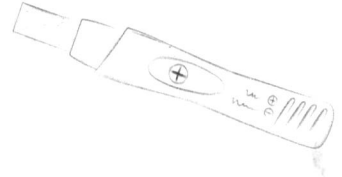

Strawberry Springs Neighborhood Watch

Jade Clark: Dean!!! Grace!!! On a date!!!

Comments:
Dale Garrett: Can you people stop talking in code???
Kerry Winsor: WHAT?! They're TOGETHER!!!
Jade Clark: Yep. She wouldn't be out in public holding hands with him if she didn't want people to know.
Hu Gh: Fucking FINALLY!!!
Tammy Jane: He better not mess it up . . .

WHEN I WOKE UP ALONE, I had a split second of panic. The bed was cold next to me, and my first thought was that he was gone.

Then I took a breath and remembered that Dean wouldn't leave. We were together now. Everything was good. I needed to trust that he wasn't going to vanish.

As I sat up, I listened for the sounds of him moving through the house. I'd bet he found a project to work on and I'd hear it from here.

When only silence met my ears, my lips pressed together. Had he gone out for breakfast?

Walking to the living room, I searched for any sign of him. His hat was still on the counter, and he hadn't packed up his stuff, but there was a note on the dining room table.

Gone driving. Needed space.

I stared at it, willing for it to give me more information. When the words didn't, I was tempted to beg the universe for more.

The note was written quickly. I'd never seen his handwriting, but I could have sworn this was done with a shaking hand. He was an electrician. His hands had to be mostly steady.

What had happened?

And why did he go through it alone?

I thought back to the day before. I'd *known* something was wrong, but I kept chalking it up to my own fears. Him coming here and telling me he had feelings for me felt too good to be true. Things like this just didn't *happen*. People didn't change.

And he had.

But waking up in a cold bed with only a note made me question that.

I should've asked. I shouldn't have ignored his distant eyes when he thought I wasn't looking. It would have been better to face it rather than let it turn into this.

He'd told me he was out of practice with relationships. I was too.

I pinched the bridge of my nose, trying to stop myself from crying. My mind conjured all the things he could be up to. Did he go find someone else? Was he alone through something terrible?

Did he just not want *me*?

A tear slipped out, falling on the paper. I put it down, the crash of emotions hitting me hard. Being pregnant made it all worse, and I wasn't sure I could survive this alone.

It was tempting to call him, but I didn't know if I should since he'd said he needed space. I didn't know *anything*, and my mind spun trying to figure out what I'd done to mess things up.

Was it that I fell asleep early? Was it something I said on the date?

I was spiraling, unhelpful thoughts making me feel worse. Pulling my phone out, I sent a message to the three people who I knew would be there for me.

> Girl meeting. It's an emergency.

WREN

> I'm stopping work for the day.

JADE

> I can open the shop late. Wanna meet at your house?

I looked around, wondering if I should have them here. The living room was a mess of half-finished projects, and his hat alone brought fresh tears to my eyes.

Why the hell had he left without his hat?

> No, not here. But not at the square either. I don't want anyone to overhear us.

MOLLIE

> My house is open. We can meet there.

The second she said it, I knew it was perfect. I thanked her for being able to host and then half-heartedly threw on a sweat-shirt before running out the door.

Even as I drove, it was a struggle to keep myself contained. I still wanted to pick apart everything I did and figure this out myself, but just the thought of him leaving sent me right back to the second I saw the note.

Wren's truck and Jade's Prius were waiting for me when I got to Mollie's house. I wiped at the tears that had escaped and knocked on the front door.

The second it opened, I was met with three women watching me with wide eyes.

"What's going on?" Mollie asked.

"Are you okay?" Wren added.

"You know I have a knife I can use." That could only be Jade.

"I'm . . . I need to vent. Can we sit down somewhere?"

Mollie pulled away first and led us to her living room. "Cain is working outside and took Jasmine with him. No one should bother us."

"Good," I replied.

"You were in such a good mood yesterday with Dean." Jade sat next to me. "Please don't tell me it was him."

"He was gone this morning," I told them. "He said he needed space."

"I'm sorry, *what*?" Jade shook her head. "What kind of space could he need?"

Wren's brow was pinched. "He said this the day after you guys went on a date? Why?"

"He has a whole life in Nashville," I said. "One that I don't know anything about. God, I barely know anything about him at *all*."

"That's not necessarily true," Wren said. "But he does keep things close to the chest."

"The note looked off. Like he wasn't in his right mind when he wrote it."

"I've been there," she muttered with a sigh. "I pulled something like that with Henry. He followed me."

"Henry could figure out where to *go*. I know . . . nothing." Tears clouded my vision again and I gritted my teeth.

A hand gripped mine, and I looked up to see Mollie. "I'm sorry. You did the right thing by calling us."

"I shouldn't have set him up. I fucked up there, and I don't know if he took my apology."

"Hang on, why are you blaming yourself?" Wren asked. "You have no idea what happened, which is the whole problem."

She was right, but I still shook my head. "I didn't treat him like other people. Not at first, when I thought it was a one-time thing, and not now after I thought . . . I should have been better."

I let him see the mess of my home. Would he have stayed if I kept my shit together?

He saw me sick. Would he be here if I hadn't let him see?

I made a mistake. He *definitely* would be here if I made the right choice.

Jade's face appeared in front of me. "Stop it."

"Wh-what?"

"I know what you're doing. You're going through all the things you could have done to be perfect."

"But if it could've *helped*—"

"No, Grace. Life isn't perfect. We all mess up. You've done it. And it's possible he's doing it right now. You don't have to take on the burden of fixing everything."

I clenched my jaw to stop myself from saying "Yes, I do." Jade wouldn't want to hear that from me.

"Hang on," Mollie interjected. "I know that look. You're stopping yourself from saying something."

"I-I'm not—"

"Say it," she said gently. "Even if it's ugly. Even if it doesn't help. You're safe to say what you think."

"Yes," Jade said. "If you disagree, tell me. I wanna know."

"I don't want to—"

"Start a fight and accidentally destroy things?" Wren asked. "I've been there and done that. With both houses and people, and then I rebuilt both of them."

"Remember what I said?" Jade's voice was softer than I'd ever heard it. "Life is messy. And we wanna see that. It's just as important as the good stuff."

Hearing my rough-and-tough best friend sound so kind broke me. All of their words did. It started with one tear and then a sob escaped my mouth. That was when the dam broke. Tears streamed down my cheeks and I said it all.

"I don't want things to be messy!" I snapped. "Not for me, at least. If I can be better, then everyone's happy with me. If I can be what they need, then I'm not taking away from *their* problems. Other people are more important. I'm supposed to be the one who handles it. And I *can't*. I've pushed myself for years, and Dean finally got me to stop, and now he's *gone*." All three of them were silent, so I continued. "He's the only one who saw me. And he needed *space*. How is that not my fault?" I put my head in my hands and sobbed.

A pair of arms wrapped around me. Then another. And then a third.

"Grace," Mollie said, "you don't have to take on all the burden here."

"But I do."

"We don't know the whole story," she said slowly.

Jade muttered, "I can't believe you're about to have me

defending a man, but here I go. I've seen how Dean is with you. He saw that struggle. He knew you were doing too much. And he took some of it from you."

"And where is he?"

"I don't know, but have you ever considered that he's doing the same thing you are? Hiding something so he doesn't bother you?"

I blinked, pulling out of the hug. "I don't want him to do that. I wanna help."

"Join the club," Wren said with a wry smile. At first, I thought she was talking about Dean. Had she always wanted to help him too?

But all of the women nodded along and their eyes were on *me*.

"Is that how you all feel?" I asked. "You just wanna help?"

"Yes."

"And you don't want anything in return?"

Mollie's hand landed on my shoulder. "This is what it's like to be loved, Grace."

"You've always been great at showing it," Jade added. "Not so good at receiving it."

Her words brought more tears to my eyes, but they were different this time. They felt lighter.

"Do you think that's what Dean's been doing?"

"Oh, yeah." Mollie said it immediately.

"Yep," Wren added while nodding.

"God, yes." Jade laughed. "He's down bad. I might not know what happened today, but he'll be back, Grace. And you don't need to apologize when he is."

"You never defend guys," I told Jade. "Not after . . . you know."

"I've seen someone I care about grow because of a man." Jade shrugged. "You've always reminded me of a geode. Beautiful, but hiding something even better on the inside."

I took a shaky breath and slumped over. "Thank you all. I swear, I don't know what I'd do without you."

"You'd stay a people pleaser forever," Jade said. "But we're not gonna let that happen."

"Are you okay?" Mollie added. "That was a lot of emotions you just felt. Do you need coffee? A nap?"

I took a deep breath. "Some quiet time. I should be good after that. Will you tell me if any of you hear from Dean?"

"Definitely," Wren said. "But we'll also be here for *you*. I now have a free day. I might as well check in on the coops and see if they need any work."

"I wanna see a cow," Jade said. "I need to bond with one."

"Need to?" Mollie asked with a laugh.

"Um, yes. I think it would add to my aura if I had a cow familiar."

As Wren and Mollie laughed, I laid down on Mollie's couch and shut my eyes. I was safe here. I would figure it out.

Whenever Dean came back.

38

DEAN

Strawberry Springs Neighborhood Watch

Kerry Winsor: Sometimes you're there for everyone else and no one is there for you . . .

Comments:
Tammy Jane: Vague posting AGAIN? Use your words.
Marjorie Brown: She's just mad she's annoying.
Tammy Jane: Pfft. You're right.
Kerry Winsor: RUDE.
Kerry Winsor: I needed a hat from Grace and the shop's closed!
Tammy Jane: Wait, seriously?
Marjorie Brown: He either fucked up or they're having one hell of a morning after.
Henrietta Brown: Sigh. Admins, delete that.

GRAVEL KICKED up from my tires and I sped into the driveway. I wanted to be back before she got up so she didn't wake up alone.

Getting to and from Shady Acres took until after the sun had risen, and I was feeling like the biggest idiot for rushing out like I did. My phone was dead, so I had no way to call her, and I had a feeling she wouldn't be thrilled if she woke up and saw my hastily written excuse for not being there.

I cursed when I didn't see her car, but I needed to charge my phone and see if there was any sign that she'd seen it.

The house was as I left it, but was silent. My heart sank. She hated how quiet it could be.

My note was still on the dining room table and I slowly walked up to it. I wasn't sure what I expected, but when I saw tearstains on it, I sucked in a sharp breath.

I fucked up. I should have *been here.*

Mom's and my conversation was needed, and I hated that I hadn't figured out my own emotions. I'd spent so long running from them that I didn't know how to process them. I wanted to be better for Grace.

And she'd woken up alone.

Checking the time, I knew the Treasure Trove would be open, so the town square was my next stop. I tried to plan out what to say to her, but my mind was spinning like a top. I had no idea how to convey that I'd only meant to be gone for a few hours, and I needed to think and didn't want to bother her.

I'd settled on some version of that when I pulled into the Treasure Trove.

Then I saw the closed sign when I tried to open the door.

My heart nearly stopped.

This was my best guess for where she could be. If she wasn't at home or here, I had no other options on where she would go if she were upset. And not knowing where she was or if she was all right sent ice into my heart.

I had to get my phone to a charger and *wait* until it turned back on before I could message her, but would she even respond?

"So, what did ya do?" I jumped when I heard a voice. Next to me, Hugh was glaring.

"Nothing," I muttered. The last thing I needed was for Hugh and the town to know what I'd done.

"She ain't here and you look guilty. You did something." He crossed his arms. "And you were together a day? That must be a new record."

I didn't have the patience for this today. All of my regret was quickly turning into anger. Could he not see that I had bigger things to do? "Yeah, okay. I messed up. I'm sure everyone was waiting for it."

"We didn't wait long at all."

I gritted my teeth and pinched the bridge of my nose, wondering how I'd managed to make things go as wrong as they possibly could've.

"So, it *was* him?" another voice asked, and I cursed.

Now it was worse.

Mark had walked up to Hugh. His eyes narrowed at me like I was a stain on his shirt.

"Yep," Hugh said. "It was him."

"Damn. It takes talent to mess things up that fast. What did you do?"

"That's what I wanna know," Hugh muttered.

"Cheating?"

"I was thinking he couldn't get it up."

I wanted to keep it together. There was something comforting about being the one that they barely liked. I didn't want them to see the reasons for how I was.

But I was also so fucking tired of being seen as something I wasn't.

"If you guys *have* to know, and I'm sure you do, I'm an idiot who didn't process all his shit before asking out his dream woman, and I realized my dad's death is half of the reason I didn't date because I'm terrified of losing someone I love again. She woke up alone and is thinking God knows what, and I need to explain myself. There, you happy?"

Both men's jaws were on the sidewalk. My chest was heaving and I tried to shake it off, but I hated talking about this. I hated telling anyone *anything*.

But that was how I got here, wasn't it?

"So, it *was* daddy issues!" someone exclaimed. I knew that fucking voice.

I turned to see her smiling so wide I would have thought she'd won the lottery.

"Of course you heard that, Kerry."

"He said daddy issues were only half, Kerry," Mark said as he crossed his arms.

Was I cursed? Had I stepped on a butterfly as a child to get here?

"Yeah, woohoo, let's all celebrate my daddy issues. Or how about we be *normal*?"

Kerry laughed. "We're never normal. That's the best part of us!"

I wanted to strangle something. Maybe someone. "Great."

"But to be fair, I'm sorry your dad died. That should have been the first thing I said, but it's unfortunately the second."

"Was it cancer?" Mark asked.

"My money's on drunk drivers." Hugh scowled. "They drive as bad as I do sober. There can only be one of us on the road at a time."

These fucking *people*. "He was a firefighter. He died in an electrical fire when he went back in to check for more people."

For once, they were all silent.

"Oh, so that's why—" Kerry covered her mouth. All joy was gone from her voice. "When was it?"

"I was ten."

"Jesus," Mark muttered.

"So, you all know my life story and soon everyone will. Great. Can I go now, or do you have more questions?"

"I always have questions," Kerry said. "Where are you going?"

"Back to Grace's. I'll wait for her there." I was turning to go to my truck, but she stopped me.

"Big mistake. Do you know why I'm so weird about gossip?"

"Because you're bored."

"No," she immediately said, but then paused. "Well, yes, but I also hate not knowing things."

"And you yap a lot," Hugh said, rolling his eyes. "Don't you ever get tired of hearing your own voice?"

Kerry glared. "Shut it. I'm trying to have a moment here and you're ruining it!"

He chuckled. "Good."

She shook her head and turned back to me. "I like to know things so I know how to help someone when they need it. Like knowing where Grace is."

Now I was listening. "You know where she is?"

"Dear God," Mark said. "Do you have trackers on us all?"

"No, better. I have a brain."

"That's news to me," Hugh said.

"Dang it! Let me have my moment," she hissed before focusing back on me. "Anyway, Jade's shop is closed too. And there aren't any banging sounds, so Wren isn't working, which means Grace contacted them for one of their girl meetings, which I wanna be invited to, by the way."

I knew that would never happen, but Kerry was being nice for once, so I kept my mouth shut. "So they're all together. Somewhere."

She put one finger up. "For real girl time, no one can over-hear. So, it wouldn't be anywhere on the square. If you went to Grace's house first—"

"Which I did."

"Then they're at Mollie's."

All of us were silent as we stared at Kerry.

Hugh broke first. "She *does* have a brain."

"Told you, old man."

"Guys, focus," I urged. "What's Mollie's address?"

"Are you about to run in for a good grovel?" Kerry asked. "Oh, if only I could be there!"

"Kerry," I said. "Please."

She sighed, but gave me the address. I didn't even say good-bye. I tore off to my truck to find Grace.

"Hey! In this town we say bye to each other!" Kerry yelled at my retreating form.

"Speak for yourself. I only say bye to people I respect, and it ain't none of you!" Hugh said back.

———

I wished I could've noticed anything about Mollie's farm, but all I could do was find the house and hope I'd found Grace.

There were many cars in the driveway, but when I saw hers, the relief that hit me was almost too much to take.

Running to the door, I banged on it. I could hear voices in the field that I couldn't care less about.

"Jade, if you got bit by a cow—" The door opened and I saw

the very woman I'd been worried about. Her eyes met mine and she paused. "Dean?"

"I'm so fucking sorry," I said. "I didn't mean to be gone so long, and I should've explained everything in my note better, but I was . . . I wasn't in my right mind when I left. That's not an excuse, though. I shouldn't have worried you and—"

She put a finger to my lips. "I think you need to breathe."

I sucked in air at her order. "I warned you I would fuck this up."

"We're human, Dean. I fear this is part of it all." Her eyes flicked behind me. "We could go inside, though. Where no one will hear us."

"Why would you do that?" Jade asked. It was followed by a loud moo. "My new cow familiar is here to take notes!"

"I'll give you the rundown later. Ask Mollie if it's okay to borrow her house."

"It's good!" a voice I didn't recognize called.

"Are you all here?" Grace asked.

"No!" three voices responded.

She sighed and grabbed my hand.

I felt like I was watching all of it through a screen. Nothing felt real. Why wasn't she angrier? She seemed . . . okay?

We walked into a small living room. This house had a similar charm to Grace's.

"There. Now we can talk. I have a feeling whatever happened shouldn't be overheard by my friends, even if they're well-meaning."

"Everyone's gonna know anyway." I shook my head. "Don't worry about it."

"They don't tell the Facebook group anything."

"Not them. I was . . . in town earlier. I ran into Kerry."

"Oh no." She bit her lip. "I should have left a note too. Or texted. I'm *so* sorry."

"It's fine."

"I know you hate running into people in the town. Especially when they're hunting for a story."

"Running into them wasn't fun, but it wasn't the end of the world. Kerry helped in the end. She deduced where you were."

"Not the end of the world?" she repeated. "Who are you?"

I shook my head. "I'm figuring that out. But you should know I don't wanna be the kind of guy who lets you wake up alone. I owe you an explanation."

I gestured for her to sit and I did the same. It gave me just a second to think about what to say. This wouldn't be elegant or perfect, but I needed to say it.

"You remember that my dad died?"

"Wow, we're going right into it?"

I only shrugged. "Why delay?"

"That's fair, and I do remember that. I'd never forget."

Talking about this wasn't comfortable. For so long, I'd avoided things like this. "I was young when he died, and I didn't realize how much I treated it like a fact, not something that changed me. I thought all of my issues with attachment came from that girl in high school, but even then, I was still scared. I just didn't know why. And yesterday, I felt the same way." She opened her mouth to say something, but I shook my head. "It was nothing you did, don't worry."

"You know me so well."

"I do. And I want to know you more. I don't have a lot of memories of my dad, but I do remember how he always seemed to know what Mom was thinking. She both loved and hated it."

"That sounds amazing."

"And it was. And then it ended." I looked down and forced myself to continue. "I've never seen Mom like that. She was broken. She begged for it to be a dream and—" My voice cracked and Grace's hand landed on my shoulder.

"It wasn't one."

"Mom and Dad were the pinnacle of love to me. But not how they felt *during* it."

"It was the end you remembered." Her voice was soft.

"I've tried not to think of that night ever since it happened, but when I finally faced what I *thought* was my fear and asked you out, it reared its ugly head." My heart hammered and I couldn't look at her, but I spoke anyway. "I had a nightmare about that night. But instead of burying Dad, I buried you."

She gasped.

"I did need space, but not because of anything you did. I should have said more, but I wasn't thinking straight."

Grace was quiet. I finally snuck a glance at her and her brow was pinched. "Where did you go?"

"I went home. Or what used to be home. Mom was awake and we talked for a while. I needed that, and now it's my goal to work through that fear."

I thought that Grace would be relieved. Everything was okay now and we could move on, but instead, her teeth sank into her lip. "I—that's incredible." Her quiet voice startled me. "I just wish I knew this was happening."

"You were tired and you needed sleep. I didn't wanna wake you up for this."

"But I wanted you to. I may not have known exactly what to say, but I could have gone with you to your mom's."

"Grace, it's too much to carry even for me. I can't put that on you."

"But you can take on *my* issues?" she asked.

I felt like I'd been sucker punched. "That's different."

"Not for me. My version of love isn't one person taking on everything. I've done that before and it's not what I want. I want you to be here for me, but I also want to do the same for you. Life is messy and heavy, and I don't wanna go through that alone anymore. You're the first person I'm *me* with, even if it's not perfect. Please let me see the same thing."

"But I—it's not . . ." I paused, not knowing what to say. I wasn't sure why I wanted to hide the hard parts of my life from her, but I could remember when she tried to do the same to me.

"You said we were a team," she reminded. "Doesn't that apply here too?"

I nodded. "You're right. I know you are. It's just a habit to do it."

"It was a habit to hide everything from everyone, but it makes sense that the fears are the hardest thing to let go of."

"I'm sorry," I said. "I hate that I fucked up on day one."

"Don't," she said softly. "We're just trying to get this right. I've messed up and you've forgiven me. And I'll do the same for you."

"I *never* want to hurt you."

Her smile was kind. "You can't always be perfect. No matter how hard you try. Trust me, I know."

"You handled this really well," I said. "Seriously, you're incredible."

"Don't give me too much credit. The girls smacked some sense into me, and I needed it." She reached out and poked my shoulder. "Next time, I want it to be you, though."

"Trust me, Mama, it will be."

GRACE

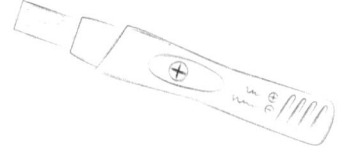

Strawberry Springs Neighborhood Watch

Kerry Winsor: Any update on Dean and Grace? I heard they already had a fight!

Comments:
Tammy Jane: Men. Ya can't trust 'em.
Hu Gh: He was all out of breath over her. I bet he resolved it.
Kerry Winsor: I need DETAILS. **@Mollie Wilson @Wren Hackett @Jade Clark**
Jade Clark: I don't know what details you want. I professed my love for a cow and was denied.
Kerry Winsor: ??? What does that possibly mean???

BOTH DEAN and I were exhausted emotionally. I couldn't keep taking over Mollie's house, so we went back to mine and talked for a little longer before we watched TV on the couch.

Virginia had reached out to both of us to make sure everything was okay, and that she wanted to make sure I had all the recipes Dean's dad used to make. There was one for a chicken and rice soup that I knew I had to make.

Dean offered to get me food, but I needed something home-cooked after the day I'd had. He didn't fight me, but he did offer to help.

And I quickly realized I should have said no.

"Wait, wait!" I grabbed at the raw chicken he was about to drop in the pan.

"What? The burner is on. Don't we need to add the chicken?"

"That's a stainless-steel pan. You need to let it get hot and then add oil so the chicken doesn't stick."

Dean frowned. "What?"

"If you let it heat up, things don't stick as badly."

"But I thought you weren't supposed to let pans get hot when empty."

"Maybe nonstick, but not this kind." He looked at me like I was explaining rocket science to him. I patted his cheek. "How about you handle dishes?"

"I don't know whether to be insulted or relieved." He stepped away from the stove as I put the chicken on a plate and washed my hands. I got the seasoning ready as the pan heated up.

Normally when I cooked, I never fully followed the recipe. I would always adjust the seasonings or other small tweaks to make it suit my taste. But with this recipe, I agreed with every single thing on it. I'd never get to meet Dean's dad, but it made me feel like I was connected to him.

Dean emptied the dishwasher as I sautéed the chicken. Once I was done with that, I took it off and cooked onion and garlic before adding in broth, seasonings, rice, and the cooked meat.

"That smells incredible," Dean said as I put the spoon down. "Are you trying to seduce me?"

"My tacos should have been the one to do that." I leaned into him as he came behind me and wrapped his arms around both me and my belly.

"Oh, they did." His lips pressed against my cheek. I was happy to stay in his embrace. The heat of his body was what I'd needed. I didn't think he would take it any further, but then he moved my hair and pressed his lips against my neck.

"Are you *trying* to distract me?"

"You're the one who's distracting." His hands rubbed my stomach for a moment before they moved upward, brushing the underside of my breasts.

My body had already started to respond. I had a feeling he would put a stop to it soon and I would have to pull out one of my dildos for a mediocre night.

"How long is left on the soup?"

"It simmers for thirty minutes," I said.

"I can work with that."

I yelped when he lifted me up and onto the counter. "What are you doing?"

Dean's eyes were half lidded and he looked at me with an expression I hadn't seen since I'd gotten pregnant. My heart skipped a beat. Was my night not about to be mediocre after all?

"I'm making up for lost time."

"But you said you wanted to wait."

He hummed as he considered it. "We agreed to do everything together, and I think this counts."

"I'll never let you hear the end of it if the soup burns."

"That's a risk I'm willing to take."

Dean's hand landed on my cheek and he tugged me toward his lips. I went willingly. I'd let him do anything to me.

"Should we go to the bedroom?" I said against his mouth.

"You need to keep an eye on the food."

If he was touching me, there was no way I could keep an eye on anything. I wanted to tell him that, but his hand slipped under my shirt onto my bare skin, and I had no other thoughts.

Pregnancy had made everything more sensitive, and every part of me he touched erupted in gooseflesh. When his lips moved back to my neck, that joined in.

I could have stayed here forever. But I also wanted more. It didn't matter what he did, I would be happy. He was all mine. How could I not?

Wrapping my legs around him, I tugged him closer. His body pressed against me in all the ways I needed him to, and I thanked all the gods I could that my counters were the perfect height for this.

Dean was already hard, and I enjoyed the feeling of him against me. There had been a time when I never thought this would happen again, and here I was, living in exactly that.

My mind was alight with all the things he could do to me. There were so many positions I wanted, but we had limited time.

Eventually, the feel of him through his jeans was no longer enough.

"I need you to touch me," I said.

"I wanna take this slow."

"*No*," I whined. "I can't wait." He pulled away and took me in. I had no doubts my cheeks were flushed. Everything felt hot. "Please," I begged. "You have to make me come. I've been waiting for this for far too long."

A slow smile spread across his face. "You know I can't say no when you beg." His hand snaked down and his mouth returned to mine. "You look fucking incredible while you do it."

I couldn't manage a response as he slid his hand past the

waistband of my sweatpants. My eyes slipped closed as he brushed across my clit.

I'd been thinking about this for months, and there was a part of me that wondered if I was playing it up in my mind.

Dean's finger traced up and down my slit and I let out a breathy moan.

"Have you been waiting for this?"

"Yes. *Yes.* I can't wait much longer."

He finally applied pressure and I sucked in a breath. My hands landed on his shoulders and they tightened as his finger rubbed circles. We must have looked wild like this, him with his hands in my pants as dinner simmered on the stove, but I loved it.

This wasn't going to take long, and I knew that as he kept the pressure on and let it build. My hips moved in time with his movements as my breathing kicked up. My body had been ready for this. It also helped that it was Dean. His hand was far better than mine.

I was hitting the edge as heat built from my core. It threatened to spill over and take me with it.

"Fuck," I said into his mouth, and he pulled away just enough to look at me as I tipped over it.

My eyes slipped shut and my entire body clenched as white-hot pleasure rippled throughout every cell in me.

"You're so fucking gorgeous like this," he said. "I mean, you are every day, but this is . . . even better."

"I'll look even better when you're fucking me."

"We'll have to test that."

My body still sang after my orgasm and I only wanted more. My hands moved from his shoulders to peel his shirt off his body. He took his jeans off and yanked my sweatpants down.

"Do you want me to get a condom?" he asked.

"Not using a condom is how we got here. Did you forget?"

"I didn't forget a second of that, but I usually use one, so I'm asking."

I bit my lip, unsure of if I could even play it safe if I wanted to. Our first time had been great, but the feeling of nothing between us was even better.

"Have you been tested recently?" I asked. I wasn't sure when he would have even had the time, but a girl could hope.

"I haven't in a few months, since right before you and I had sex."

"And how many other people were you with?"

"None."

I wasn't sure I heard that right. "None?"

"I told you it was only you."

"But you didn't even . . ."

He pressed a kiss to my lips. "I didn't want anyone else."

I stared at him, still not comprehending that when I thought he'd been distant, it was still only me. I made it my job to read people, and yet I'd missed that.

"Only me?"

"Only you since the day I met you."

My throat closed up. I didn't want to ruin the moment by crying on him, but I didn't know how much he'd cared, even from the beginning.

"You okay?"

"I am. I'm just shocked." I tugged him closer. "I wanna feel it all. No condom."

Dean lined himself up and I shut my eyes, eager to feel his piercing enter me. As he pressed in an inch, I bit my lip.

It wasn't as good as I remembered. It was better.

"Fuck," he said, his voice tight. "There's no way I can make this last."

"Five months has you at the edge?"

"*You* have me at the edge."

I didn't care how long he lasted. I just wanted to feel him.

Besides, I could have it all again any time I wanted.

"Make me come again," I said. "And as long as I feel you, I'm good."

"Yes, ma'am."

I figured he would pull out and use his hand again, but managed to get one of his hands in between us and on my clit.

Sensation blossomed from two areas. Dean was slowly entering me and my swollen clit was getting pressure from his fingers. I gasped at the burning pleasure.

"Let me hear you," he said. "Don't hold back."

Dean pulled out and pressed back in, earning a sharp cry from me. Feeling the cool metal press against my G-spot and the pressure on my core was worth it.

He didn't waste any time. He pushed in and out of me, gaining depth slowly as he went. I was still tight around him, and both of us loved the feel of it. His jaw clenched with every inch he moved. He was enjoying this as much as I was.

It was too much in the most perfect of ways.

"I'm gonna—" I couldn't finish the sentence.

"Me too," he said in a near growl as he let loose and pummeled into me.

If my first orgasm was heat, then this one was fire. It overtook every part of my body, stealing my vision as it burned through me. I lost track of time. I lost track of Dean. All I could do was *feel*.

"Goddammit, Grace." Dean's lips covered mine again as he came too.

I swore I could feel him coming inside of me, and I savored every second of it. His body stayed pressed against mine, and instead of pulling away, both of us stilled.

It was how I'd wanted it to be the whole time.

Even though I didn't want it to, reality crept in.

Mostly because my ass was numb.

"One of these days, we need to have sex on a bed," I said. "I'm getting too pregnant for this."

"We've got all the time in the world."

I was about to agree when the last bit of pleasure left me and I finally remembered that we were in the middle of making dinner.

"Shit, the soup doesn't! I need to stir it!"

40

DEAN

Dad Company (But Sometimes Good Advice)

Dean Briggs: I know you all were waiting on the edge of your seats, but my plan failed. I'm now dating the mother of my child.

Comments:
Ryan Kim: You had us in the first half, not gonna lie. Congrats, man!
Robert Colt: Hell yeah! An actual happy ending!
Oliver Brian: Shouldn't we be on topic? This is a dad advice group . . .
Robert Colt: Shh, I'll bend the rules this once. I'm living vicariously through others.

INSTEAD OF WAKING UP ALONE, I woke up warm. That worry about how this ended hit me before I could enjoy it, but I remembered Mom's words and tugged Grace closer. Her back was plastered to my front and she snuggled closer in her sleep.

This was what I'd always dreamed of. It had faded in adulthood, hidden by fear and resentment, but now I felt like *me*.

Instead of focusing on how it could end, I thought about what I would do next. I wanted to finish the few projects on her house that I'd started. I wanted to move my stuff into her room and go full force on the nursery. I wanted to make her breakfast and talk to her about our days.

I tried to pull away and go get coffee started, but her arms tightened on my forearm.

"Not yet."

"You're supposed to be asleep," I said.

"I had a feeling you were trying to leave." Her voice was still soft and sleepy, but I knew me leaving in the middle of the night had done damage.

My heart sank as I rubbed her back. "I'm just gonna make breakfast for you. And coffee. I won't be going anywhere."

"I don't have anything for you to make."

"I can go to the store."

She blew out a breath. "Stay here. With me. I sleep better when you're around."

"Really?" I asked. "I've heard that sleeping gets harder later in pregnancy."

"You're actually an incredible cuddler," she said with a laugh. "I didn't even need my pregnancy pillow to fall asleep."

"You were exhausted."

"Oh, trust me, I've been kept up by this little one when I've been exhausted."

"Are you keeping your mama up, baby? That's very rude."

"It's more like my body does."

"Shh, I'm talking to my kid."

She went silent, but I could see her cheeks turn red. I sat up, getting a better view of her belly.

"I can't wait to meet you so you can kick me instead." I rubbed my hand over the skin there. "Your mama has been doing too much work."

"I've not. Just my job and growing a kid."

"That's still a lot."

She laughed. "Perfect boyfriend material."

I didn't know why I was so afraid of this with her. It was easy. Like coming home after a long time away.

Our moment was interrupted when her stomach growled.

Her lip poked out. "I'm not gonna say you're right."

"And I know better than to ask for you to. What are you in the mood for?"

"Gummy bears and ice cream?"

"Somehow I feel like you should also have nutrients too."

"Boo."

"How about gummy bears and yogurt?"

"That's not a terrible idea."

I pressed a kiss to her cheek. "Be right back." I got up and threw my shirt on while she groaned. "Shut up and let me feed you."

"I like it when you talk dirty to me!" she yelled as I left. I couldn't keep the smile off my face as I drove into town. I got what I needed from Food 'n' Things and walked up to the checkout.

I'd dealt with the people in town enough to know when one of them was about to strike up an annoying conversation, and Dale was bouncing on his feet when he saw me.

"So, you and Grace are in hot water already, huh?" He sounded like that would be the best news in the world.

I sighed and leaned on the counter. "Let me guess, it's what everyone's talking about."

"Definitely. Now, has she kicked you out of her house yet? I kinda thought this would happen. Corruption doesn't last."

That gave me pause. "What?"

"You and her. You corrupted her a little, but she saw the light of day and moved on."

I couldn't believe what I was hearing. These people *still* thought that? Even after I'd been here for weeks and shown them I didn't want to corrupt anyone?"

Dale continued on, oblivious to my glare. "I have a record with bets, and I knew I'd win the long game, you know."

"We're not broken up," I ground out.

"Wait, really? But you had some kind of fight."

"And we talked it out."

"What did you do that for? There goes my record."

"We're not just bets. We're people."

Dale paused as he scanned the items. "Touchy," he muttered.

"I didn't corrupt her," I muttered right back.

"Well, you did something." He laughed as if it were nothing and then told me my total. I gritted my teeth and paid as quickly as I could. I needed to get the hell out of here.

Once I was back in my truck, I hoped I would calm down, but my bad mood stuck around until I got back to the house.

Grace was in the shower, and I worked on putting food together while trying to push away my annoyance.

"Food?" I heard only moments later.

"Yes. And coffee." I handed her both and she gave me a grateful smile before plucking a gummy bear to eat.

I thought she hadn't noticed that I was still tense, but I was wrong.

"So, what happened in town?"

I sighed. "Do you wanna enjoy your breakfast before I tell you the drama?"

"Nope. I'm always here for it. Unless it's about Hugh being naked in more places. I'll have to pass on that."

I wanted to laugh with her, but Dale's words played back in my mind.

"What happened?" she repeated, her voice softer, and she grabbed my hand.

"I thought most of them had come around. I was wrong."

"Who?"

"Dale. He said something rude and I forgot that I wasn't in the clear. He said I corrupted you and was hoping you'd seen the light and left me."

"He *what*?" she nearly yelled. I jumped at her sharp tone. It was one of those ones that would send a chill up a kid's spine.

She was going to make a terrifying mother.

"Hang on, finish breakfast first—"

"No, I'm not gonna sit here while he insults you and me like that. Maybe Kerry was onto something when she compared him to Hugh."

"Grace, it's fine." It wasn't, but I still didn't want it to bother me anymore. "Half of the people here probably think the same thing."

Her jaw dropped before she shook her head. "That's not fine to me."

"It is what it is. I own the reputation I had before I met you."

"And? You being a playboy doesn't give them the right to say what they want."

"They don't like me, and this is how people treat those they don't like." I shrugged, even as my chest hurt thinking about how Shady Acres had become in the end. "They all are like this eventually."

Grace pressed her lips together. "Not here. We care about each other."

"They care about *you*. Not me."

"I should—"

"Grace," I said gently, "I don't want you fighting this for me. It was one person, and I can deal with that."

"People *do* like you here," she said. "I know I do."

"And that's what matters." I squeezed her hand. "It's all I care about."

———

"You don't have to do this, you know." Grace crossed her arms as we both looked at the antique shop in front of us. "You could hide out in the Treasure Trove until he forgets he contacted you."

I laughed and shook my head. "Here's one thing about grumpy old men, if they're asking for help, it's dire. I wouldn't be surprised if he has a fire hazard in there right now."

"Hugh *is* the fire hazard," Grace replied. "But it's very nice of you to help him. Even if he drives you up a wall today."

"I'll survive, and then I'll go work on the house a little more."

"See you at home," she said before giving me a kiss and turning toward the Treasure Trove.

"I think I preferred it when you two were fighting."

I jumped. Hugh had somehow snuck up on me.

"You're quiet, do you know that?"

"You're too busy staring at Grace to notice me." He crossed his arms. "Now, are you here to help or not?"

I wasn't sure what to expect when Hugh called me, but him having a job for me to do wasn't one of them.

The weeks that had passed had been more than decent. They'd actually gone well.

I hadn't officially decided if I was moving here, but I was close to it. Despite everything that should've made me hate this place, I was still reluctant to leave Grace. The farthest I'd gone was Knoxville to catch up with Clyde and tell him things had worked out.

Hugh's antique shop was packed to the brim with things all from a bygone era. For a man with such a reputation, I wasn't sure what kind of things he would stock. There were a lot of hand-painted plates and oil lamps, as well as old soda bottles. It was a mix of trash and treasure, but I could see myself finding something to buy here if I wanted to.

"What's the issue?" I asked.

"This outlet shocks me whenever I use it."

Yeah. That was an immediate problem. "How long has it done it?"

"Eh, about fifteen years."

I turned to him with wide eyes. "You know that could have turned into a fire."

"It didn't." He shrugged as if it were nothing. "I was waiting for someone I halfway liked to fix it." He gestured to me.

"Nice compliment," I said. "I'll save the lecture because of that."

"Since when does being nice get you anything?"

"Since the beginning of time, Hugh."

"Sounds like a scam," he muttered.

I only shook my head to hide my smile and got to work. As I did, Hugh vanished to do something else. I had to run to my truck a few times, but I was able to get it in working order in just a few hours.

"I suppose you wanna be paid, huh?" he said when I was done.

I had a feeling he didn't have a ton of money lying around. "It's fine. Call it a favor."

"I don't take handouts, boy. Stay right there."

I wiped my hands and sighed. My rates were higher than he

could probably afford—not that I'd charge that to most of the people here anyway. I would accept a crisp one-dollar bill if it made him feel any better.

But Hugh didn't give me a one-dollar bill. He actually walked out of a back room with a huge wad of cash in his hand. "Here."

He threw it at me, and I had to make sure they didn't fly everywhere. At first, I thought it was a pile of ones, but when I looked closer, I saw what it really was. Twenties and tens.

"What? I don't need this much."

He shrugged. "Well, I have it. And you'll need it when I kick your ass in poker." Hugh nodded and turned away, but then he paused. "So, you and Grace. You're in it for the long haul?"

Oh, here it was. "Yes, sir."

"I guess you owe me a thank you," he said. "For the hotel mix-up."

I'd put *that* out of my mind, not wanting to relive seeing him naked. But I did know that staying with Grace had pushed us together.

"It was more of a bad circumstance, but I suppose I do owe you a thanks."

He laughed, which was an odd sound from him. "I knew you'd call her. And I knew she'd let you stay. Never have I ever been so glad I know how to bribe, boy."

That gave me pause. "Wait a minute, what did you just say?"

"You think that hotel is ever full?" He shook his head. "I know the girl at the front desk. She's saving up for a car. I helped her along and she gave me a key."

"You are unbelievable."

"It worked, didn't it? And I made it back on my bet. Enjoy

391 AS I GROW

your girlfriend, kid! Just remember it was me who made it happen!"

This time he truly walked away, and I only had confusion and a wad of suspicious-looking cash to show for it.

This town was *so* fucking weird.

And yet, a smile made its way onto my face as I left to go to the bank.

After getting a raised eyebrow from a teller, I deposited my crumpled-up cash into my account and got a few things to work on the front yard of Grace's house. She wasn't much of a gardener, so the front was overgrown and the grass was getting tall. It was a warm day, but a decent one, so I figured I'd take care of it.

After finding an old mower that worked, I got the grass cut down before I trimmed the bushes. The sun beat down on me, and eventually, I pulled off my shirt to cool off.

Grace found me right as I was finishing up.

"Oh my *God*." Her jaw was on the ground as she got out of the car.

"Like what you see?"

"Very much," she said, but her eyes were on *me*, not the work.

"Eyes on the prize, Day. You can see this whenever you want."

"You're shirtless in a cowboy hat while *glistening*. Nothing else could be more important than this."

I shook my head. "You're objectifying me."

"Yep. What are you gonna do about it?"

I rolled my eyes and made my way over to her, kissing her senseless.

Grace's breaths were heavy when I pulled away. "Now, can we focus?"

"No," she pouted. "I want you to take me to bed and—"

If she finished her sentence, I would give her whatever she wanted. So I turned her around to look at the cut grass and bushes.

Once I was out of her field of view, she saw all that I'd done. "Wait, did you mow my lawn and trim my bushes?"

"That's what I was *trying* to show you."

"Well, cover up next time so I can focus."

"Yeah, yeah."

Grace turned around and faced me. "Seriously, though. Thank you. I hate yard work. I owe you one."

"You owe me nothing," I reminded her. "We're a team, remember?"

When she smiled, she *glowed*. I didn't help her out to get anything in return, but if I did, this would be the gift I needed.

"I'll handle dinner as a thank-you. I actually stopped at the store to get a few things."

"I'll take your food any day," I said as I walked over to the car to grab the bags. "What are you cooking?"

"A Day specialty," she said. "Chicken alfredo."

"Will it be good enough that I'll want to marry you?"

She laughed. "Probably. You should have bought a ring."

I needed to get one. Immediately.

I finished up outside as she cooked dinner. When it was done, I helped her plate it and set the table before getting to experience another one of her perfect dishes.

This was the life. Getting to spend time with someone I cared about each night for dinner. For right now, it was just the two of us. Eventually, our baby would join in.

I couldn't wait.

Halfway through the dinner, Grace paused on eating, feeling her stomach.

"Are you okay?"

"Yeah, I'm fine." She still kept a hand on her bump. "The baby's just kicking."

"Really?"

"I thought it was gas, but this feels real."

We'd known that she would be able to feel them any day, but she hadn't brought it up. I knew many first-time moms didn't realize it was happening until later.

"Can I feel?"

"I don't know if you'll be able to feel anything," she said. "But yes."

All other thoughts vanished as I placed a hand on her belly. At first, I didn't feel any movement, but I did feel connected to them in a way I hadn't before. Life was always one job after another. Work and more work. But this was far more than that.

"Hey," I said. "It's your dad."

And I swore I felt the tiniest movement.

Grace gasped. "That was definitely a kick."

"I felt it too," I said quietly.

"They like you."

"Or my voice is annoying."

"You do realize this baby is gonna adore you, right?"

I wasn't sure, but I wanted them to. I'd loved Dad, but I still didn't remember how he'd acted. I would do my best.

"They'll adore you just like I do," she added softly.

I could only meet her hazel eyes and stare.

Because I knew Mom was right. This moment, even if it was all I had, was worth all the fear.

And I had no regrets.

41

GRACE

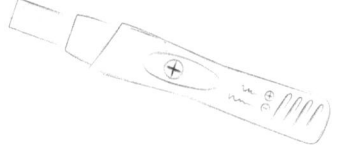

Strawberry Springs Neighborhood Watch

Hu Gh: ONCE AGAIN, MY FREEDOMS ARE BEING IMPEEDED ON. WE NEED TO BAN DECAF COFFEE!!! I CAN DO WHAT I WANT.

Comments:
Tammy Jane: That was your eighth cup! Touch some grass, old man!
Henrietta Brown: Tammy, touching grass doesn't always help. Marjorie touches it all the time and she never calms down.
Marjorie Brown: Shut up! There are cops in this group.
Kerry Winsor: @SherriffMike Finch
Marjorie Brown: KERRY!
SherriffMike Finch: I have other things to deal with. Can you people leave me alone?

"I DON'T UNDERSTAND how picking a simple yellow color can be *this* stressful." I stared at the wall as if it were offending me. Over the last couple of months, I'd put off working on the nursery. With only six weeks left until my due date, it was time. The small bed was pushed into the corner, and Virginia sighed and looked again.

"I still like the one on the right." She crossed her arms. "Though, it's very bright."

"It'll be *too* bright on all the walls."

Virginia hummed and nodded.

We'd been at this ever since Virginia had arrived hours ago. She'd offered to come and stay for a few days, and now that Dean slept in my bed with me, we had the room. First, we worked on cleaning out most of the nursery, leaving only the bed and a nightstand.

This was one of the last things left on our list of things to do before the baby. My house was finally presentable again because of Dean, and I already couldn't wait to show it off to the girls. The yard was mowed and in shape, and inside, all cracks had been repaired and painted over, and anything that was left on the floor was put up and organized.

It finally felt like a home, not just a house. Most days, I woke up thrilled that Dean came into my life.

This was the main thing still bugging me.

I was about to go back to staring at yellow swatches when my phone went off. I figured it would be from the girls or Dean, but a name I didn't expect to see flashed on the screen.

BROOKE

Hey! It's me. I'm performing at a sing off out in Nashville and I would really love it if you could make time for it. I've been really wanting to show you all I've been working on. I hope to see you there!

I stared at it. We hadn't talked much since her half apology. I was still on the fence about how I felt about her, but I figured she would show up one day and we would see how it went.

The last thing I ever expected was for her to *invite* me to something.

All this time, her life in Nashville seemed separate from her life here. She would come here to tell me about it, not ask me to see anything.

She didn't reach out. She showed up.

This was a change for her.

Had anything else changed?

I wanted to go see.

But the bar was in Nashville. That was three hours away, and I didn't want to even *think* of driving that far by myself.

"Let's take a break," Virginia said. "You seem lost in thought."

"S-sorry. I was thinking about something else." I forced myself to look at the paint samples on the wall and still wasn't sure which one I liked better. "But I should take a break, you're right."

"It's dinnertime anyway. Dean should be back in about an hour."

"Do you really think traffic will be that nice to him? He's coming from Knoxville."

Dean had been splitting his time working for Wren and Clyde. The only jobs he took were in Knoxville, but it was over an hour away, and that led to some late nights.

Between the maintenance on my house and his job, he'd hardly slowed down. Dean had told me he wanted to have savings so he could take time off and help with medical bills. I hated that he had to consider it, but even I could see the money would be helpful. I would have done the same thing, but I could only work so many hours before my body demanded I sit.

"Could you try to show me how to make a pasta sauce again?" Virginia asked. "I'm determined to figure it out."

"Yeah, of course." Cooking was mainly practice, though Virginia needed more help than I expected. Still, I enjoyed spending the time with her, especially when Dean was at work all day while the shop was closed.

We moved to the kitchen where I got everything we would need. My pasta sauce recipe was an amalgamation of many different ones, but I made sure to slow down and tell her why I was doing what I was doing. She'd seemed focused, but when she asked me if she could substitute tomato paste for tomato sauce, I knew she would need more time.

The front door opened as I was draining the pasta, and Dean appeared in the kitchen.

"Baby, what did I tell you about leaving the front door unlocked?"

I shook my head and accepted a kiss from him. "I was home all day, so it's fine."

"You forgot to say hello," Virginia reminded him.

"I have to lecture her first."

"You're lucky she likes you," she said with a roll of her eyes. "Never forget your manners."

Dean sighed. "Hello, baby. Please lock the door."

"No," I said as I stuck my tongue out.

Dean shook his head and muttered about how unbelievable I was before going to wash up for dinner.

"By the way, how often is the store closed?"

"Two days a week," I replied. "Though, I've been sneaking in a few more since all of this happened."

The third trimester had taken its toll on my energy. Things like bending down were more difficult, and running a shop was hard.

"People'll get over it," Dean said.

"You know, my last client back in Shady Acres canceled her service. I could maybe help out on a more permanent basis."

"You absolutely don't have to."

"But I want to. I was thinking about living here anyway." She said it casually, but I felt like I'd been gobsmacked.

"Wait, seriously?"

"I don't know where I'll live, but it's the plan."

"You can stay here!" I said it immediately. "I have the space."

"Until the nursery is built," she said softly. I deflated at the reminder. It felt like no one lived here, and I had an extra room that was never used.

It was too bad it was Brooke's.

I wondered if she would even notice if I did let someone use it. After all, she was barely here.

But then I remembered her inviting me to one of her shows and I felt bad. She was trying. It was in her own way, but I saw it.

"I'll only stay until the nursery is done. Then either a house will sell or I'll get an apartment." She looked a little green at her own suggestion.

"We'll figure it out, just like with everything else."

Virginia smiled gratefully and then turned to her son. "Dean? Didn't you have something to mention to Grace?"

"Oh, this should be good," I said. Dean and I talked about almost everything, but there were times when he didn't know how or what was appropriate in relationships. Since Virginia was around, he would ask her. Most of it had been small stuff, like if things we were doing were too fast, or how not to start a fight while setting a boundary.

"You didn't have to say it like *that*." He sighed. "I just need to stay in Nashville for a few days."

"Oh," I said. I couldn't pretend that I loved the idea of him being gone for days at a time, but he still had an apartment there, and I knew this was coming. "When are you leaving?"

That was when he winced. "I need to start getting things figured out to permanently move here before my lease ends. So, tomorrow?"

"He forgot about all of this," Virginia added. "I promise he didn't keep this from you that long."

But I wasn't mad. I was thinking about something else that was also tomorrow.

"What if I go with you?" I asked.

"Why would you want to do that?"

"Dean, she wants to spend time with you." Virginia said it like it was obvious. And while she was halfway correct, I did have another reason.

"Is that why?" Dean asked.

"I *do* want to spend time with you, yes. But there is a thing I wanna go to out there. Brooke reached out and invited me to a show. It's late tomorrow night, and if we leave early enough, we could make it."

"*She* reached out?" he asked.

"Yes, which she never does. I might be reading into things, but this might be her way of asking to catch up."

"But you're thirty-four weeks pregnant. Is it fair of you to drive all that way to see her?"

"Not really. I wasn't sure I could swing it on my own, but since you're going, I could make it work."

I would understand if Dean said no. I knew it wouldn't be because of me. He hated Brooke, and I didn't blame him for that.

But Dean had said he wouldn't stand in the way of me trying with her, so I had hope.

"I'm fine with that on one condition."

"Tell me your terms."

"If it's anything about what happens in the bedroom, at least let me leave the room," Virginia said immediately.

My cheeks burned. "No, I highly doubt it's that."

"Mom, why would I even—no!"

"Just kidding. I like to see the two of you squirm." Virginia laughed and took another bite of her food. I shook my head. I had a feeling she knew what Dean and I got up to, no matter how quiet we tried to be. Normally, she didn't mention it.

Now I knew I might die of embarrassment if she did.

"The condition is that you do something for yourself in Nashville."

"Will you have time for that?"

"I'll make time for it."

"Your conditions are steep," I said with a sigh. "But I think I can handle doing something for myself."

"And it can't be food related."

"What? But I've heard Nashville has great food!"

"It does, and I'm taking you to those places anyway. It needs to be something fun and for you."

I had to think about it for a moment. "There are a few plus-sized thrift shops I could go to there."

"Now *that's* what I'm talking about," Dean said. "We'll be doing that."

42

DEAN

Strawberry Springs Neighborhood Watch

Hu Gh: Slightly used casket for sale. Cheap price. Get it while you can.

Comments:
Jade Clark: I'm sorry??? Slightly used??? By who???
Kerry Winsor: You never did tell us what happened to your wife, Hugh! PLEASE tell me it's not what I think this is!!!
Tammy Jane: What the hell, old man?
Hu Gh: I didn't use it for its intended purpose!!!! Y'all leave my wife out of this. She just left me!
Marjorie Brown: You're not getting any younger, Hugh. Maybe you should keep it. I bet you'll have a use for it soon!
Jade Clark: MARJORIE OH MY GOD
Hu Gh: YOU BETTER NOT BE CALLIN' ME OLD!!! YOU AIN'T A SPRY CHICKEN EITHER!!!

A DAY LATER, I pulled up to my apartment building.

Normally, I'd have been thrilled to be back home, but this time, it felt different. Instead of seeing the place where I went to relax, I saw a three-story white building that I spent time at.

When had that changed?

"Wow, it's loud," Grace said as she looked around.

"We're near a big road."

"All of them look like big roads," she replied with a laugh. "It's not bad. It's just different."

She'd probably said that just for me. But I'd noticed how the noise had gone up since we got into town. Grace's house was an oasis. There was no one around for what felt like miles. Here, everyone was so close together you could hear everything they were doing.

"Definitely different."

"I bet you're glad to be back for a little while, even if it is to wrap up."

I looked around once more. I enjoyed the work I did here, and the time spent with Clyde. But the rest? I didn't miss the cars or the loud neighbors I had below me. I didn't miss the traffic or the way that I couldn't see nature.

"Strawberry Springs isn't so bad."

"Really?" she asked with a raised eyebrow.

"There're good parts. Even if the people love to be up my ass." I tried to mutter it, but it was weird not expecting someone to waltz up and ask about my day. Here, they wouldn't. They would walk right past me and not look twice.

"Well, you have a break from it," she said. "Are you ready to show me your bachelor pad?"

"Hopefully it's not too bad." I knew it wasn't as cozy as her place was, but I had put art up, at least.

My apartment was on the third floor, and as we walked up the steps, I made a plan for what I wanted to keep versus what I wanted to get rid of. I was used to these things, and it took me far too long to realize Grace had paused.

"Hang on a second." She gasped. "I'm . . . just needing to catch my breath."

I ran back down, feeling like an idiot for leaving her behind. "Are you okay?"

"Yeah. The baby's just pressing on my lungs. I promise I'm not *this* out of shape."

"It wouldn't matter if you were. These stairs are rough for almost anyone. I should have thought about it."

"I'll be fine." She tried to wave me off, but I wasn't having that.

"Come here," I said, and before she could try to lie again, I picked her up bridal style.

"D-Dean!" She was still breathless, but her cheeks were faintly red.

"What?"

She shook her head. "You don't need to carry me in."

"But I will. Or at least to the door. I would go the whole way, but my door is locked."

I knew she wanted to keep fighting it, but I started moving and her arms tightened. I liked having her this close. I liked helping her.

Grace watched me the whole time, and I wasn't sure if she wanted to kiss or kill me.

I hoped it was the first one.

"There you go. One free ride."

"It better be the first of many," she said lowly.

I'd completely forgotten about the third option.

Me carrying her turned her on.

"I can make that happen," I said as I unlocked my door.

Grace barely looked around to see my apartment. The one

bedroom I lived in was nothing compared to her house, and I didn't mind that she was focused on me.

The second my door was shut and locked, she pulled me to her. I noted that I was right about *two* things as she kissed me.

"Have I ever told you how hot it is that you do things for me like that?"

"Have I ever told you how hot you are every fucking day?"

She giggled and brought my mouth back to hers. I didn't know where this would go, nor did I care. She got to take the lead since she was the one growing my child. Some days she loved the idea of sex. Others, her body was too sore to even think about it.

Slowly, she swiped her tongue over my bottom lip and the kiss quickly turned heated.

"You have a bed here, right?" she asked.

"We just got here," I said.

"You told me to do something fun. And I have something *very* fun in mind."

"This doesn't count. You better have something else planned."

"Shut up and fuck me," she said, and then looked around. "After you show me your bedroom, that is."

My bedroom only had a bed and a nightstand, but she didn't seem to care.

It must have been being in Nashville, but I remembered times when I would treat this like a last time. Where I would purposefully try not to get to know someone and focus on the feeling.

But there was none of that with her. Hell, I'd failed at it before I'd even started.

I was in my own place, but I felt like a different version of me. I felt like I was visiting something from my past, but I didn't want to be here.

Suddenly, my choice to move solidified in my mind. I knew I was doing the right thing.

Grace must have sensed that I was in thought because she pulled away and looked at me with a raised eyebrow. "Everything okay?"

"Everything's perfect," I said, pulling her back into a kiss. I put my all into it, proving to her that next to her was exactly where I wanted to be. Nothing could be wrong when I was with her.

I pulled away only with the intent of making my way down her body. I stopped at her neck, and then at her nipples, taking off layers as I went. She'd been sensitive since she'd gotten pregnant, so my mouth in just those two places had her letting out a high-pitched noise that my neighbors could *definitely* hear.

Oh well. I was moving anyway.

Grace was already wet when I put my mouth on her clit. I knew the way to make her come quickly, but instead, I took my time. I went near her clit, but not on it, and with my other hand, I teased her opening.

"Oh my *God.*" She gasped. "More."

I usually gave her what she wanted. This time, I didn't. She caught on quickly.

"Dean," she said, an edge now in her voice.

I gave her one direct swipe of my tongue and went back to it.

Grace's hips arched and her thighs tightened. She moved me right to where she wanted me, and with how hard she squeezed, it was almost like a punishment.

When she finally released me, I looked up at her. "Can't handle taking things slow?"

She was a picture as she sat on my bed, propped up and flushed red. "You got me pregnant before we were together and now we're moving in together. Obviously not. Now make me come like only you can. Or I'll do it myself and hold it over you forever."

Her hand drifted lower and I pushed it away and went back to her pussy.

Once I was fully on track, Grace didn't need to do a thing. I gave her the attention she'd asked for, and her breathing immediately picked up.

My other hand went from teasing her entrance to fully fucking her. I arched my fingers, going for the very spot that set her off.

"Dean, *fuck!*" She arched off the bed and her thighs tightened around me, but it was for a different reason. I felt when she came, and she went from wet to absolutely soaked.

I kept going until she shied away from sensation. I didn't even need to ask if she wanted more, because I knew she was too sensitive.

"God, you're so good at that," she said, her voice light.

"We could go to dinner," I replied. I was painfully hard, but I didn't care. We had plans for the evening, after all.

"I want you to fuck me," she said.

"Even if it makes us late?"

"Yes. Who cares about plans?"

"What you want, you get." I kissed the inside of her thigh as I took off my shirt and pants. As I did so, my eyes caught on her. I'd seen her naked many times, but she still made my heart stop.

The best part of it was seeing her belly round with *my* baby. I noticed it in passing throughout my day, but now it was even better.

"You're so fucking incredible." I whispered it in awe of what all she had been doing.

"You sure know how to make a girl feel special."

"I want you to feel that every fucking day," I said as I finally got my boxers off and hovered over her.

Grace smiled and brought my mouth to hers.

We kissed leisurely for a moment as I lined myself up. I still took things slow and I wasn't sure who enjoyed it more.

"Just fuck me," she said. "Don't ease into it."

"But—"

"It's like you said, we have plans."

"But I don't wanna hurt you."

"You just gave me one of the best orgasms of my life. Trust me, I'm ready. And if it hurts a little—" She bit her lip. "I don't mind that either."

I never once wanted her to be in pain, but I had imagined what it would be like to not have myself so close to the edge after working my way inside of her.

And I had said she would get what she wanted.

"Are you sure?" She nodded. "And you'll tell me if you change your mind?"

"Dean." Her hand landed on my cheek. "I trust you. And you have to trust me to know my own limits."

"Okay. What you want, you get."

I was still lined up with her, and instead of pushing inside of her just an inch, I pushed in all the way in one ruthless thrust.

"Yes, fuck," she hissed.

I wasn't sure which was worse for me, fucking her quickly or taking my time. Maybe I was *way* too into her.

"You did so fucking good," I said as I began to thrust. "God, you feel incredible."

She scrambled for my hand. "Touch me," she begged. "I need to come again."

"Yes, ma'am." I balanced on a forearm, moving my other hand right where she needed it. Nearly every part of us was touching. It felt like I was melting around her. And this was something I wouldn't have done with anyone else. I never would have let it get so intimate.

Grace didn't get every one of my firsts, but she got all the ones that mattered.

I'd give her all the rest too.

She muttered half-formed sentences as she came again. There was no way I could hold back from moving as she tightened around me. I began fucking her earnestly. There was no way I could last, not with the gorgeous vixen under me.

"Yes, yes, *yes*. That's what I need." Grace's legs locked around me.

I wanted to compliment her again, but my words were lost while I was inside of her. All I could do was feel.

It was Grace's turn to shock me, though, because she pulled me down by the nape of my neck and whispered into my ear.

"Be a good boy and come inside of me."

I came the second she said it. Hell, it felt like I'd died and gone to heaven as I emptied myself.

Then I could finally think.

"Did you just play an Uno reverse card with praise?"

She laughed. "I did. And it definitely worked."

I pressed my forehead to hers. "We really need to think about dinner now."

"Oh, we definitely do. I'm starving after that."

"What are you in the mood for?"

"Spicy food."

"I think I can manage that."

GRACE

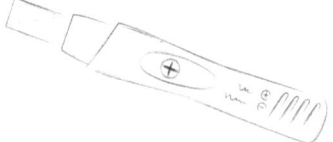

Strawberry Springs Neighborhood Watch

Kerry Winsor: @Grace Day, did you get a weird text from Brooke? She wants me to go to some concert in Nashville.

Comments:
Marjorie Brown: You got that too? I thought she'd lost her mind. Who would invite ME to a concert?
Tammy Jane: I got it too. I don't even like the girl. I bet it's one of those scams.
Mollie Wilson: How did she even get my number???

WE WOUND up at an Indian restaurant in the bottom of a hotel. Dean had mentioned that Nashville was known for its hot chicken, but the idea of fried food nearly made me sick, so he pivoted.

It was a fantastic choice considering how delicious the naan alone was. The curry was even better, and I got to try two different kinds since Dean was willing to share. We weren't able to stay too long, but it was nice to fill up on something good before seeing Brooke.

The drive to the bar was short, and I grew nervous as we got close. I wasn't sure why, since she'd been the one to invite me to this, after all. Why would she be anything but happy to see me?

"Say the word and we'll leave," Dean said lowly. "And if she hurts you, you're leaving anyway."

I wished I could say that she wouldn't hurt me, but this was Brooke we were talking about. Anything was possible with her.

"Okay," I said. "Fair enough."

He nodded and got out of the truck to open the door for me.

If I thought Nashville was loud, a bar in Nashville was even louder. It hit me like a train the second we walked in. Someone was singing a country song on stage, and the speakers were at max volume. Despite that, people were still talking. And yelling.

I found a corner to get us into that wasn't packed with people. I hoped it wouldn't be as loud, but it was. The baby moved. I wondered if they hated this too.

Still, I'd been invited, and I searched the bar for my sister. She was in the front row wearing another pink cowboy hat.

Was she nervous? I would be if I were in her shoes.

We'd gotten to the bar just in time. As the first singer was done, everyone erupted in cheers. Brooke stood and rushed on stage. She had a guitar in hand and waved at everyone.

"Hi, y'all! Welcome to the sing off."

She didn't even sound like herself. She sounded like all the other country singers from Nashville. Her drawl was exaggerated and syrupy. And not to mention, it was very fake.

"I'm Brooke Day and I'll be singing an original for you." She strummed a note on the guitar. "I want to dedicate this to the one who shows up. The person who's been here from the beginning." I nearly froze. Was she actually about to dedicate this to . . . me? "Jude, I know you're out there. This one's for you!"

My hope crashed. She was talking about Jude. Of course she was. My shoulders slumped in disappointment. Dean's hand slid into mine and he raised an eyebrow, a silent offer to leave.

I shook my head and faced the front.

Brooke started playing. I was no music expert, but I could hear a difference between Brooke's performance and the one before it. She'd improved since her days in the shower, but I wasn't sure how she stacked up against all of the other incredible performers in Nashville.

Judging by Dean's wince, he heard it too. Thankfully, he didn't say anything bad about the performance. Unfortunately, there was nothing *good* to say either.

When her song was over, most people clapped, but I saw the whispering going on. We weren't the only ones who'd noticed she'd been a little off-key.

"I'm gonna go say hi," I said to Dean as she got off the stage. Brooke was talking with someone I didn't recognize, but her eyes flicked to me and she did a double take.

"What are you doing here?" she asked when she saw me.

I jerked back. "You invited me."

Her eyes narrowed. "I did? Huh. Maybe I did." She shrugged as if it were nothing. "You're huge, by the way."

Dean must have been behind me. He cleared his throat and shook his head. Brooke took no notice. I wasn't sure what to say. My hope had fallen when she dedicated the song to Jude. Now it was crushed.

"Anyway, I need to mingle. Hope you enjoyed!" She ran off with a wave, not taking a second look at me.

"Wow," Dean said, his voice tight. "That was . . . something."

"Let's go," I said, trying to not let my voice crack. "It's way too loud in here."

Dean tugged me out of the bar, and in the warm air, I finally felt how hot my cheeks had gotten. Brooke had completely dismissed me, and the act hurt more than I wanted to let on.

But one thought was louder than the rest of them. I'd given Brooke so many chances and she let me down each time.

I was *so* tired.

"Grace," Dean said.

"Can we not right now?"

"I'm sorry. I really am."

"You should be telling me that we shouldn't have come. And you'd be right."

"I'm not gonna do that."

"You should."

He grabbed my hand. "She's your sister. Your last family. It isn't a bad thing that you're trying with her. She's the one who doesn't deserve it."

I closed my eyes and took a breath. I refused to cry on the streets of Nashville. "I don't understand how she can only care about herself. I couldn't imagine treating people like she does."

"Of course you can't imagine it. You're kind. That's one of your best qualities."

I needed to hear that. I needed comfort instead of punishment. I leaned into Dean's warm, solid body and let my emotions wash over me.

"Can we go back to your apartment?" I asked. "It would be nice to have a night in."

"Whatever you want."

I was quiet on the way back, but it helped to think through all that Brooke had done to me. I'd continued to give her passes and let her hurt me. All for the sake of family.

But I didn't seem like family to her tonight. Just another inconvenience.

When had I become that to her?

I still felt down when he pulled into his place. We took the stairs slowly, stopping at the second flight.

"Need another ride?" he offered.

"No, but thank you. I want to master these myself." I heaved out a breath. "After I catch my breath, though."

He laughed and leaned on the wall.

Someone else came down the stairs, a woman with blonde hair in a high ponytail. She was in athletic wear and absolutely beautiful.

"Dean!" she exclaimed. "God, it's been forever since I last saw you."

His shoulders went tense. "Oh, hi."

I had a feeling I knew where this was going. Dean's past wasn't a mystery to me. I knew he'd slept around, and most of the time, it didn't bother me.

But while I was facing this beautiful human, a thought hit me hard. One that I'd worked on not having in years.

Why the hell was he with me when he could have women like that?

I always tried my best not to be insecure, but my body was changing in ways I was never ready for. I was at my highest weight, and every day, I saw a new stretch mark on my stomach, legs, or boobs.

As much as I wished I would never feel insecure again, it was a lie. I'd loved my body before pregnancy. Eventually, I would love these changes the same way, but that took time. And I was in a delicate place after seeing Brooke. Especially after the only thing she said about me was that I was huge.

I'd face this. I'd love my body and try my best to never feel this again.

But not until tomorrow.

The woman's eyes drifted to me, and then to my stomach.

"Oh, do you need help?" she asked. "Dean's always great about that."

"She's my girlfriend," he said firmly.

Her eyes widened, then turned downward. "But you told me you didn't date when we . . ."

"Things changed."

She looked in between us, as if wondering *how* and *why*.

I wanted to melt into the floor. I didn't wait to hear the rest. I gave her a polite nod and booked it up the rest of the stairs. I was out of breath, but at least I was alone and could *think*.

My feelings were already bruised. The woman was undoubtedly jealous. None of that was my fault.

But it all felt terrible.

"Grace, hang on. Take it easy!"

"I'm fine." My voice was harsher than I'd ever let it get. "Just give me a second." I needed my logic to come back to me. But looking at Dean, beautiful, *perfect* Dean . . . it hurt.

"Don't worry about her. She's in the past."

"I'm trying not to. I just feel . . . a lot right now." Was it my changing body? Probably. Did I sometimes wonder why Dean had chosen me of all people? Yes, on bad days. "Seeing a past fling of yours didn't help. I have a feeling she would've liked to pick up right where you left off."

"I'm yours," he said, grabbing my hand. "No matter what happens."

"I know. I promise I believe that. I'm just having an off day."

"Come inside." Once the door was shut, he grabbed a pen and handed it to me. "Write your name."

"What are you—"

"Grace, listen." His words were firm. "I want you to know there's no other woman for me. So, write your name."

"Like, on your hand?"

His lips twisted as he considered it and then shook his head. Then he pulled his shirt off.

"On my chest."

Dean being shirtless always had my heart racing, but this was a new level. "Why?" I asked softly.

"Because I know how I feel, but I want you to see it too."

My cheeks burned. I never thought of myself as being the kind of woman who wanted to mark a man. But I wanted to see my name there. I *needed* this reminder.

Slowly and with a shaky hand, I wrote my name. When I stepped back to survey it, my name looked like it belonged.

"Thank you," I whispered.

"We can write it again any time you need the reminder."

"I'm trying not to be insecure," I said. "And normally I'm not, but everything is changing so fast, and some days it's hard to stay confident."

"What's changing?"

"I'm gaining weight, obviously."

"You're still beautiful, no matter what weight you're at." His words echoed a lesson I'd had to teach myself a long time ago, and I needed the reminder.

A long time ago, I'd accepted my weight would change. Now there were new things to work on accepting.

"And then there's the stretch marks."

"Show me."

My cheeks went hot. "I'd rather not."

"Grace, you're always gonna be beautiful to me. Whether you have stretch marks or not. And I'll prove it to you."

I took a breath and I lifted my shirt. Dean fell to his knees, fingers gently running over the marks I was still learning to love.

"Beautiful," he said.

"You don't have to—"

"No, it is. All of it is. It's a reminder that you're growing our child, Grace. And you're doing it so well."

I grew warm. "You really don't hate them?"

"No, I love them. Just like I love—" His eyes flicked up to mine, and his throat worked as he struggled with whatever he wanted to say.

I knew what it was, and while I wanted nothing more than to hear those words, I knew why they were terrifying for him.

Reaching down, I cupped his cheek. "Take your time. I'll be right here."

I could wait however long he needed to. It could be minutes or months, but I *knew*.

He closed his eyes to get his thoughts together. When he opened them, they were shiny. "I love you. A lot, actually, and you don't have to say it back—"

"Dean, I love you too. Now get up here and kiss me."

He didn't waste any time. My emotions still felt sore in ways only time could heal, but this was a moment I'd always remember.

Warmth and love covered all of it like a Band-Aid. I was still emotionally hurting, but it felt easier to take now. This was exactly what I'd wanted when I told him I wanted us to deal with our problems together.

This was what *love* was.

I pulled away, fighting a yawn.

"Bedtime?" he asked. "It's been a long day."

"I should head in that direction. I just wonder why Brooke acted like she didn't invite me. You saw the text."

"She probably just wanted one more supporter." He shrugged. "I don't know if logic applies to her."

I blew out a breath and took out my phone. It had been on silent throughout the night, but I did have a tag from the Neighborhood Watch group. I opened up the notification and my jaw dropped when I read it.

"It was a *fucking* mass text." I showed him the post. "Everyone got it."

"Are you kidding me?" he asked.

"It must have been a marketing thing."

Dean shook his head, jaw locked tight. It matched how I felt. I was starting to hate Brooke. Maybe I should have felt like this a long time ago.

"I wouldn't blame you if you wanted to go home. Mom could come and get you and you could still take time away from the shop."

It was tempting, but I shook my head. "No. Fuck that. I wanna enjoy Nashville and get time with you. I'm having fun tomorrow. She doesn't get a say in that."

"That's my girl."

"And I'm unsubscribing from her stupid text chain." When it was done, Dean was smiling softly at me.

"Feel better?"

"I do, and now it's time to finish cleaning your apartment and have fun." I wanted to start tonight, but I broke out into another yawn.

"Tomorrow?"

I sighed. "Yeah, we'll start tomorrow. Who knew growing a child would be so exhausting?"

44

DEAN

Strawberry Springs Neighborhood Watch

Mark Bell: Had some youngins in here visiting and they called me "unc." What the hell does that mean???

Comments:
Jade Clark: Er, don't worry about it. It's short for uncle.
Mark Bell: Do I look like I'm an uncle to you???
Kerry Winsor: You know, Tommy says that all the time. I had no idea it meant that! He doesn't even have an uncle, though.
Nicole Rudder: Jade, you gotta stop this. Unc means old. Mark, you got called old.
Mark Bell: Of all the people in town, ME??? I'm cool! They should have said that to Hugh or Dale.
Dale Garrett: Hey!!!

"DEAN." A soft voice pulled me out from sleep. "Deeeaann."

"Hm?" I cracked one eye open and found Grace peering down at me.

It was the best way I'd woken up in a long time.

"Good morning."

"Morning, Mama." I snaked a hand around her and tugged her closer. She moved and swung a leg over to straddle me. Now I was really awake. "Need something?"

"You," she said before leaning down to kiss me.

Grace already looked to be in a better mood. It had killed me to see Brooke treat her like she had, but I saw a spark of defiance in Grace that told me she wasn't going to be down-and-out for long.

My lips moved against hers and I stroked her cheek. Until her, I'd shied away from intimacy during sex, but since we'd gotten together, I'd slowly added it in.

And it made it all better.

Grace had gone to bed in a nightgown. She said it was one of the most comfortable things she owned, while I tried and failed to be a gentleman and not stare at her legs as she climbed into my bed. After the day she'd had, I promised myself I would let her rest.

All bets were off now.

I pulled back to witness how gorgeous she looked above me before I took one of her breasts into my mouth. She gasped as I did, but it was muted as if we were back at the house.

"No one's here," I said. "Be as loud as you want."

"Fuck yes," she said as I went back to her nipples. They'd grown as she'd gotten further into pregnancy. Some days they were too sensitive to mess with. On others, it was exactly what she needed.

Grace shamelessly ground herself on my cock, which had hardened the second she climbed on top of me. She must have not been in the mood to be patient, because she pulled away to slide her underwear to the side and free me.

The second I felt her, I let out a loud groan. "You're so fucking wet."

She rolled her hips with a moan. Or maybe it was mine. I wasn't sure whose it was. It was so tempting to find her entrance and start pushing inside her, but I knew she loved having the control of moving on top of me. We had to be flexible in what we were doing because certain positions became uncomfortable in her third trimester. This had quickly become one of her favorites.

I'd never been with anyone long enough to know their favorite, but knowing her felt like knowing myself.

And when she paused, I knew what was happening.

"Need to move?" I asked.

Her cheeks were red. "Sorry. My hip doesn't like this."

Being pregnant came with a whole host of aches and pains. I was sure Grace expected me to be inconvenienced, but I refused to be bothered. After all, I wasn't the one going through them.

"Prop up on my headboard," I said as I patted her thigh.

She slowly did so, and I took over the work. I gave her one more kiss before moving to her breasts and then down to her core.

With one taste, I was reminded of the fact that I'd take this over coffee. Over water itself. She tasted incredible, and the sounds she made were even better.

I was reminded of the first time we'd been together, when neither of us knew a thing about each other. Back then, all of the sounds she made were new. I thought I'd liked the newness of each encounter I'd had, but really, knowing that I made someone I cared about more than anything feel so good was even better.

Knowing which movements she enjoyed made her get to the edge quickly. I knew when her moans increased in pitch and her thighs tightened around my head that she was there, and when she tumbled over that peak, she grew impossibly wetter.

"Do you want more?" I asked. It was tempting to stay down here forever, but I knew she liked coming on my cock more than on my mouth. I was fine either way.

"I need you now," she said.

I grabbed one of her legs and threw it over my shoulder, pressing my cock into her entrance.

"Take this part slow. I wanna enjoy it."

"Yes, ma'am," I said as I captured her lips in a kiss. I bit her bottom one before pulling away.

Her pussy was so wet it felt like she was inviting me in. It was hard for me not to press all the way inside of her, but I knew how much she enjoyed it, and I knew she liked one other thing.

"You look so fucking hot like this, taking my cock so perfectly."

"Oh, *God*."

I pressed in just a little deeper.

"It's like you were made for me." I pulled out as I swirled the head of my cock right at her entrance where she was more sensitive.

Now she was biting her lip, her breathing heavy. Grace's head tipped back as I concentrated on not letting this make me finish too soon.

Her body would let me in at any second, but keeping us both on the edge with my shallow thrusts made everything feel more intense.

"*Fuck*," she said, and then her legs locked around me, making me slip just a little farther inside of her.

"Can't take it anymore?" I asked.

"I could come just from this," she said.

I lifted an eyebrow. "Really?"

"I-I think so."

I wanted to see if she could. Despite her attempts to keep me closer, I pulled back and continued on.

"I didn't mean that as a challenge."

I paused. "Want me to stop?"

She immediately shook her head. Grace was soaked, and every time I slipped in, she would tighten. It was like her core was begging me to stay inside of her, but I continued my work.

"G-God, I'm gonna—" Her jaw dropped open and she tightened again. That was when I pushed deeper, filling her entirely. "*Yes*," she said, arching into me as she was lost to pleasure. I smiled and returned my face to her neck. I was ridiculously proud of myself, but I also was ridiculously close to coming, so a break was exactly what I needed.

Eventually, I wasn't at the edge and I lifted my head to kiss her as I finally moved. I could tell by her high-pitched moans that she was still feeling the aftershocks of her second orgasm.

"Keep moving," she begged.

"These sounds," I said, my voice tight. "I can't last long with you sounding like that."

"Then don't. Come in me." Her legs tightened. "I wanna feel it."

Her words were like adrenaline. Feeling her pussy around me was already getting me close again, but that sent me. I made it another minute thrusting in and out of her when I felt it. I covered her mouth with mine again, and that was when I blew my load. It hit like a tidal wave, taking every bit of my consciousness with it.

That was the thing about fucking someone I loved. Everything was more intense. Everything came with a side of something warm and comforting. It made it all the better.

I could have stayed there forever, feeling her body close to mine, but then her stomach growled.

Grace blushed. "Guess I'm hungry."

I could only laugh. "Then it's time to find something to eat. I'll need it to recover from that."

We wound up going to an eatery that she had found. She was in a better mood today, smiling and laughing with me like she normally did.

And I was relieved.

Love was a little like having a part of my heart walking outside of my body. I felt her pain and her sadness at the same time she did. It was always a terrifying feeling, but the joy I felt *with* her was better than what I felt alone.

As we worked on clearing my apartment out and then all the fun things Grace wanted to do, I wondered how I'd made it so long going through life by myself.

And if I ever truly knew happiness before her.

45

GRACE

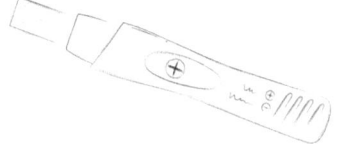

Strawberry Springs Neighborhood Watch

Mollie Wilson: I say this lovingly, but if any of you break my rules at Grace's baby shower, you WILL meet God.

Comments:
Jade Clark: Oh, I'm stealing that.
Kerry Winsor: Threats are against the group rules!!!
Mollie Wilson: I have immunity when it comes to planning a baby shower.
Hu Gh: How do I get that immunity??? MY posts keep getting taken down!

TWO WEEKS LATER, I was trying to find a recipe for punch when I was faced with a very stern Mollie.

"Grace, *sit*." Mollie pointed me to the couch. "If you get up, I *will* kick you out of this house."

"It's my house," I said with a laugh. "You can't kick me out."

"When I'm planning a party, it's our house. And I say you aren't doing a damn thing."

Dean laughed. "Good luck with that."

"You too, cowboy hat. Sit the fuck down or so help me God."

His eyes went wide. "You're not playing."

"I *will* wrap you up like I wrap up the chickens."

"Maybe we should listen," Dean said as he sat. I shook my head and followed suit.

The town had been hounding Dean on whether or not I would have a baby shower. I had been on the fence about planning yet another thing, and I didn't know if Mollie had the capacity to do it.

Then she offered, and I realized how she wrangled kids and handled a farm. She was a fucking force of nature.

"You're so bossy," I said. "But thank you."

"I'm dedicated, and my mom planned an amazing shower for me. I consider this me returning the favor."

"And I get to get pictures!" Virginia said as she came around the corner. She immediately snapped a photo. "Oh, I'm so happy to be here."

Now that I was nearing full-term, all three of us had finished the nursery. I'd gone with a light yellow and found a crib, plus some small furniture. Virginia and Dean had put it all together.

Once there wasn't room for the guest bed any longer, Virginia had increased her efforts to find an apartment, but both of us could tell she wasn't happy.

That was when I offered to have her stay in Brooke's room.

After what she'd done in Nashville, I didn't want to talk to my sister. She'd made her life there, and I was making mine here.

She wouldn't be happy when she found out, but I wasn't

sure that I cared. I doubted she would come home anytime soon, at the very least.

This was the first time my house was guest ready. All of the mess Brooke had left had been put in the basement by Virginia and Dean. We'd slowly gotten to most of the things that needed to be fixed or cleaned, and now it felt like a home again.

Jade and Wren arrived as Mollie finished the punch. She directed them on last-minute decorations while I watched from the couch.

"All right, that's all settled." Mollie put her hands on her hips. "Just in time for the first guest that wasn't called early."

"And who's that?" I asked.

Mollie laughed. "Kerry. Who else?"

"Hello, hello!" Kerry said as she walked in. "Where is the expecting couple?"

"Back here! I've been tied to the couch!"

"Don't say that!" Mollie hissed. "Do you want me to get in trouble?"

"Maybe."

She narrowed her eyes at me. "You're not as nice as everyone says you are."

"She's not," Dean added as Kerry came around the corner.

"Hi!" Kerry said. She had a massive present in her hands. "Oh, you look beautiful. Pregnancy suits you."

"I'll take the present," Mollie said.

"Thank you, but no peeking."

"I am absolutely peeking," she said. "I'm making sure you all brought things from the registry."

"Oh, come on." Kerry laughed. "Do you really expect me to break the rules?" Everyone was silent. "Well, I didn't! Look inside, it's not a diaper cake."

"Is a diaper cake a problem?" I asked.

"Oh, yes it is." Mollie shook her head. "They're cute in the beginning, but a nightmare later. Do you know what it's like to have a poop explosion in process and have to unpin a diaper?"

"But they're cute," Kerry whined. "Do you know how much it killed me to be basic and pick something from the registry?"

"Don't play with me, Kerry."

The older woman huffed and crossed her arms. I'd never seen someone stand up to the town gossip like Mollie did.

Well, until Dean.

It was good to know Kerry could be tamed.

"So," Kerry said as Mollie took the present, "am I still banned from talking about this beautiful baby with Grace?"

"You're clear," Dean said with a laugh. "It was just while the town adjusted."

Her shoulders slumped in relief. "Oh, thank God. So, how are you feeling? Is your crotch on fire yet?"

"S-sometimes," I admitted. Of all the questions to ask, why was it that one? "But it's not too bad."

"I felt like I couldn't walk with Tommy. But then again, he came out with a massive head."

I didn't spend a lot of time thinking about her son Tommy's head. But as the younger version of him crossed my mind, I realized his head *was* quite large.

"Did he hurt coming out?"

Kerry opened her mouth and then paused. "No, I don't think he did." I had a feeling she was lying to me. "Oh, by the way, Dean, do you install recessed lights? I might have some jobs for you."

"Nice subject change," I said with a laugh.

"No need to dwell on what must happen. You'll just freak yourself out."

Dean asked about what she wanted in her house while others arrived. Many congratulated us and brought presents that Mollie continued to audit.

Eventually, we got separated. Jade and Wren returned with snacks, and I immediately went to hunt that down. Cain and Henry arrived and pulled Dean into a conversation about something.

"They're planning a guys' night," Wren said. "Cain and Mollie agreed to give each other one night off a week, and I'm sure Dean will do the same."

"He will," I replied. "It's nice to see him making friends."

As Dean laughed at something Henry said, it was nice to see that he'd built a rapport with the guys. Come to think of it, he'd built a rapport with almost everyone. I knew he preferred the city, but he seemed to be doing well here.

But I knew he had one friend in Nashville that he was going to miss, and that friend had been invited today. I'd been excited to meet Clyde. Virginia said the person he was most social with was Dean, and not to expect us to be best friends, but I was happy to meet anyone who was close with him.

A person I didn't know walked in. He was a larger man and held a small gift in his hands. I excused myself from a conversation with Jackie and nearly ran to him. Dean and I got there at the same time.

"Clyde," Dean said. "It's good to see you."

His eyes shifted to mine and a slow smile spread to his face. "Uh, hi, Dean. And you must be Grace." He handed over a gift. "It's nice to meet you."

Mollie watched us closely and I knew she wanted to make sure the gift was from the registry. I had a feeling that would stress poor Clyde out.

"It's so nice to meet you too. I've only heard good things."

"Me too," he replied. "When I get to see Dean, that is."

It was paired with a chuckle that was well-meaning, but Dean's smile dimmed.

"Sorry."

"Don't be." He shrugged. "I bet this is a nice little town. And you're kinda close to Knoxville. There's work there. A lot, actually."

"Still. We won't be working together *that* regularly. It sucks."

"Well, I wouldn't say that."

"You live in Nashville and that's three hours away." Dean's brow furrowed. "The only time we'll hang out is when you happen to take a job in Knoxville."

"I'll be doing that more often. I think maybe my home base should be there."

Dean straightened. "Really?"

"Yeah, there're a lot of jobs out here and I don't wanna be three hours away from the closest thing I'll ever get to a grand-kid." He glanced at Dean. "If that's okay with you, of course."

"Yes, that's definitely okay," Dean said, clapping Clyde on the shoulder. "More than okay. I'm happy to have you closer."

Dean took him over to Virginia, who was the one other person he knew. She greeted him like an old friend and intro-duced him to some of the people in town. Clyde seemed tense, but I knew he would blend in just fine.

Dean was watching closely and I gave him a thumbs-up before we all started playing games. We got through four before my table was a mess and everyone seemed to prefer talking over playing.

That was when the last guest arrived.

The entire party went quiet when he walked in, and I knew why.

Hugh was *not* the kind of guy to come to a baby shower. Unless it was the bar, he avoided town gatherings. But here he was, a present in hand, even though he looked angry about it.

"This is one hell of a hike," he grumbled.

"Hey, Hugh." I walked up to him. "Thank you for coming."

I heard Mollie whispering to Wren in a panic. I doubted Hugh had let anyone know he was coming, and she had no idea what kind of gift he brought. That made two in a row she didn't know about.

I wasn't worried. It could be a pair of old socks and I would still think it was sweet.

"This kind of thing is too loud for me, so I won't stay long. Where's your other half?" Hugh looked around.

Dean was in the back checking in on Mark and Clyde, but he'd started walking over when he saw Hugh.

"Hey," Dean said. "You looking for me?"

"I got you both a present for the mini-you." He shoved it at us and sniffed. "It ain't much, but I hope you like it."

Dean held the bag as I grabbed whatever it was. It was heavy.

I pulled out a music box. It was a rich wood one with intricate carvings. I stared at it for a long time, feeling like I'd seen it before.

"This is beautiful," I whispered. I couldn't stop staring at it. "It looks familiar."

"Your mom brought it in a long time ago. She needed the money, so I gave her double what it was worth." He shrugged like it was nothing. "I figured I'd keep it and give it back someday."

"This was Mom's?" I knew we had money troubles, but never knew that she'd had to pawn anything off. I'd always thought she'd had magic with her ability to make things happen.

"It was. I liked her. She was as sweet as you are."

I felt tears in my eyes. All this time, I thought I had everything of Mom's that she left behind. I also thought that I knew her, that she had somehow managed to do it all without ever needing help. It looked like I was wrong.

Hugh leaned away. "And that's my cue to leave. Come by the shop sometime, though. I have stories for ya."

With a wave, he left the party.

I thought the only piece of my family was with Brooke. The same girl who'd signed me up for a text chain rather than talking to me. But there were other things that could keep me connected, and they weren't toxic.

My real family seemed to be here, in the people who cared about me and the memories I still held on to.

46

DEAN

Dad Company (But Sometimes Good Advice)

G. Singh: I'm back again with the hellions. They're flushing every chemical in my house down the toilet to rid the world of sharks.

Comments:
Robert Colt: You've really got to lock those up, man. They could drink them.
G. Singh: They were locked. I have the only key. They broke in.
Ryan Kim: Man, you've got problems.
Oliver Brian: Swap the bottles with water.
G. Singh: Kids said it didn't taste the same and it wasn't good enough. Not sure if they're joking or not.
Robert Colt: Do those kids need an exorcism?

GRACE HAD BEEN tired for hours, but I knew she was really hitting a wall when she finally sat. The baby shower had dwindled to just a core group of people. Mom, Jade, and Wren had stayed to help clean up so Mollie could go home. She'd fought, but a meltdown from Jasmine told us all it was time for her and Cain to go.

"That's your future," Mom had said to me. "How excited are you?"

"So fucking excited," I said. "I can't wait."

And it was true. Watching Cain with both his son and daughter renewed my excitement for this. I wanted to be a dad. It was the final piece of the puzzle.

"Mollie should be the party planner from now on," Jade said as she picked up any remaining cups. "That was so smoothly run."

"She does own a farm," Grace said from where she lounged on the couch. "She *has* to be good at planning."

"Also, we need to talk about how you two got a gift from Hugh." Jade's eyes were wide. "You're miracle workers."

"I'm as shocked as you are," Grace said as she tried to fight a yawn. "But it was sweet."

"We'll get outta your hair," Wren said as they collected the last of the trash. "You two need rest."

"But—"

"Thanks," I interrupted. "You're right."

Grace huffed, but I knew she needed the rest, and it would be nice to have some quiet time.

"My feet are killing me," Grace muttered when the house was finally empty. As she was nearing the end of the pregnancy, she'd been having more and more aches and pains.

"Here," I said, moving her legs so I could sit and rub them.

"Thanks." She let out a sigh of relief. She'd taken all of the changes like a trooper, but I could see it was also taking a toll on her. In the kitchen, Mom was doing more cleaning, which meant there was even less for Grace to do.

I was relieved Grace and Mom got along so well and that Grace had let her stay in Strawberry Springs for a while. It was nice having her close, and even nicer that we had the extra help.

There was a feeling I couldn't shake that this phase would be ending soon. I hadn't told Grace because I was sure it was just my nerves talking, but I was mentally preparing for birth any day now.

Our gentle peace was interrupted by the sound of the door opening. Grace gave me a shocked look, and I knew that she probably hadn't locked the front door.

"I'll take care of it," I said, gently moving her legs off me. I got up. I thought maybe a party guest had forgotten something and simply didn't knock.

That was not who I found.

"Brooke," I said. "What are you doing here?"

Grace had made it a point to not invite her. Why should she have, after everything Brooke had done and said? We should have known she would show up anyway.

"Where's Grace?"

"She's resting. What can I help you with?" I asked evenly. I knew nothing good would come of me being an ass to her, no matter how much I disliked her.

"How about you let me walk into my own house without questions?"

"You moved to Nashville," I said slowly. "This isn't your house. It's not even where you live."

"Brooke?" Grace asked. I crossed my arms, knowing she didn't need this right now. "What are you doing here?"

Brooke's arms drew tighter around herself. "I had an agent come to my show. He didn't sign me."

"I'm sorry to hear that," Grace said as she made her way over to us. "But—"

"He's an idiot, I know. But my roommates all agreed with him, and when I called them out for also being stupid, they told me to get out for the night. I figured I could come here and show everyone what a real star looks like."

My jaw tightened. Nowhere in any of Brooke's words was a lick of self-awareness. She'd ignored Grace when she came to her show, but the second she needed something, she expected Grace to be there.

"That room isn't available," I said.

"What, are *you* staying in it?" Brooke glared and looked back at Grace. "I told you that was *my* room."

Her words made my temper flare hotter.

"No, it's not me."

"Who else would it be? And why would you let this happen?"

Grace's shoulders went tight. "You moved out, Brooke."

"But it's still *my* house."

Grace took a breath and tightened her shoulders. "It's *my* house. And I'm not sure if you're aware, but things are busy here because I'm having a baby soon. Dean's mom is staying in your room because she's been helping."

Brooke blinked, obviously not expecting Grace to say no. "Well, she can get a hotel. Hopefully, for forever."

"No, *you* can." The room went silent. Grace's fists were tight. I could see she hated this, but she was doing it anyway.

I'd never been prouder of her.

"Excuse me?" she said lowly.

"Virginia was here first. She also *asked* if she could stay. You haven't talked to me in weeks, and you showed up here with no warning. That isn't fair to me or anyone else here."

"I'm obviously *busy*. Can't you see that I have bigger things in my life than you?"

Grace's voice came out harder. "Watch it, Brooke."

"No, *you* watch it—" She stepped toward Grace, and that was when I'd had enough. I didn't know what Brooke would do, but I had a feeling it wouldn't be good. Grace hadn't told her no before. There was no telling how Brooke would react.

I used my arm as a barrier. "Get out."

"What?" Her voice was high-pitched. "Are you fucking kidding? You're doing this on the worst day of my life?"

Grace looked away.

"We are," I said. "She's got enough going on without you making it worse."

Brooke finally stared at me. "I guess Daddy is protective, huh? You'll regret this."

"If it means you stay out of my woman's hair? Gladly."

Brooke rolled her eyes and stomped out of the house, slamming the door behind her.

"Did she just threaten you?" Grace asked. "God, what is *wrong* with her?"

"What's wrong with who?" Mom came around the corner. "What happened?"

"That was my sister," Grace said.

"I'll tell you the whole story later." I looked back at Grace. "Are you okay?"

"Y-yeah, I'm . . . sorry about her. Her selfishness knows no bounds."

"It's okay, Grace."

She took a breath, but then shook her head. "This isn't over," she warned. "This is only the beginning of her tantrum."

"Tantrum? Isn't she a grown woman?" Mom asked.

"Physically, yes." I said it harshly.

"Whatever it is," Mom said, "we'll handle it. You don't need to worry about a thing, Grace."

"She's *my* sister."

"She is, but you're not alone in this. You have Dean and me. And we're making sure nothing happens to you."

Grace considered it. Normally, she would put up a fight, but this time, I could see that she didn't have it in her.

But that wouldn't happen anymore. Not with me around. And not with Mom around either.

"Thank you," she said. "Seriously, thank you both."

"It's no problem," I said.

It was late that night when I got a call from Mark. I was in bed with Grace and dead to the world, but I always kept my ringer on just in case an emergency happened.

"So," he began, "I don't know if you'll be happy with me waking you up, but I don't wanna stress Grace out."

"That's a good call. What's going on?"

He let out a sigh. "Brooke is here and she's . . . she's wild tonight. More so than usual."

"I'll get her," I replied. "I'll be there in a little bit."

"Thanks, Dean. I owe you one."

He didn't. But Brooke sure as fuck did.

As I drove, I tried to figure out what to say to get her head out of her ass. I'd never had siblings, so I was out of my element, but I would gladly be there for Grace.

When I walked in, Brooke was dancing on a table, a bottle in hand. Mark was glowering at her.

"She took the whole thing!" Mark yelled when he saw me. "What the hell is wrong with her?"

"I'm having fun!" Brooke yelled as she swayed her hips.

Then her eyes landed on me. "Oh. You're here." Her distaste for me was obvious.

"Time to go," I said.

"Everyone gather round! He's gonna yell at me."

People did turn, though some seemed to want nothing to do with this. I didn't blame them. I didn't want to be here either.

"Brooke, you have to know this is wrong. Your sister simply said to get a hotel."

"Because she's pregnant and life is sooooo hard." Brooke rolled her eyes. "You can stop playing the part now. She's not here."

"I'm not playing a part."

"Oh, you are." She stumbled off the table, causing more eyes to turn to us. She made it halfway to the bar before I stopped her by grabbing her arm. That must have set her off. "Be real. You aren't attracted to her. You only care about her because it makes you look good. Because you want everyone to like you."

I didn't even want to give her the time of day. It was the best thing to do in a situation like this. "Put the bottle back and go to the hotel. You're done."

"Am I? I have a few other things to say."

"No, you don't."

"You're temporary, Dean. A guy like you doesn't stick around."

"You would know a lot about not sticking around, Brooke. Where have you been?"

That only made things worse.

But the truth was going to.

Brooke muttered something under her breath, but I couldn't hear it. I did, however, hear Grace's name.

"What was that?" I asked as I leaned in. If she was bad-mouthing Grace of all people, then I would drag her out of here myself.

"Grace'll dump you when she sees this."

I didn't have time to ask what she meant because her lips were on mine. My ears rang, but I could hear gasps ring out across the bar.

I jerked away, mouth on fire. "What the—"

Brooke slapped me before I could finish my sentence. "Did you seriously just kiss me while my pregnant sister is at home asleep?"

"What? No, I—"

"Everyone saw it," she said. "And everyone knows I would *never* kiss someone here. But the kind of guy you are?" Now she smiled, and I saw what kind of monster she truly was. "You sure would."

GRACE

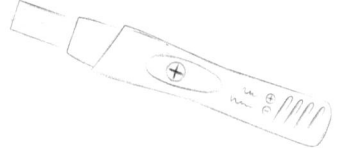

Strawberry Springs Neighborhood Watch

Kerry Winsor: I hate to be the person to do this again, but I must issue a warning about the new baby daddy in town. Brooke sent me a voice note along with many messages. Dean kissed her in the bar while Grace was at home. He's apparently been making moves on Brooke since they met! Who else was at the bar and can confirm?

Comments:
Dale Garrett: I was. I couldn't believe my eyes when I saw it.
Kerry Winsor: A man from out of town with a history of breaking hearts kissing Brooke while with Grace? I can't believe I helped him!!!
Tammy Jane: I'm so tired of these men cheating on our girls! Damn playboys always think they're slick!!!
Mollie Wilson: @Jade Clark @Wren Hackett RED ALERT
Kerry Winsor: Finally telling the girls who he is?

Mollie Wilson: Kerry, this is NOT appropriate for the group. Second, I'm alerting the girls so we can clear this up with the people involved . . . You know, like real adults.

Jade Clark: Oh, I'm past being an adult. ADMINS FUCKING DELETE THIS SHIT NOW BEFORE I SAY ENOUGH BAD WORDS TO GET THE GROUP REMOVED.

THERE WERE many reasons I would wake up in the middle of the night.

But on this night, it was a bad feeling that settled deep in my stomach. My eyes were still heavy from sleep, but I slowly sat up.

That was when I saw my phone was lighting up brighter than a Christmas tree.

I reached for it, wondering if Brooke had enacted her revenge.

> **KERRY**
>
> I'm so sorry about what Dean did. I'm heading to bed, but if you need to chat tomorrow, I'm here for you!
>
> **TAMMY**
>
> I didn't trust him. You say the word and I'll ban him everywhere.
>
> **JADE**
>
> Grace. Do NOT go into the Facebook group. I'm serious. You don't need this kind of worry right now. The girls and I are handling it.

I, of course, didn't listen. I immediately opened it up. The top post told me everything I needed to know.

Brooke and Dean had kissed at the bar, and everyone was talking about it.

I could only stare at the words on the screen, trying to wrap my mind around Brooke and Dean, of all people, kissing. I read through all of the comments. A lot of the top ones were people saying never to trust a playboy, but some were asking more questions.

I was asking more questions.

Dean hated Brooke. There was no way to fake that kind of body language I'd seen when she was around. There was no way he'd suddenly kissed her.

Besides, he'd told me I was it for him. He'd shown me it a hundred times.

I trusted Dean. But did I trust Brooke?

I got out of bed, wondering if I should go down to the square to see what had happened. This had all gone down only half an hour ago.

When I got halfway down the hallway, I ran right into someone else.

"Grace," Brooke said. "There you are. I really need to talk to you."

She smelled awful. Like beer and alcohol. Her lip gloss was smeared and I knew exactly why.

"About what?" My voice was flat.

"You can't trust Dean," she said immediately, hands gripping my arms. "He—"

The hallway lights flipped on and Virginia came out of Brooke's room. My sister sneered the second she saw the other woman.

"What's going on?" Virginia asked, her voice heavy with sleep. We must have woken her up.

"Of course there's an audience." Brooke rolled her eyes. "Let's go to your room to talk."

"Anything you need to say to me can be said in front of her."

"No, it can't. She'll take *his* side."

"Not necessarily," Virginia said. "What happened? Grace, why do you look upset?"

"Your son assaulted me."

I flinched at the words.

"What?" Virginia asked. Her eyes grew wide and she crossed her arms. "That's not like him."

"Oh, I'm sure you *think* you know him."

"What did he do?" she asked slowly.

"He found me at the bar and forced me to kiss him."

"He . . ." Virginia blinked. I could tell she was trying to listen to Brooke, but she knew Dean just like I did. Neither of us could see him doing this.

"Brooke, what really happened?" I asked.

"I'm telling you what happened."

"You're drunk and angry," I said. "Which means you're gonna act out. Did Dean really kiss you, or did you do it to him?"

Brooke's jaw dropped open. "I can't believe you would accuse me of that."

But then the front door slammed shut. I heard thudding footsteps heading right toward us.

When Dean came into view, he looked like a wreck. His hair was a mess. His eyes red. One of his cheeks was red too. I'd never seen him so torn apart.

"Grace, I need to . . ." He paused when he saw Brooke.

"I got here first," she said, but I knew that voice. It was the one she used when she got the doll from me and cried that I was trying to take it. The same voice she used to garner Mom's sympathy.

"I didn't kiss her," Dean rushed to say. "I would *never* ever betray you like that."

I knew. I'd known the whole time.

This was why I hadn't ever told Brooke no. Because I'd seen what she was capable of. I'd seen how she threw a fit.

"Okay, we need to get the story straight." Virginia looked at Brooke. "I want to believe you, but you're accusing my son of something serious."

"I'm not a liar."

"But you are, Brooke." Every set of eyes turned to me.

"What?" she asked.

"You *are* a liar. And a manipulator. And a fucking *bitch*."

She jerked back from me. "How dare you!"

"Shut up." I stepped close, getting right in her face. "I'm so sick of you. You have steamrolled my life whenever you remember I exist, and I tolerated it because I hoped, deep down, that you cared about me because I'm your sister. But you don't. You're a spoiled brat trying to ruin what I have because I told you no. But guess what? I see right through you and I don't believe you."

"B-but we're *family*."

"Not anymore. You've hurt me a lot over the years, and I shouldn't have let that slide. But you're not going to hurt someone I *love*. I draw the line there. So get out of my house."

My cheek erupted in pain. It took me a second to register that she'd slapped me. Virginia gasped, and Dean had Brooke's arms in a tight hold before I could even take a breath.

"Don't fucking touch her!" he yelled.

"I can do what I want!"

"Oh my God!" Virginia hurried to my side. "Are you okay, honey?"

"I'm fine." My voice was flat as I stared at Brooke. Instead of seeing someone I cared about, I saw a girl who'd never faced consequences for her actions.

And it was time she did.

Taking a deep breath, I grabbed my phone and called the one person I never thought I would.

"'Ello?"

"Mike, I need to report an assault. And an unwelcome person in my home."

"Grace?" Now he sounded awake. "Shit, kid. I'll be right there."

Once he hung up, I turned back to the scene in my house.

"Are you okay?" Virginia asked again.

"Yeah. Her bark's worse than her bite."

Brooke tried to wrestle her way out of Dean's grip. "Let me go!"

"So you can run from what you've done?" he snapped. "No. You're facing this. All of it."

"Mike lives five minutes away," I said as Virginia wrapped her arms around me. "Thank you for holding her, Dean. Especially after what she did to you."

"She hurt someone I love." His voice was firm, but his eyes were soft as they landed on me. "And I won't let that happen again."

A heavy silence settled on us all before Mike arrived. He took Brooke from Dean and put her in handcuffs. I watched the whole time, even as she tried to talk her way out of this.

"It's not that big of a deal," she tried to reason. "Grace will let this go. I just had a bad night."

Mike looked at me with a raised eyebrow.

"She slapped me while I'm nine months pregnant, Mike. Please get her outta here."

"Are you pressing charges?" he asked.

"I am."

"Me too," Dean said.

"Good. I'll get her locked in the car and I'll get my notebook."

"No!" Brooke yelled as he dragged her out. "Grace, come on. Just let it go. I won't ever do anything like this again."

And she was right, but not because she would change.

But because I wouldn't save her this time.

DEAN

Strawberry Springs Neighborhood Watch

Wren Hackett: Since you all are STILL on this, let's clear a few things up. If anyone knows Dean's character more than Grace, it's me. I've worked with him for years, and he's not the kind of man who cheats on someone. You all are jumping on the new guy in town and I am VERY disappointed in you!!!

Comments:
Mollie Wilson: And let's not forget, Brooke loves to cause problems! Like, hello???
Kerry Winsor: Oh, sure. But how do you explain that he was out at a bar instead of being with his pregnant girlfriend??? That's weird!!!
Mollie Wilson: He can still have a life, Kerry.
Mark Bell: I can actually answer that. I called him instead of Grace to come get Brooke, since I didn't wanna stress her out.
Kerry Winsor: Oh.
Wren Hackett: See??? You guys better hope he never joins this group and sees this.

I wasn't sure if I was shaking with rage, fear, or misery. Maybe it was all three. I'd never seen Grace go so long without making a single facial expression, but she looked like a ghost of herself.

It killed me.

Our statements were taken by the sheriff, who promised that she would be in jail for the night. Mom drifted between us both, eyes wide with unshed tears and shock before she offered to go get new locks.

Grace went inside to sit on the couch when Mike left, and I followed. I silently sat next to her and pulled her to me.

That was when she lost it. Tears streamed down her cheeks and she fell into me, sobbing *hard*.

Tears escaped me too. I'd been holding back. I was only thinking of getting to her and explaining. Only thinking of how to make this right.

And then Brooke hit Grace, and I had to hold myself back from getting in trouble myself.

It was all terrifying, and I wasn't made of stone. I thought it was over. I thought Grace was hurt. And all of my fears were happening tonight.

"I'm so sorry," Grace said through her sobs.

"Why are you sorry?" I asked. She'd been through just as much, if not more, and that was unacceptable. "She hurt you."

Grace pulled away and let her cool hand rest on my cheek. "She hurt you too."

"Who cares about me?"

She frowned. "I do."

And that was it, wasn't it? We both cared about each other. This was an equal partnership, where either she or I gave everything without wanting anything in return. We were a team. We loved each other.

And Brooke tried to ruin that.

I tugged Grace back to me, and all we could do was exist in each other's embrace.

Mom wound up making us some tea before sitting in the extra chair in the living room, giving us space and silence to process. It reminded me of the night after Dad's funeral, when neither of us knew what to do.

But this time I did.

We would feel sad for a while. We would slowly learn how to feel okay again. And life would go on.

But this moment? It was terrible.

Grace's phone kept going off, and eventually, she pulled it out.

"Wh-what are they saying?"

"Honey, don't worry about that," Mom said. "You barely even like these people."

I pressed my lips together. Her statement *was* true, but deep down, I was gutted by the idea of them hating me. I felt like something I'd grown used to was irrevocably changed. It was a different kind of heartbreak, but one I'd felt before.

It was when Shady Acres lost its way.

"You do care, don't you?" Grace said softly.

I wasn't going to pretend I didn't; she would see right through that.

"I do," I muttered. "I'm not sure when I started to, but . . . it was nice. Being a part of them for a while."

I'd known how this would end, which was why I tried to keep my distance, to stay in denial about it. Yet here I was, desperately wanting to know how badly this looked on me. Could I salvage this?

I wanted to, and that was terrifying.

"I'm so sorry," Mom said.

"They should know better," Grace added. "And they will."

I saw her go to Facebook before she angled the screen away from me.

"What are you doing?" I asked.

"Saying something that's on my mind."

"You don't have to—"

She leveled me with a flat stare that shut me up. "They know how Brooke is, and by now, they should know you too. Sure, some of them didn't like you at first, but that doesn't mean they should take Brooke's side."

"So, you're yelling at them?"

"Exactly." She typed furiously. "All right, done. They can all have fun with that. I'm turning my phone off."

"Thank you," I said. "Do you think they'll ever trust me again?"

"They might be stupid sometimes, but they see sense when it's knocked into them. Hopefully what I said did it."

"Thank you, Grace." Virginia said it softly. "That was sweet of you."

Grace stifled a yawn and looked in between us. "So, do we just sit here and process?"

"I think we should sleep," I said. "If we can."

"I'm not opposed to that." She sighed. "But before you do, will you make sure the door's locked?"

That was her best idea of all. I immediately sprang to my feet. "Gladly."

Strawberry Springs Neighborhood Watch

Grace Day: Hi. I know that the last few hours have been full of drama, but let's not forget that times with Brooke usually are. I'm aware of what happened. I'm handling it.

I'll just say this. I've listened to you all complain about

Brooke for years. You all know what kind of person she is. You also know what kind of person Dean is. Especially the longer he's been in town. So why, without any questions or thoughts, did some of you take her side? Anyone with two brain cells knew she was on a tirade and Dean was trying to stop her.

We're a community, and I appreciate that you all want to protect me. I've taken a lot over the years, especially with Brooke. I don't need you vetting who I choose to spend my time with. I'm capable of doing that myself.

I'll pose the real question you should ask yourself. Did you all believe what you heard because it confirmed a predisposed belief you had of Dean? Were you all ready to jump on an outsider again, just like you did with Cain?

Because it seems like you did. Grow up.

As I grow and change, I'll find people who care about me, and you don't get to oust who you don't get a good first impression of.

And by the way, Brooke is no longer allowed in my home. I'm sure you'll hear she's spending the night in jail for assaulting Dean AND me. All of your protection didn't do anything.

Do better.

Comments:

Jade Clark: Holy shit, Grace. This is the most badass thing I've ever seen. (And for the rest of you, I fucking knew I was right. I'll accept apologies in the form of buying candles from the shop.)

Wren Hackett: YES, QUEEN.

Tammy Jane: Heard, Grace. Wren already gave me an earful. I'm gonna do better from now on.

Hu Gh: You all are gullible as hell. You let BROOKE pull the wool over your eyes? Shameful.

Grace's phone was still off the next day, but mine wasn't. And
that was when the texts came in. I figured I was about to catch
all the flak for what had happened.

It wasn't that.

CAIN

> Heard about what happened. Pay the town no
> mind. They'll get their heads out of their asses
> eventually. Let me know if you need anything.
> I'm so sorry for what happened.

UNKNOWN

> Hey, kid. It's Tammy. I was an idiot and
> believed a punk kid who's never done any
> good for this place. You're good for Grace and
> I hope this doesn't scare you off from us. The
> next few meals are on me at the diner. Get
> however many burgers you want.

KERRY

> I heard about Brooke. I'm SO sorry for
> believing the wrong thing. I must be losing my
> touch because I've always known that Brooke
> is such a pain to Grace. You deserve better
> from us.

"Do I need to make you turn your phone off too?" Grace
asked from beside me. She sat up with a wince.

"Are you feeling okay?"

"Yeah, just some Braxton-Hicks. It's normal right about
now." I was tempted to ask about it more, but then she glared.
"But no changing the subject. What are you on your phone
for?"

"I got a few texts overnight. A lot of people are . . . apol-
ogizing?"

"Good," she said. "They finally saw sense. I hoped they would."

"They listened." My voice was soft with disbelief.

"We're not terrible here." She laughed. "But I'm sure I probably scared some of them. They've never heard me talk like that."

"You didn't have to do that."

"It's you." She said it like it was obvious. "Yes, I did."

GRACE

Strawberry Springs Neighborhood Watch

Kerry Winsor: Moving on from the . . . incident. Let's talk about something fun! Will anyone be at the farmers market???

Comments:
Jade Clark: Oh, Grace got her GOOD. I've never seen Kerry move on from anything.
Kerry Winsor: Helloooooo, I wanna know about the farmers market, Jade! No more talk about how I was wrong.
Mollie Wilson: I had a good harvest this year. I'll have some strawberries and blueberries.
Kerry Winsor: Yes! Oh, and I bet we'll finally have good coffee this year too! **@Theo Murf**, are you attending?
Theo Murf: The shop'll be open. You all can come in.
Kerry Winsor: But you can never chat when you're working! Someone needs a social life . . .

I KNEW the third trimester wasn't going to be fun, but this was worse than I could've ever imagined. My cramps were terrible, but I'd heard of women thinking Braxton-Hicks contractions were the real deal, and I refused to drive to the hospital for anything but something serious.

Add that to the fact that I had to deal with what my sister had done, and I was feeling even worse.

I was sure this was stress from processing the incidents with Brooke while also figuring out the best way to make sure that she got what she deserved. Some days, I felt like the worst sister in the world. Other days, I felt like I was doing exactly what I should have been.

All of it had taken its toll, though. Over time, I started to feel worse and worse, and now that I was at the end of pregnancy, there was a physical exhaustion to add to it all.

"Listen," I told both Dean and Virginia. We were sitting at the table with coffee, talking about how we were going to deal with Brooke. I'd spent the morning looking into what it would cost to hire an attorney and keep her in jail. "I just want a restraining order at this point. At least for what she did to me."

"She assaulted a pregnant woman," Virginia reminded. "That's a serious offense."

"But we also have to think about the medical bills that are coming up. Having this baby won't be free, and there isn't going to be some magical thing that saves us."

"I want to do it all." Dean said it shortly. "She can't get away with this."

"Technically, she'd be getting a restraining order," I said softly, but even I knew that it wasn't enough.

"Mom, you're on my side here, right?"

Virginia pressed her lips together and thought about it, then sighed. "Sometimes this is how justice goes. Only those with enough money get it."

"I can work with Clyde more," he added. "I can save up for both."

"Don't you wanna be here with the baby, though?" I asked.

That got him.

He sighed and leaned back. "Yeah, I do."

I fought against a twinge in my stomach, another reminder that what was coming was imminent. We were on limited time. Even if I made it to forty weeks, that was only a month away. I didn't want to spend that in court if I didn't have to.

"So, a restraining order for both of us," I said.

"And I'm asking the town to keep a lookout," Dean added. "Some have offered."

"That'll also help. I'm sorry we can't do more."

"It's okay. She'll be away from us."

There was a part of me that was sad it had come to this. Maybe I always would be, but me being sad didn't mean I was making the wrong decision. It just meant that I felt something about it.

She was the one who pushed me too far, and I knew without a doubt that my life would be more peaceful without her in it.

"Are you opening your shop today, Grace?" Virginia asked. "I could go and help out."

"You don't need to do that."

"We're family," she reminded softly. "And I haven't gotten nearly enough practice to take it over when the baby is here."

I'd been taking too many days off and knew I *had* to go in, even if it was just for a distraction.

But I did *not* feel up to it.

"You know what? I should open it today. Dean, would you like to join? You don't have a job right now."

"I'm tempted to find one for extra money," he muttered, but then sighed. "But I won't. I don't think Wren or Clyde would let me work with how little sleep I've had."

"And I don't think I will either. You didn't sleep well, did you?" Virginia asked.

He sighed. "Not really. Or maybe I did but I'm just too exhausted."

"Get some rest," I said. "I'll be back tonight."

Dean fought it up until he broke out into a loud yawn and knew he had lost the battle. Virginia and I got ready and headed down to the shop.

I tried to keep it cool, but I was feeling worse and worse. The contractions went from being dull and achy to more and more intense. I couldn't wait for them to stop.

"You know," she said as she folded clothes, "Dean came pretty early."

"Really?"

"He was the size of a full-term baby too. Sometimes, PCOS can make the babies a little bit bigger. It's probably good that they come early."

"I'll have to keep that in mind for when I really go into labor."

She eyed me. "So, how are you feeling today?"

"I'm mostly fine. I'm glad that the town texted Dean to apologize and that Brooke shouldn't be bothering us anymore. I'm still emotionally all over the place, and that's causing other things."

"Like the way you keep wincing?"

Looked like I was caught. "Braxton-Hicks," I said. "It's nothing major."

"You could finish out the day and get that checked out."

"I don't wanna be one of those moms who panics and goes for nothing." I waved my hand. "I've heard so many stories about being turned away at the hospital. I'm sure it's nothing."

"How long has it been going on?"

As I said the answer, I knew what she was going to think. "Since this morning."

Virginia's eyebrows went up. "It's been quite a few hours. Normally they're supposed to stop if they're Braxton-Hicks contractions."

"It would be my luck that my body wanted a little bit of extra practice before the real event. Besides, there's still time for them to stop."

"Are they regular? Do they have a pattern?"

I wanted to say no, but they *had* been pretty regular. Though, I could have been making that up considering I wasn't timing them and my mind had been focused on other seemingly more-pressing events.

"I'll be fine. I bet this is nothing." I waved her off again, convinced that I was right.

Of course, my body must have had a great sense of humor.

Because that was when my water broke.

50

DEAN

Dad Company (But Sometimes Good Advice)

Dean Briggs: So, any advice for birth?

Comments:
Robert Colt: Have a plan. Then throw that plan out the window. It never happens like you expect it would.
Ryan Kim: Whatever you do, don't look down.
Robert Colt: Eh, it's not that bad.
Ryan Kim: He could be squeamish! The last thing you want is to be one of those idiots who faints in the birth room.
Graham Hamilton: At least you don't have to see it if you faint . . .
Ryan Kim: The more I learn about you, the less I like you.

THERE WAS something that was preventing me from sleeping. I knew Grace wanted me to rest, but I had a bad feeling that something was going on.

Maybe it was the fact that the last forty-eight hours had been wild. My brain simply couldn't stop. All night while holding Grace, I had tossed and turned, trying to doze off. I'd gotten a few hours in, but not nearly enough.

But this time, my feeling was correct, and I knew it the second Mom called me.

"Hi, honey, are you resting okay?"

"I'm fine. What's up? Are you with Grace?"

"Yes, I am." She talked slowly, which was a thing she did whenever she was trying not to make someone panic. "We need to head to the hospital actually."

"What happened?" I ground out. "Is something wrong?"

"No, nothing's wrong, but you might want to get ready for a big life change. Grace is in labor."

I heard her groan in the background, and it felt like my heart stopped. She was in pain and I wasn't there. "Where are you guys?"

"We're five minutes out from the house. Can you be ready to go to the hospital?"

I'd never moved so fast in my life. I jumped out of bed and threw on new clothes. The second I was done, I ran out to the car and right to her.

"Baby, I'm here."

"Oh, thank God." She grabbed my hand and pulled me into the back seat with her. "This *hurts*. And we're not even sure I'm in labor!"

"We'll find out when we get to the hospital. Everyone, hang on!"

I'd never seen Mom drive like a maniac, but when there was a woman in labor, she didn't mess around. We made the drive in forty minutes and were ushered into the triage area where they tested to see if her water truly had broken.

"I'm very sure it did," Mom said when the nurse left.

Grace shook her head. "It still could be—"

"I know you're scared," I said. "And I know it's tempting to be in denial, but we've got this whether you are or aren't."

Her bottom lip poked out, but she nodded. "You're right. God, I'm so glad you're here."

"It seems like you have it, Dean," Mom said. "I'll go get some things from the house for you two."

"Even if I am, first-time moms take forever," Grace said. "Don't rush."

"I'll rush just because I want to be here too," Mom said with a smile. "Let me know if you two need anything else."

Mom dashed out the door and I returned to keeping Grace calm.

When a nurse announced her water really had broken and we were being moved to a room, I knew it was go time.

For a while, I helped her through the labor. We dealt with her being hooked up to an IV, her contractions, and all the interruptions from those contractions.

Grace was brave for a few hours. We hadn't had time to come up with a full birth plan, but we knew some of the things to expect in labor. She tried to take deep breaths and listen to her favorite music, but eventually, I could see it starting to take a toll on her.

"I can't do this," she said on hour four.

"Are they getting worse?" I asked, brushing her hair from her face.

"They're hitting like a *fucking* train now. Is that normal? God, how am I supposed to do this for longer?"

Her voice rose in pitch, and I could feel her panic sink into me. Neither of us had a clue of what we were doing. But I wouldn't show her a damn thing other than support.

"We can call a nurse to do another check."

"I was only five centimeters last time," she groaned. "There's no way I'm any further along."

"Weird things can happen."

"No, I know how first-time babies are. This is supposed to go slow. My body doesn't know what it's doing."

"What if it does?"

"No, there's no way." She gritted her teeth and shut her eyes as another contraction hit her. They were lasting longer now, and she was hooked up to a graph that measured how hard they were. They looked really intense on that piece of paper.

"Then at least let's ask for something to distract you."

"I want the damn epidural," she muttered.

"You sure?"

"Very. Fuck this."

"All right then." I placed a kiss on her forehead before getting a nurse.

"We'll do a check before we call the anesthesiologist," the nurse said. "I'm sure she's fine, though."

"She's in a lot of pain."

"Poor thing. First-time moms can take a while."

"Between you and me, I have a feeling this is going faster."

"All the first-time parents say that. The baby will be born when it's ready to be."

I understood that it was very easy to fall into habits of first-time parents. Maybe I just wanted this to be over. I took a deep breath to calm myself and then walked into the room with Grace to keep her levelheaded.

Soon after, the nurse walked in to wash up and put gloves on. Grace grumbled about having to get checked, but only gripped my hand as it happened.

I figured both she and I would get relief when it was over with and she got the medicine she needed.

What neither of us expected was for the nurse to freeze.

"All right, change of plans."

"What's wrong?" Grace asked. "What's happening?"

"It's time to push, my dear."

"*What?* But I—"

I resisted the urge to say "I told you so," but the nurse didn't stay long. She didn't even let Grace finish her question because she was calling all kinds of people into the room.

I'd never seen people filter into a place so quickly. I thought I would be used to the unexpected after everything that had happened over the last few months.

I didn't think I would ever get used to it.

"I seriously can't do this," Grace said as she grabbed my hand desperately. "I wanna go home."

"Grace, you've got this." I hated that she even had to be here. I hated that she had to be in pain at all, but this was always coming ever since we found out she was pregnant. I wished I could've taken it from her, but all I could do was be supportive.

"I don't think I do." Her eyes were wide and she looked terrified. I didn't blame her for being that way because I was too.

Dr. Anderson came in, laser focused on what was going on. I held one of Grace's legs as she bore down. There was nothing I could do but tell her how strong she was, even if it didn't help.

After this, I would be changing every fucking diaper. I'd wash all the clothes. She'd done enough.

The doctors timed the pushes while Grace groaned through each one. Her grip on my hand was tight enough to almost break bones, but I didn't care. I kept hoping that each one would be the last.

"This should be the last one!" the doctor called. "Gimme one last push!"

I heard cries only seconds later. It felt like time slowed down as the doctor handed our baby off to a nurse and then they were placed on Grace's chest. It felt like a dream as I reached out to stroke their tiny little hand.

They formed a fist, wrapping their fingers around mine. I knew they would be my world when they were born, but this cemented it. This was *my* baby, born from the woman I loved, and I would do anything for either of them.

"A beautiful baby boy," the doctor said. "Congratulations, you two."

A boy. A son. God, we had a *kid*.

"Dean?" Grace asked through her tears.

"Yeah, baby?"

"Did we pick out a name?"

I was a mess of emotions, both from the last day and from witnessing my child being born. I didn't know how Grace was having any thoughts at all.

But her question was fair because we hadn't picked out a name.

"Uh . . . oops?"

"All this time and we didn't talk about that?" She shook her head. "I don't even know what to call him!"

I had no idea why this was the first thing on her mind after giving birth, but she could think of whatever she wanted to after going through that.

"We'll figure it out just like everything else." I put a hand on her head. "But you did it."

Her head rested against the back of the hospital bed. "I did. That sucked, though." She looked down at our baby, whose cries had finally slowed. He would need to be cleaned up, but I could see that he had Grace's nose and my chin. I wanted to study his features and know what he'd gotten from each of us. "I think I want more."

I let out a shocked laugh. "Let's figure out what the hell to do with the first one."

She nodded, and nurses came around to get his weight and length. Both of our gazes followed him the whole time.

I'd once said that being in love sometimes felt like my heart was walking outside of my body. Now, it was split in two. Half with Grace, and half with the little boy we'd be raising.

And I couldn't be happier.

51

GRACE

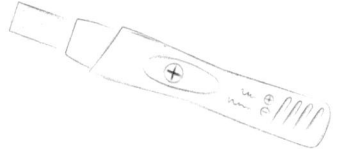

Strawberry Springs Neighborhood Watch

Dean Briggs: Grace invited me to the group to say the baby is here. He's nine pounds and doesn't have a name. Please DON'T drop suggestions. This is hard enough.

Comments:

Tammy Jane: Where are the pictures?? Come on, you can't leave us hanging like this!!!

Hu Gh: The baby's probably ugly.

Kerry Winsor: HUGH! Don't say that!

Hu Gh: What??? It swims around in juice for nine months and then gets squeezed out like toothpaste! None of us looked good when we were first born!

Jade Clark: Didn't need that visual, but thanks. (The baby is very cute.)

Tammy Jane: You better not be holding out on us. LET'S SEE THAT BABY!!!

"PETER?"

"No, that doesn't fit."

"James?"

"Too boring."

"Mason?"

"That makes me think of the glass jar brand."

I blew out a breath from my comfy spot on the couch. Dean was currently bouncing our unnamed son as he tried to get him to sleep. He was a natural with this, or at least it seemed like it. I knew him well enough to figure out that he'd done as much research as he could.

I'd done well enough to simply birth the baby.

Our kid was adorable and I loved him more than anything, but I was still figuring out how to take care of him. I was still figuring out how to go from the Grace who was simply pregnant to the Grace who was now a mom.

Two days after giving birth, and I didn't know how I would have done this by myself. I was given strict orders to rest, and I was exhausted just doing that. Unless it was feeding the baby—which was only me, considering that I was breastfeeding—Dean did everything else. Literally everything else.

I would have felt bad if I hadn't given birth.

"Don't you have to pick the name by today?" Virginia asked, coming around the corner with two plates. The hospital hadn't been thrilled that we couldn't settle on a name before I was discharged, so they'd sent home the packet to fill out and told us we had to figure out what to name him and turn it back in soon.

I'd gotten nowhere with figuring it out.

And it wasn't like I had time.

After we came home, Virginia had insisted she take care of the house while we recovered. Dean tried to tell her she didn't have to do that, but she wouldn't accept no for an answer.

I might have cried about it.

After the detonation of my relationship with Brooke and giving birth, my emotions were in a delicate place. Virginia had warned me these were the baby blues, but I felt like I was tearing up at every given moment.

Thank God Dean knew not to judge me. If he'd been any less of a perfect partner, I might have killed him.

But between Dean and Virginia, I had the support I needed. I didn't realize how many clothes we'd go through in just a few days, but she'd made sure we never ran out and that the house was clean.

The town had also come through for us, both with apology treats for Dean and other food for us so none of us had to cook. Since I was the best cook out of the three of us by a long shot, we needed the help.

"Yeah, we do," Dean replied. "Nothing seems right, though. I want something that matches his personality."

"Well, if we're going by personality, we have three options." Virginia began counting on her fingers. "Eat. Sleep. And poop."

"Already considered those," Dean said. "Grace told me they weren't name-y enough."

"Whatever you choose will be perfect," she said. "They'll grow into the name."

"Boy names are hard," I groaned. "None of them sound right."

I expected Dean to agree with me, but he was looking at the baby pensively. I thought he was staring in awe again. I'd caught him doing that often when he was holding him.

But the longer he went, the more Dean seemed to be deep in thought.

"Do you have something?" I asked.

"I was . . . thinking about it. But it might not fit."

"Tell me," I said. He only got like this when he had an

emotional connection to something, and I knew I needed to consider it.

"Samuel," he said. "For my dad."

"Oh." Virginia's eyes instantly got wet. This was the first time she'd had any reaction to a name. "That's . . . well, Grace, what do you think?"

This meant a lot to them, and I knew how much Dean had loved his dad. There were times when I wished I could have met him. I looked at the sleeping baby in Dean's arms, imagining calling him some version of that for the rest of my life. I knew my answer immediately.

"I love it," I said. And I did. It was the only thing that felt right.

"Really?"

I nodded. The name fit him perfectly. It had a lot of nickname potential too. After calling him different pet names for the last few days, both Dean and I would love giving him something for just him. I gazed at our perfect son and realized I had everything I could ever want.

Then I was tearing up again. Dean walked over and silently rubbed my shoulder as I got myself together.

"We'll have to fill out that paperwork from the hospital finally," I said as I wiped my eyes. "I need to do that, and probably check my mail."

"I'll handle that," Virginia said. "Be right back."

"Thank God for your mom," I said to Dean.

"She's never gonna leave. I hope you know that. She's been wanting grandkids since the day I was born."

Most people would be bothered by that, but for the first time since Mom died, my house felt *alive*.

"You know, if the hospital bills and court cases aren't that bad, which is a pretty big if . . . part of the basement could be refinished into a mother-in-law suite."

"You're willing to let your future mother-in-law live here?"

"That would require you to marry me."

"Oh, Mama, I have plans for that. I just need this one to not poop and throw up as much."

I laughed and cleared my throat. Emotion was already back to clogging me up, and I wanted one hour where I wasn't shedding tears. The baby blues couldn't leave fast enough.

"To answer your question, no, I wouldn't mind it. She's the best mother-in-law I could ask for."

"She's amazing, and I know she'd love that. I think life was a little . . . boring for her after Dad died."

"Then let's hope we don't get screwed by all the bills we have."

"Let's hope," he repeated.

"The mail is mostly junk," Virginia said, walking into the room. "Though, this looks quite official. It was shipped overnight, which means it must be important."

"Might be the first bill," I muttered as I took it from her.

"I don't think insurance processes that fast," Dean said.

"With our luck, they did it immediately."

Dean could only shrug. No one in the room could deny that we'd had our brushes with bad luck, and ever since Brooke tried to ruin things with us, nothing felt like it was going my way.

Opening the envelope, I braced for a large number.

But the first thing I saw was a letter.

To Grace and Dean,

The entire town wrote to the grant asking us to cover any legal expenses related to an incident with your sister, Brooke. We are happy to approve those funds.

But I'd like to go one step further. I heard you had a baby recently, so I'd also like to cover any medical expenses related to

ELLE RIVERS

*that, plus anything else that may come up. Attached is a check
that should cover all of this.*

    Congratulations to you both.
    The STM Grant Founder

My jaw dropped. I had to reread the letter three times to make sure it was real. Once I realized the words *weren't* changing, I finally spoke. "Oh my God."

"Don't worry about the amount." Dean was quick to assure me. "I'll work more and we can do a payment plan—"

I flipped the letter over and covered my mouth. This was more money than I'd ever seen in my *life*.

"Honey, tell us, what's happening?" Virginia's voice was soft, but I could hear her worry.

"The town applied for the grant for us to pay for a lawyer to make sure Brooke never bothers us again."

"The grant. The STM one?" Dean asked. "Did it not cover it?"

I turned the check around. Dean went pale. Virginia gasped.

"Is that a check?" she asked. "A real check?"

"No way did they send that much money," Dean said as he shook his head.

"I've never—I don't understand." I looked at it again, flipping over both the letter and the check, looking for some sign it was fake.

Instead, I saw a Post-it stuck on the back.

*You of all people deserve this, Grace. Cash the check. The money
will go through.*

.   .   .

I stared at the handwriting. I dimly recognized it, but the letters were shaky. It was either that they were nervous . . .

Or they were older.

"We should cash it," I found myself saying.

"You really trust this thing?"

"I have doubts, but I think it's . . . someone I know. Someone who cares."

Dean looked over my shoulder and read the note. "I'll take it to the bank and try it. Who knows if the money will go through."

"And if it does?" Virginia asked.

I spoke before Dean could. "Then I think we just found our solution to . . . *everything.*"

Dad Company (But Sometimes Good Advice)

Justin Holloway: Had a one-night stand and she's pregnant. How do I make sure we stay friends? I don't really date, so friends is all we'll be.

Comments:
Robert Colt: Oh, boy. **@Dean Briggs**, you wanna weigh in on this? You're the expert, after all.
Ryan Kim: Here we go again.
Dean Briggs: I see I've been summoned. Who was the one-night stand?
Justin Holloway: A girl I met at a bar. She was fun and I couldn't get her out of my mind . . . Guess I know why.
Dean Briggs: All right, buddy. Have a plan. Throw the plan out the window. And tell us everything. I'm just glad it ain't me for once.

I was late getting home.

Grace would have made Sammy dinner and gotten him started in his bath by now. I didn't plan on getting back this late, and I slowly opened the door, wondering if she would be mad.

I found her as she was washing Sammy's hair. Even while his hair was wet, the ends still curled. He'd gotten Grace's hair texture but my lighter color. His eyes were hazel, just like Grace's too. Once we'd both figured out how to be parents, we loved raising him. Grace still worked at the shop, but she always looked forward to coming home to see him. I did too, which is why she cocked an eyebrow at me when I walked in at bedtime.

"I would have stopped for flowers, but that would've made me later." I'd still ordered some. They would be delivered tomorrow.

"It's fine, Dean."

Sammy looked at me and smiled wide.

"Still, I never try to be this late. I owe you coffee in the morning at the very least."

"I'll take the coffee," she said. "Did work keep you?"

"Something like that."

Sammy was done in the bath, and he let us know by trying to throw water out of the tub. Grace yelped and immediately pulled the plug and got him out. I helped her get him ready for bed before she met me in the hallway.

My life had calmed down ever since she'd given birth to Sammy. Sometimes, I thought back to that time and wondered how the hell we'd survived. Hell, I wasn't sure how Grace had survived Brooke for so long. But now that we were surrounded by people who cared about us, there was less drama.

Luckily, Grace would never have to deal with her again. Brooke didn't get a long sentence, but it was the kind that would stay on her record forever. We were awarded a restraining order for both of us and a promise from Mike that he would come immediately if she ever tried anything.

Her restraining order was strict enough that she would either wind up with hefty fines or go back to jail if she couldn't pay them. Considering how hard the restraining order was to get, I was glad for the extra money the STM grant had provided.

We both got the peace that we deserved, and we had the money to renovate some of the basement into a mother-in-law suite for Mom, who was thrilled to stay as long as she could. I was ecstatic to be able to have a little more privacy when Grace and I got time alone.

I had told Mom what my plan was and why I would be late. So she was spending her time in her suite because she knew that Grace and I would need some time alone once I revealed what I'd done.

"So, are you gonna tell me what you were up to?" She put a hand on my chest and I nearly jumped straight into the air. She raised an eyebrow.

"Okay, okay. I'll tell you. It's just sensitive right now."

"Did you get injured at work?" She narrowed her eyes. "Clyde should've called me."

I shook my head. "Come here."

I took her to our room and peeled off my shirt.

"You're not gonna distract me with—"

"Look at my chest."

Her eyes flicked over me. At first, she missed it, and then her eyes widened.

It was her name, exactly the way she'd written it just over a year ago. I'd taken a picture and found an artist who could replicate it. Back then, I wasn't sure if I would go through with a tattoo, but I wanted the option of it to be open.

"Oh my God," she said. "You got my name tattooed? Don't you know you're never supposed to get a name?"

"Oh, yeah. I got a long lecture about it, but when does a lecture ever stop me?"

"Who all lectured you?"

"The tattoo artist, Mark, Mom, Tammy, you name it. They all knew I was gonna go through with it, though."

"You don't have to prove your dedication to me. I know you're staying."

"I'm not proving anything. I wanted this. And when Sammy gets old enough to write his name, I'll get his too."

"You are . . . something else."

"I've been called worse."

She laughed, but her eyes were wet. Grace didn't openly cry ever since her baby blues resolved, so seeing her wipe at her eyes meant she was feeling a lot about this.

"Do you like it?"

"Like it? You know this is the most romantic thing I've ever seen, right?"

"I try."

"And to think, all I got you for our anniversary was flowers." She blew out a breath. "I need to up my game."

"Oh no, Mama." I pulled her close. "Trust me. You've given me everything I could possibly need."

And it was true. I'd lived my entire life thinking I would always get shallow evenings where I'd inevitably end up alone.

But now life was fuller than I could ever imagine.

I wouldn't take it any other way.

I had milk in one hand and a latte in the other. Sammy was being carried to the table by Grace as I waved to Theo and Kelsey.

"Excuse us," Grace said to the woman behind us. She

jumped out of the way before I could see her, but then I paused. I'd seen that bright blonde hair and reaction to other people before. I knew her.

She must have seen me at the same time because her eyes widened. "Hey, you're that guy."

"You know each other?" Grace asked. Her voice wasn't harsh in any way. I was sure both the tattoo and the fact that I was obsessed with her had proven that I wasn't going anywhere. There had been a few times when my past had been brought up, but she took it well each time.

The woman looked at Grace and then at me. "Oh, um. Yeah. We met once. But don't worry. Absolutely nothing happened."

"It's okay," Grace said. "I'm not the jealous type when it comes to him."

"It was after I met you, so of course nothing happened." I turned back to the woman. "Your name was . . . Piper, right?"

"Yeah. And you're Dean. You told me about *Renovating with Love.*"

"I did. Are you seeing the town it took place in?"

"I'm . . . trying something new. I moved in upstairs a few days ago."

"You got the apartment?" Grace asked. "I was wondering when someone would move in. Welcome to the town."

She held out her hand and Piper looked a little like a kicked puppy. "I'm sorry, I . . ."

"Don't worry about it." She picked up on Piper's discomfort immediately. "It's just great to meet you. If you need anything, I'm Grace."

"Piper."

"Enjoy the coffee," I said. "It's the best in town."

Grace gave her one more glance before we got to our table. Then she looked again.

"Wait a second," she said. "Is Theo staring at her?"

I shook my head without looking. Theo didn't stare at anyone. Then Grace gave me a flat look that told me I would be in trouble if I didn't look, and she turned out to be right.

"Oh, shit." I said it immediately. I'd never seen Theo look at someone like that. His cheeks were red, and instead of the brief glances he gave everyone else, she had his full attention.

I couldn't hear what they were saying, but I heard him try his best to talk with her. She got her drink and then walked off.

That was when I made my move. I was running up to the counter before Grace could stop me.

"Looks like you need some tips."

"You saw nothing," he muttered.

"Oh, I saw enough. And as the most recent resident to get his love story, there are some rules to try and follow. Don't add to the population, don't subtract—"

"Leave the poor guy alone," Grace said as she cut in. Then she looked at Theo. "Sorry about him."

"It's fine." Theo's eyes were back to his POS machine. "Nothing is gonna happen."

Grace hummed and tapped her chin. "My money's on you being wrong. I guess we'll see in a few months."

Theo's glare was downright vicious, but both of us only laughed and walked away. As we got to our table, Piper was glancing back at him when he wasn't looking.

"Finally, a bet that I can participate in." I rubbed my hands together. "How much is the starting bid?"

THANK YOU

Some novels are easy to write. This was unfortunately not one of them. I'm so proud of where this book ended up, but it was a journey getting here. I always had an image in my mind of where I would be in my own life when this book came out. I had goals that unfortunately I could not achieve because my health didn't allow it, and that made Grace's journey in particular very difficult for me.

But despite all of those challenges, I was able to write a book that I love. Throughout everything, I adored who Dean and Grace become in the end, and I'm so proud of myself for finishing this. While struggling, I kept reminding myself of this moment, the one where I was done with the book and only had to write my thank-yous, and it kept me going. Now that I'm here, I can say that I was right.

To Mae, my superstar PA and editor, thank you for being patient while I flip-flopped on what I wanted this book to be. You're the one who listened to my three different ideas and was excited about them all. To Kasey, my copy editor, thank you for all your hard work in fixing all the errors my dictation software made. I also have to thank my cover designer, Summer, who knocked this one out of the park. I love everyone I work with and couldn't do it without each of you.

WANT MORE?

Get a bonus chapter about Grace and Dean here!

ALSO BY ELLE RIVERS

ABOUT THE AUTHOR

Elle Rivers writes fun romance books filled with real-world problems wrapped in beautiful, heartwarming happy endings. When not writing, she can be found speed-reading other authors' amazing romance novels, curling up next to any warm object she can find, or singing obnoxiously loud to Taylor Swift.

Elle was born and raised in Nashville, Tennessee, and she considers herself one of the few native Nashvillians who does not like country music. She has eight cats who fight for the spot on her lap and eight chickens who couldn't care less about her unless she is bringing them food. She lives with her romance hero of a husband who endlessly supports her writing endeavors, and her son, who is the biggest, but most adorable, distraction.